SLIME SHOP

Created by **Karina Garcia**
With text by **Kevin Panetta**
Illustrations by **Niki Smith**

▼ VERSIFY

Imprints of HarperCollinsPublishers

HARPER
alley

To my supporters who have been on this slime journey with me. —K.G.

To my wife, Brook, and dog Bertie (and also my other dog Albie, who would eat a bucket of slime if I let him). —K.P.

For all my slime-loving pals, you know who you are! —N.S.

Versify® is an imprint of HarperCollins Publishers.
HarperAlley is an imprint of HarperCollins Publishers.

 For information address HarperCollins Children's Books, a division of HarperCollins Publishers, 195 Broadway, New York, NY 10007.
www.harperalley.com
ISBN: 978-0-35-844645-3 — ISBN: 978-0-35-844644-6 (pbk.)
The illustrations in this book were done in Clip Studio Paint on a Cintiq and iPad.
Flatted by Kori Michele
Typography by Phil Caminiti
23 24 25 26 27 GPS 10 9 8 7 6 5 4 3 2 1
First Edition

Contents

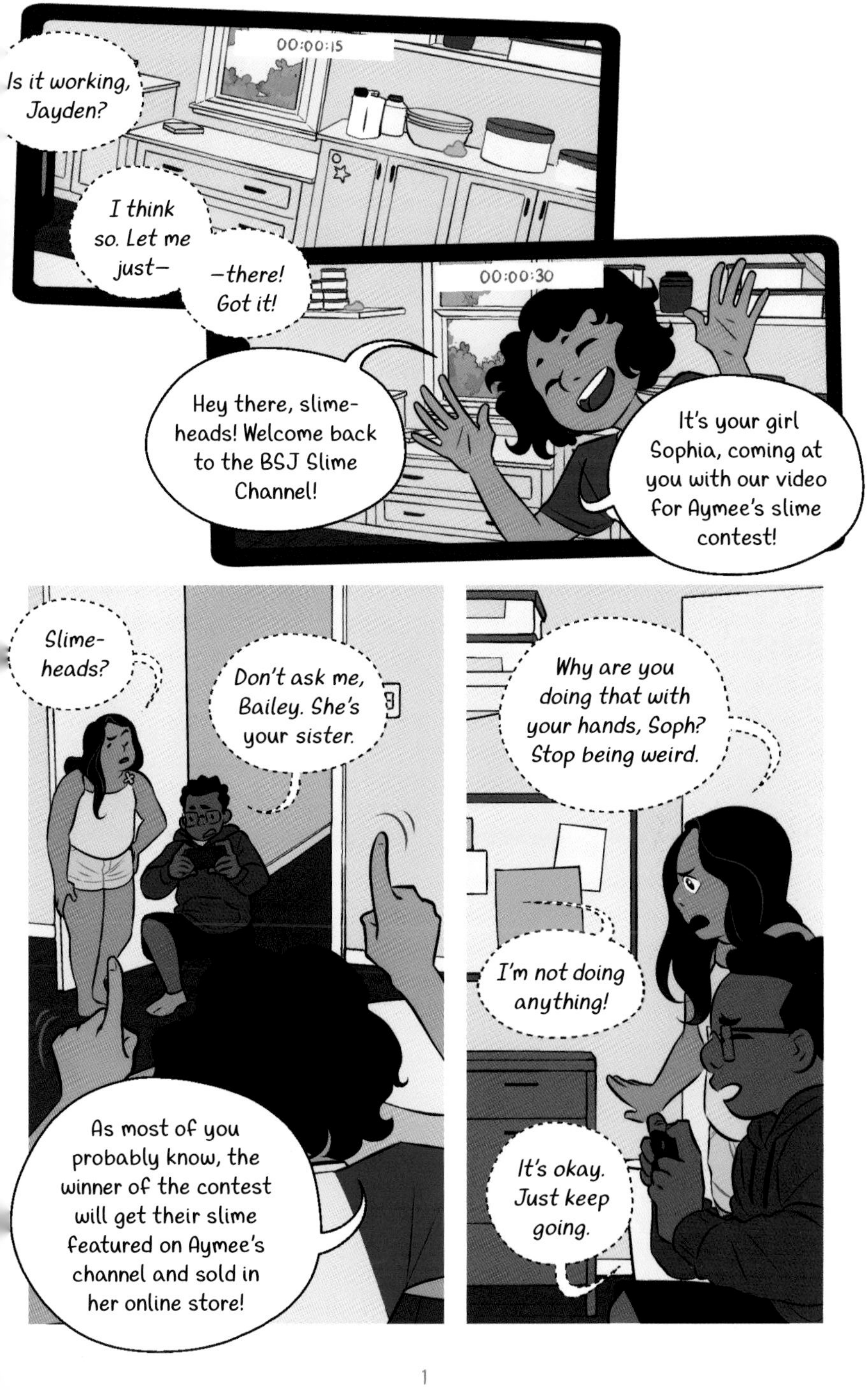
00:00:15
Is it working, Jayden?
I think so. Let me just—
—there! Got it!
00:00:30
Hey there, slime-heads! Welcome back to the BSJ Slime Channel!
It's your girl Sophia, coming at you with our video for Aymee's slime contest!
Slime-heads?
Don't ask me, Bailey. She's your sister.
As most of you probably know, the winner of the contest will get their slime featured on Aymee's channel and sold in her online store!
Why are you doing that with your hands, Soph? Stop being weird.
I'm not doing anything!
It's okay. Just keep going.

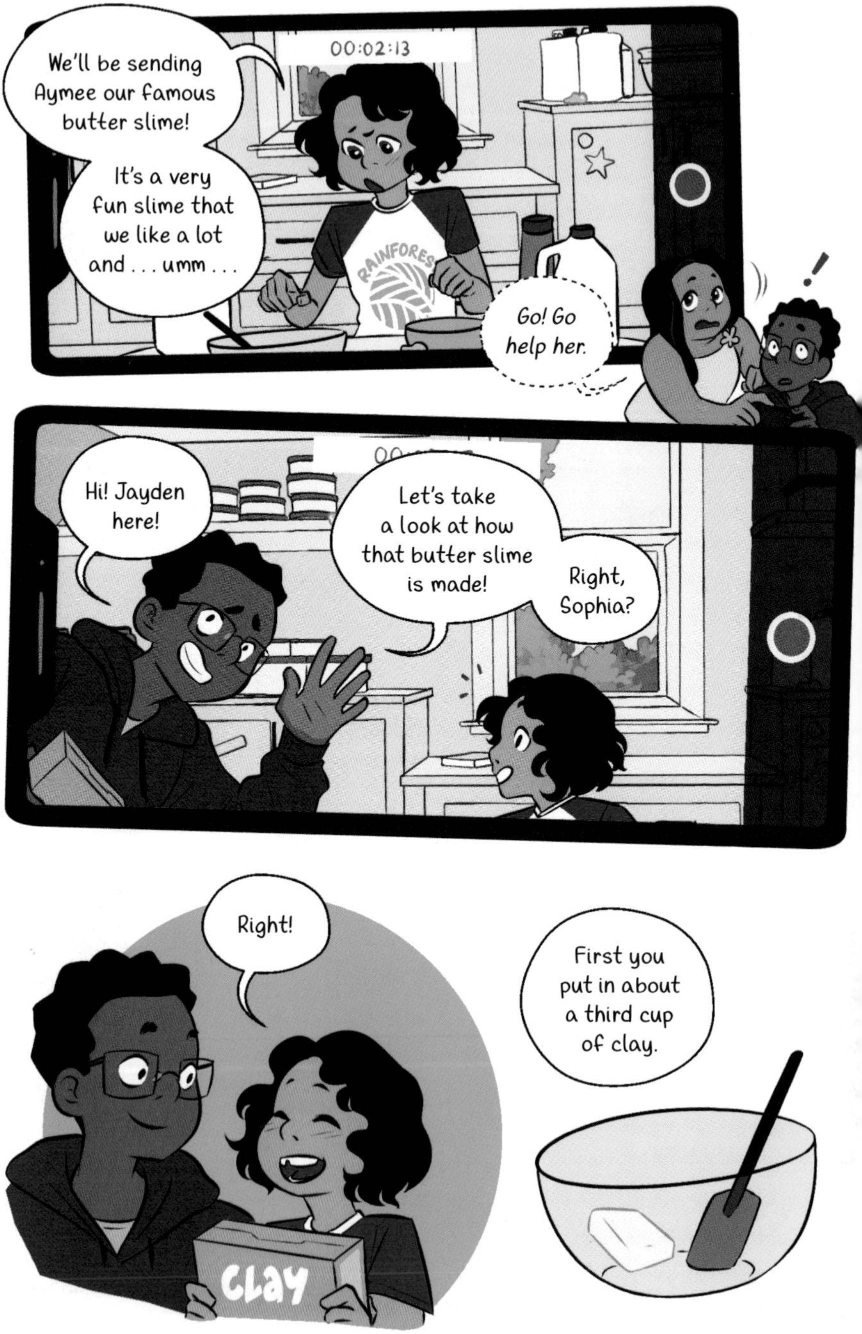
00:02:13
We'll be sending Aymee our famous butter slime!
It's a very fun slime that we like a lot and . . . umm . . .
RAINFORES
Go! Go help her.
!
Hi! Jayden here!
Let's take a look at how that butter slime is made!
Right, Sophia?
Right!
First you put in about a third cup of clay.
CLAY

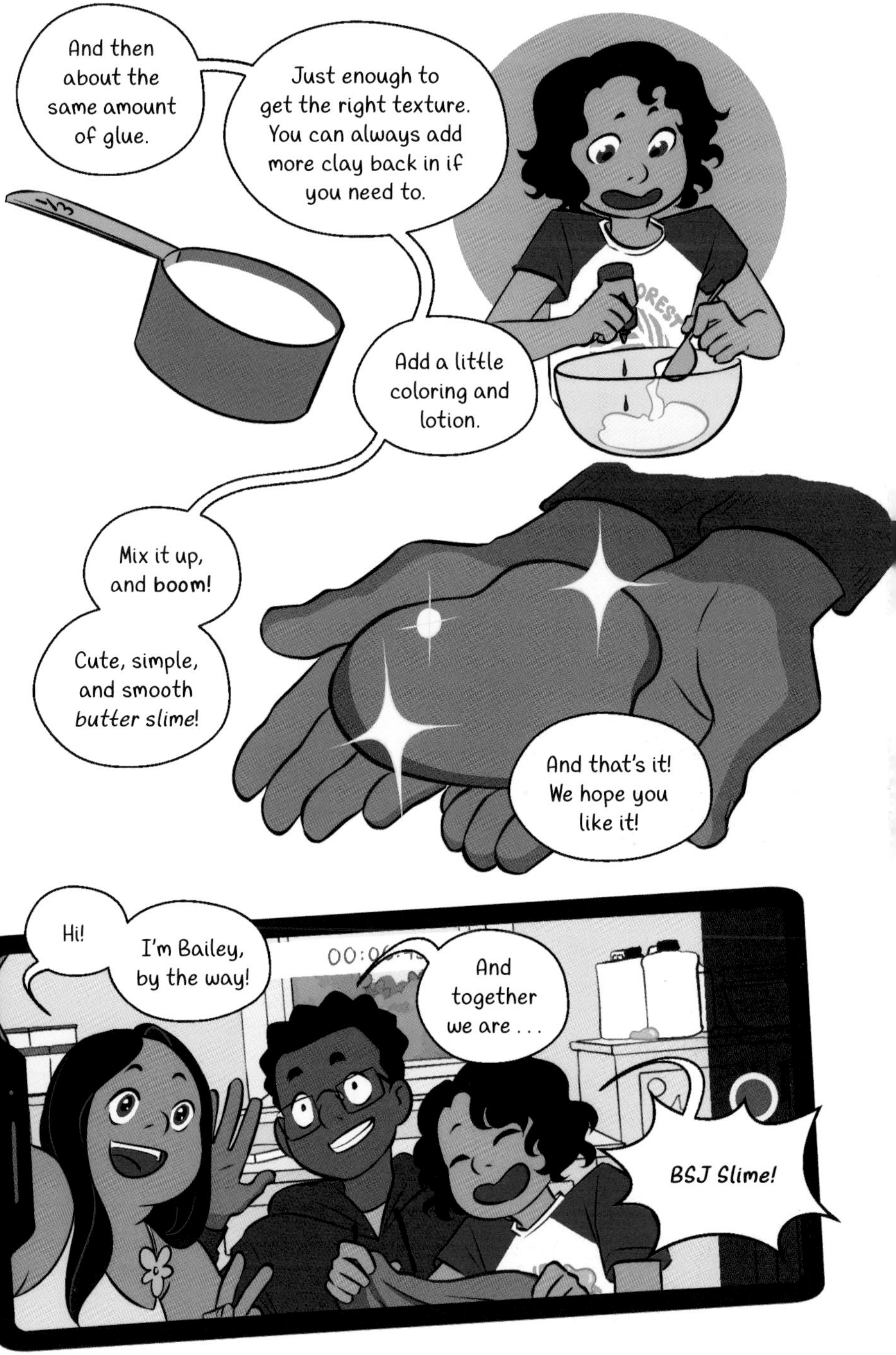
And then about the same amount of glue.
Just enough to get the right texture. You can always add more clay back in if you need to.
Add a little coloring and lotion.
Mix it up, and **boom**!
Cute, simple, and smooth *butter slime*!
And that's it! We hope you like it!
Hi!
I'm Bailey, by the way!
And together we are . . .
BSJ Slime!

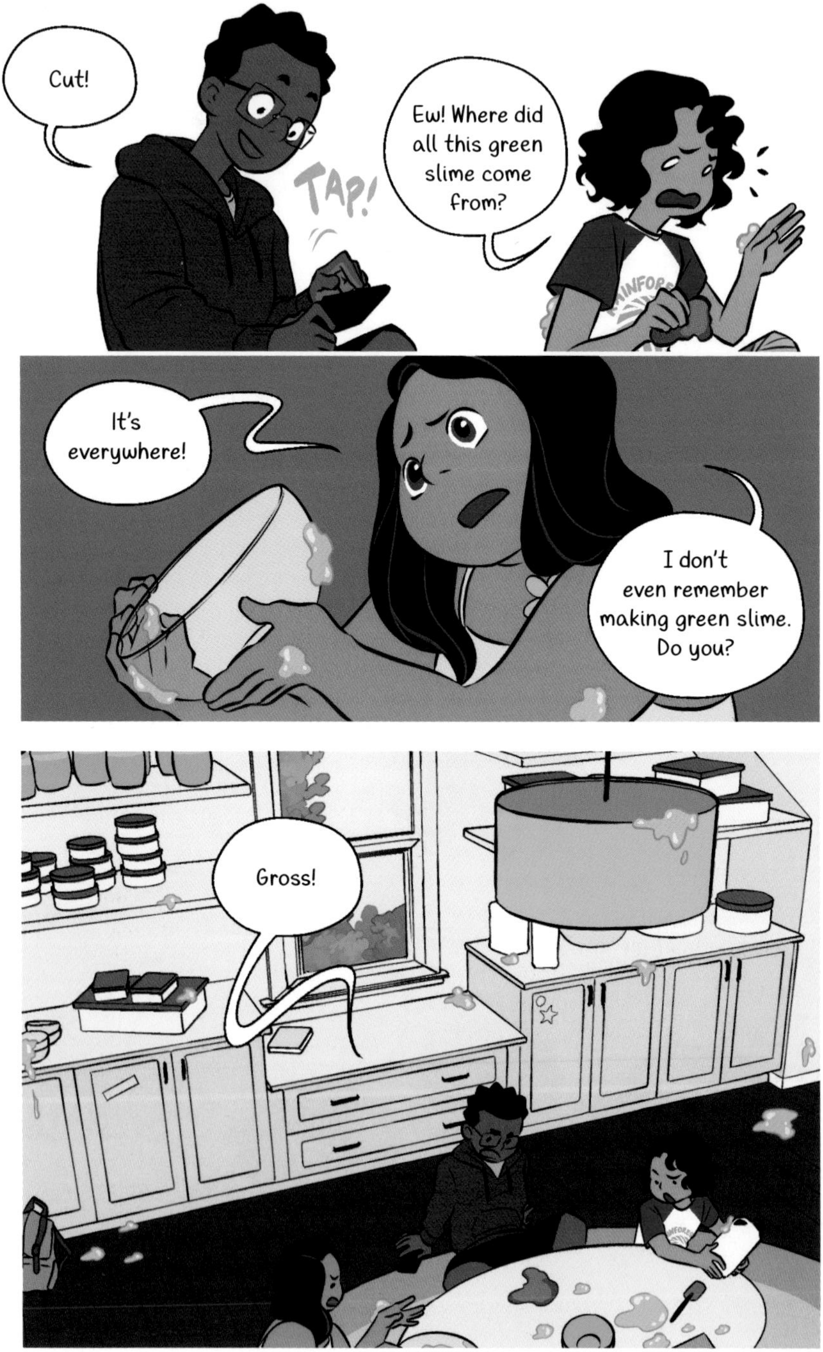
Cut!
TAP!
Ew! Where did all this green slime come from?
It's everywhere!
I don't even remember making green slime. Do you?
Gross!

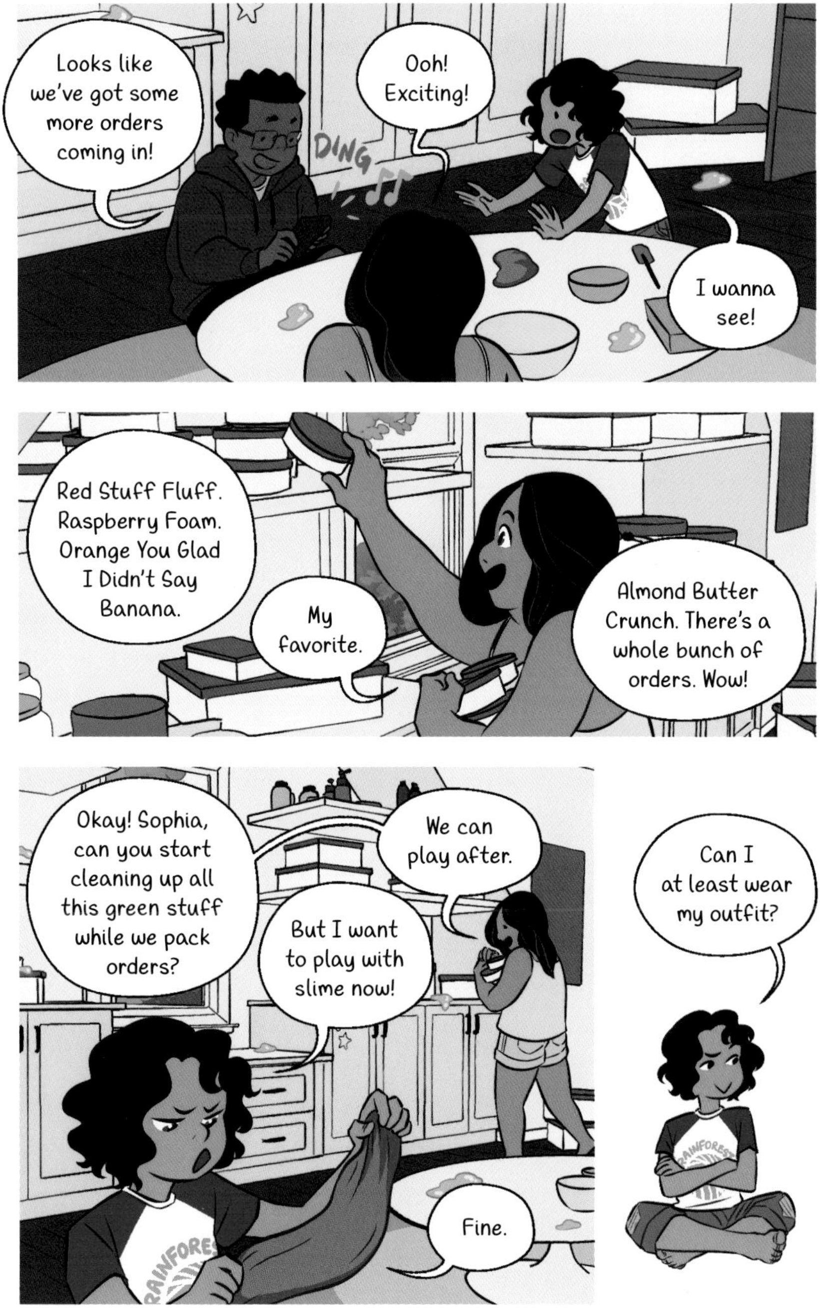
Looks like we've got some more orders coming in!
DING
Ooh! Exciting!
I wanna see!
Red Stuff Fluff. Raspberry Foam. Orange You Glad I Didn't Say Banana.
My favorite.
Almond Butter Crunch. There's a whole bunch of orders. Wow!
Okay! Sophia, can you start cleaning up all this green stuff while we pack orders?
We can play after.
But I want to play with slime now!
Fine.
Can I at least wear my outfit?
RAINFOREST

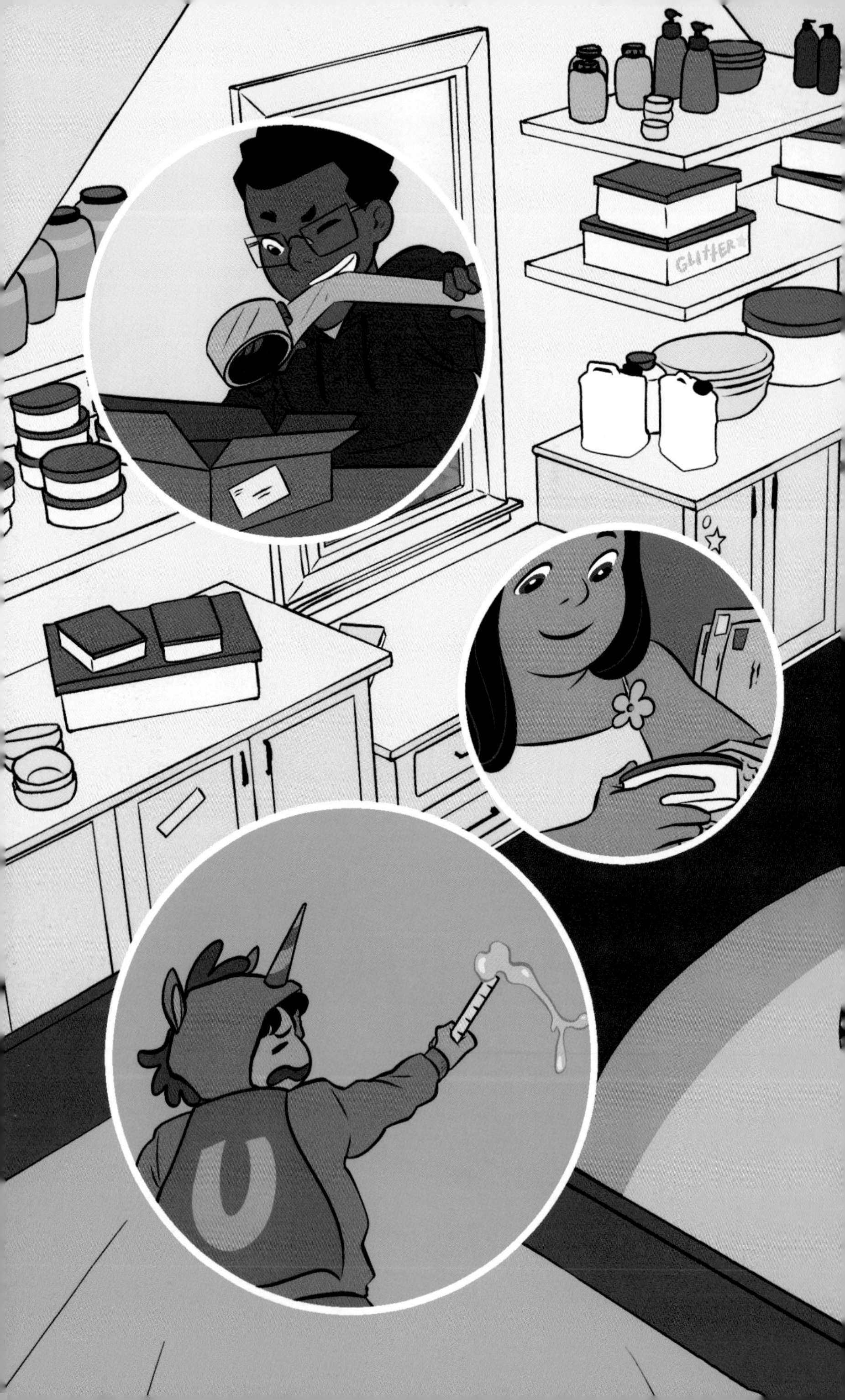
GLITTER

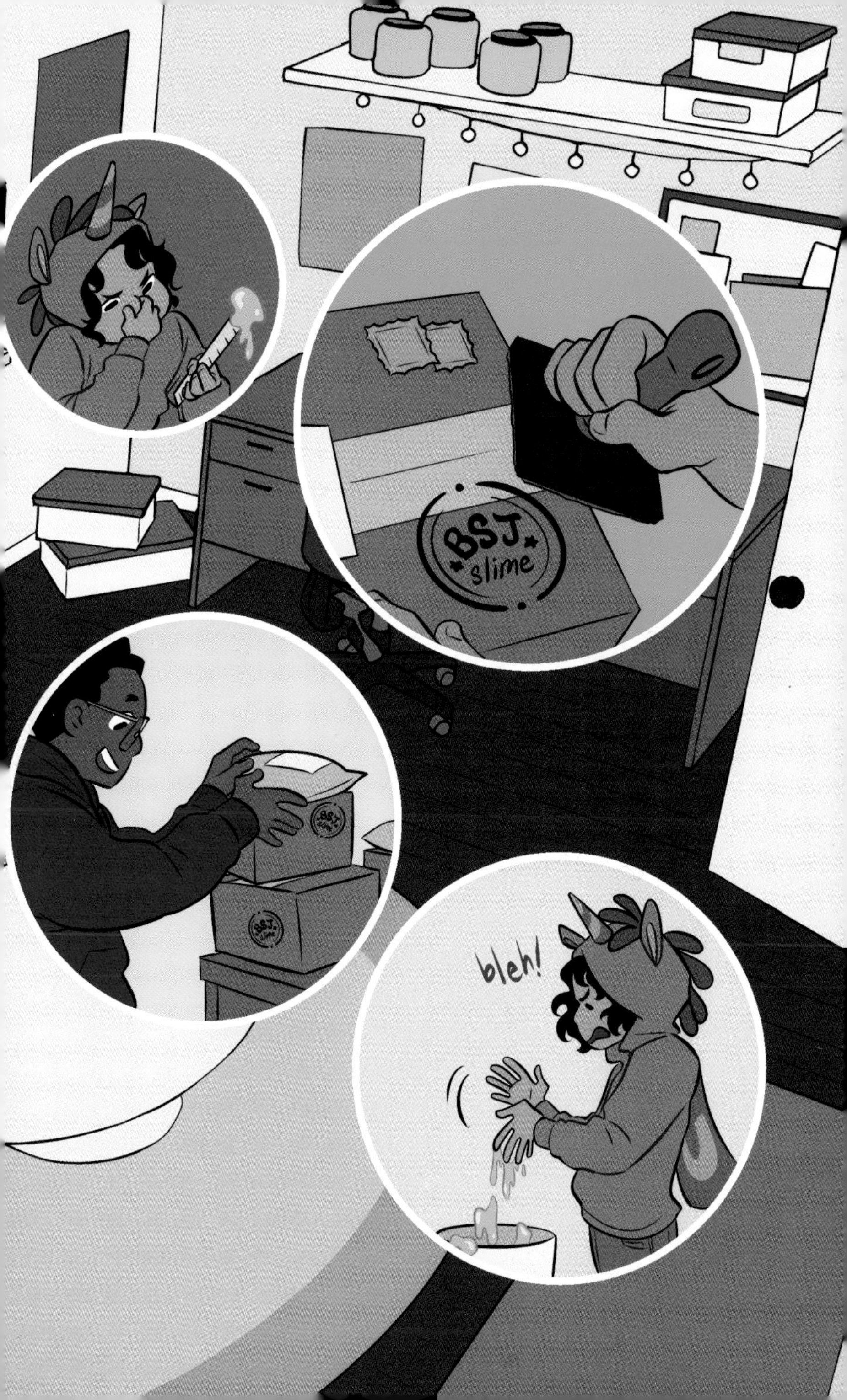
BSJ
slime
bleh!

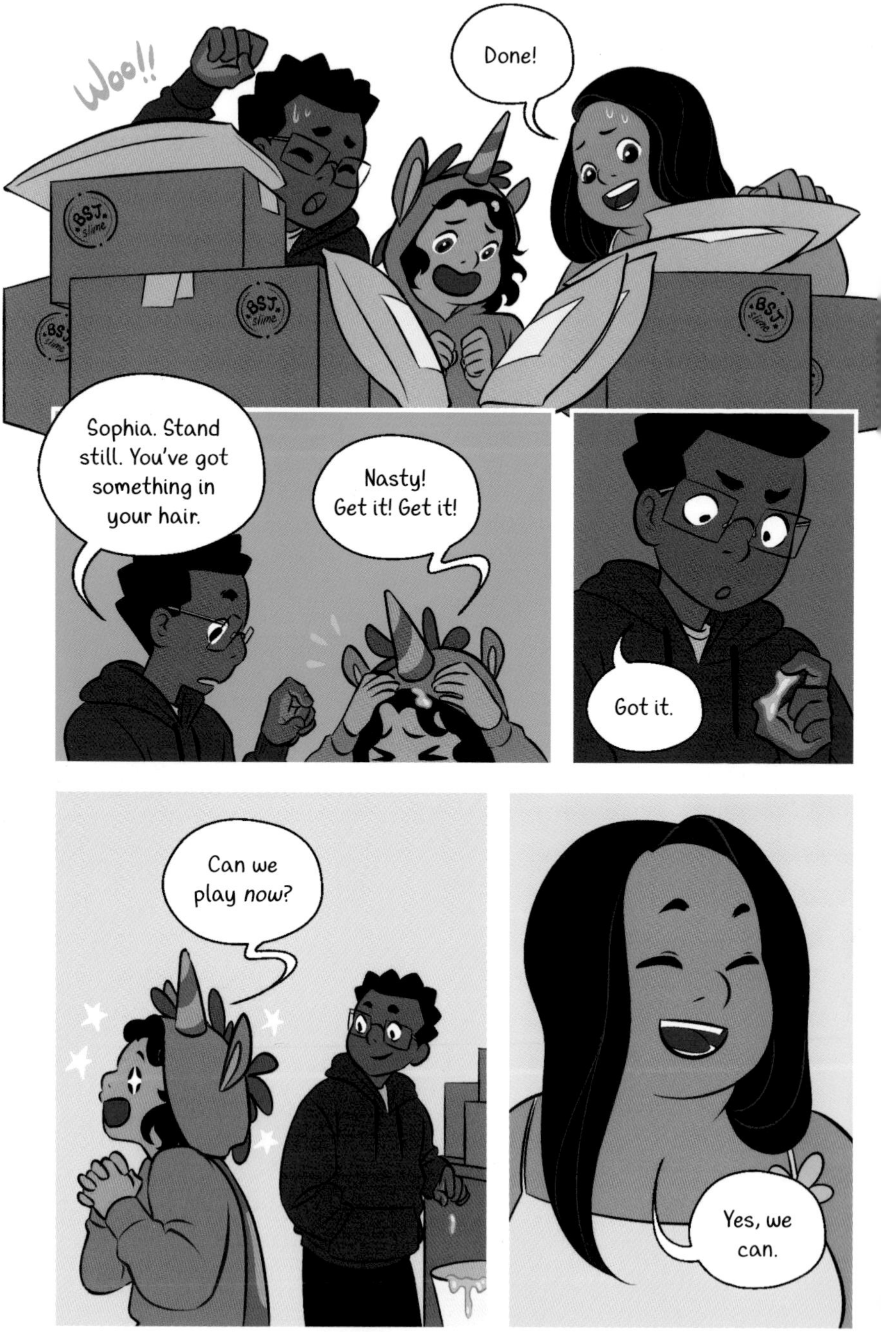
Woo!!
Done!
Sophia. Stand still. You've got something in your hair.
Nasty! Get it! Get it!
Got it.
Can we play now?
Yes, we can.

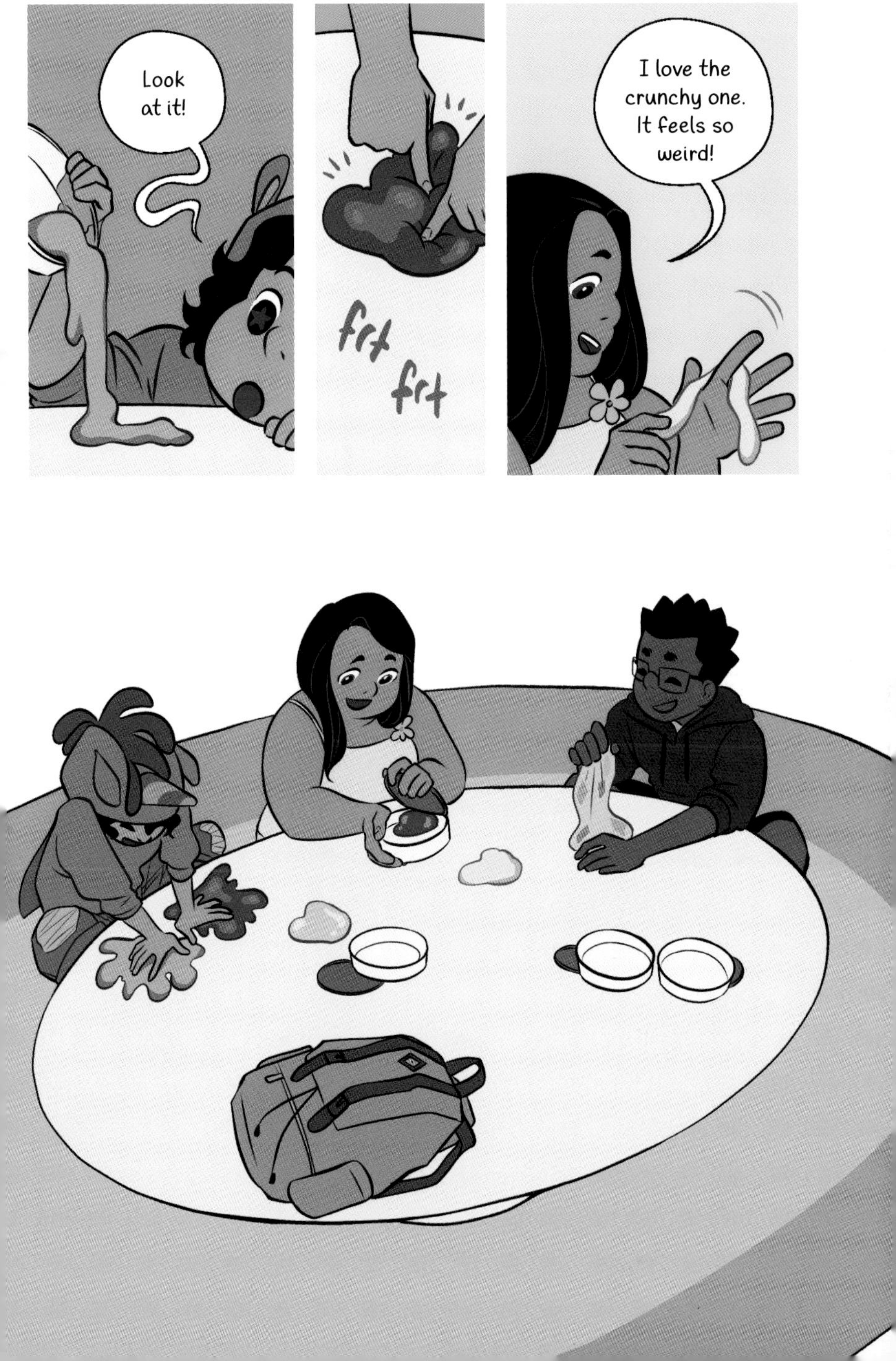
Look at it!
frt frt
I love the crunchy one. It feels so weird!

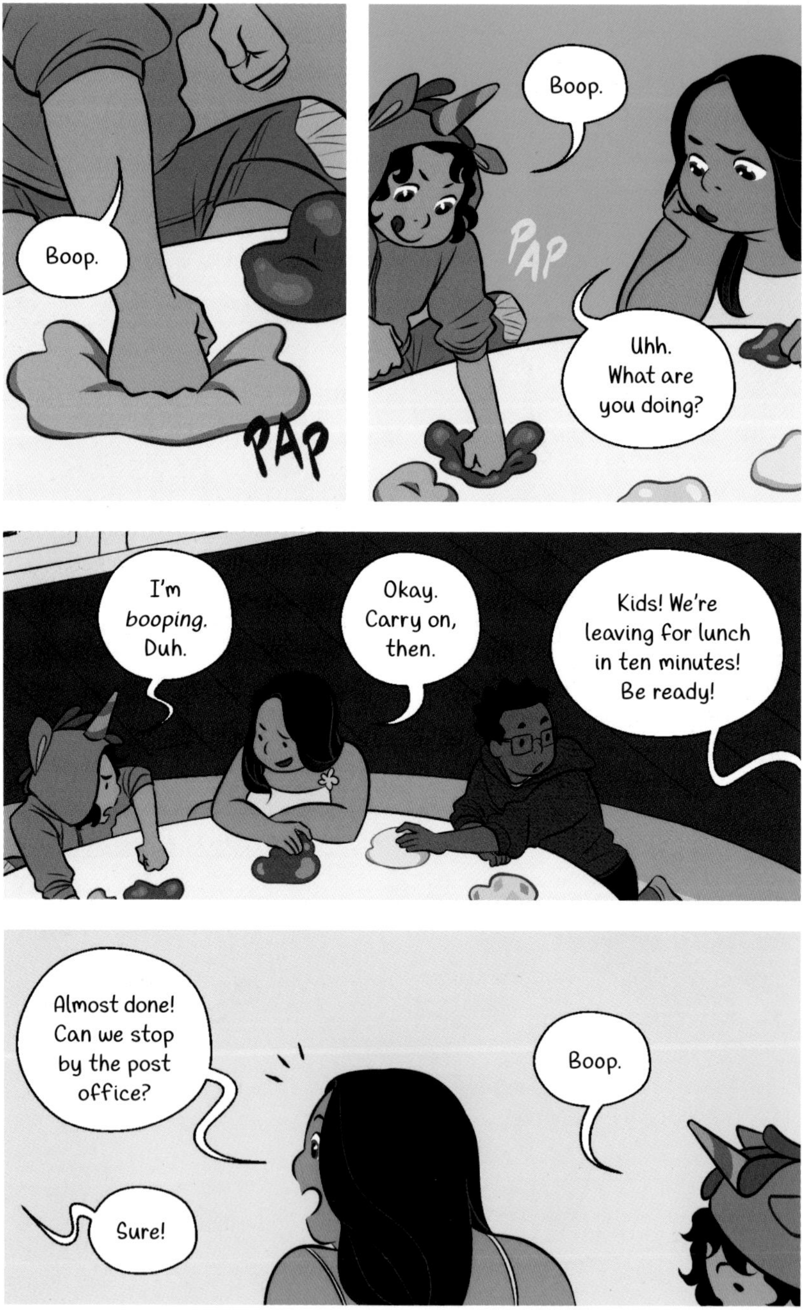
Boop.
PAP
Boop.
PAP
Uhh. What are you doing?
I'm *booping.* Duh.
Okay. Carry on, then.
Kids! We're leaving for lunch in ten minutes! Be ready!
Almost done! Can we stop by the post office?
Sure!
Boop.

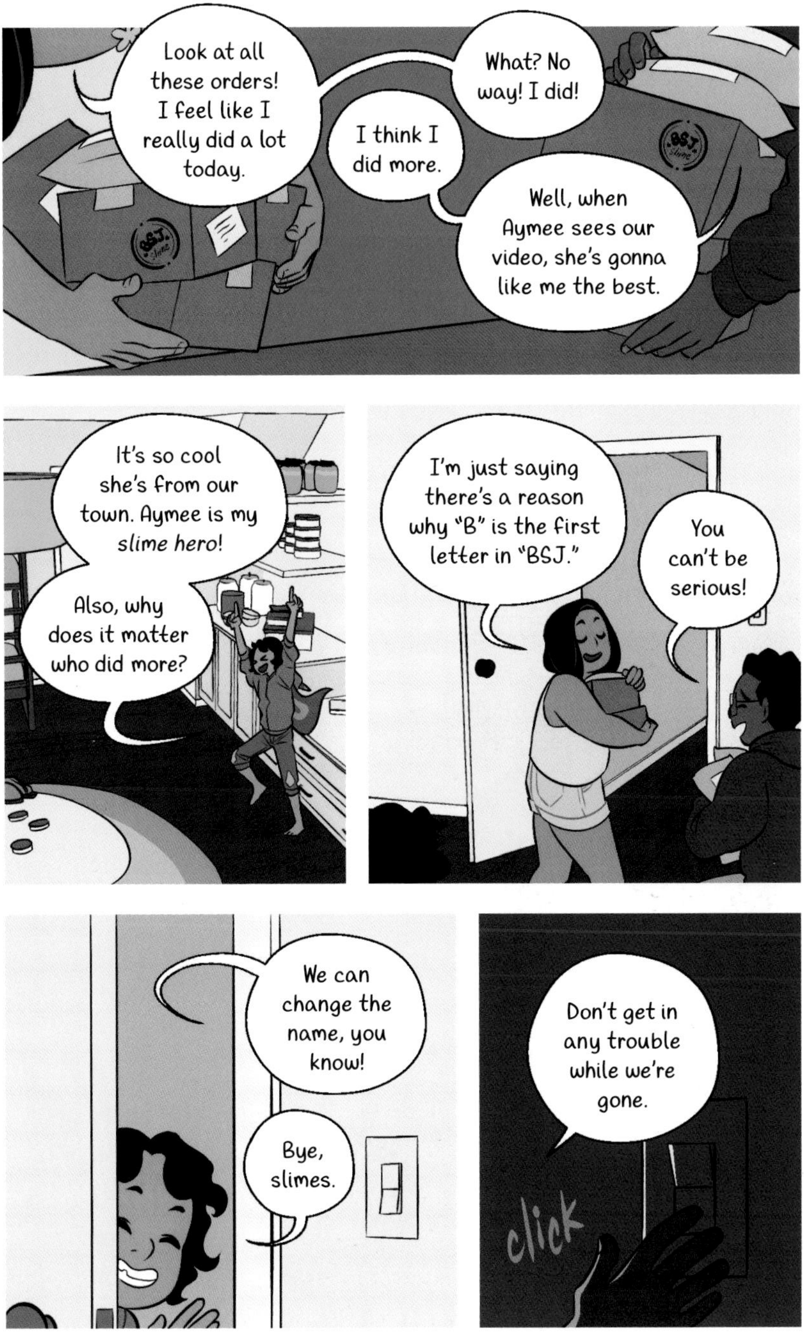

Look at all these orders! I feel like I really did a lot today.
What? No way! I did!
I think I did more.
Well, when Aymee sees our video, she's gonna like me the best.
It's so cool she's from our town. Aymee is my *slime hero*!
Also, why does it matter who did more?
I'm just saying there's a reason why "B" is the first letter in "BSJ."
You can't be serious!
We can change the name, you know!
Bye, slimes.
Don't get in any trouble while we're gone.
click

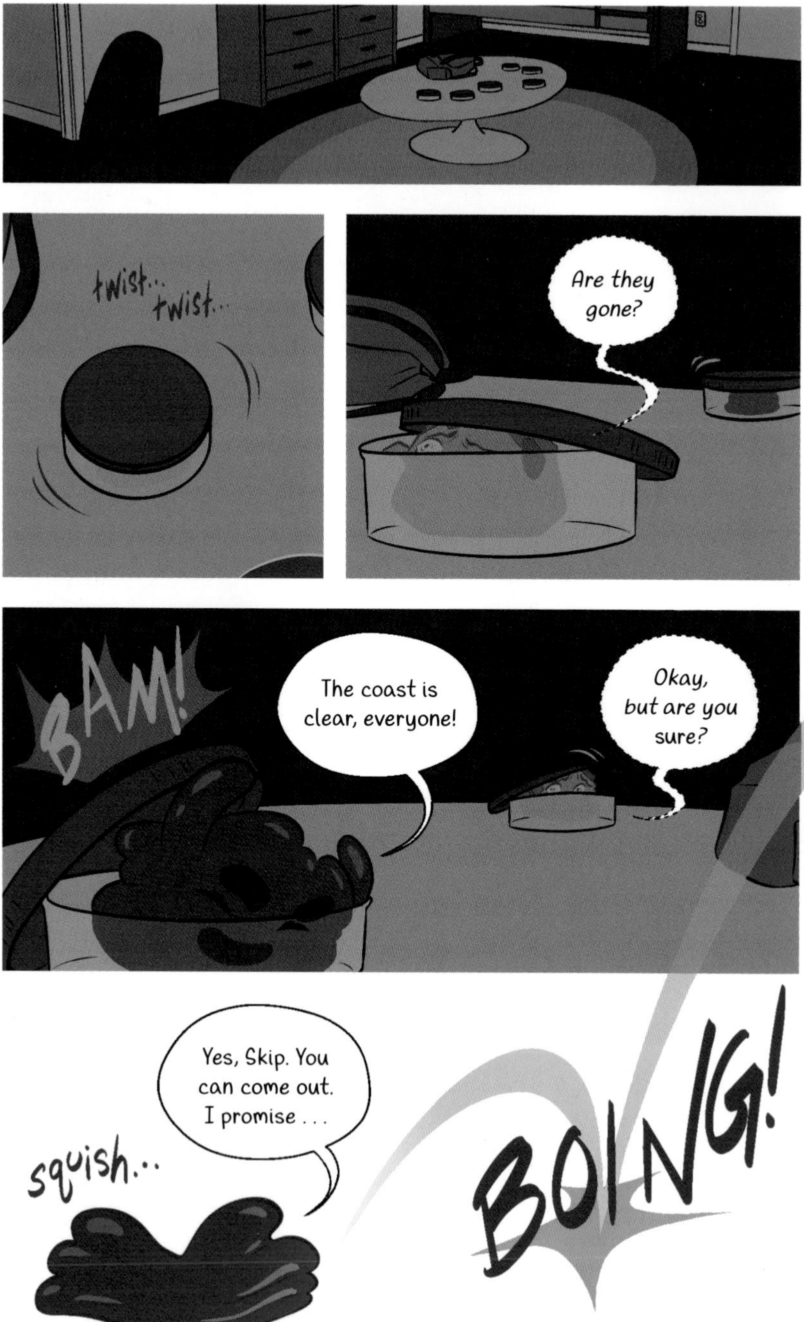
twist... twist...
Are they gone?
BAM!
The coast is clear, everyone!
Okay, but are you sure?
Yes, Skip. You can come out. I promise . . .
squish...
BOING!

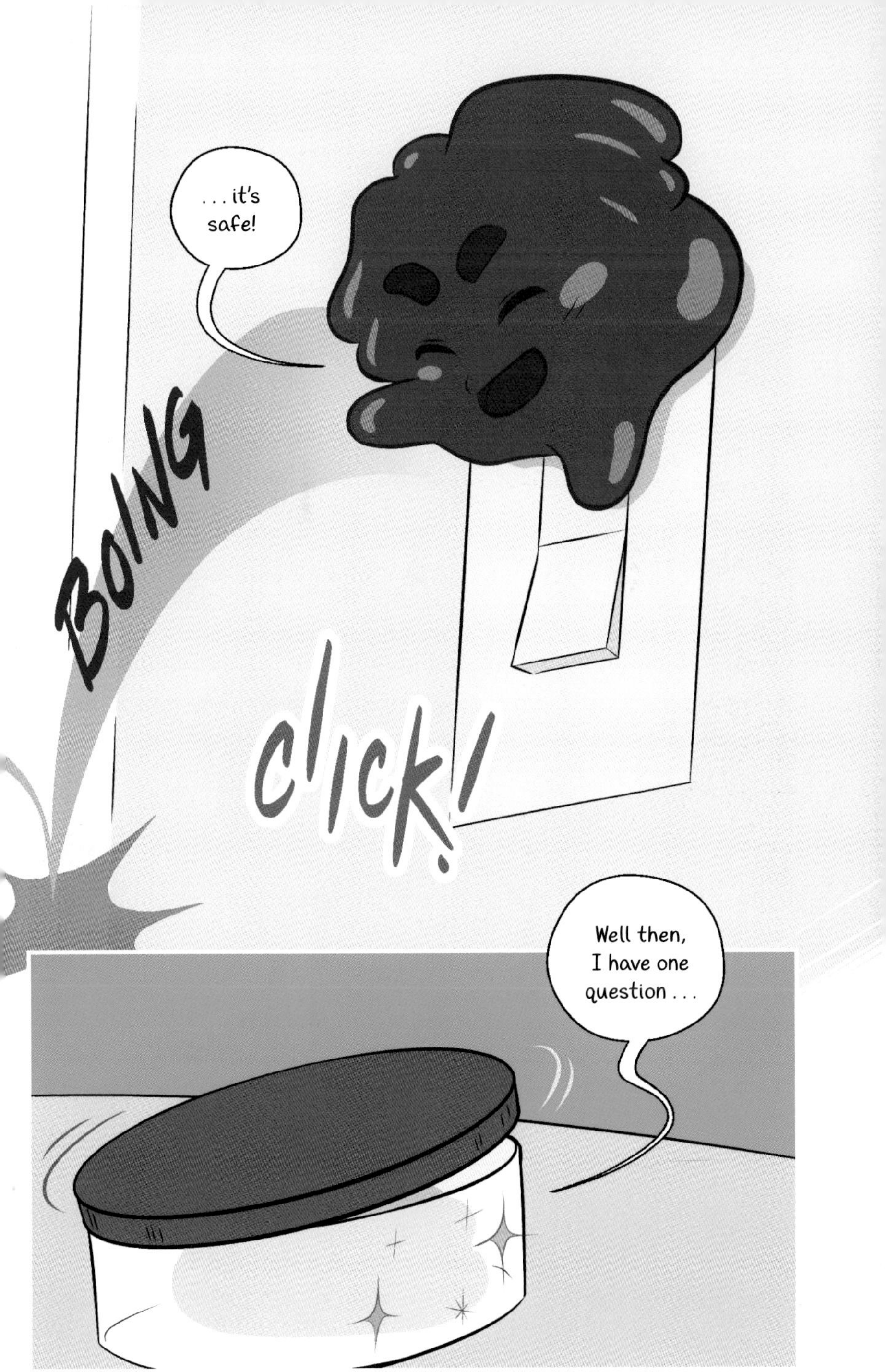
. . . it's safe!
BOING
CLICK!
Well then, I have one question . . .

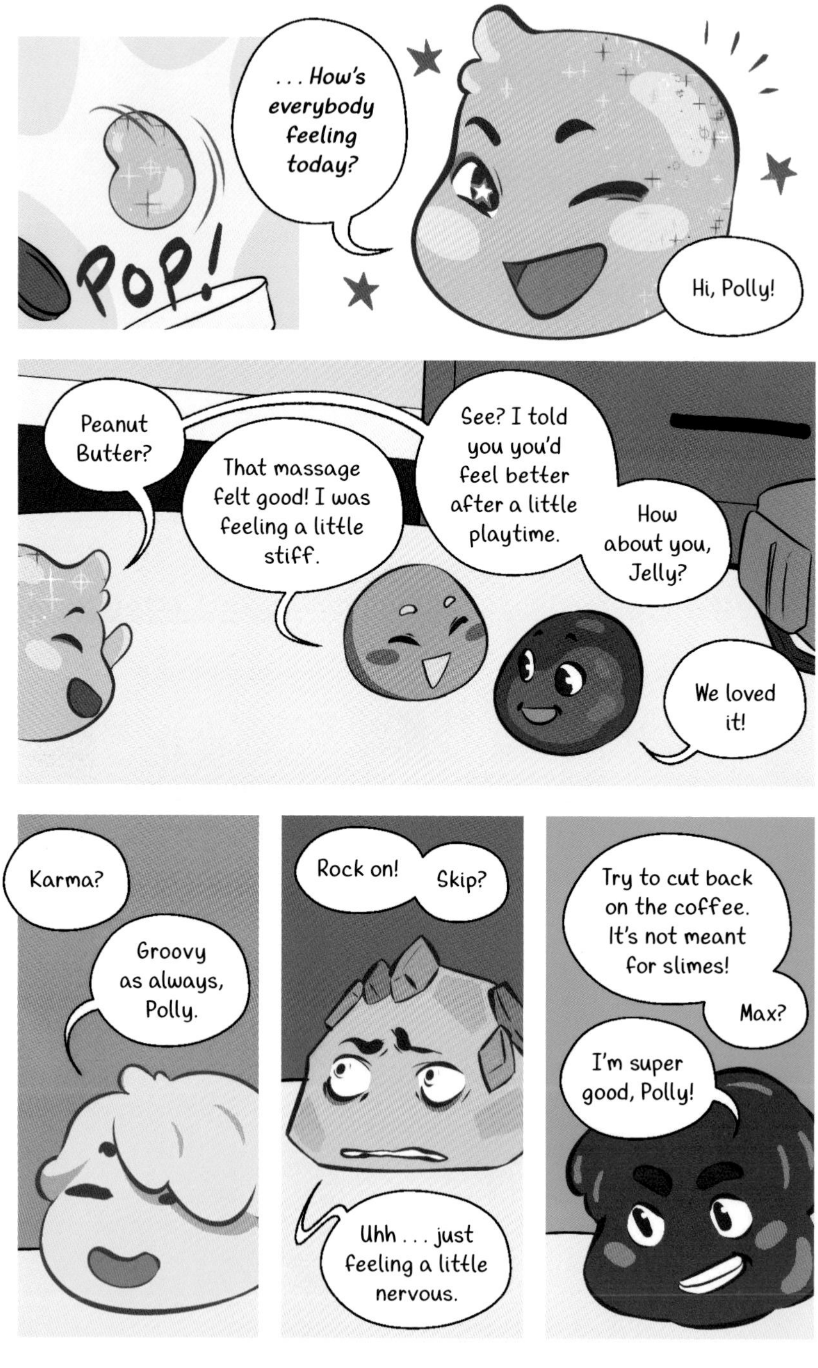
POP!
. . . How's everybody feeling today?
Hi, Polly!
Peanut Butter?
That massage felt good! I was feeling a little stiff.
See? I told you you'd feel better after a little playtime.
How about you, Jelly?
We loved it!
Karma?
Groovy as always, Polly.
Rock on!
Skip?
Uhh . . . just feeling a little nervous.
Try to cut back on the coffee. It's not meant for slimes!
Max?
I'm super good, Polly!

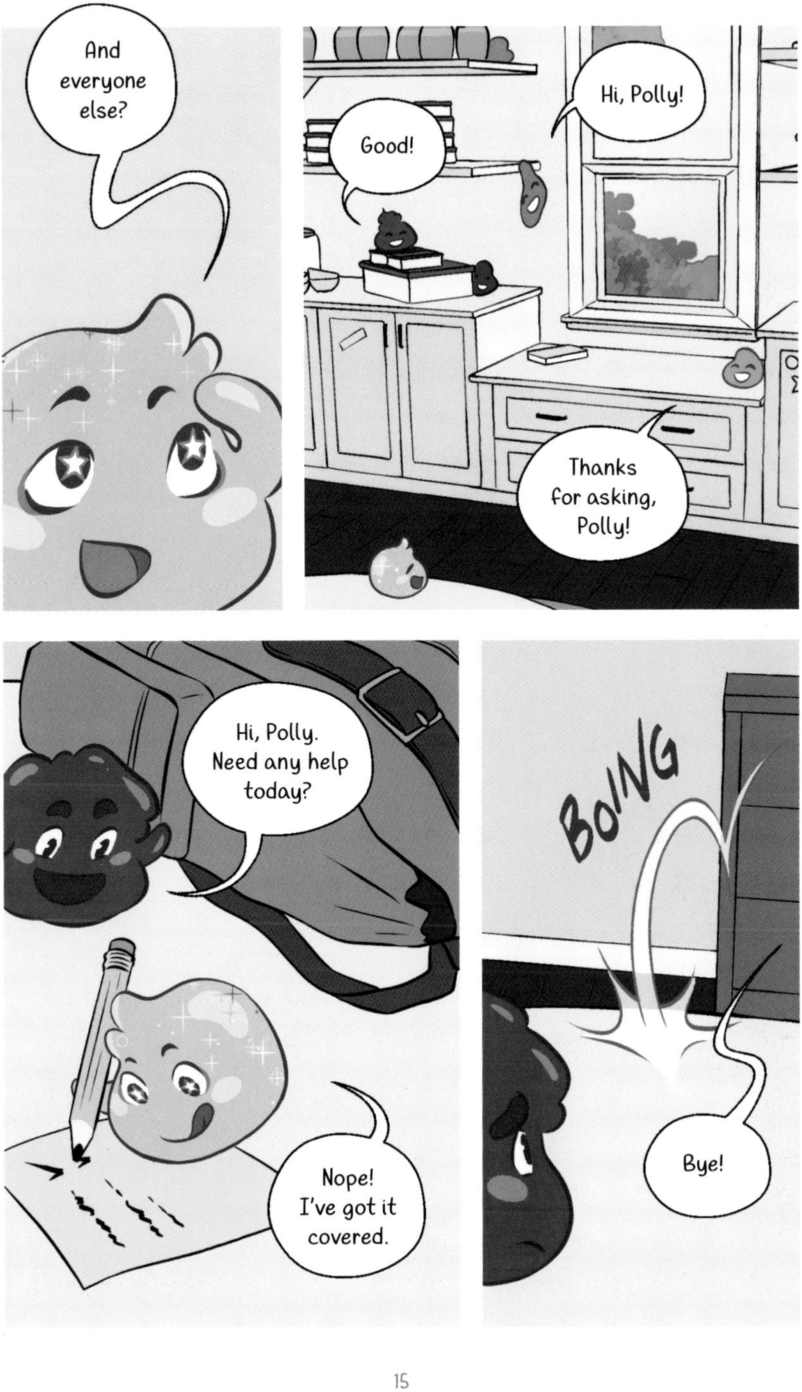
And everyone else?
Hi, Polly!
Good!
Thanks for asking, Polly!
Hi, Polly. Need any help today?
Nope! I've got it covered.
BOING
Bye!

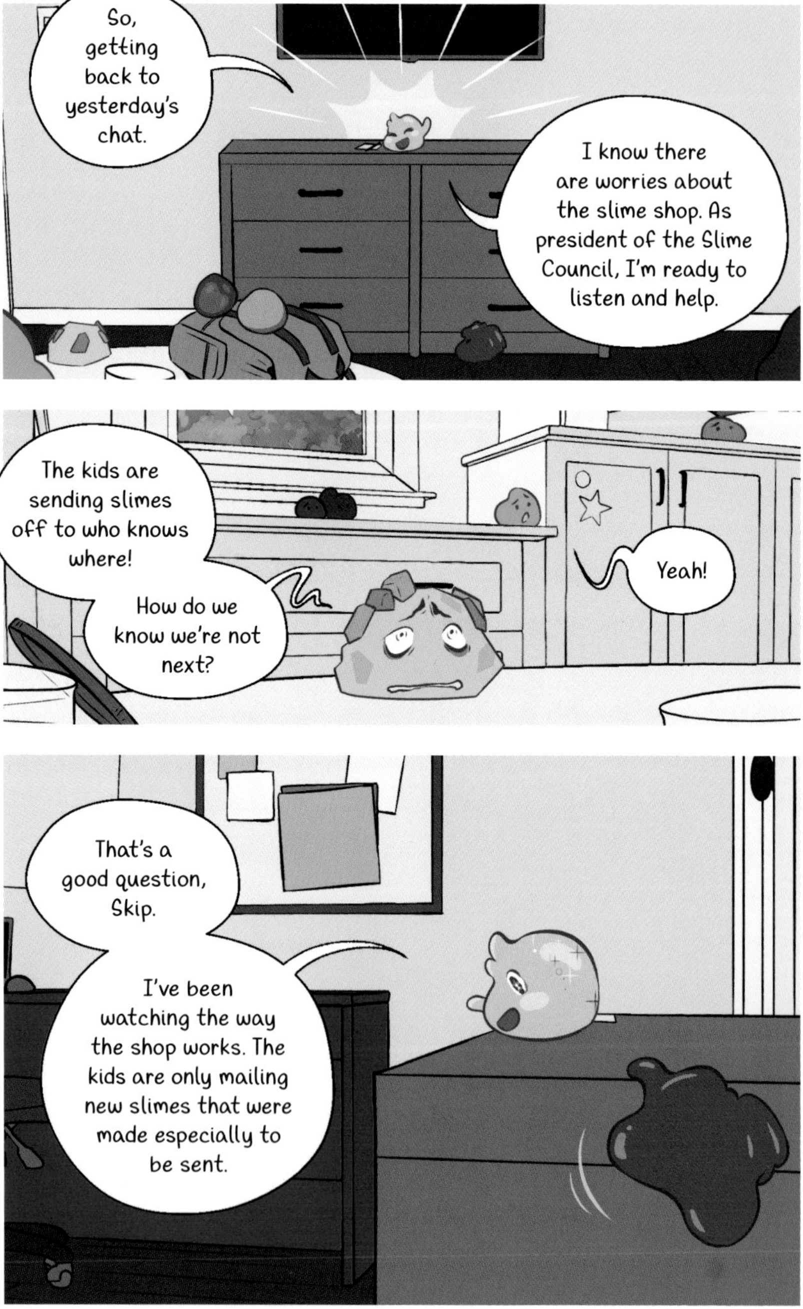
So, getting back to yesterday's chat.
I know there are worries about the slime shop. As president of the Slime Council, I'm ready to listen and help.
The kids are sending slimes off to who knows where!
How do we know we're not next?
Yeah!
That's a good question, Skip.
I've been watching the way the shop works. The kids are only mailing new slimes that were made especially to be sent.

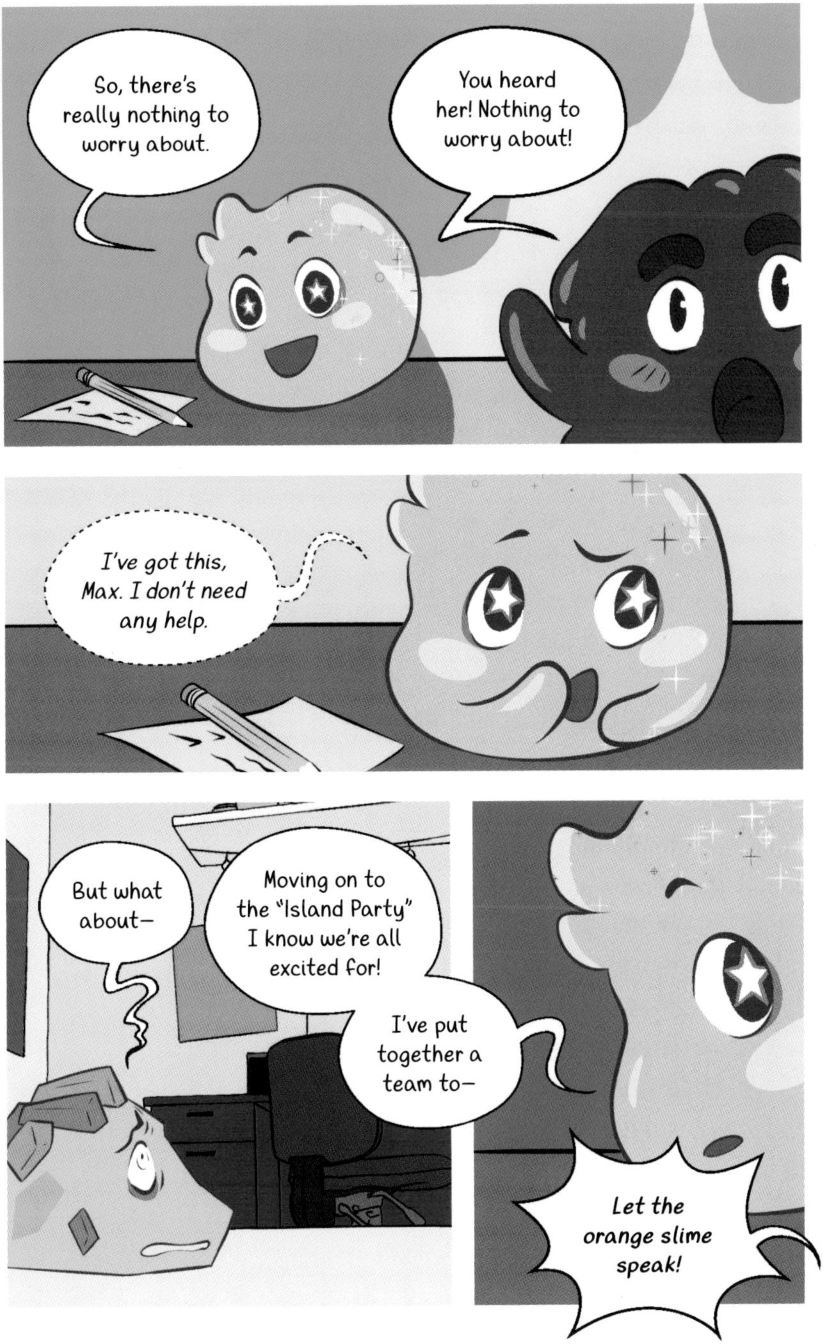
So, there's really nothing to worry about.
You heard her! Nothing to worry about!
I've got this, Max. I don't need any help.
But what about—
Moving on to the "Island Party" I know we're all excited for!
I've put together a team to—
Let the orange slime speak!

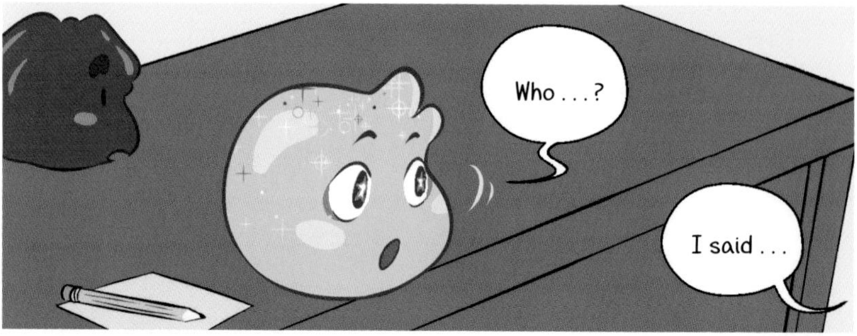
Who . . . ?
I said . . .

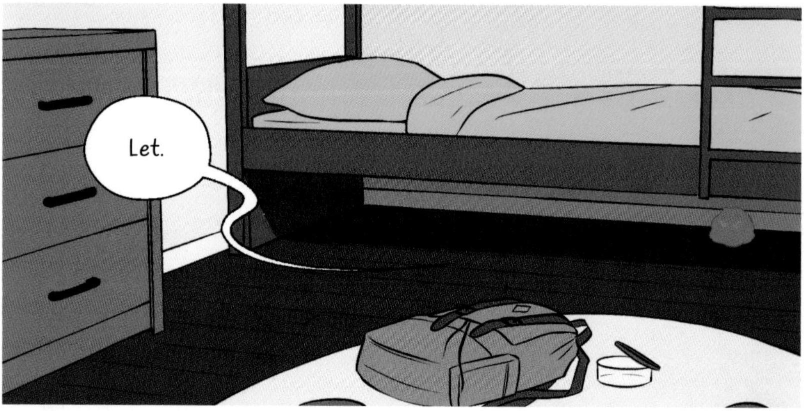
Let.

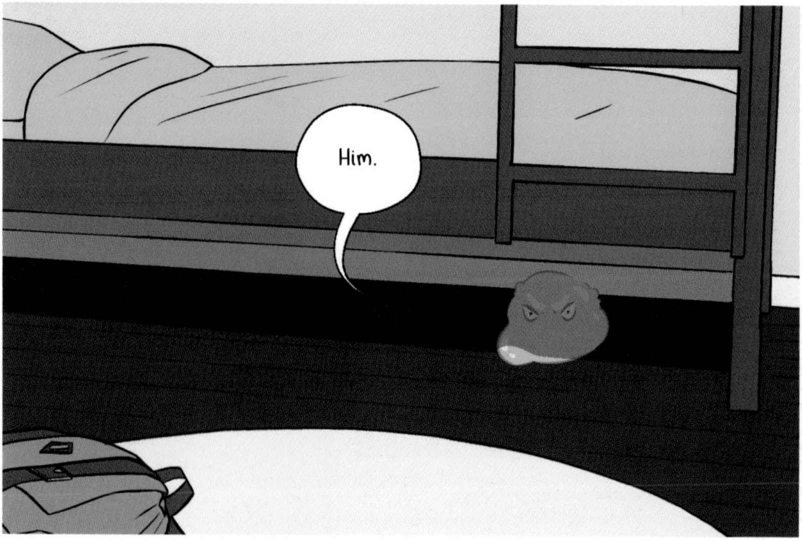
Him.

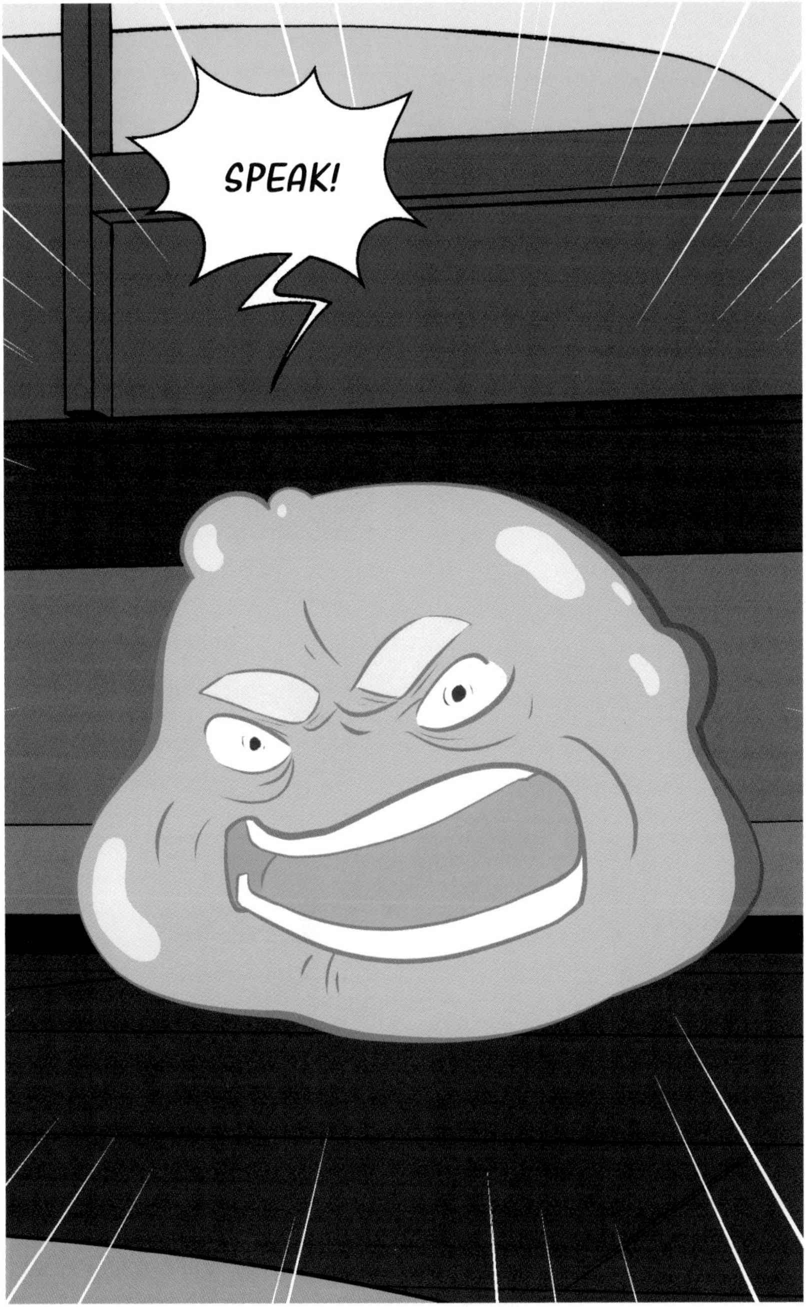
SPEAK!

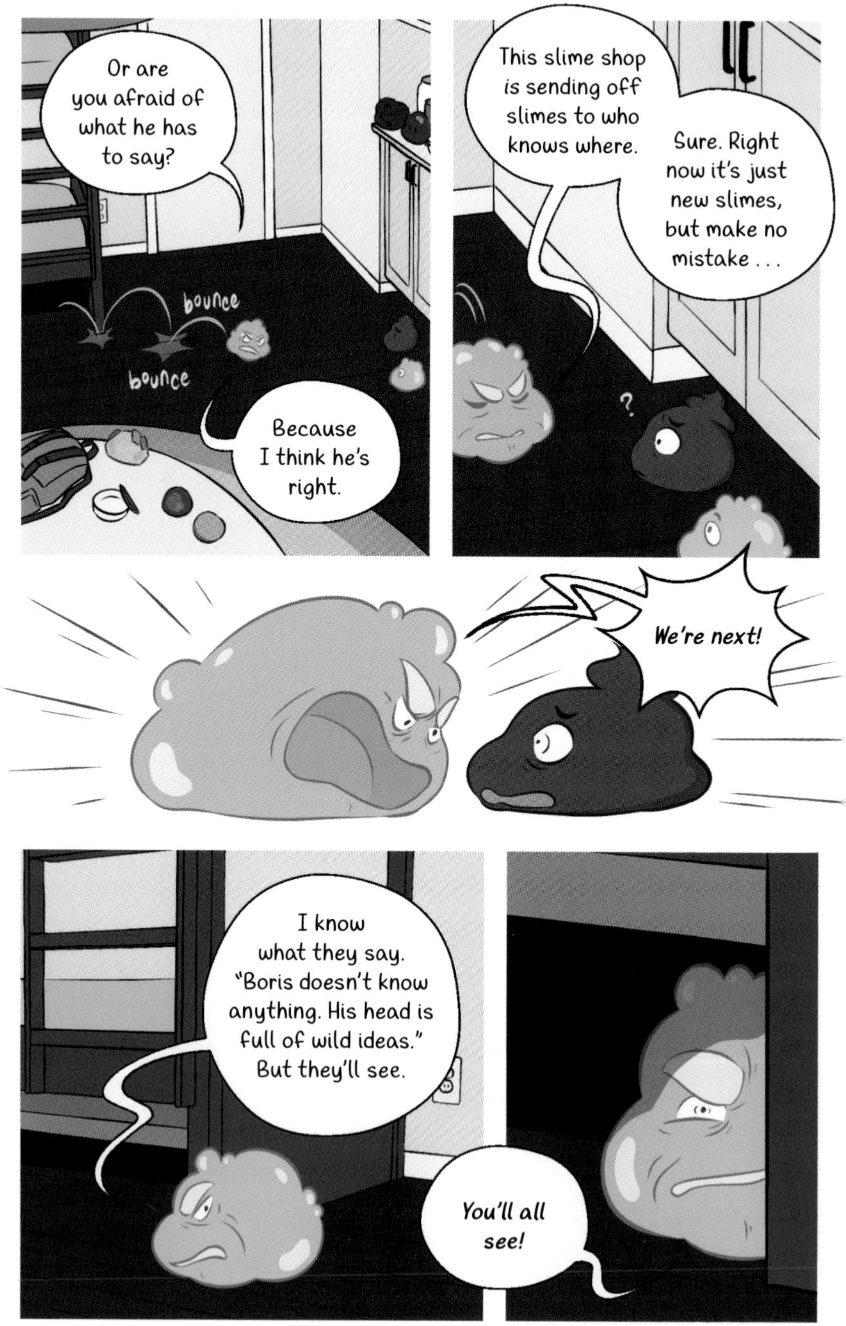
Or are you afraid of what he has to say?
bounce
bounce
Because I think he's right.
This slime shop is sending off slimes to who knows where.
Sure. Right now it's just new slimes, but make no mistake . . .
?
We're next!
I know what they say. "Boris doesn't know anything. His head is full of wild ideas." But they'll see.
You'll all see!

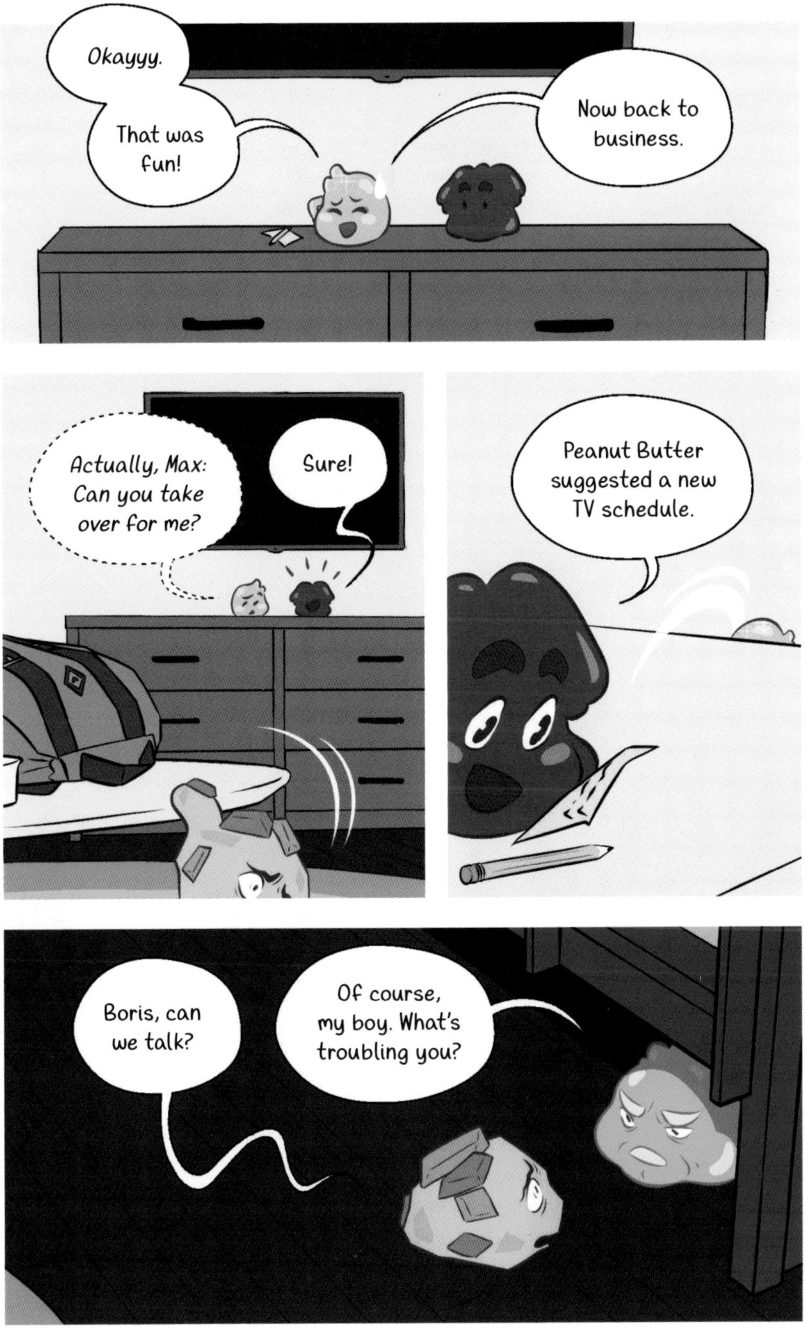
Okayyy.
That was fun!
Now back to business.
Actually, Max: Can you take over for me?
Sure!
Peanut Butter suggested a new TV schedule.
Boris, can we talk?
Of course, my boy. What's troubling you?

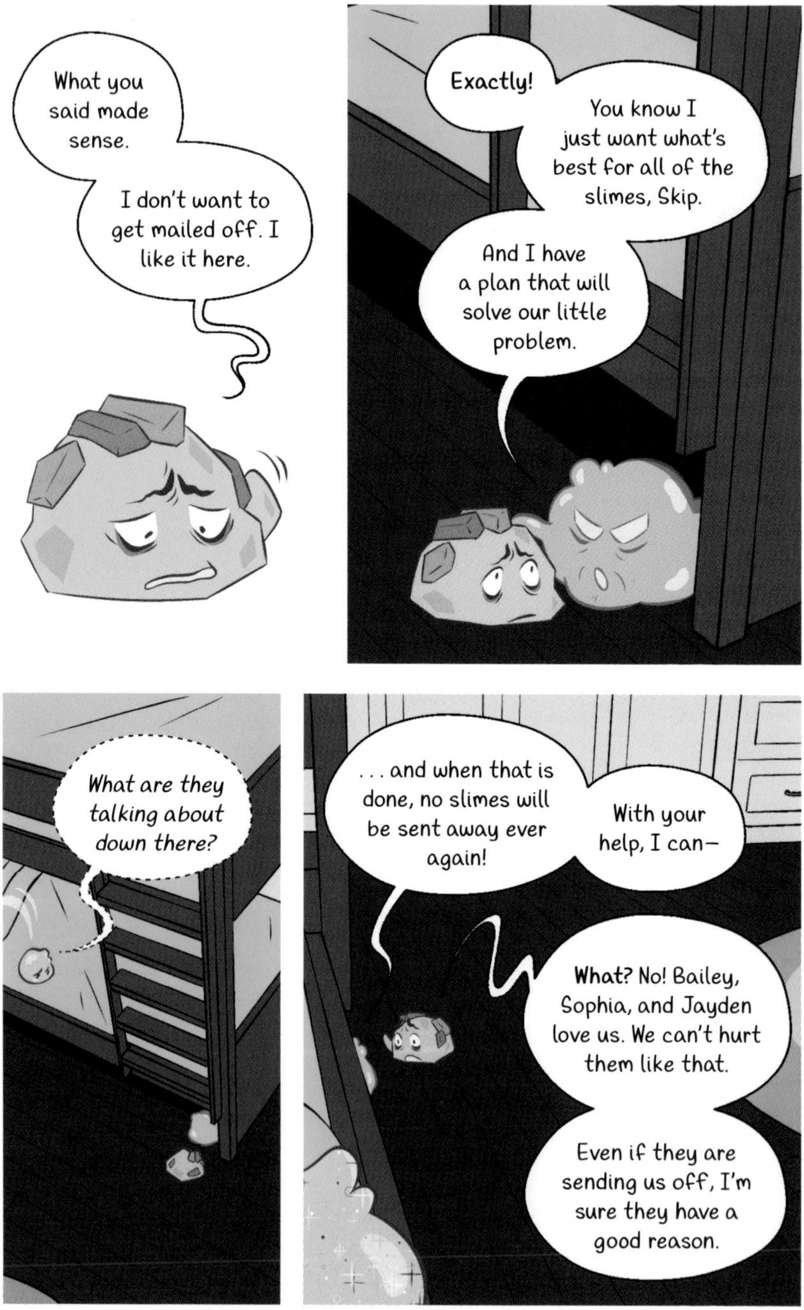

What you said made sense.
I don't want to get mailed off. I like it here.
Exactly!
You know I just want what's best for all of the slimes, Skip.
And I have a plan that will solve our little problem.
What are they talking about down there?
. . . and when that is done, no slimes will be sent away ever again!
With your help, I can—
What? No! Bailey, Sophia, and Jayden love us. We can't hurt them like that.
Even if they are sending us off, I'm sure they have a good reason.

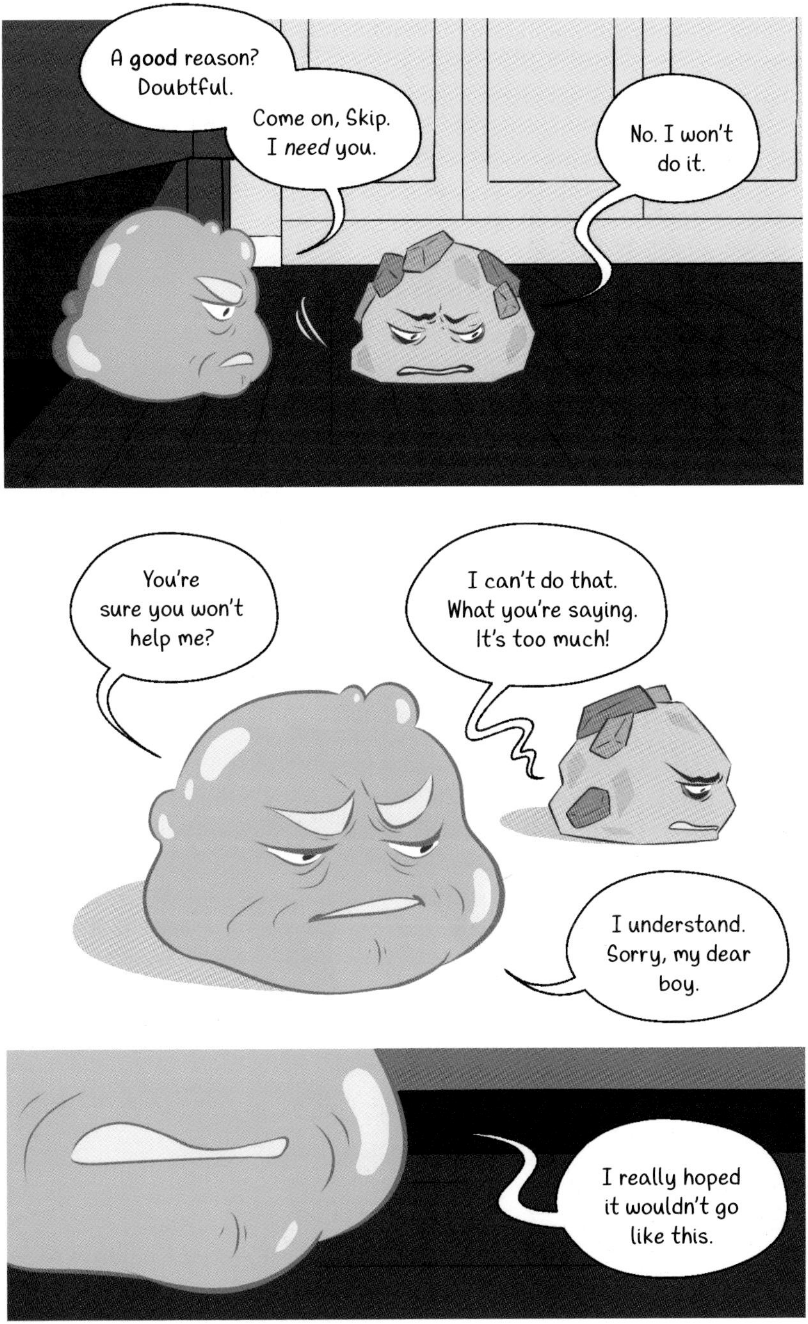
A good reason? Doubtful.
Come on, Skip. I *need* you.
No. I won't do it.
You're sure you won't help me?
I can't do that. What you're saying. It's too much!
I understand. Sorry, my dear boy.
I really hoped it wouldn't go like this.

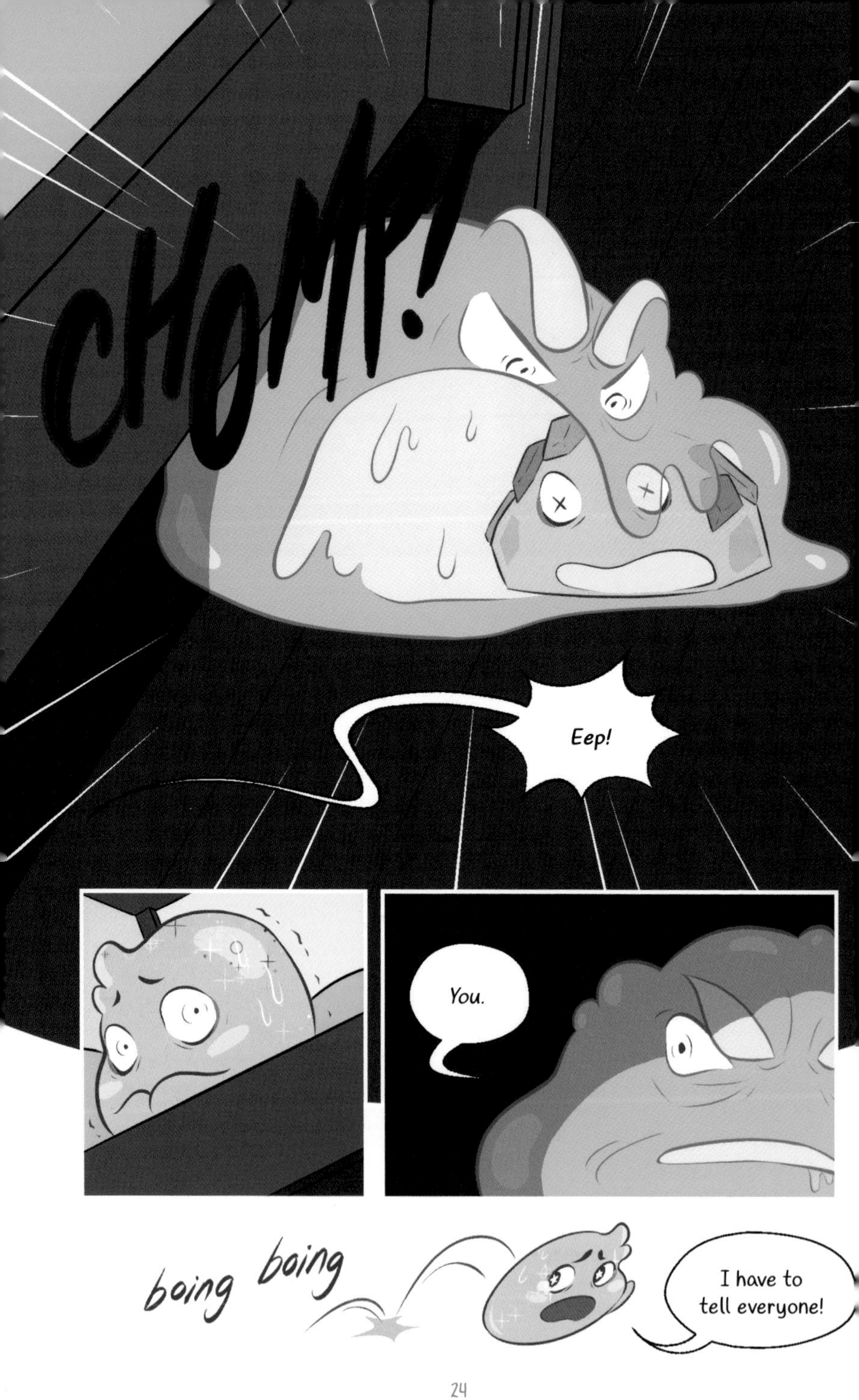
CHOMP!
Eep!
You.
boing boing
I have to tell everyone!

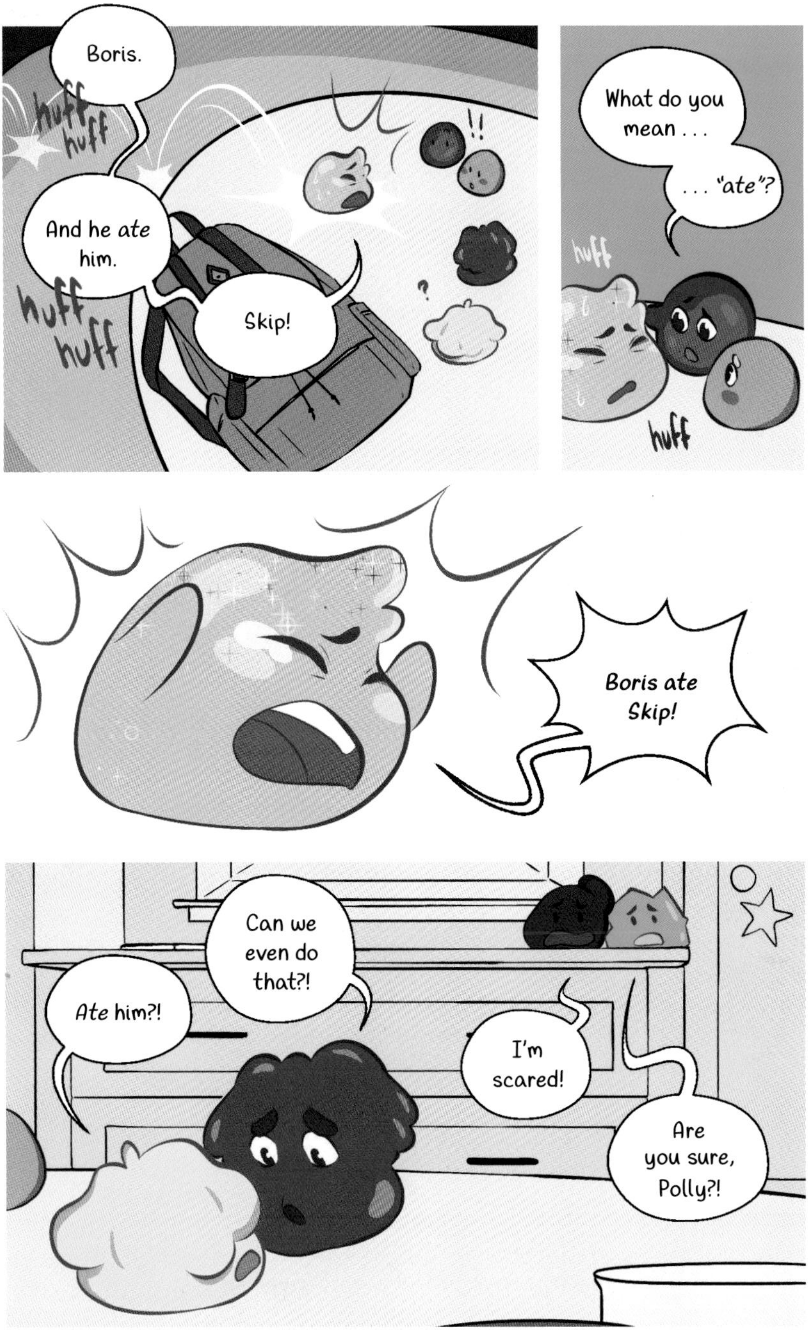
Boris.
huff huff
And he ate him.
huff huff
Skip!
!!
?
What do you mean . . .
. . . "ate"?
huff
huff
Boris ate Skip!
Ate him?!
Can we even do that?!
I'm scared!
Are you sure, Polly?!

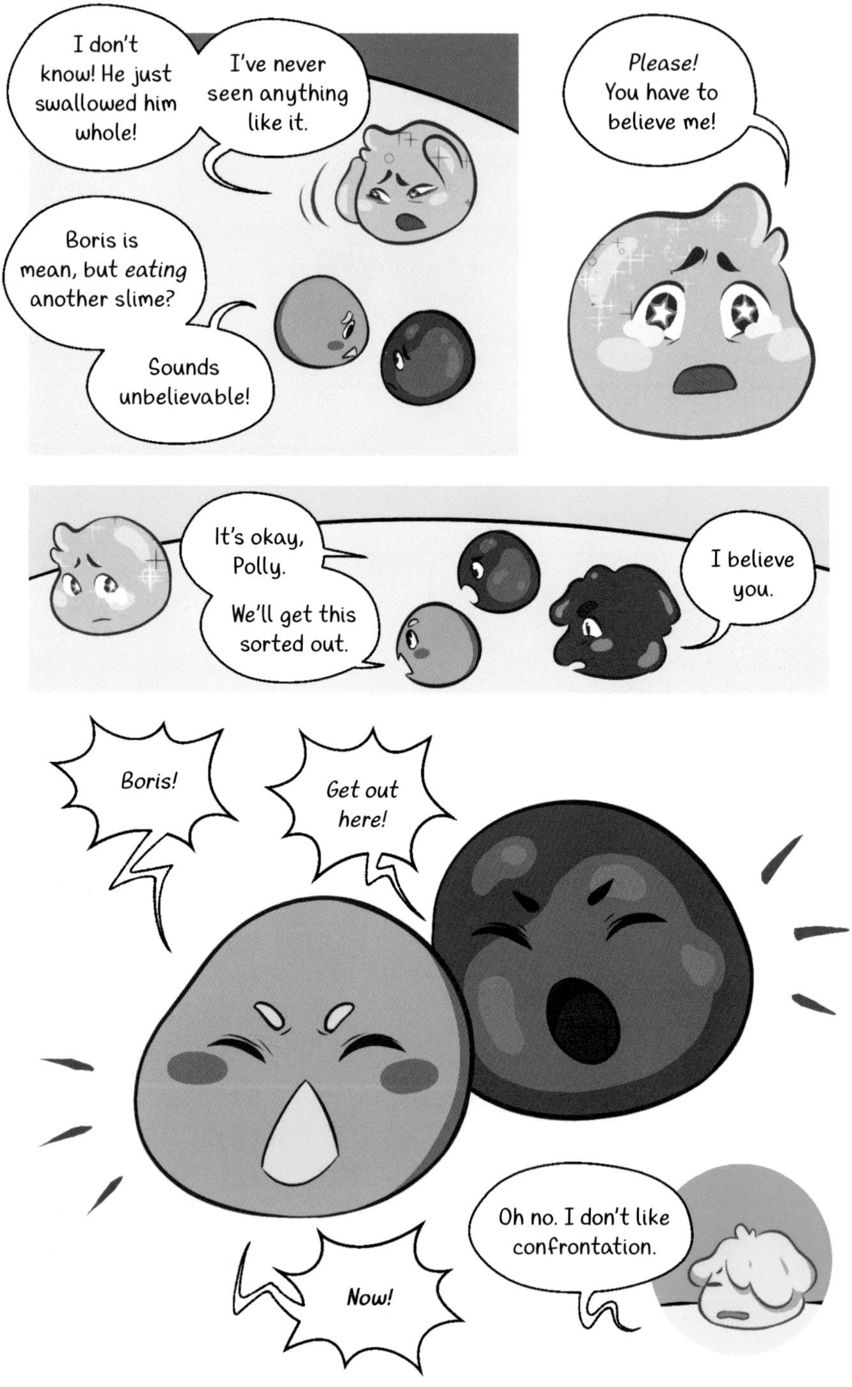
I don't know! He just swallowed him whole!
I've never seen anything like it.
Boris is mean, but *eating* another slime?
Sounds unbelievable!
Please! You have to believe me!
It's okay, Polly.
We'll get this sorted out.
I believe you.
Boris!
Get out here!
Now!
Oh no. I don't like confrontation.

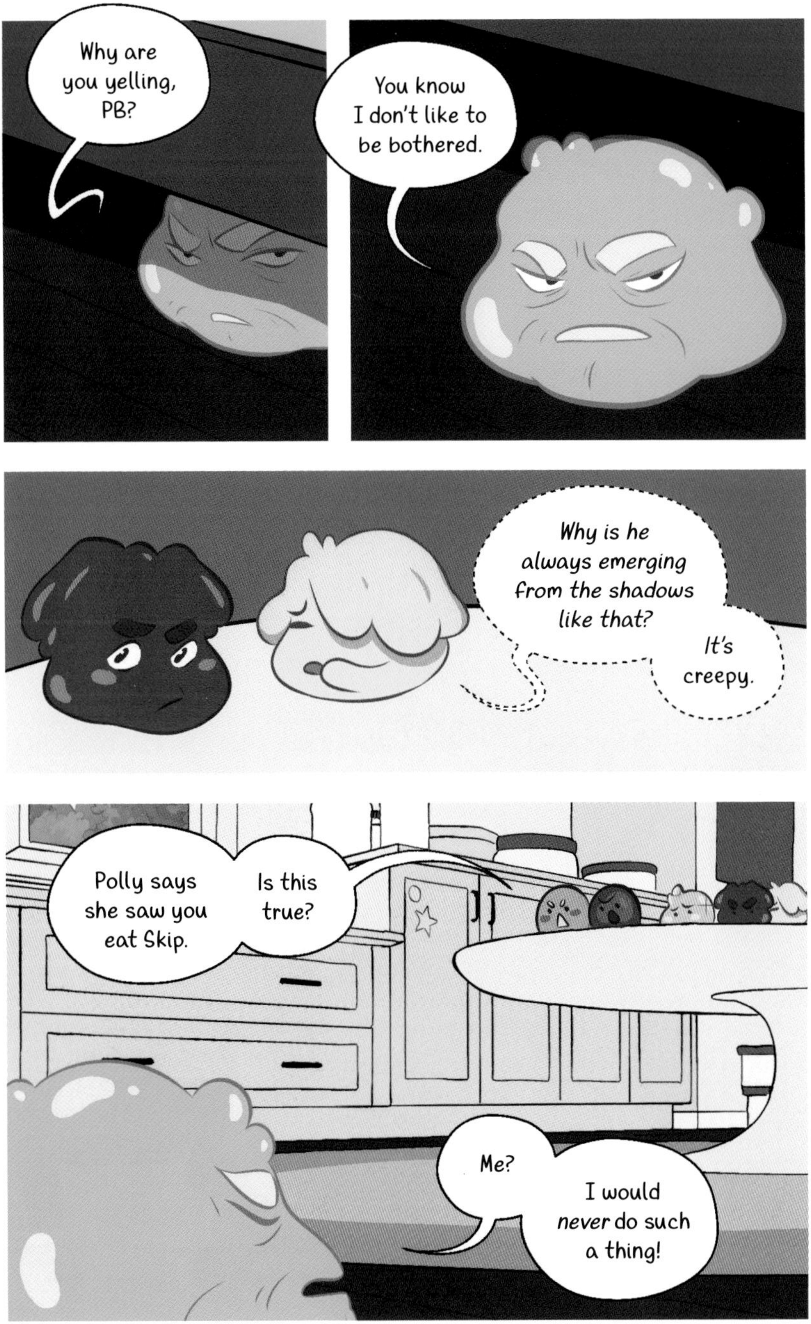
Why are you yelling, PB?
You know I don't like to be bothered.
Why is he always emerging from the shadows like that?
It's creepy.
Polly says she saw you eat Skip.
Is this true?
Me?
I would never do such a thing!

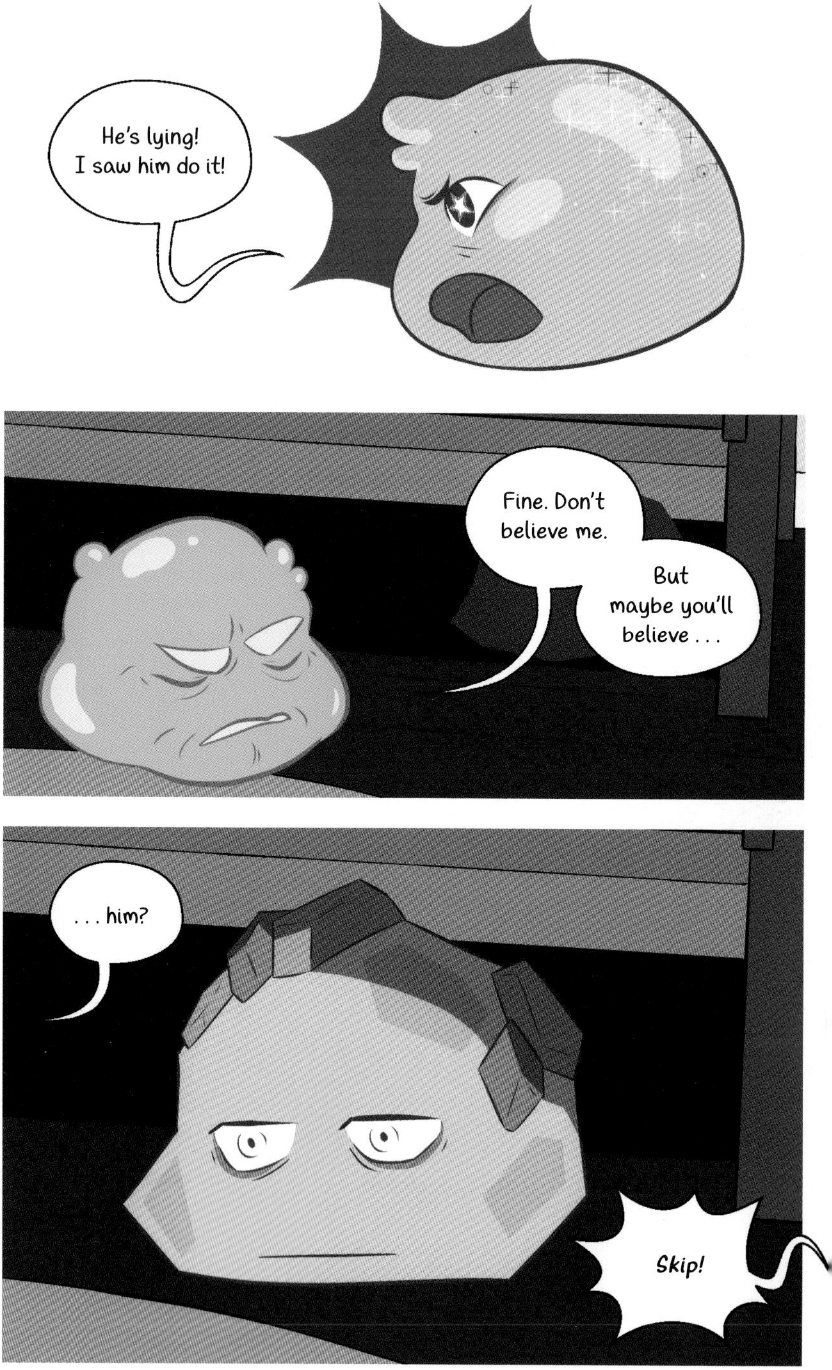
He's lying! I saw him do it!
Fine. Don't believe me.
But maybe you'll believe . . .
. . . him?
Skip!

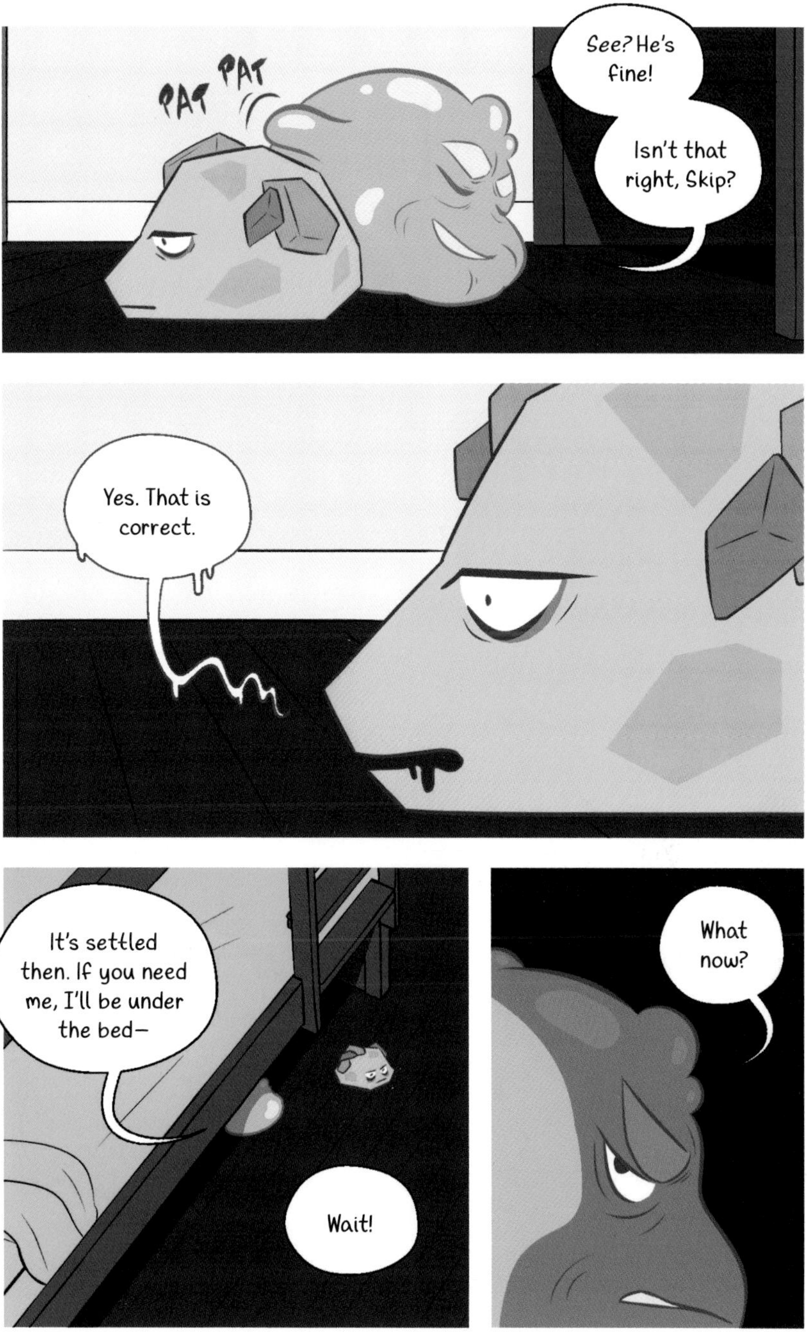
PAT PAT
See? He's fine!
Isn't that right, Skip?
Yes. That is correct.
It's settled then. If you need me, I'll be under the bed—
Wait!
What now?

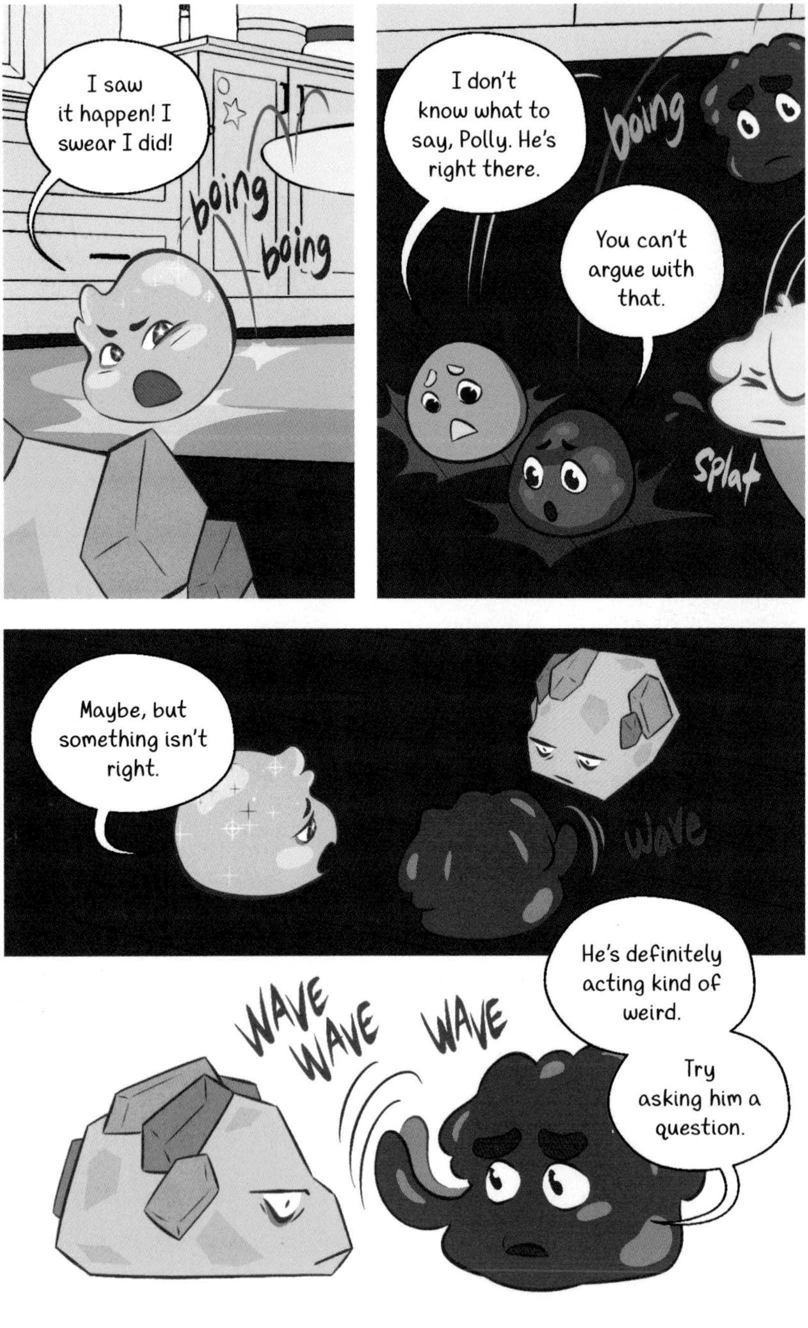
I saw it happen! I swear I did!
boing
boing
I don't know what to say, Polly. He's right there.
boing
You can't argue with that.
Splat
Maybe, but something isn't right.
wave
He's definitely acting kind of weird.
Try asking him a question.
WAVE
WAVE
WAVE

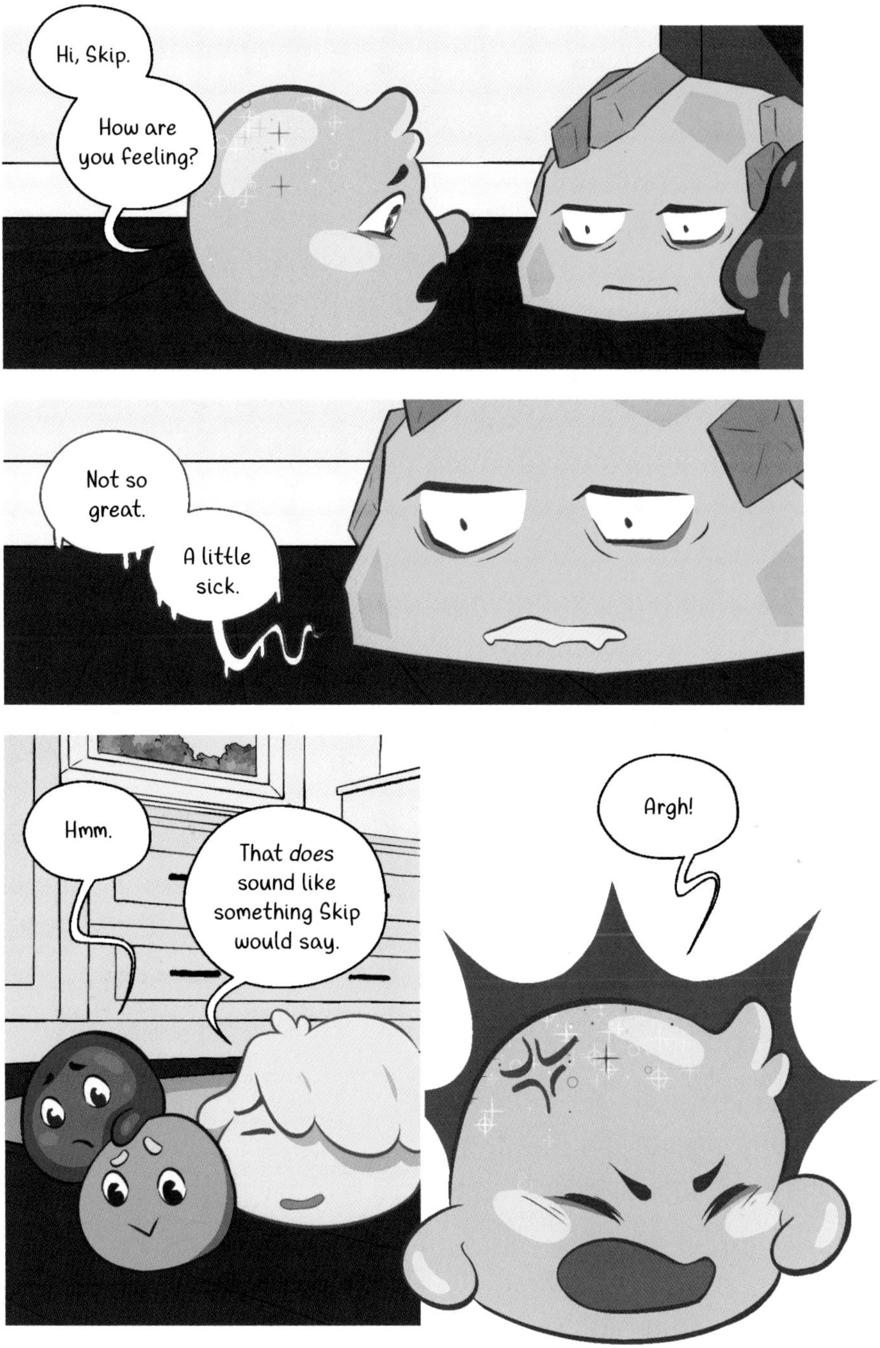
Hi, Skip.
How are you feeling?
Not so great.
A little sick.
Hmm.
That *does* sound like something Skip would say.
Argh!

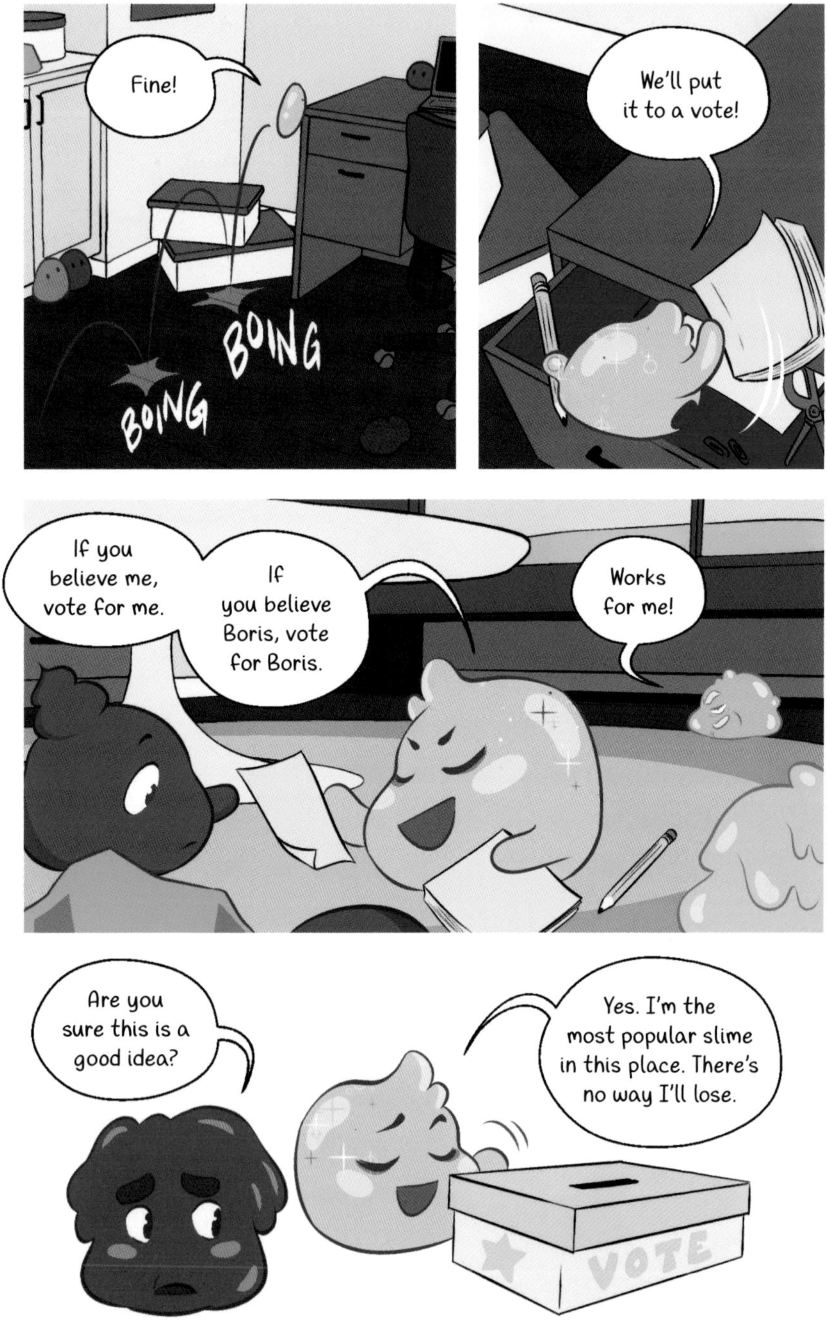
Fine!
BOING
BOING
We'll put it to a vote!
If you believe me, vote for me.
If you believe Boris, vote for Boris.
Works for me!
Are you sure this is a good idea?
Yes. I'm the most popular slime in this place. There's no way I'll lose.
VOTE

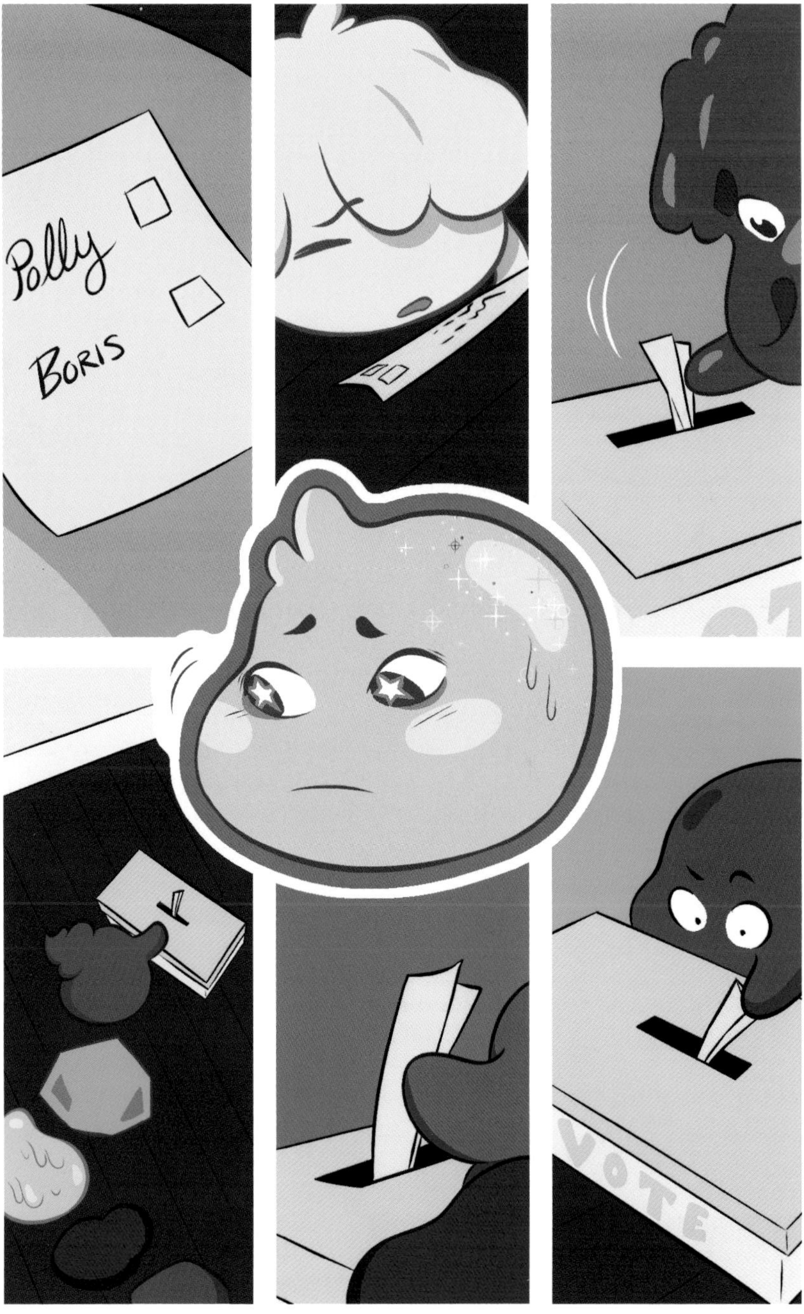
Polly
Boris
VOTE

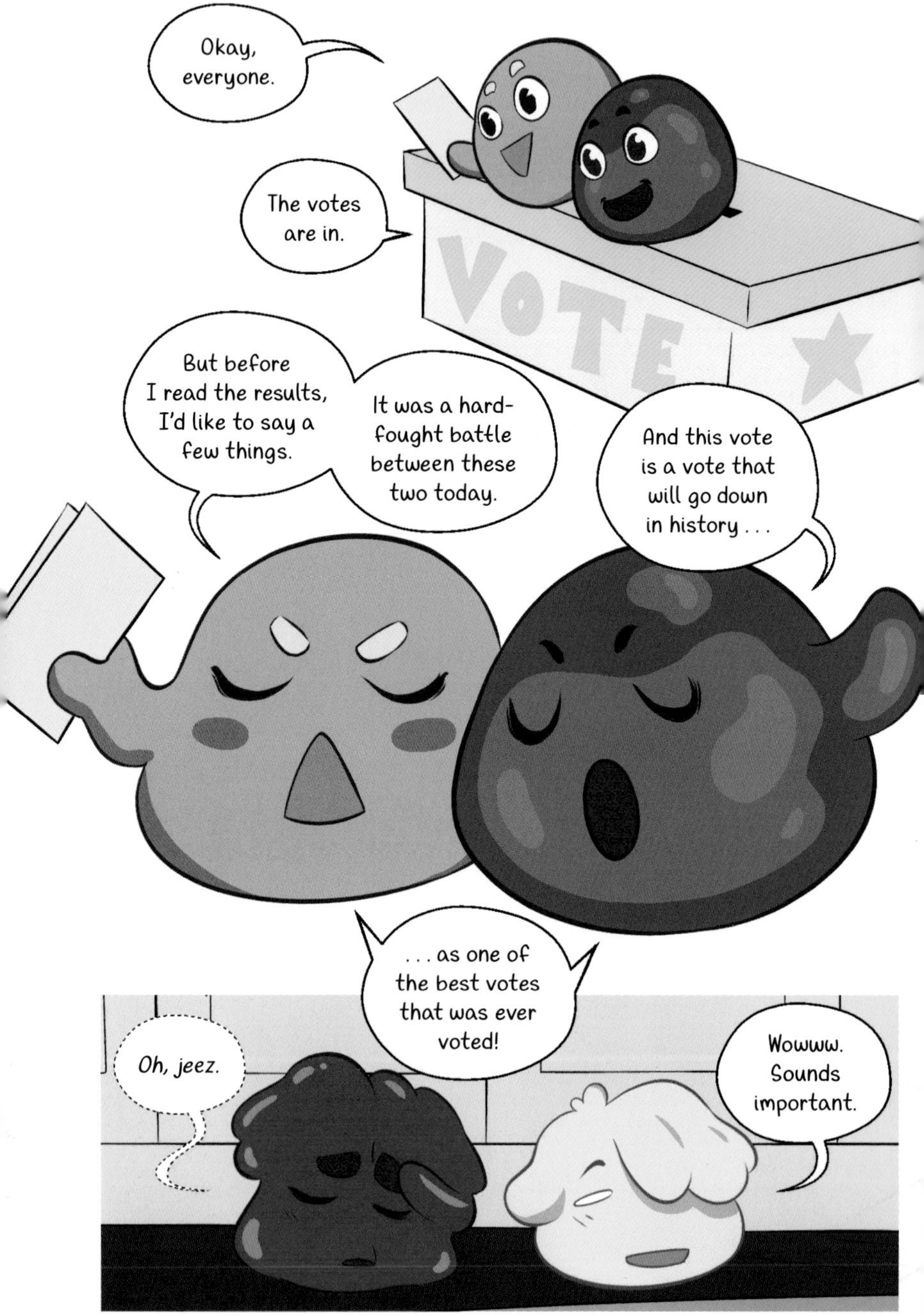
Okay, everyone.
The votes are in.
But before I read the results, I'd like to say a few things.
It was a hard-fought battle between these two today.
And this vote is a vote that will go down in history . . .
. . . as one of the best votes that was ever voted!
Oh, jeez.
Wowww. Sounds important.

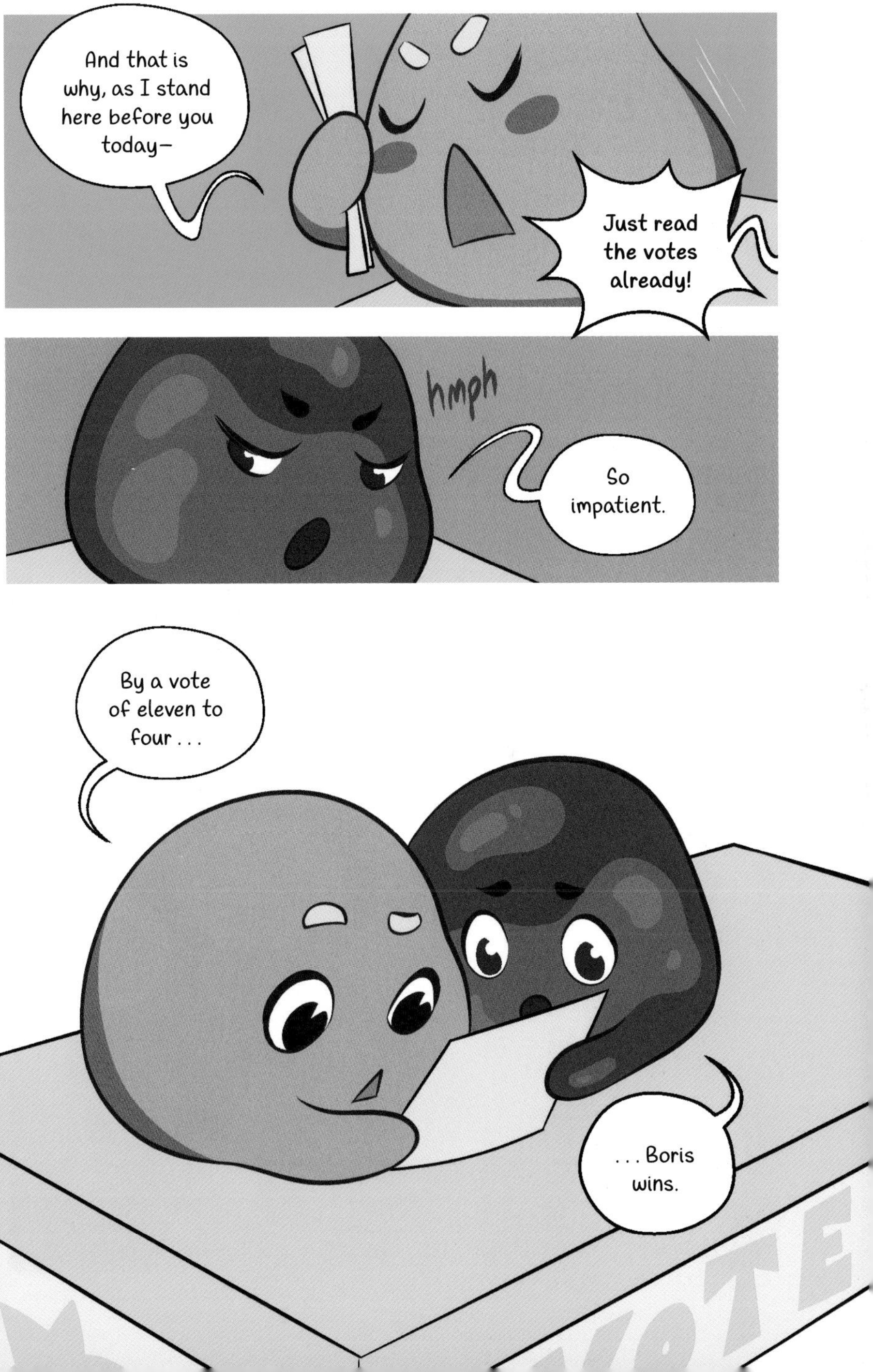
And that is why, as I stand here before you today—
Just read the votes already!
hmph
So impatient.
By a vote of eleven to four . . .
. . . Boris wins.
VOTE

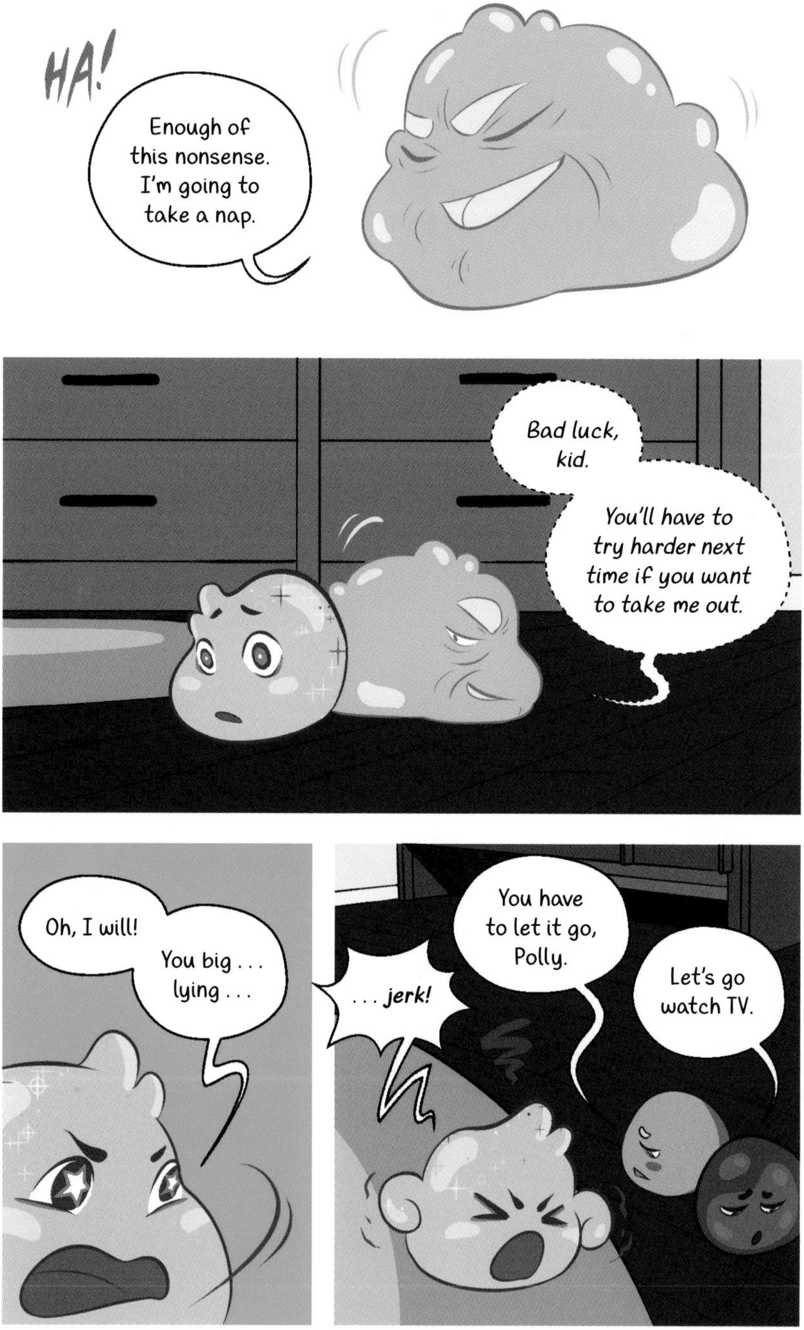
HA!
Enough of this nonsense. I'm going to take a nap.
Bad luck, kid.
You'll have to try harder next time if you want to take me out.
Oh, I will!
You big . . . lying . . .
. . . jerk!
You have to let it go, Polly.
Let's go watch TV.

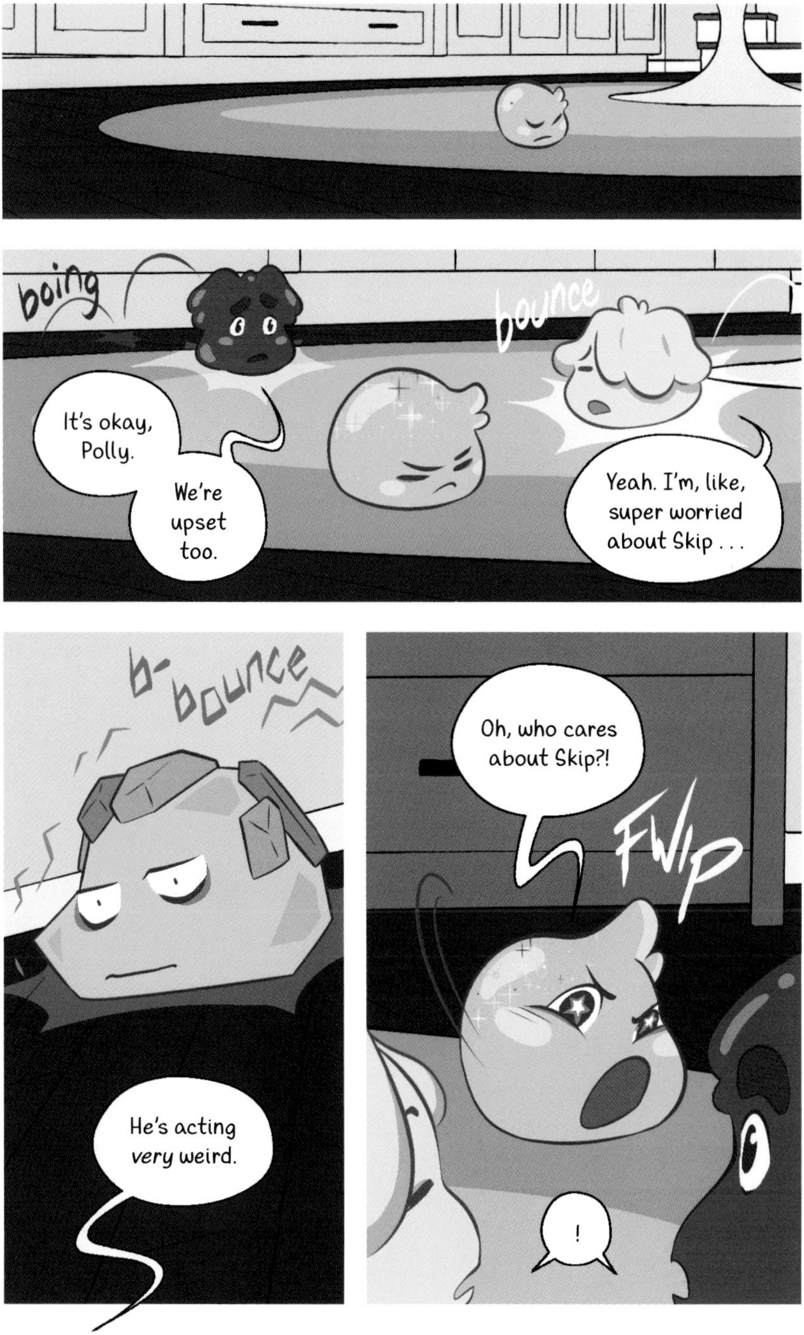
boing
bounce
It's okay, Polly.
We're upset too.
Yeah. I'm, like, super worried about Skip . . .
b-bounce
He's acting very weird.
Oh, who cares about Skip?!
FWIP
!

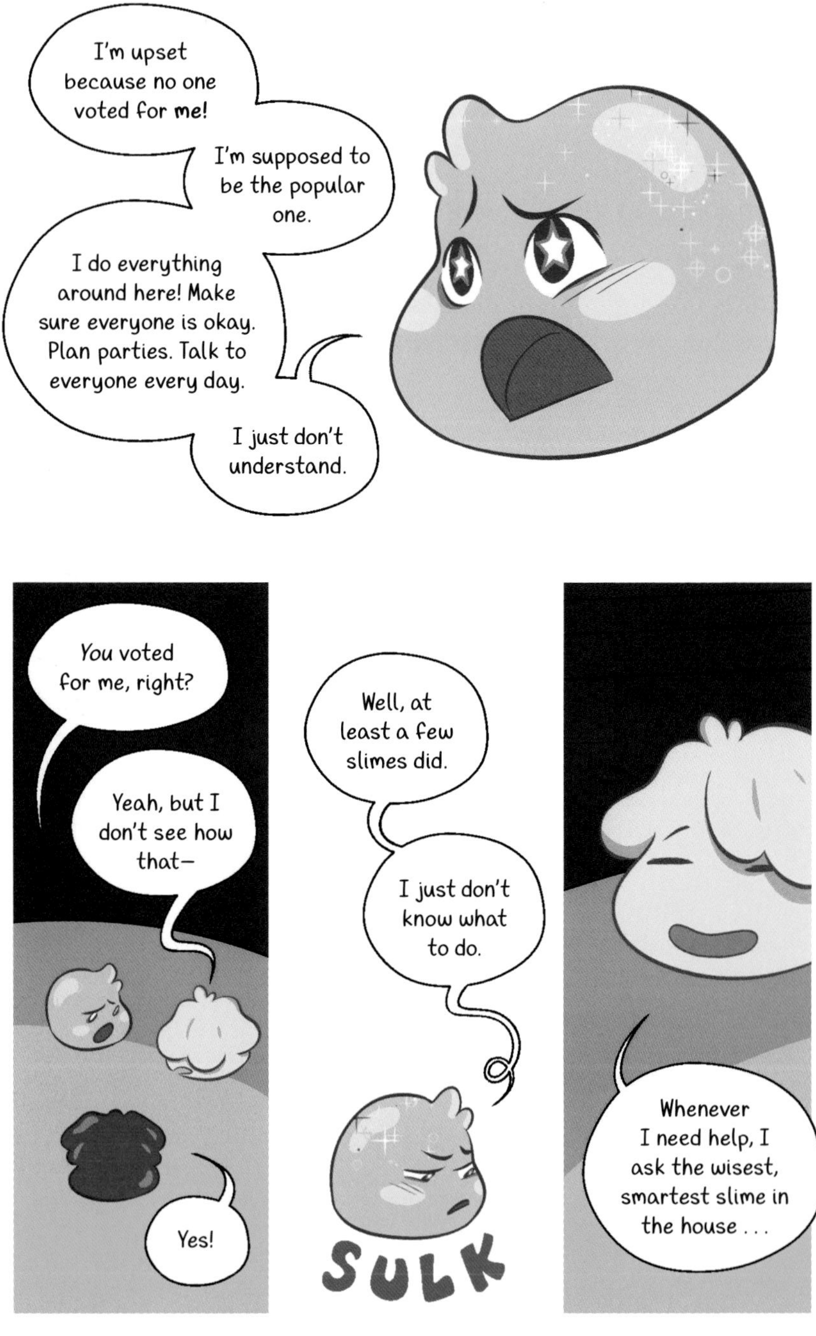
I'm upset because no one voted for **me!**
I'm supposed to be the popular one.
I do everything around here! Make sure everyone is okay. Plan parties. Talk to everyone every day.
I just don't understand.
You voted for me, right?
Yeah, but I don't see how that—
Yes!
Well, at least a few slimes did.
I just don't know what to do.
SULK
Whenever I need help, I ask the wisest, smartest slime in the house . . .

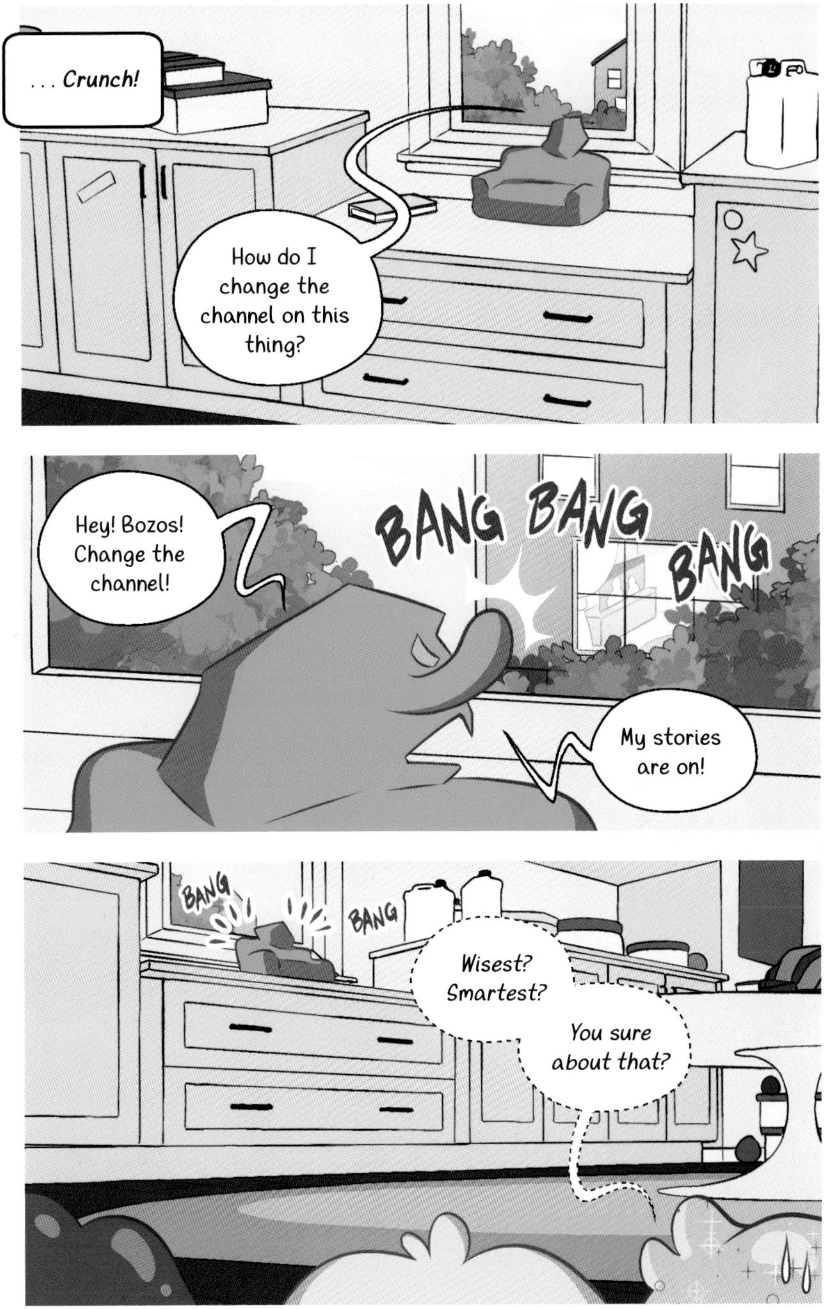

. . . Crunch!
How do I change the channel on this thing?
Hey! Bozos! Change the channel!
BANG BANG BANG
My stories are on!
BANG BANG
Wisest? Smartest?
You sure about that?

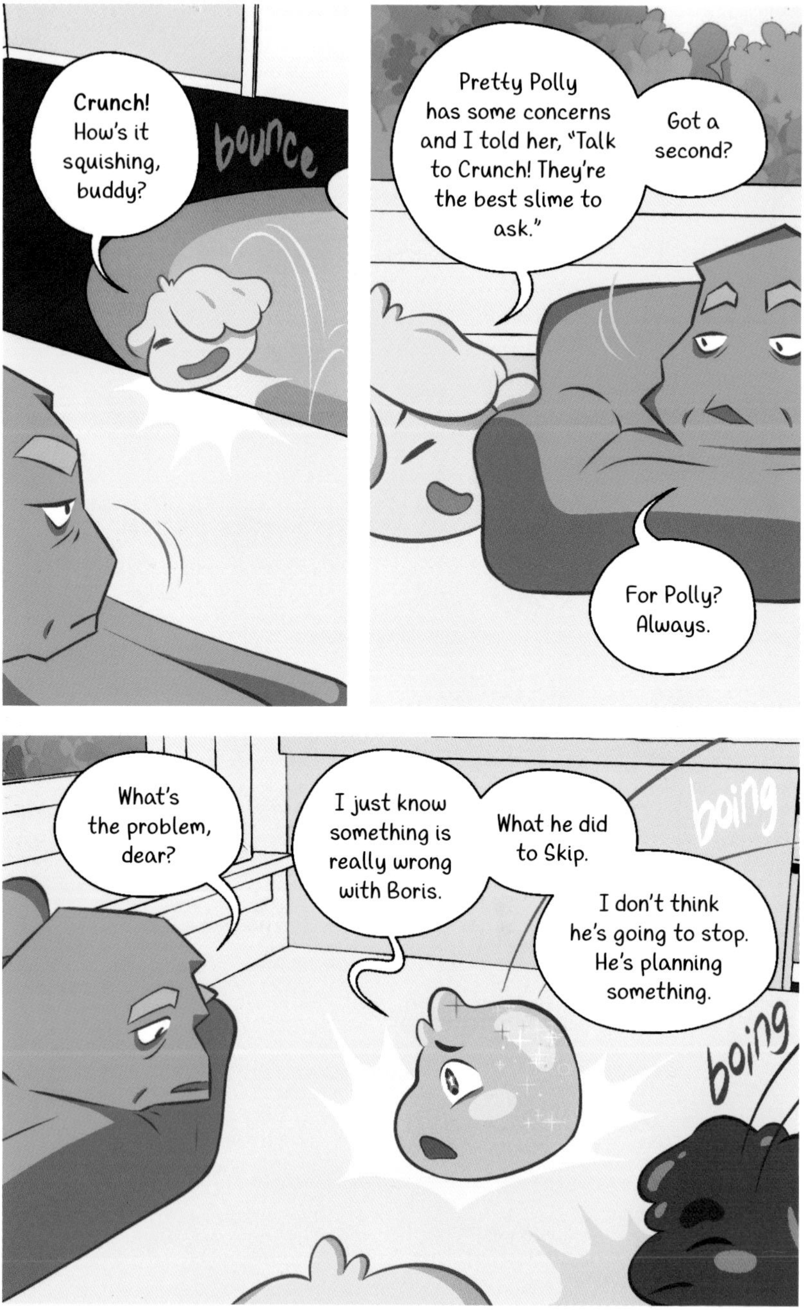
Crunch! How's it squishing, buddy?
bounce
Pretty Polly has some concerns and I told her, "Talk to Crunch! They're the best slime to ask."
Got a second?
For Polly? Always.
What's the problem, dear?
I just know something is really wrong with Boris.
What he did to Skip.
I don't think he's going to stop. He's planning something.
boing
boing

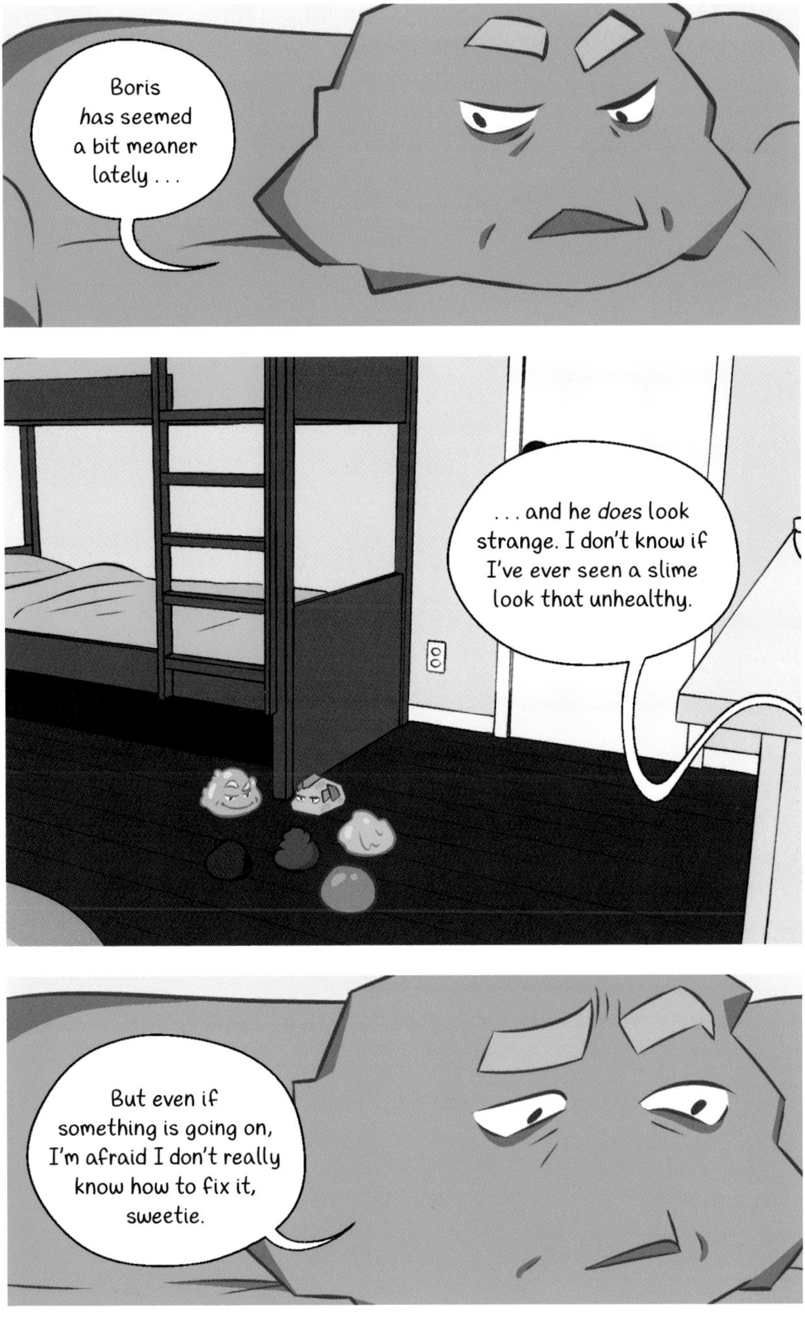
Boris *has* seemed a bit meaner lately . . .
. . . and he *does* look strange. I don't know if I've ever seen a slime look that unhealthy.
But even if something is going on, I'm afraid I don't really know how to fix it, sweetie.

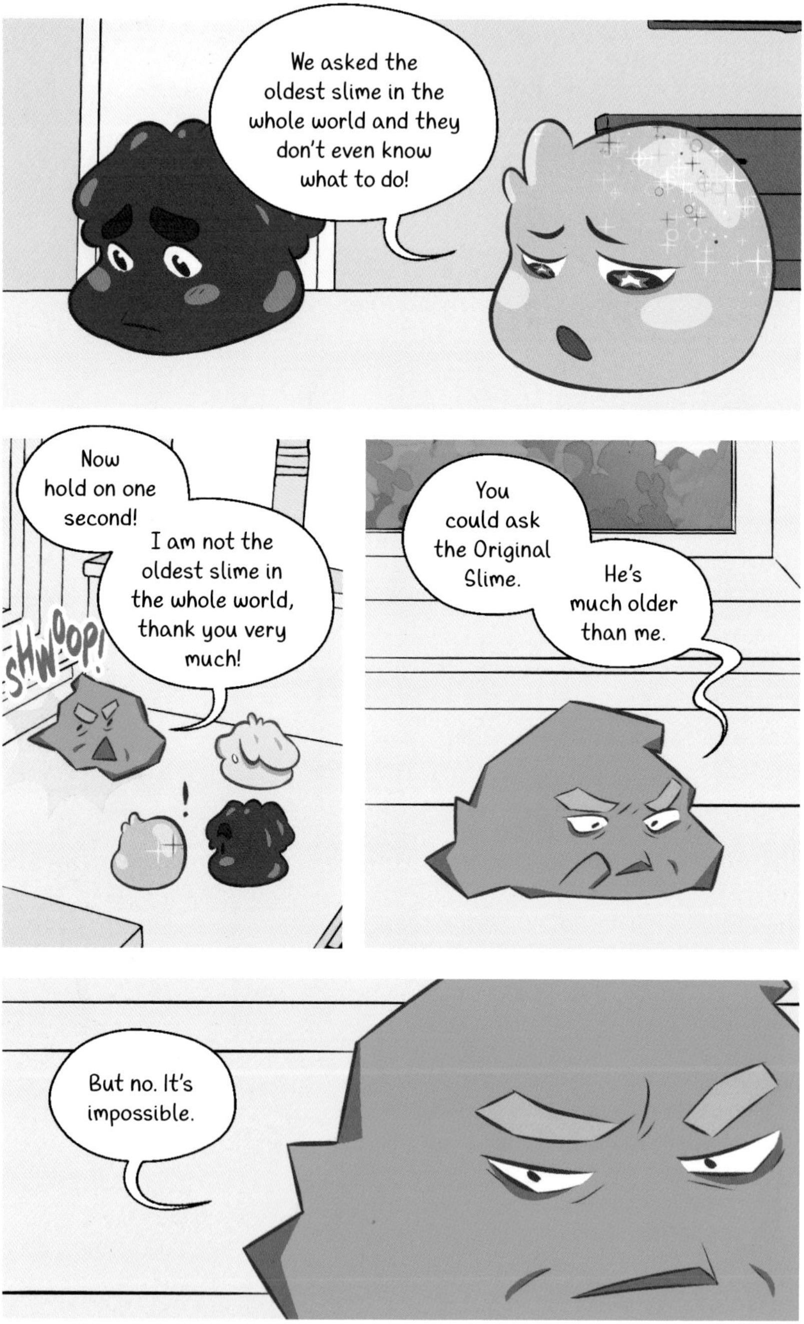
We asked the oldest slime in the whole world and they don't even know what to do!
Now hold on one second!
I am not the oldest slime in the whole world, thank you very much!
SHWOOP!
!
You could ask the Original Slime.
He's much older than me.
But no. It's impossible.

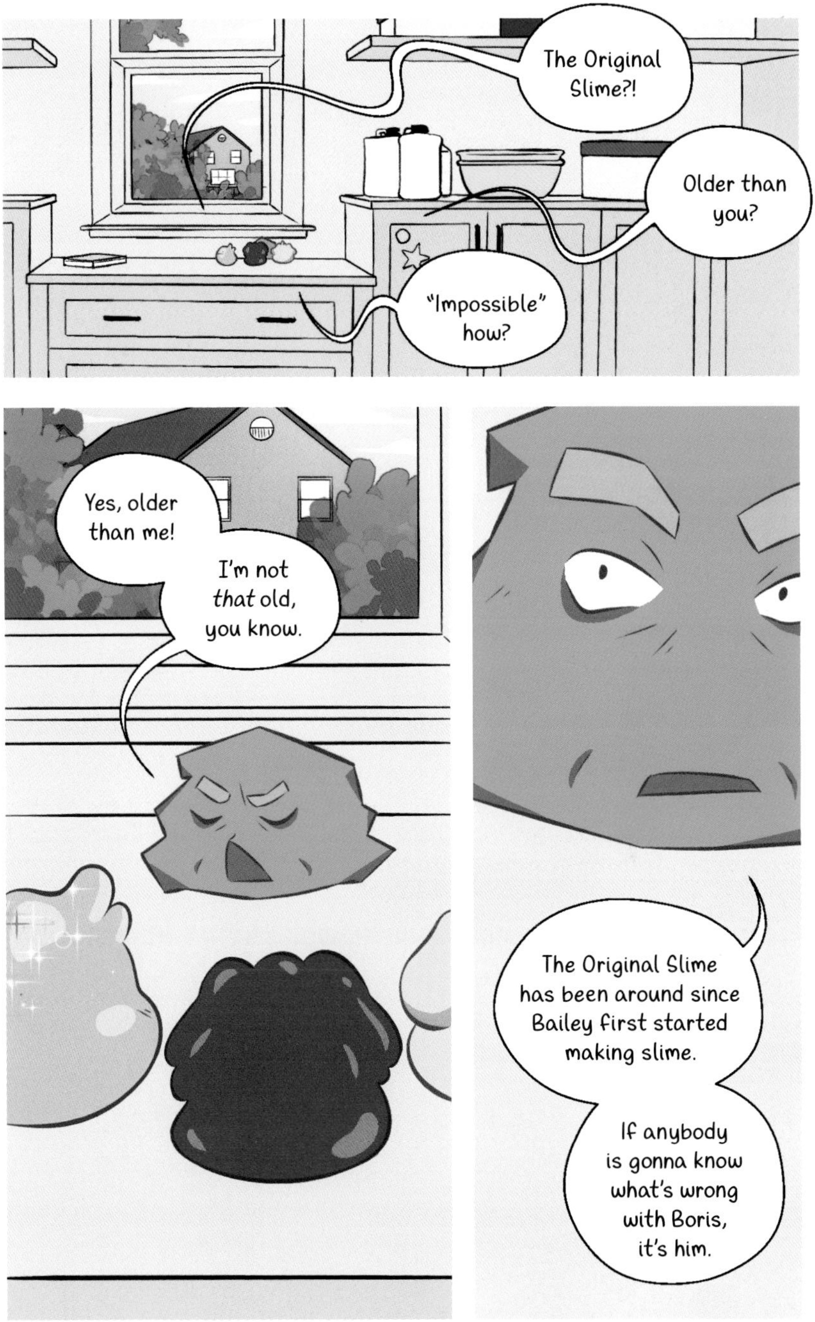

The Original Slime?!
Older than you?
"Impossible" how?
Yes, older than me!
I'm not *that* old, you know.
The Original Slime has been around since Bailey first started making slime.
If anybody is gonna know what's wrong with Boris, it's him.

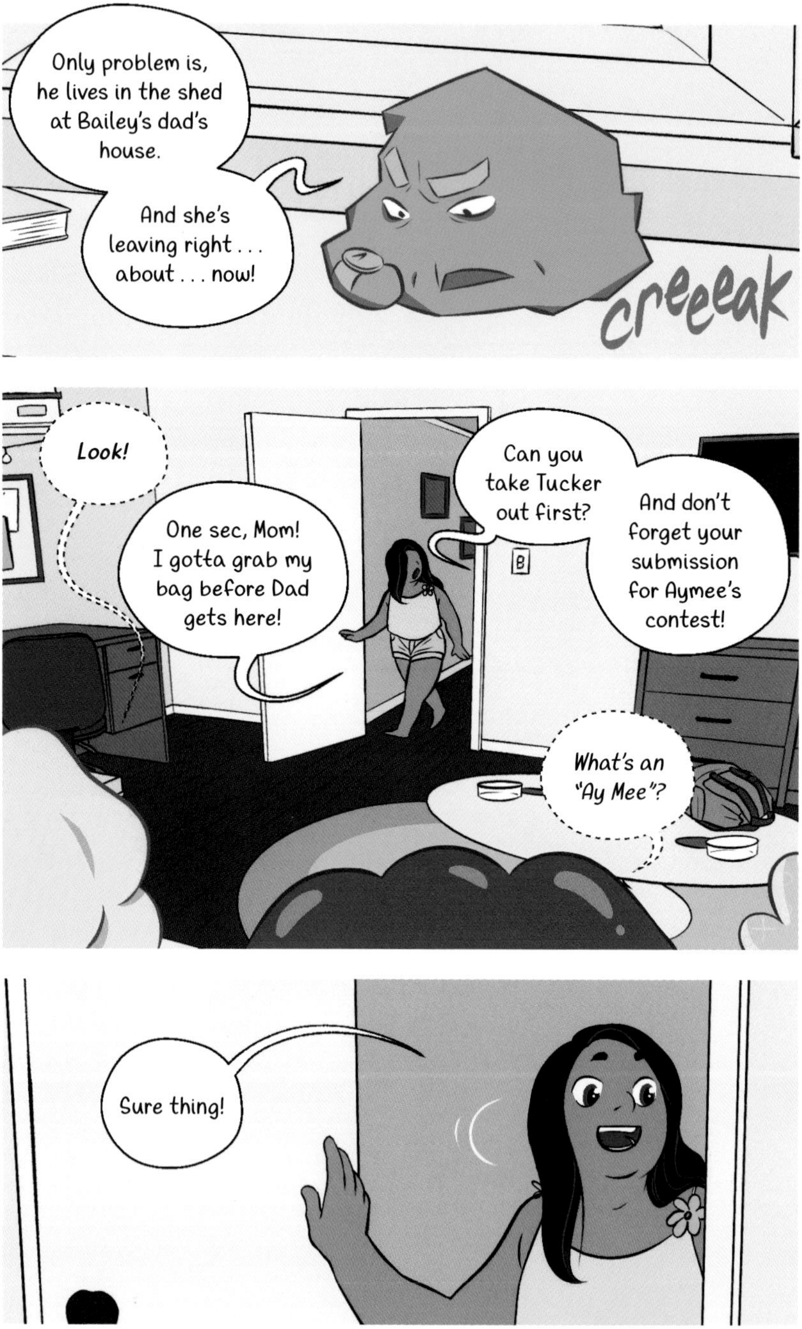
Only problem is, he lives in the shed at Bailey's dad's house.
And she's leaving right . . . about . . . now!
creeeak
Look!
One sec, Mom! I gotta grab my bag before Dad gets here!
Can you take Tucker out first?
And don't forget your submission for Aymee's contest!
What's an "Ay Mee"?
Sure thing!

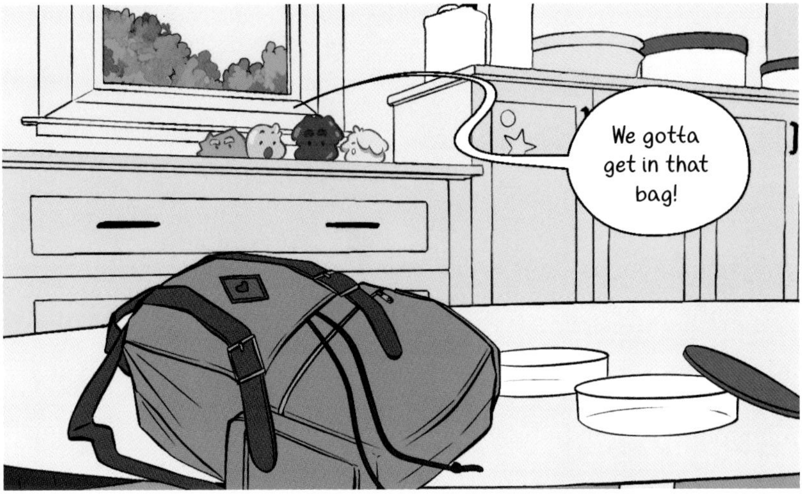
We gotta get in that bag!

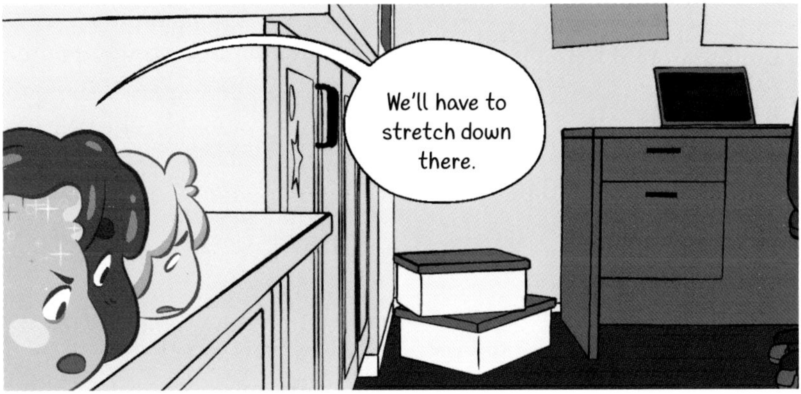
We'll have to stretch down there.

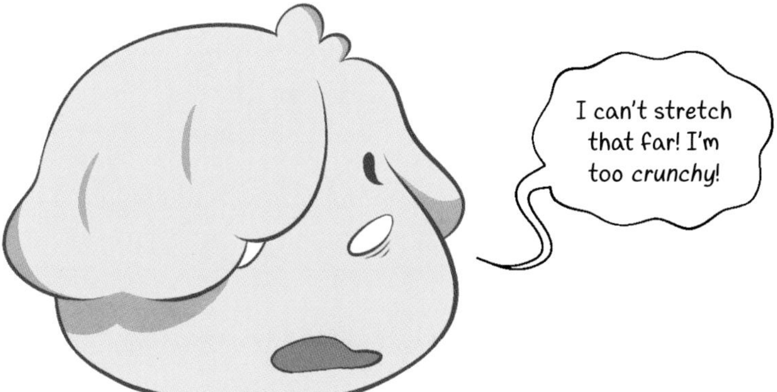
I can't stretch that far! I'm too *crunchy*!

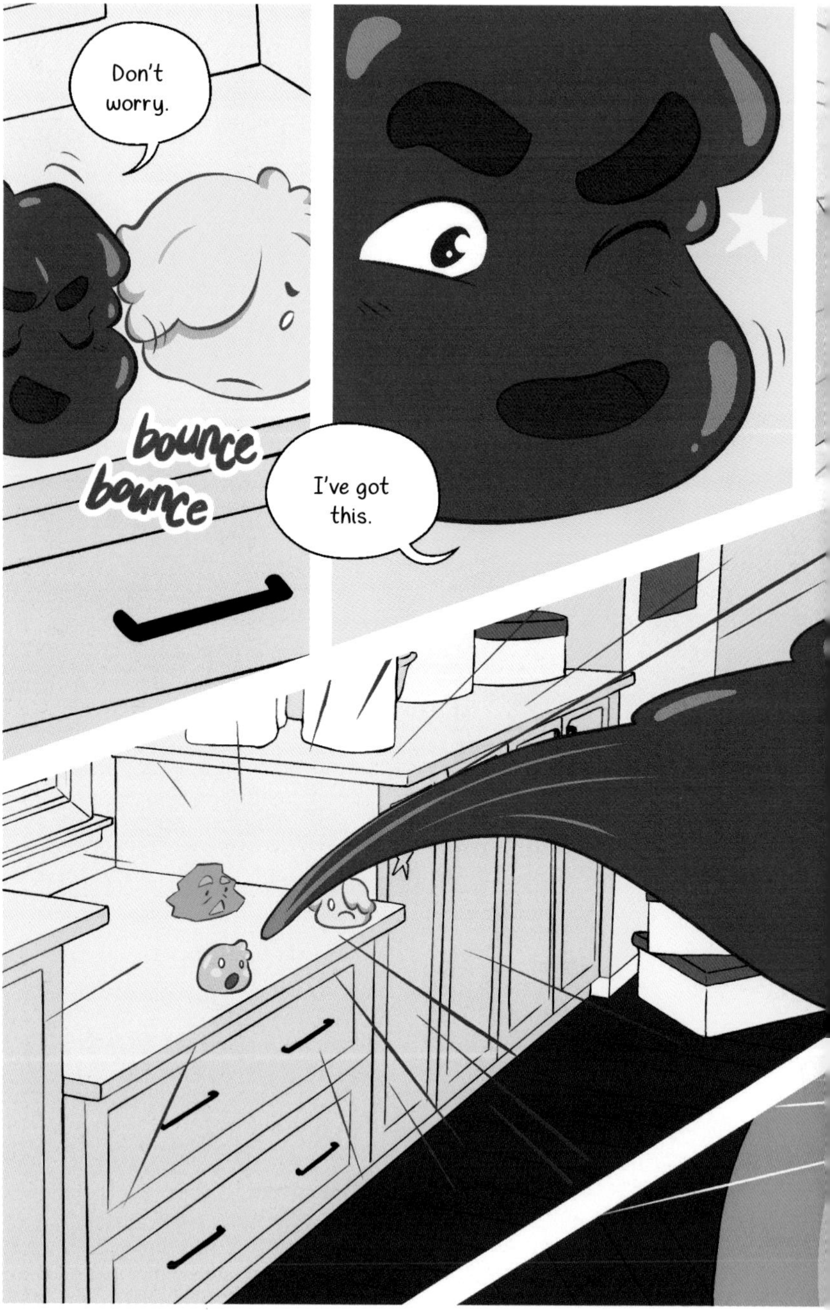
Don't worry.
bounce bounce
I've got this.

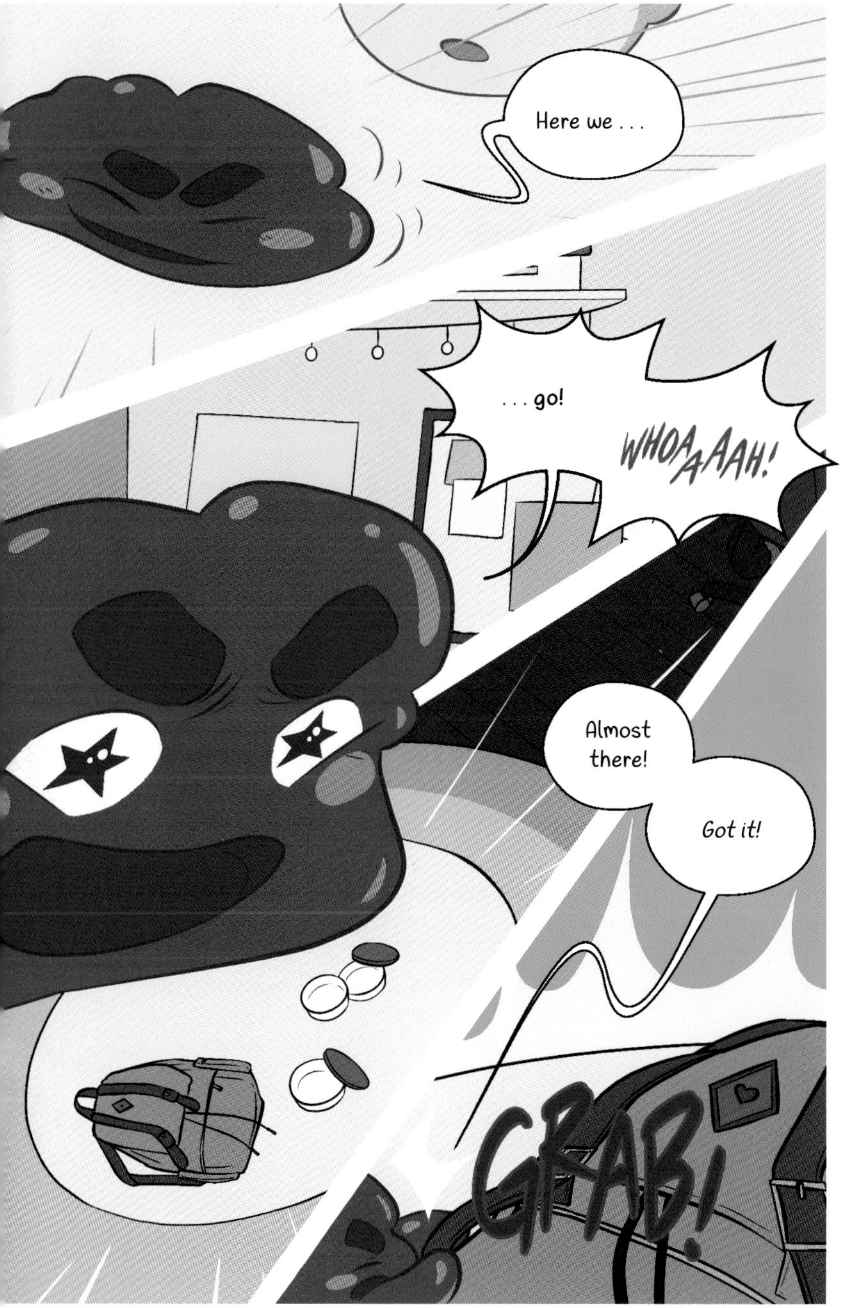
Here we . . .
. . . go!
WHOAAAAH!
Almost there!
Got it!
GRAB!

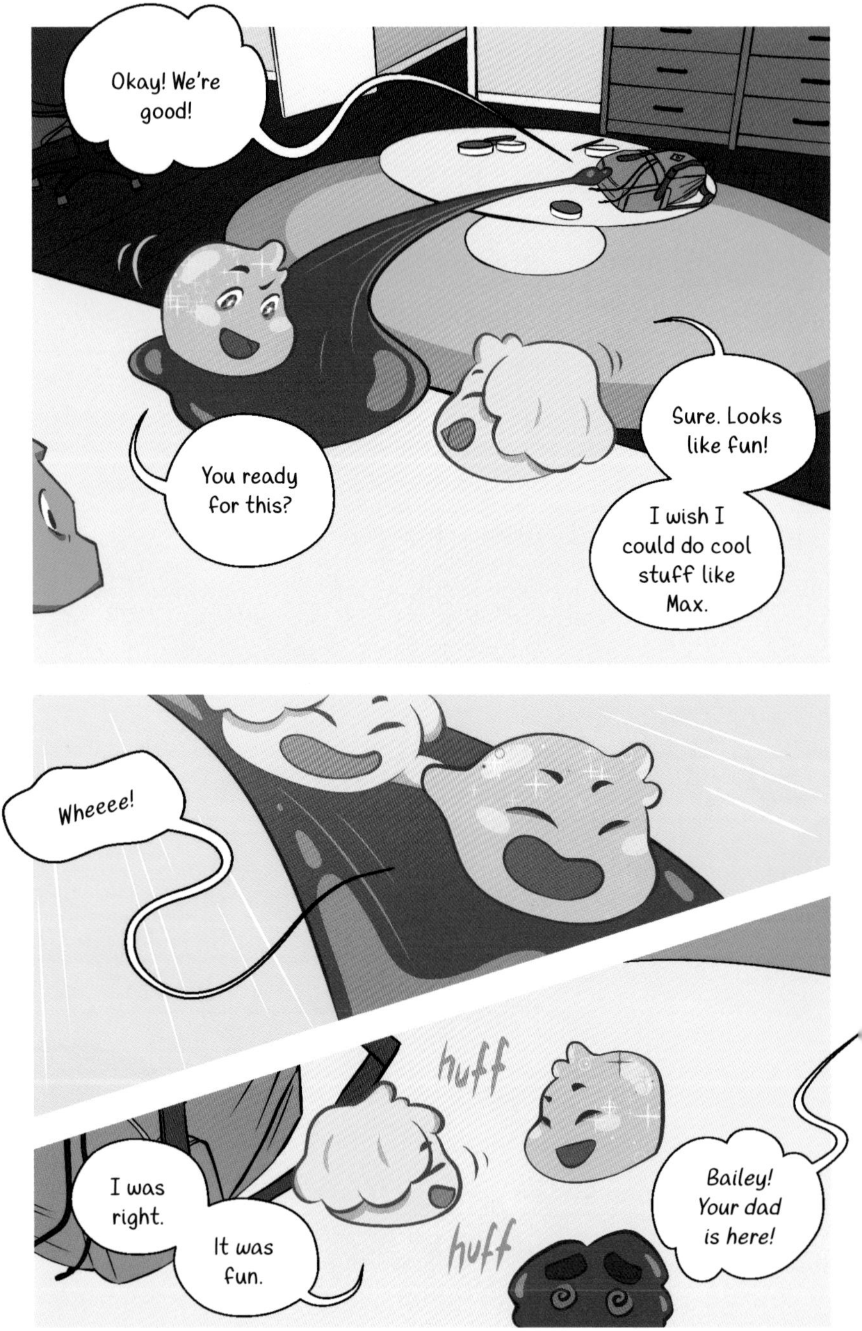
Okay! We're good!
You ready for this?
Sure. Looks like fun!
I wish I could do cool stuff like Max.
Wheeee!
huff
huff
I was right.
It was fun.
Bailey! Your dad is here!

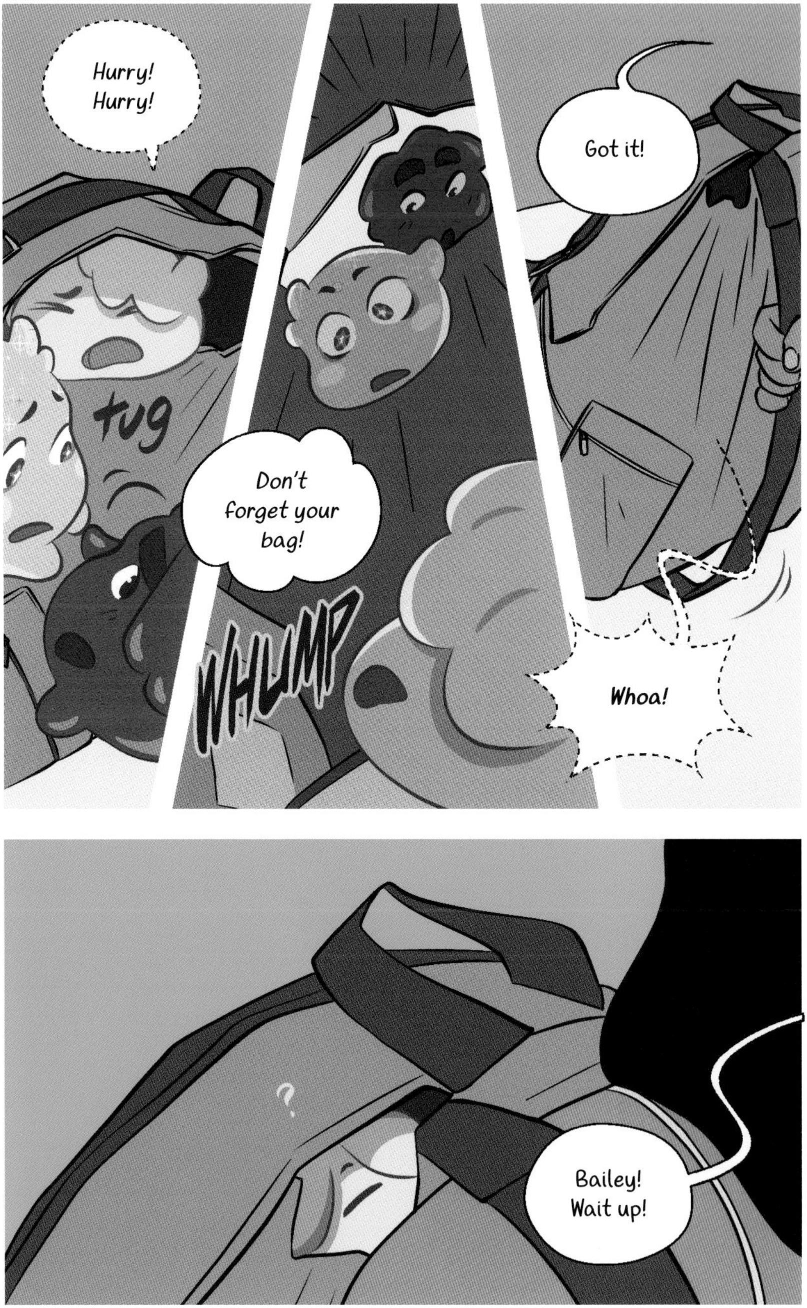
Hurry!
Hurry!
tug
Don't forget your bag!
WHUMP
Got it!
Whoa!
?
Bailey! Wait up!

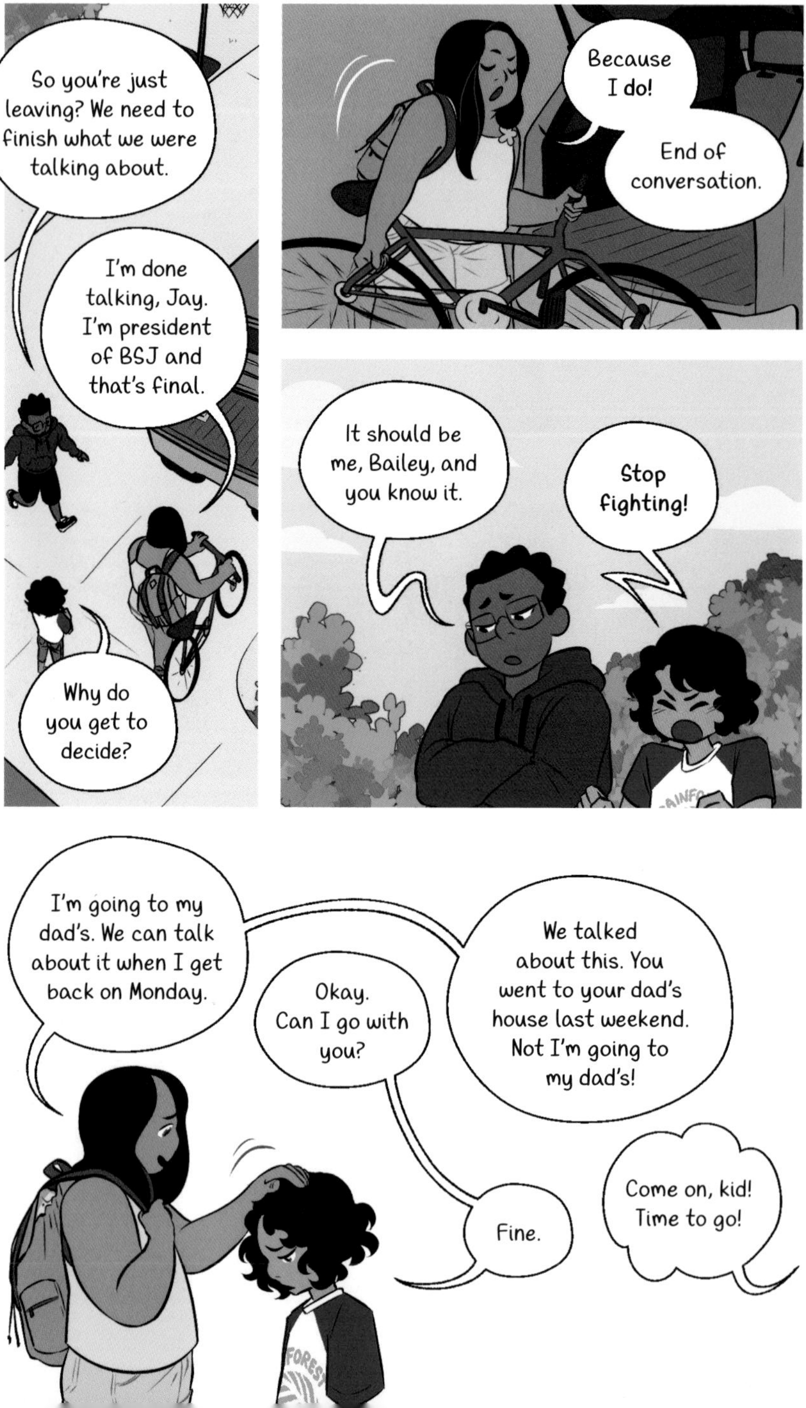
So you're just leaving? We need to finish what we were talking about.
I'm done talking, Jay. I'm president of BSJ and that's final.
Why do you get to decide?
Because I do!
End of conversation.
It should be me, Bailey, and you know it.
Stop fighting!
I'm going to my dad's. We can talk about it when I get back on Monday.
Okay. Can I go with you?
We talked about this. You went to your dad's house last weekend. Not I'm going to my dad's!
Fine.
Come on, kid! Time to go!

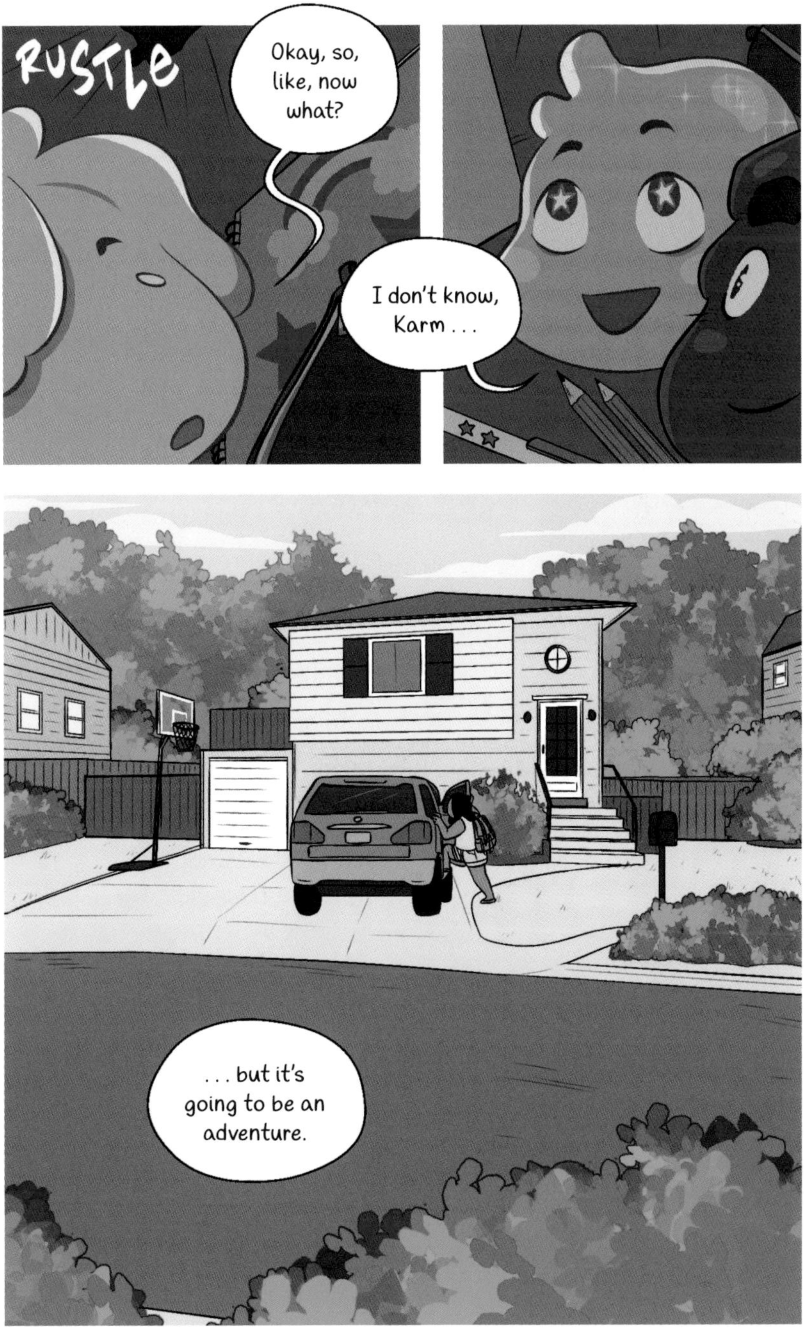
RUSTLE
Okay, so, like, now what?
I don't know, Karm . . .
. . . but it's going to be an adventure.

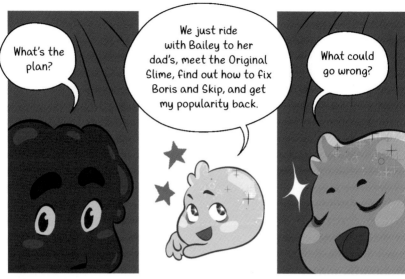

What's the plan?

We just ride with Bailey to her dad's, meet the Original Slime, find out how to fix Boris and Skip, and get my popularity back.

What could go wrong?

Um. A lot.

I think it'll be cool. Maybe I can learn some cool stretchy tricks like Max.

I just want to see the world! I'm tired of being stuck in that room.

And hang out with Polly, of course.

Hey!

Karma, can you check and see what's going on out there?

On it.

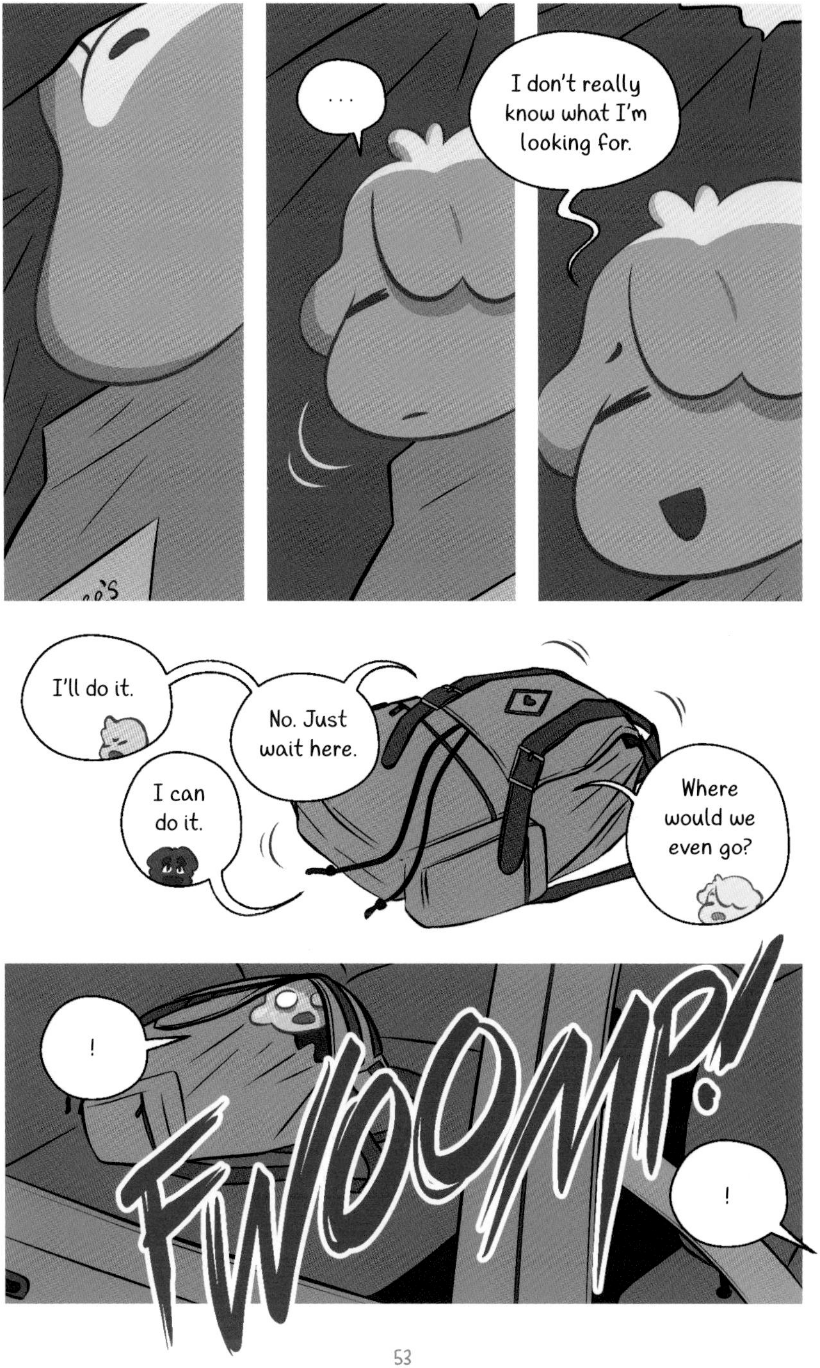
. . .
I don't really know what I'm looking for.
I'll do it.
No. Just wait here.
I can do it.
Where would we even go?
!
FWOOMP!
!

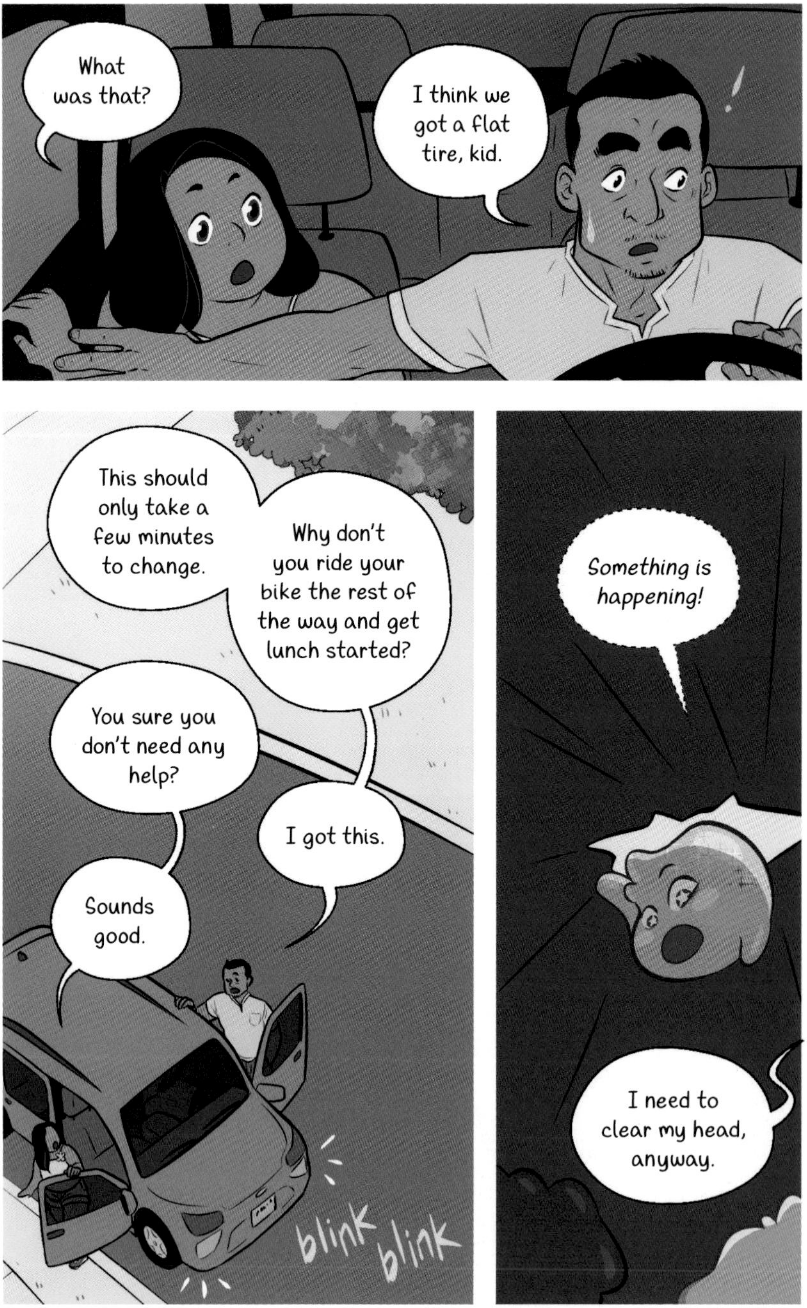
What was that?
I think we got a flat tire, kid.
This should only take a few minutes to change.
Why don't you ride your bike the rest of the way and get lunch started?
You sure you don't need any help?
I got this.
Sounds good.
blink blink
Something is happening!
I need to clear my head, anyway.

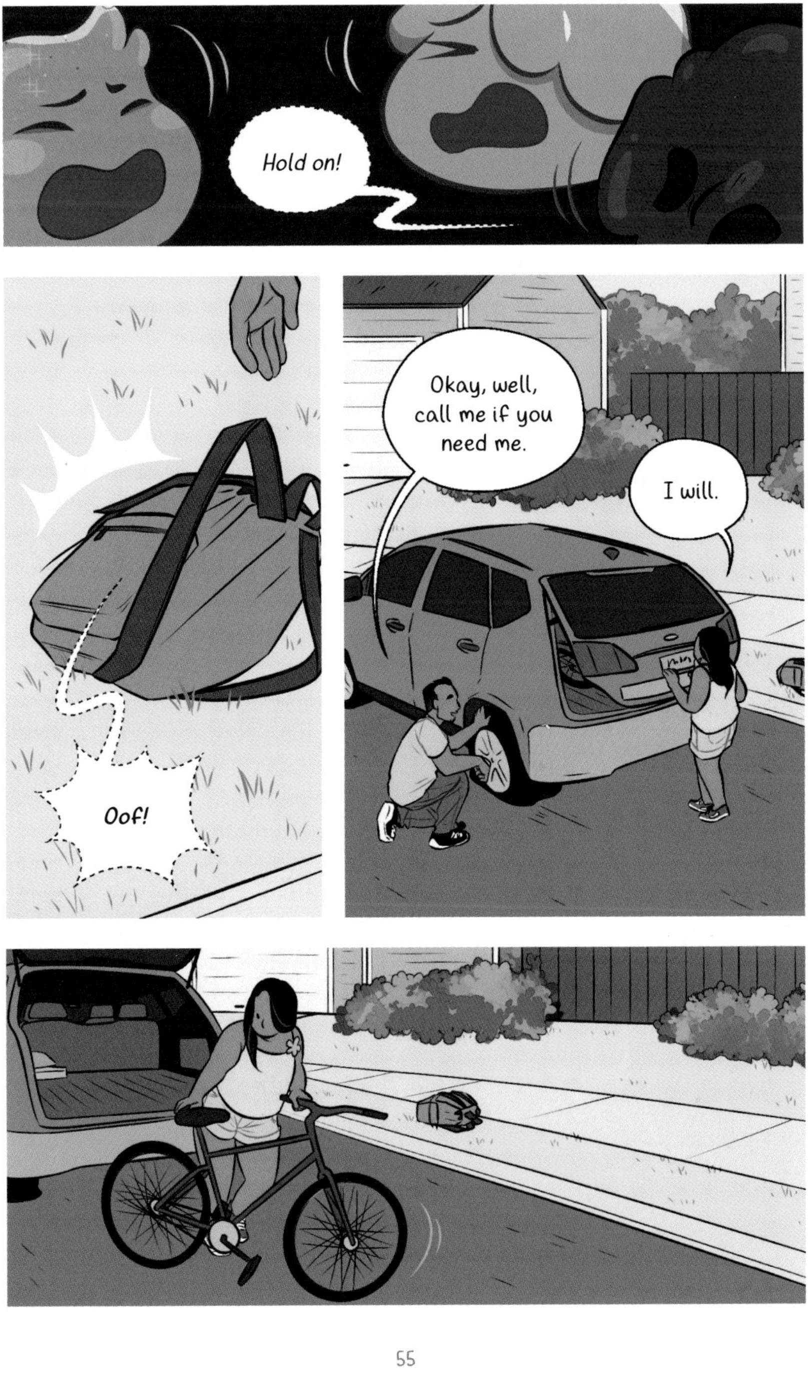
Hold on!
Oof!
Okay, well, call me if you need me.
I will.

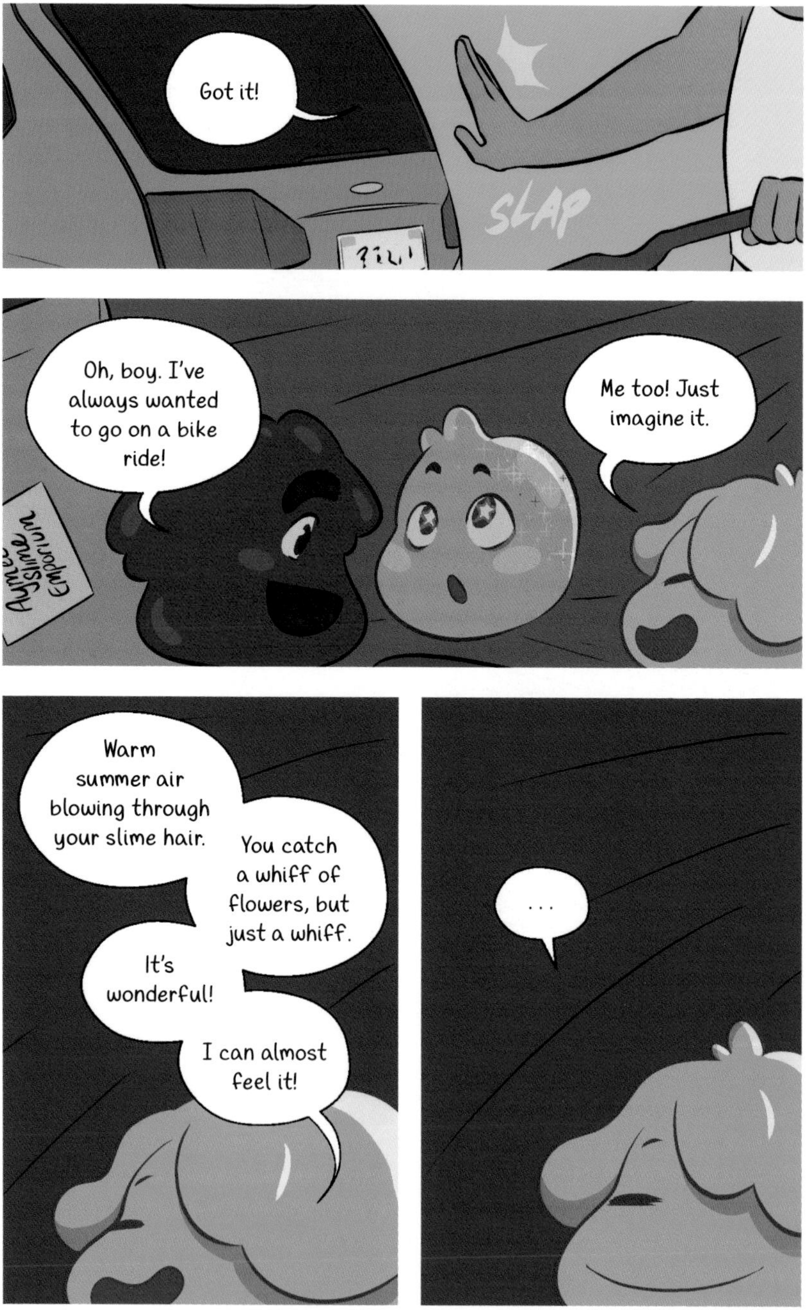
Got it!
SLAP
Oh, boy. I've always wanted to go on a bike ride!
Me too! Just imagine it.
Aymee's Slime Emporium
Warm summer air blowing through your slime hair.
You catch a whiff of flowers, but just a whiff.
It's wonderful!
I can almost feel it!
...

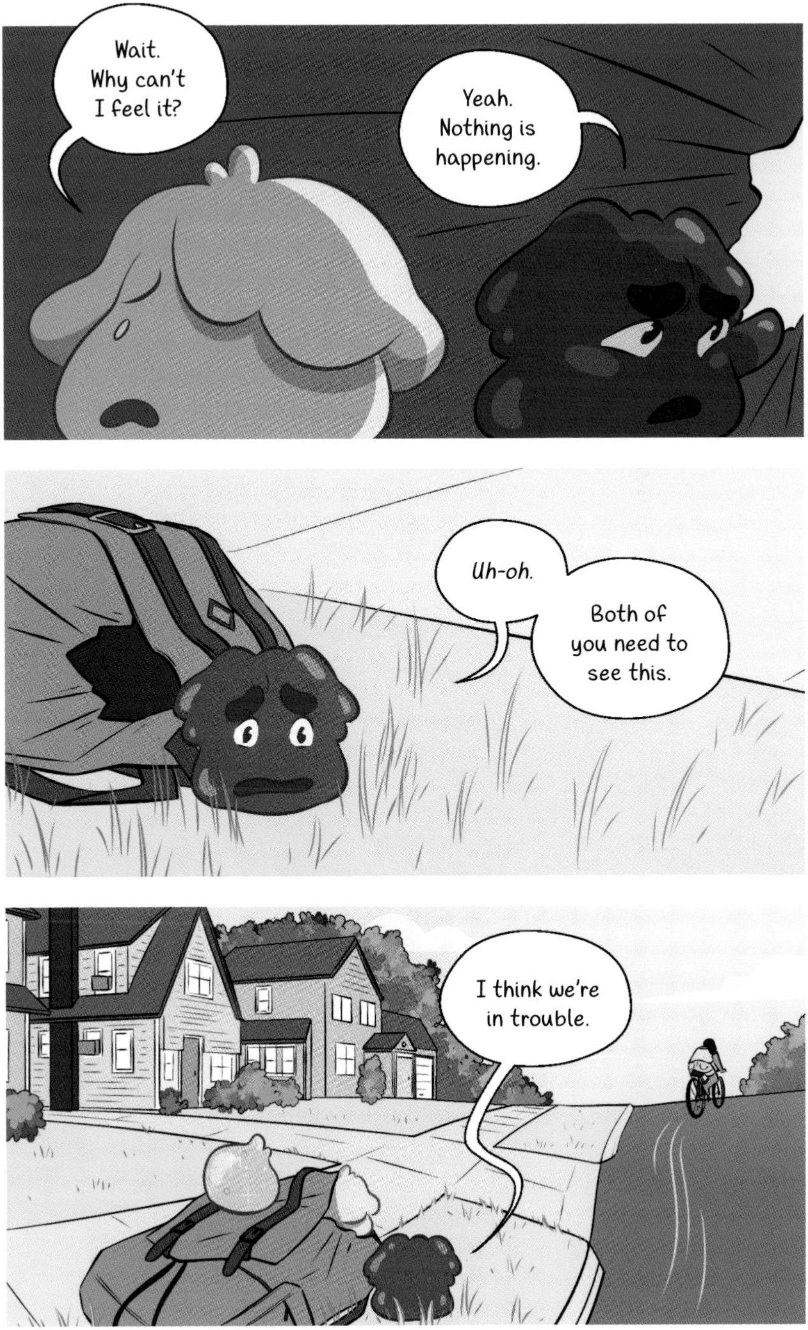
Wait. Why can't I feel it?
Yeah. Nothing is happening.
Uh-oh.
Both of you need to see this.
I think we're in trouble.

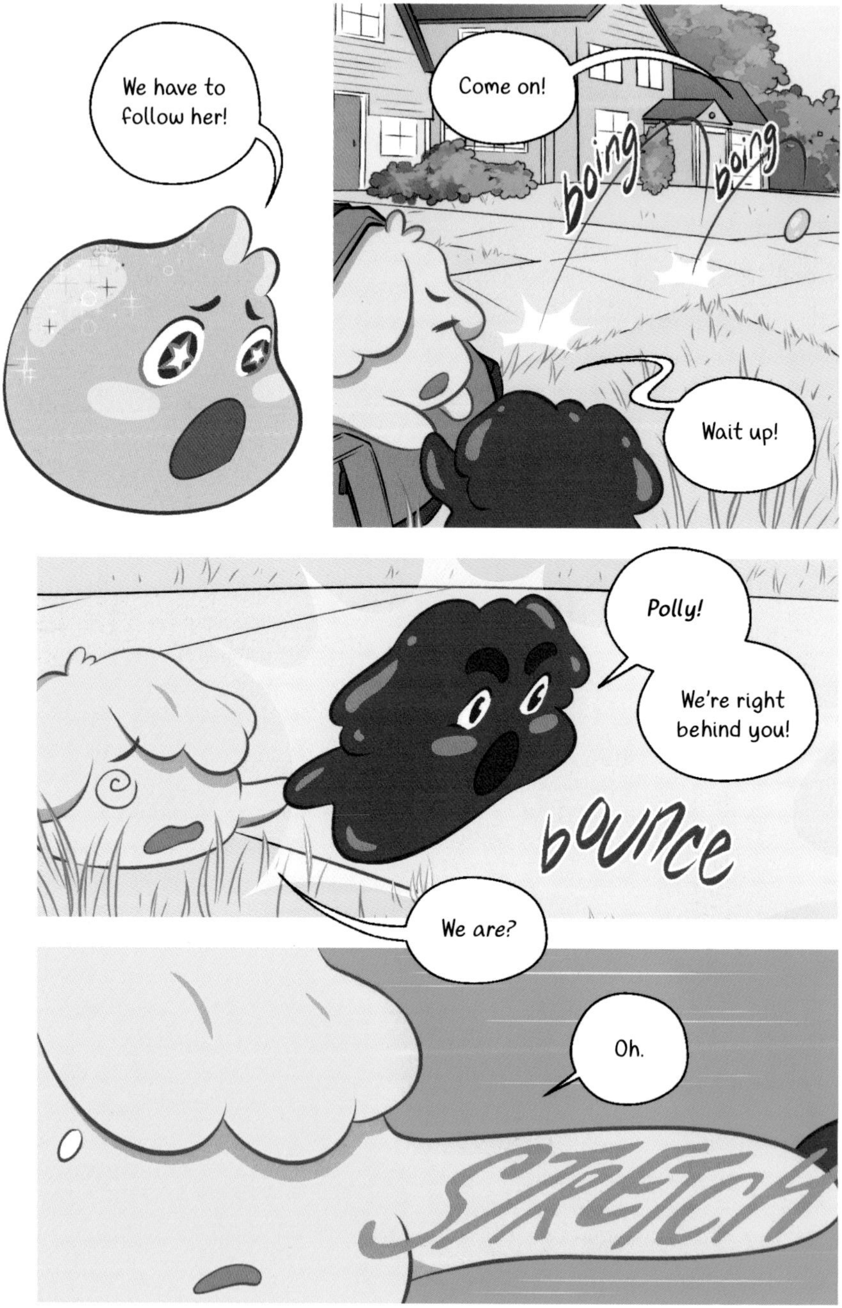
We have to follow her!
Come on!
boing
boing
Wait up!
Polly!
We're right behind you!
bounce
We are?
Oh.
STRETCH

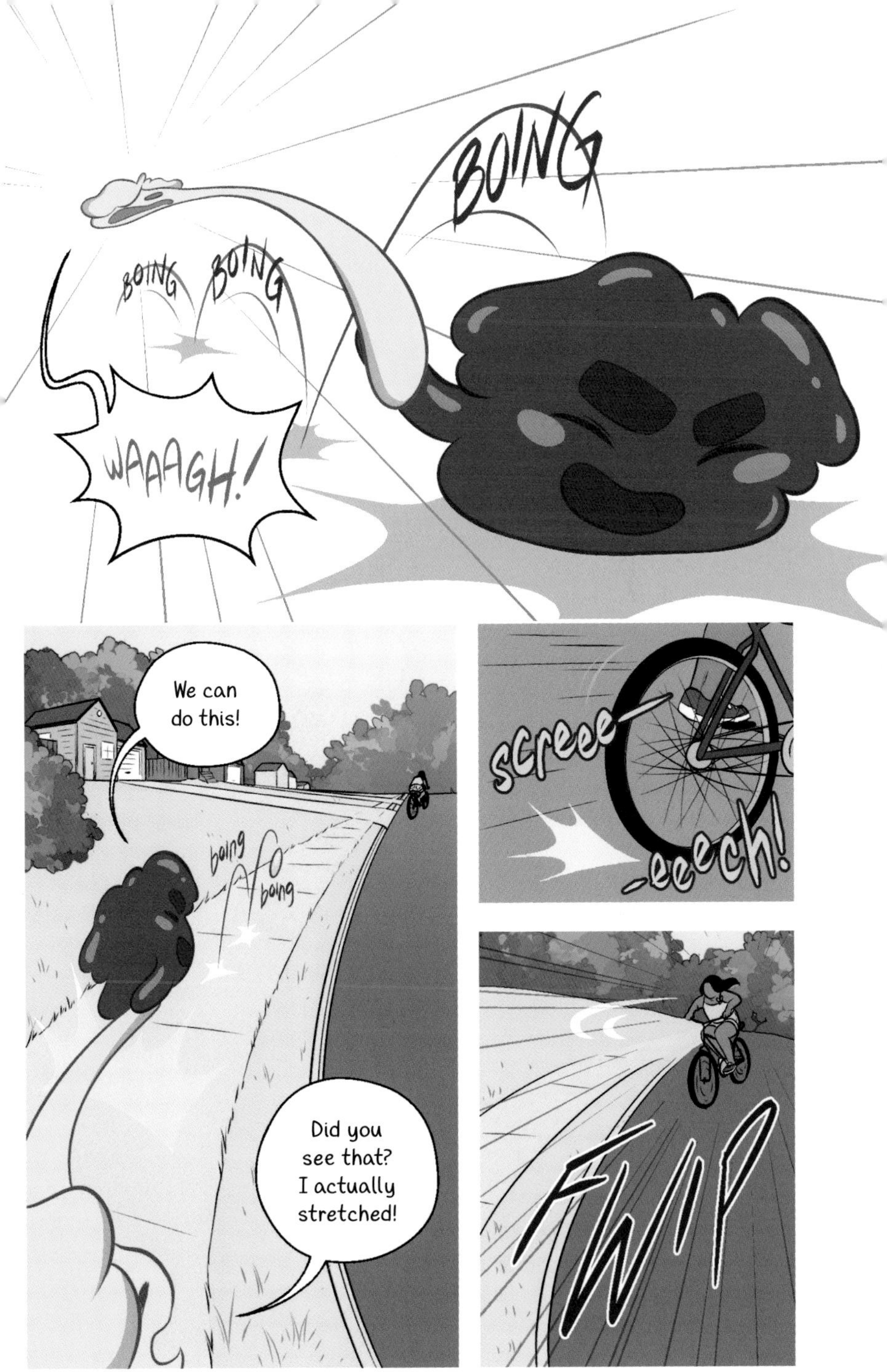
BOING
BOING BOING
WAAAGH!
We can do this!
boing boing
Did you see that? I actually stretched!
screee-
-eeech!
FWIP

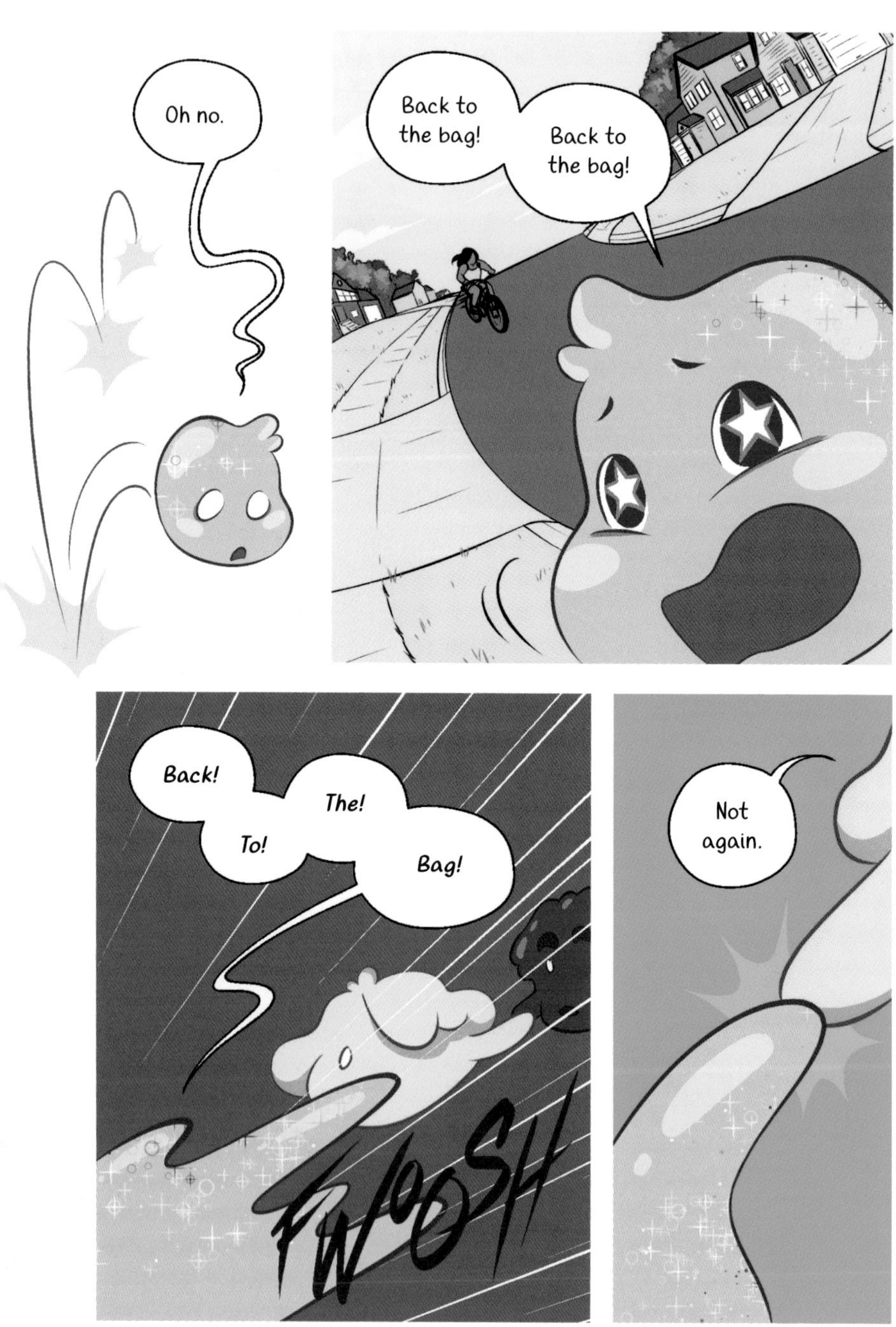
Oh no.
Back to the bag!
Back to the bag!
Back!
To!
The!
Bag!
FWOOSH
Not again.

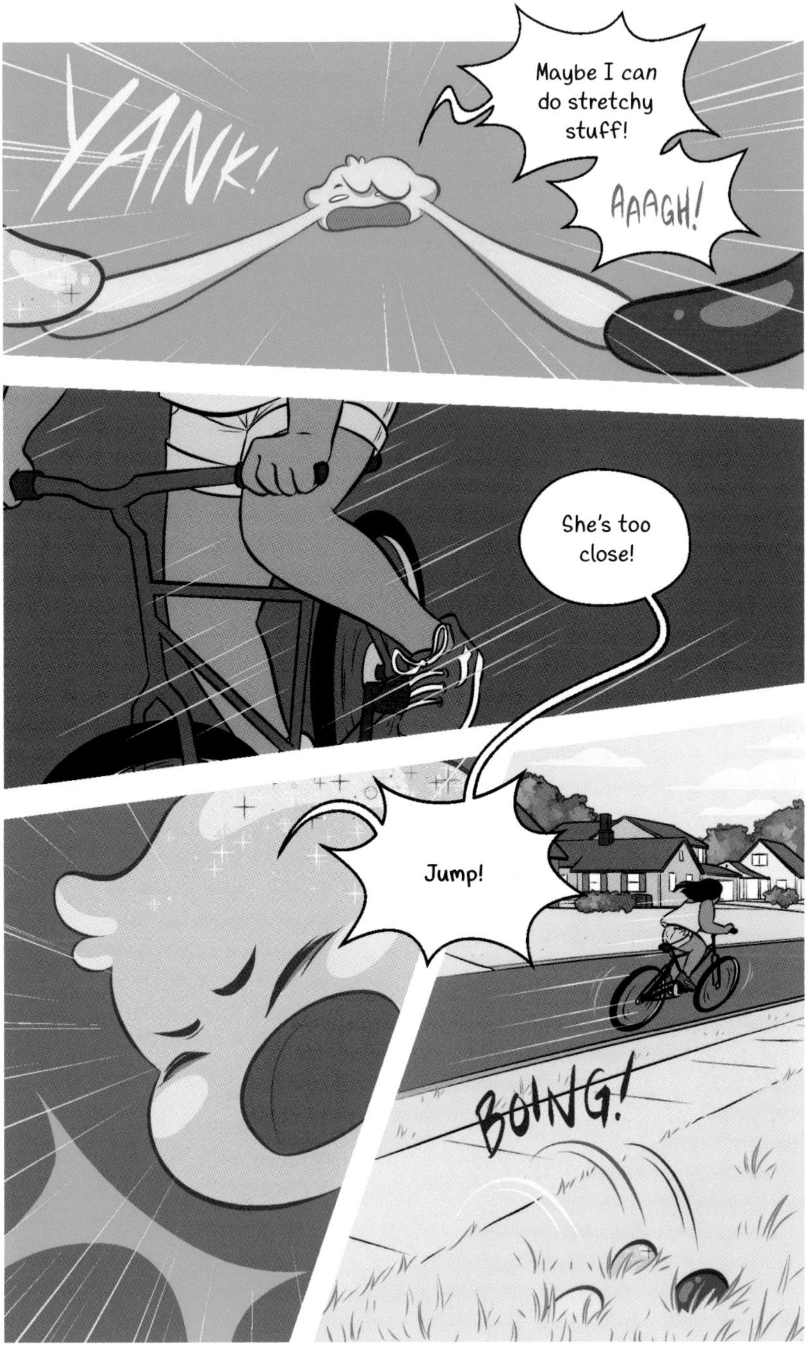
YANK!
Maybe I can do stretchy stuff!
AAAGH!
She's too close!
Jump!
BOING!

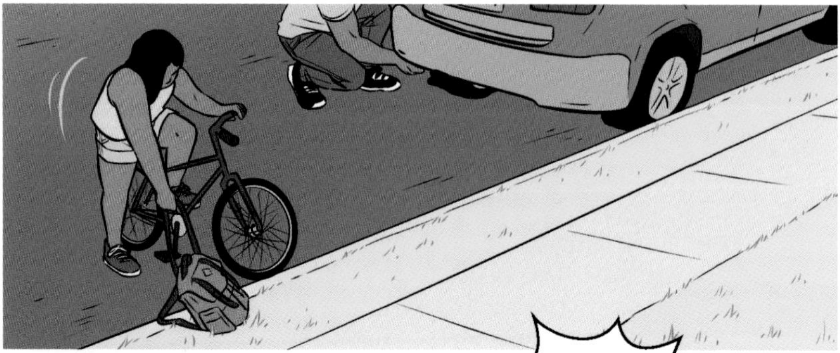

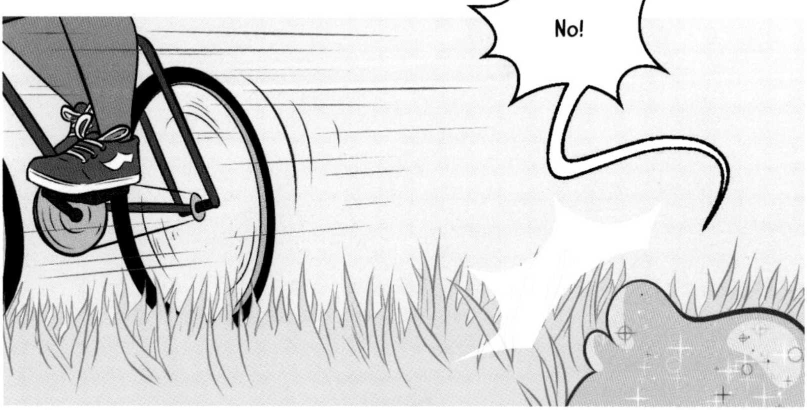
No!

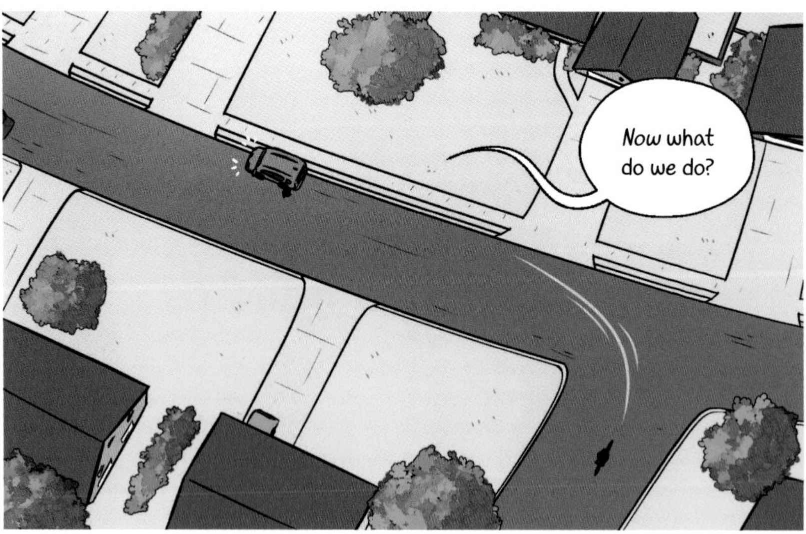
Now what do we do?

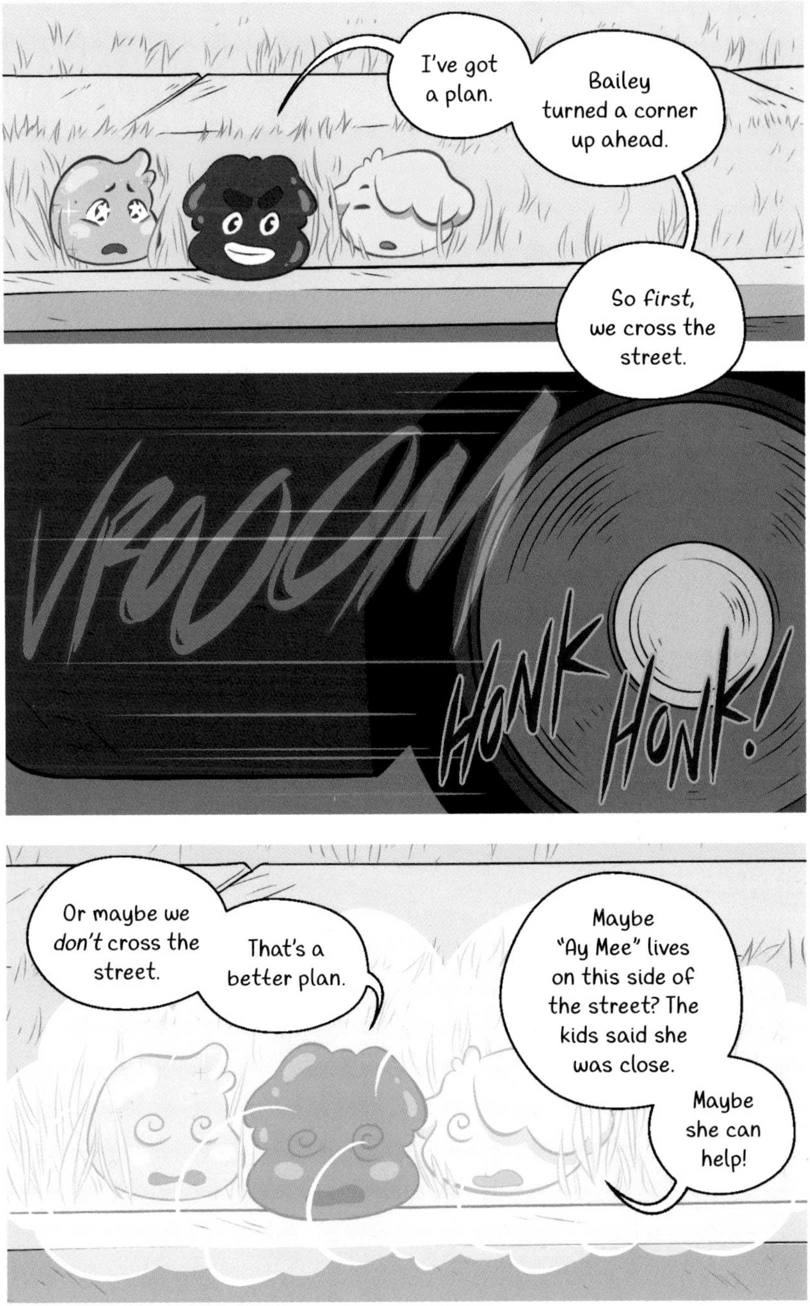
I've got a plan.
Bailey turned a corner up ahead.
So first, we cross the street.
VROOOM
HONK HONK!
Or maybe we *don't* cross the street.
That's a better plan.
Maybe "Ay Mee" lives on this side of the street? The kids said she was close.
Maybe she can help!

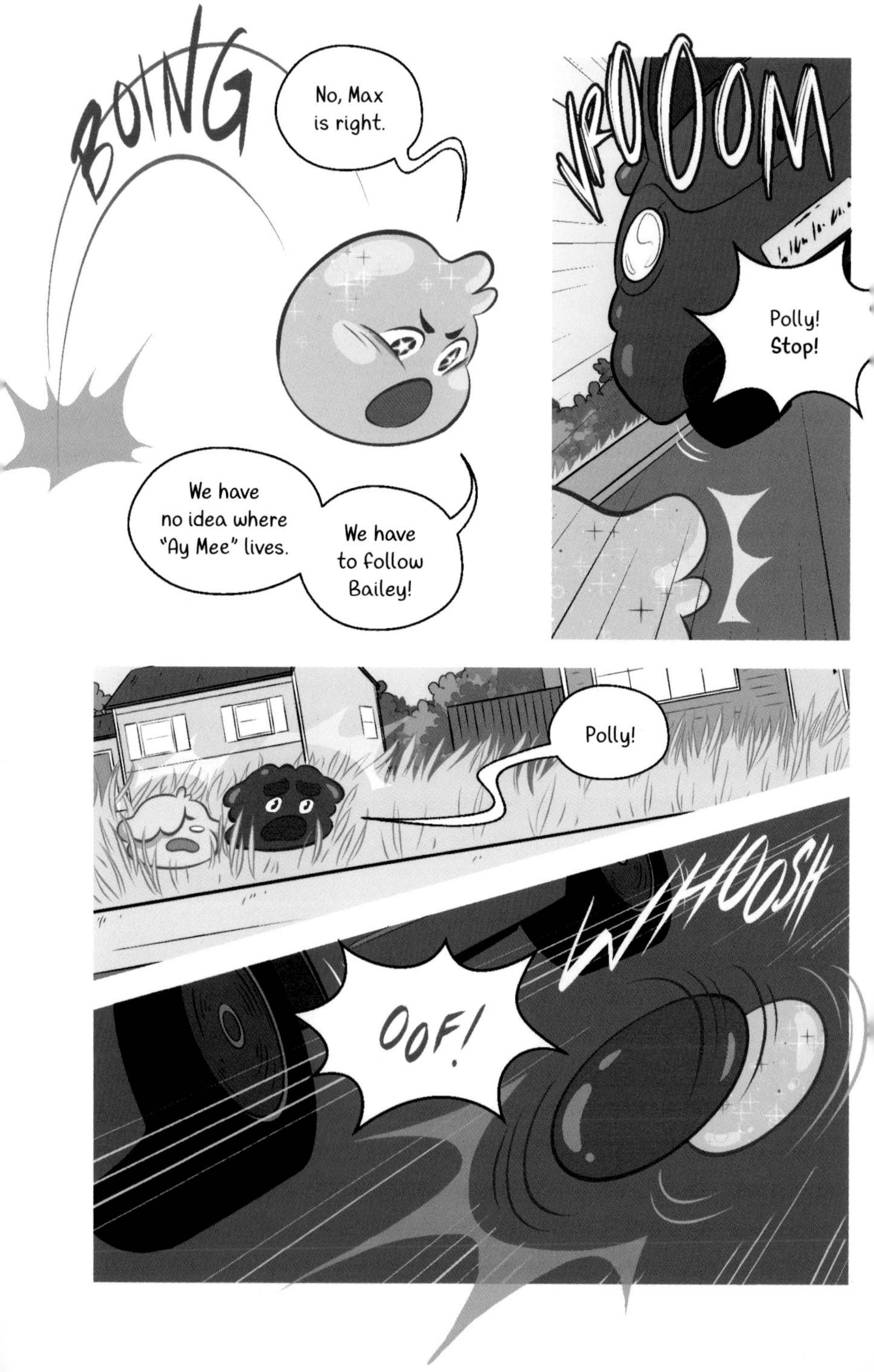
BOING
No, Max is right.
We have no idea where "Ay Mee" lives.
We have to follow Bailey!
VROOOM
Polly! Stop!
Polly!
WHOOSH
OOF!

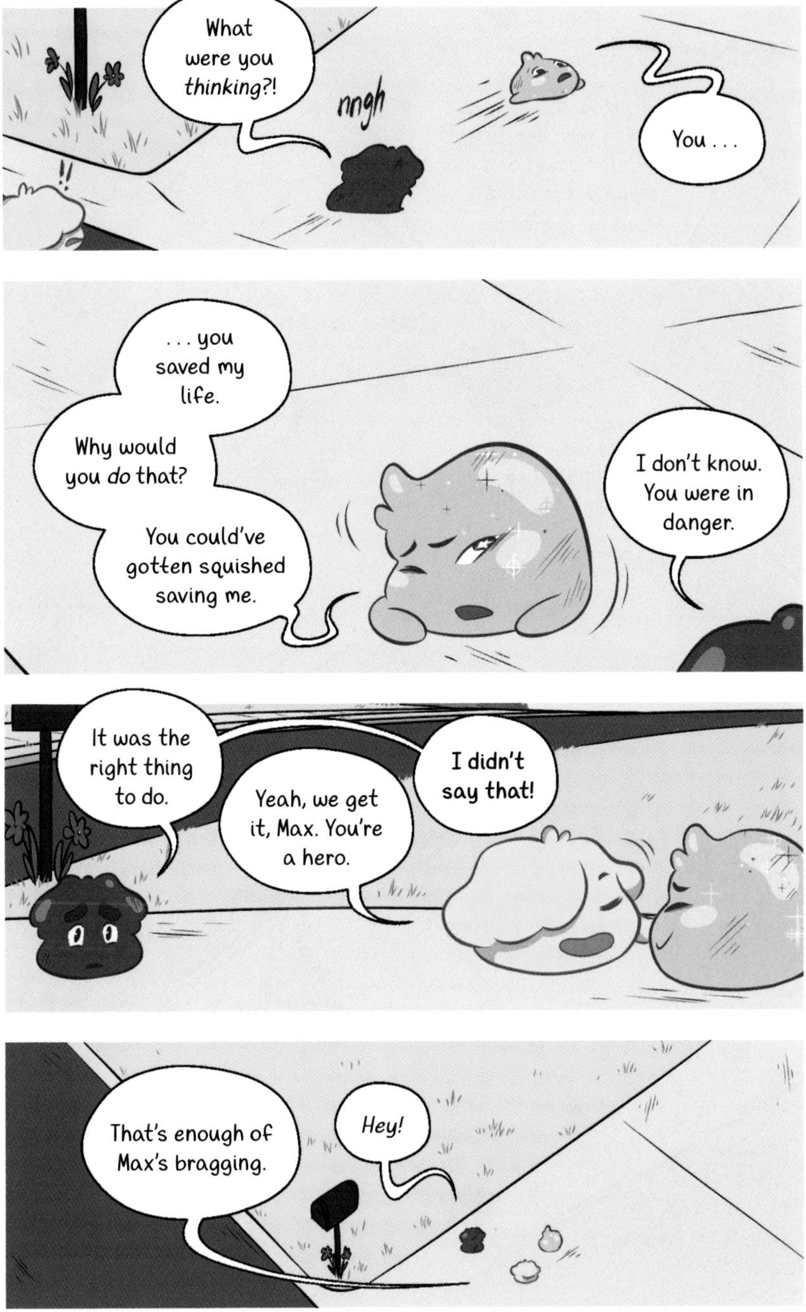
What were you *thinking?!*
nngh
!!
You . . .
. . . you saved my life.
Why would you *do* that?
You could've gotten squished saving me.
I don't know. You were in danger.
It was the right thing to do.
Yeah, we get it, Max. You're a hero.
I didn't say that!
That's enough of Max's bragging.
Hey!

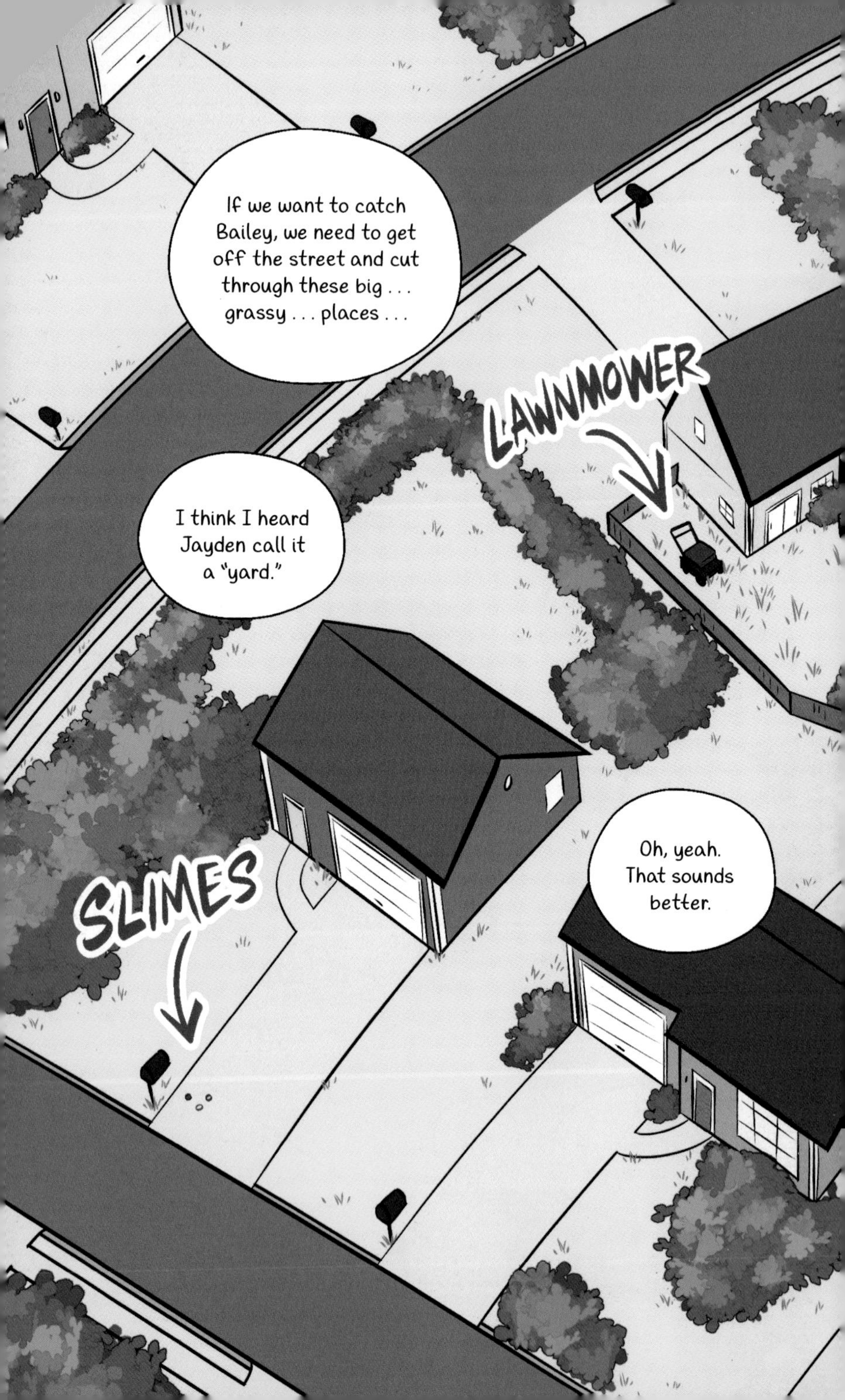
If we want to catch Bailey, we need to get off the street and cut through these big . . . grassy . . . places . . .
LAWNMOWER
I think I heard Jayden call it a "yard."
SLIMES
Oh, yeah. That sounds better.

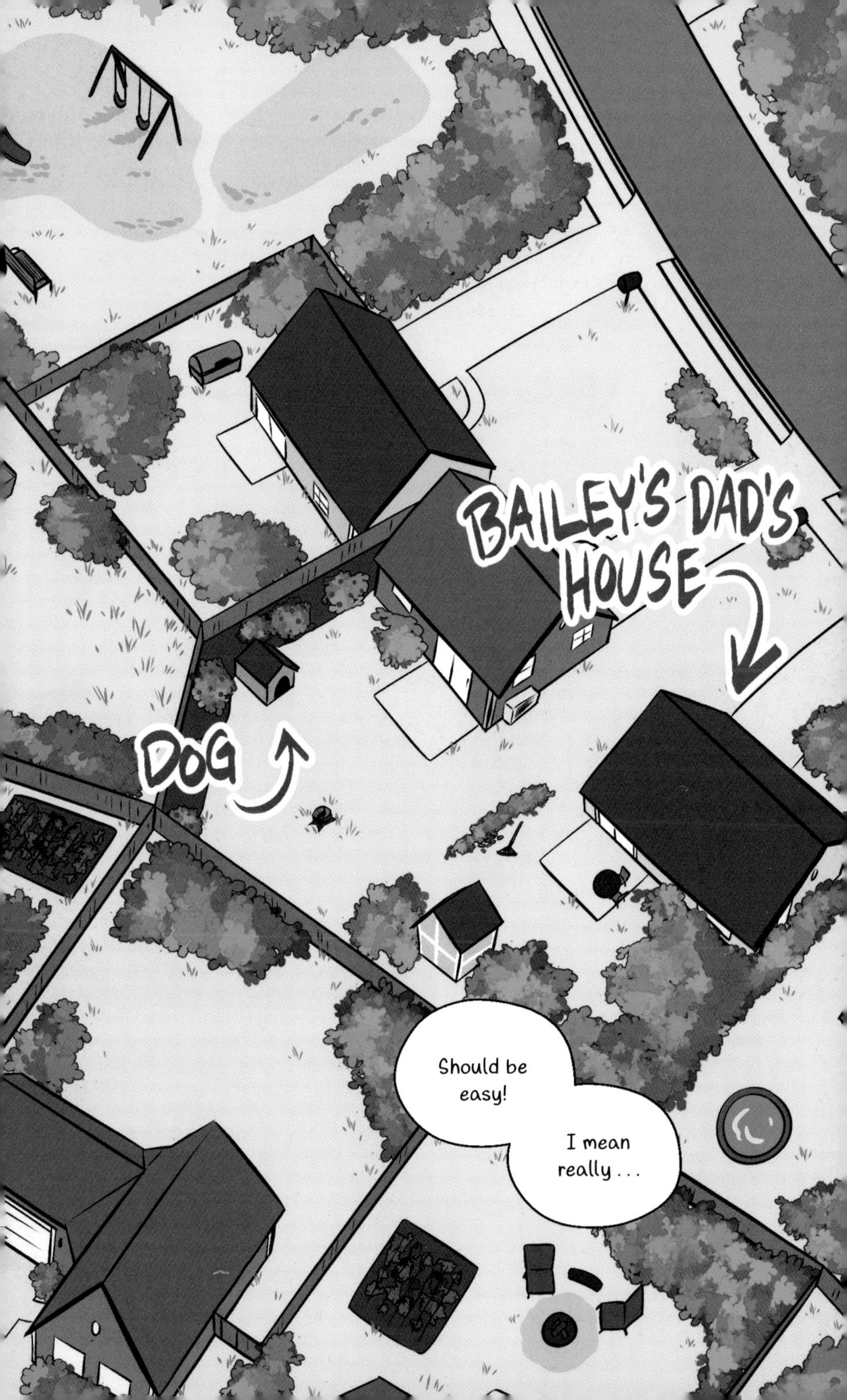

BAILEY'S DAD'S HOUSE
DOG
Should be easy!
I mean really . . .

"... what could go wrong?"

Everything is going wrong!

It's just like I said.

These *kids* are sending slimes off to their *doom!*

Stop it, Boris!

You're scaring him.

Fine. Fine.

And now they've even gotten rid of your precious Polly and her silly friends.

If it could happen to them, why not *you?*

I don't believe it!

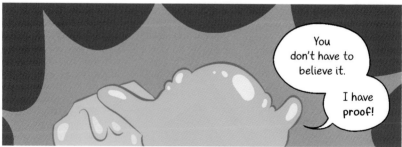

You don't have to believe it.

I have proof!

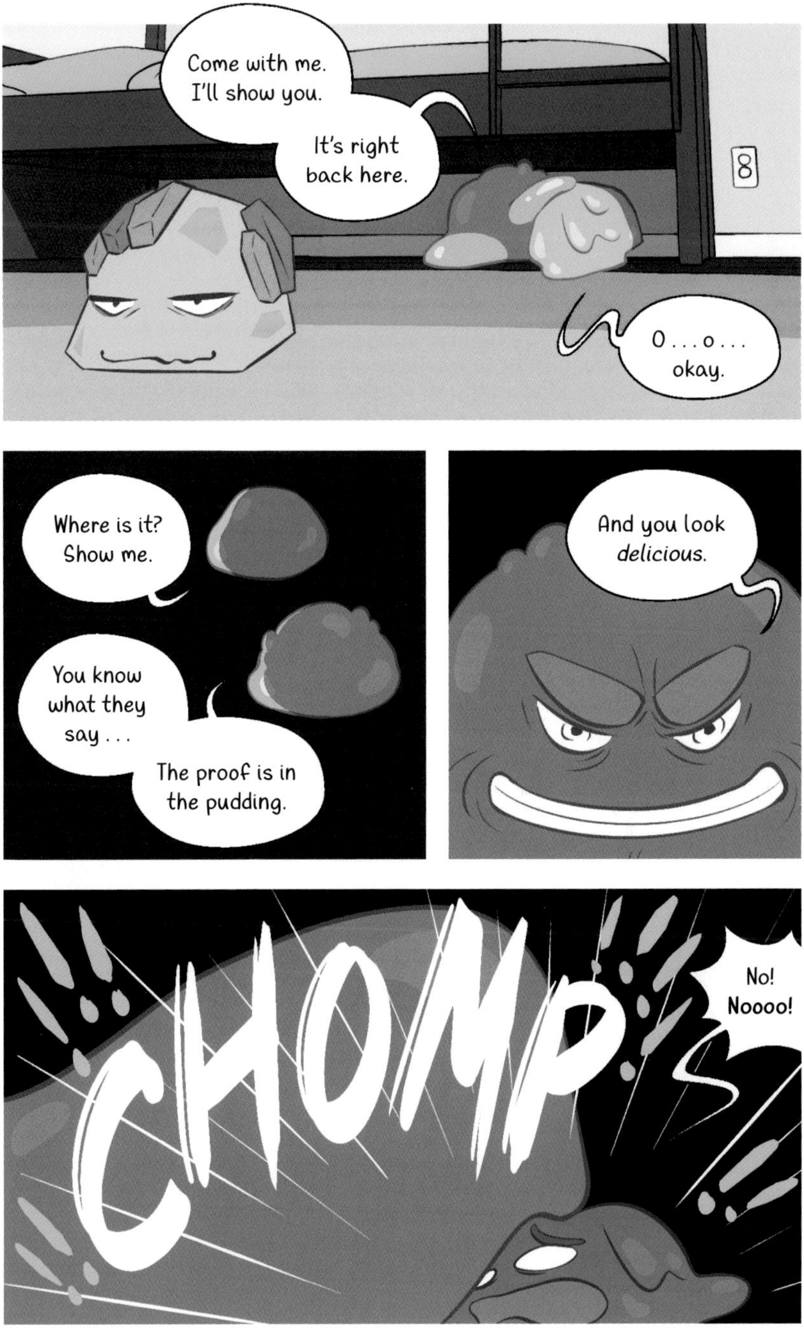
Come with me.
I'll show you.
It's right back here.
O . . . o . . . okay.
Where is it? Show me.
You know what they say . . .
The proof is in the pudding.
And you look *delicious.*
CHOMP
No! Noooo!

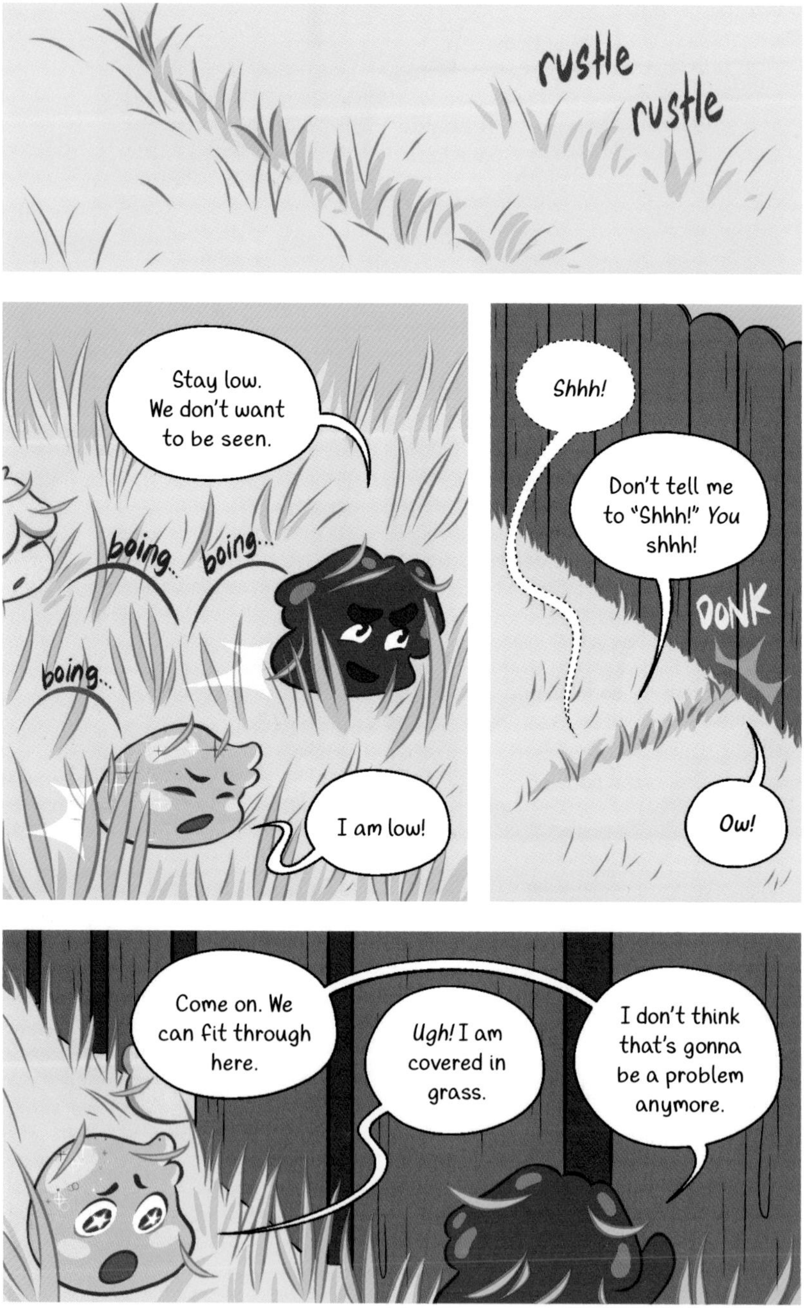
rustle
rustle
Stay low. We don't want to be seen.
boing... boing...
boing...
I am low!
Shhh!
Don't tell me to "Shhh!" *You* shhh!
DONK
Ow!
Come on. We can fit through here.
Ugh! I am covered in grass.
I don't think that's gonna be a problem anymore.

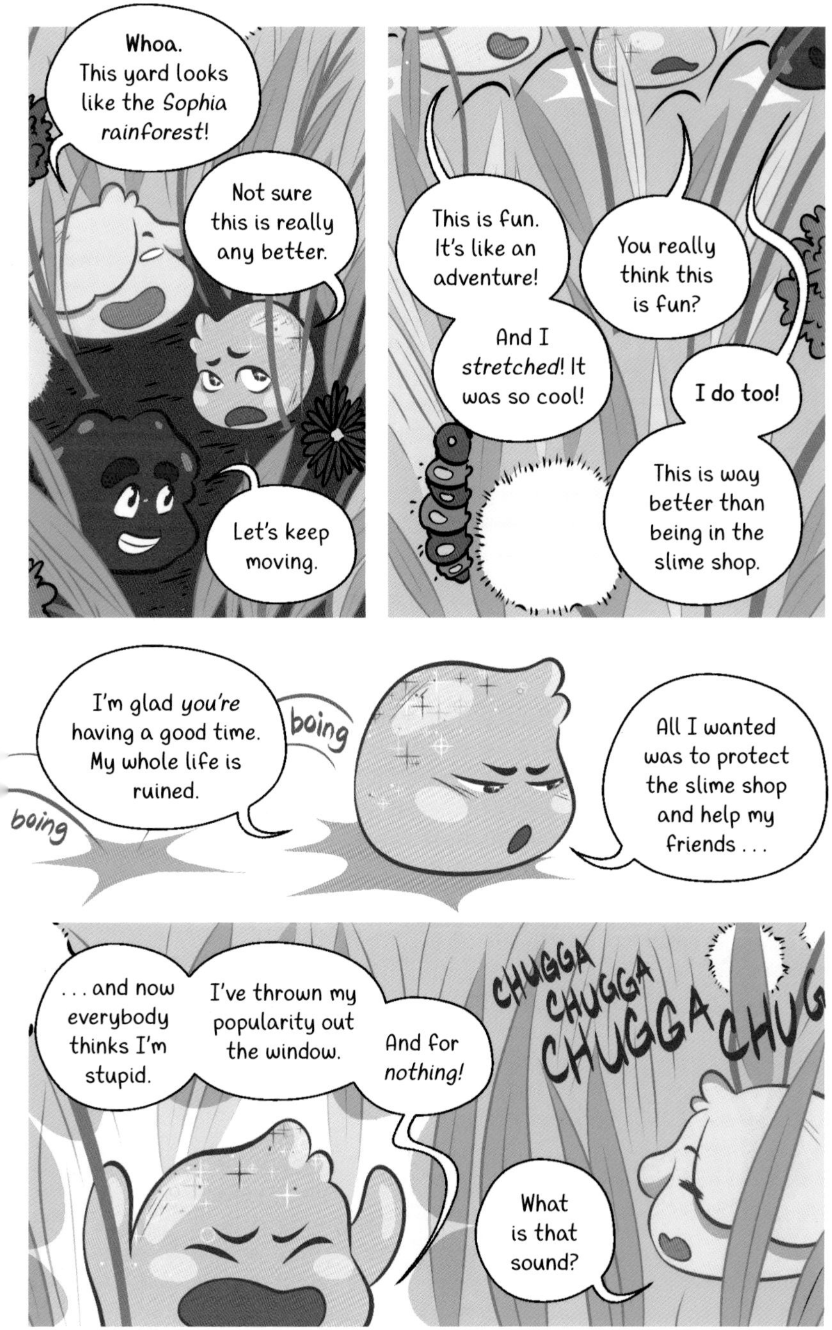
Whoa. This yard looks like the *Sophia rainforest*!
Not sure this is really any better.
Let's keep moving.
This is fun. It's like an adventure!
You really think this is fun?
And I *stretched*! It was so cool!
I do too!
This is way better than being in the slime shop.
I'm glad *you're* having a good time. My whole life is ruined.
boing
boing
All I wanted was to protect the slime shop and help my friends . . .
. . . and now everybody thinks I'm stupid.
I've thrown my popularity out the window.
And for *nothing!*
CHUGGA CHUGGA CHUGGA CHUG
What is that sound?

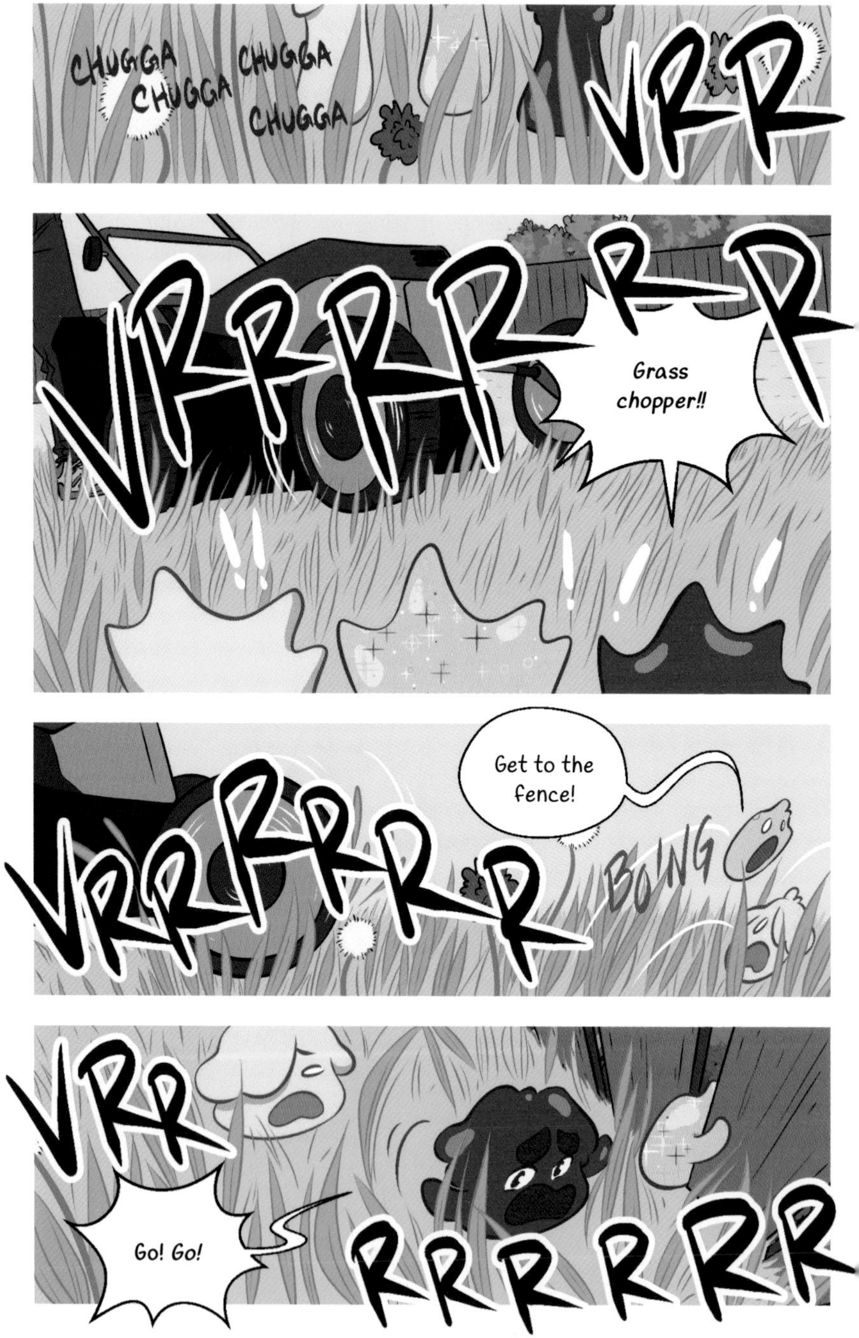
CHUGGA CHUGGA CHUGGA CHUGGA
VRRR
VRRRRR-R-R
Grass chopper!!
!!
!
!
VRRRRR-R
Get to the fence!
BOING
VRR
Go! Go!
RRRRRR

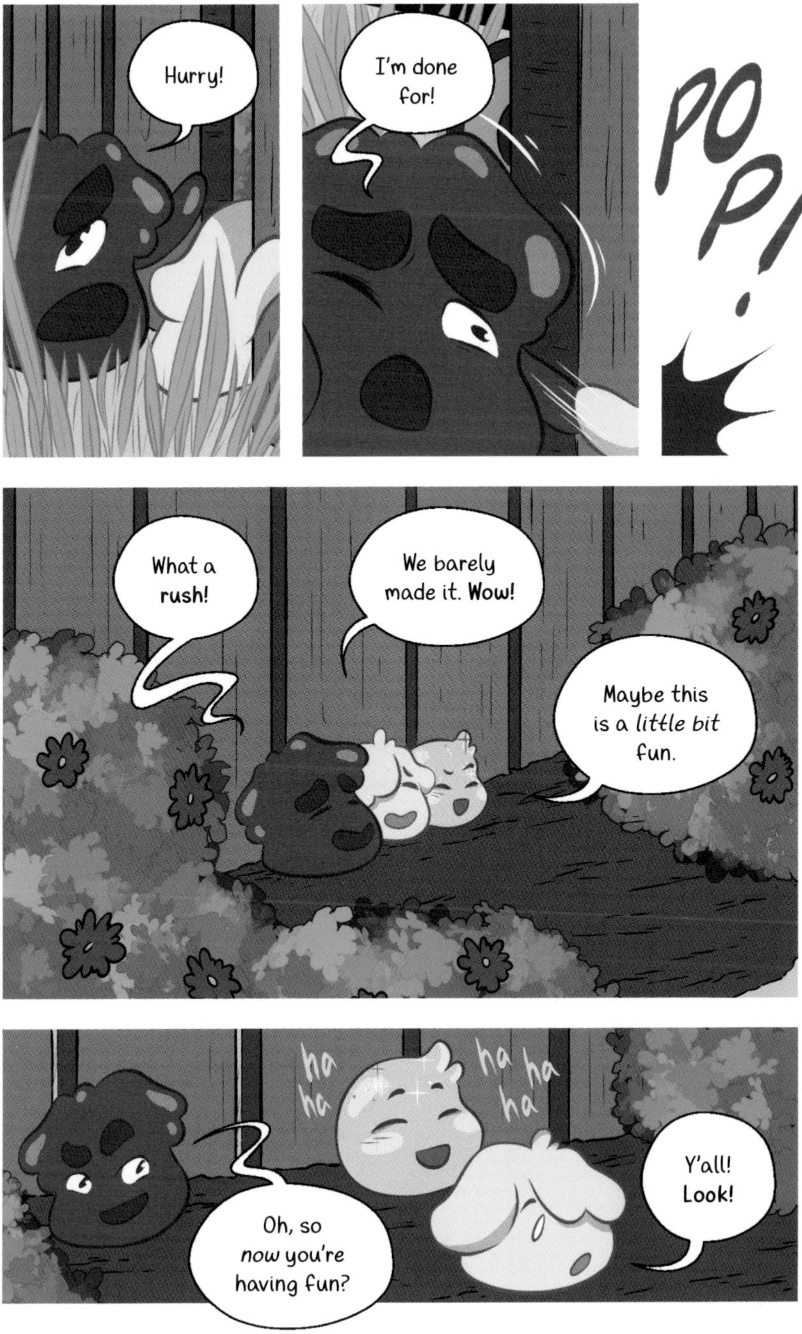
Hurry!
I'm done for!
POP!
What a rush!
We barely made it. Wow!
Maybe this is a *little bit* fun.
ha ha
ha ha ha ha
Oh, so *now* you're having fun?
Y'all! Look!

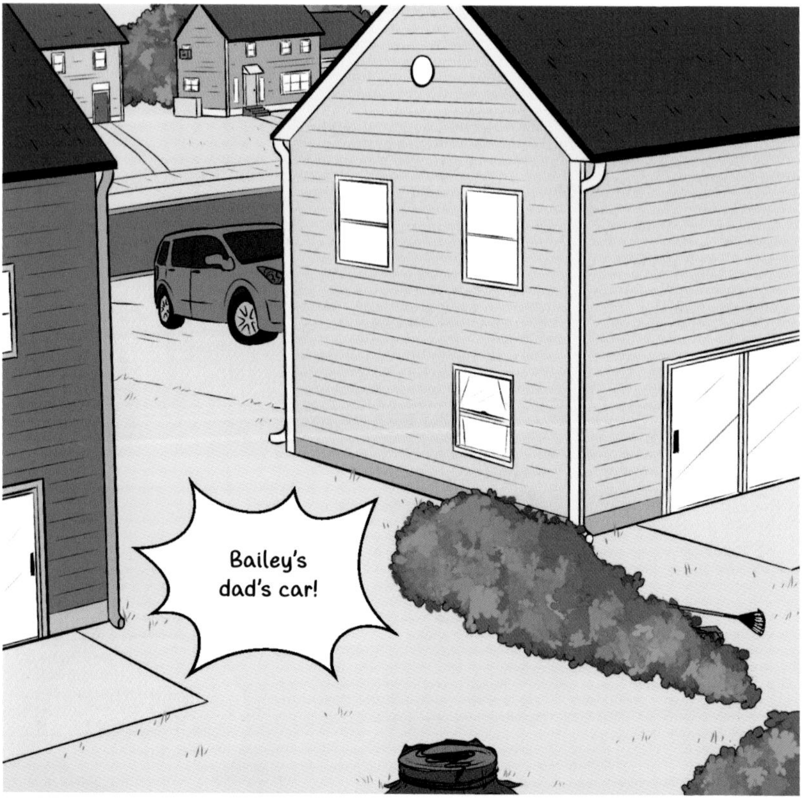
Bailey's dad's car!

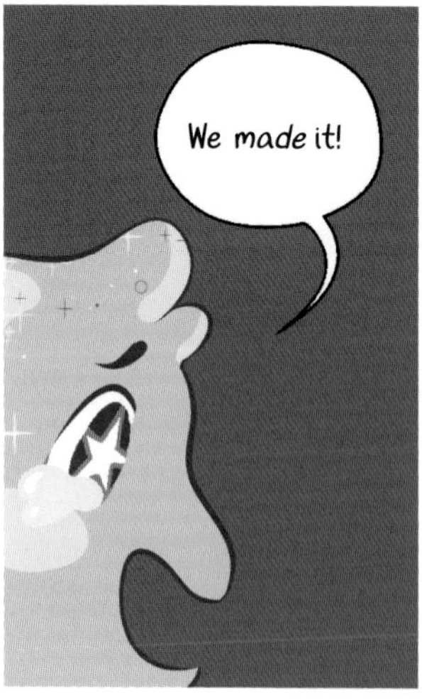
We made it!

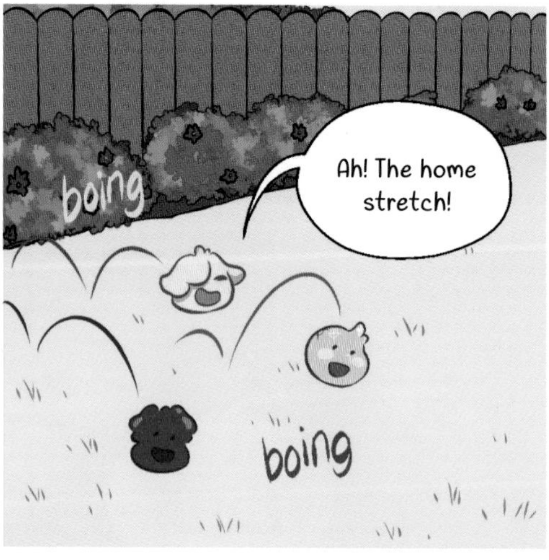
boing
Ah! The home stretch!
boing

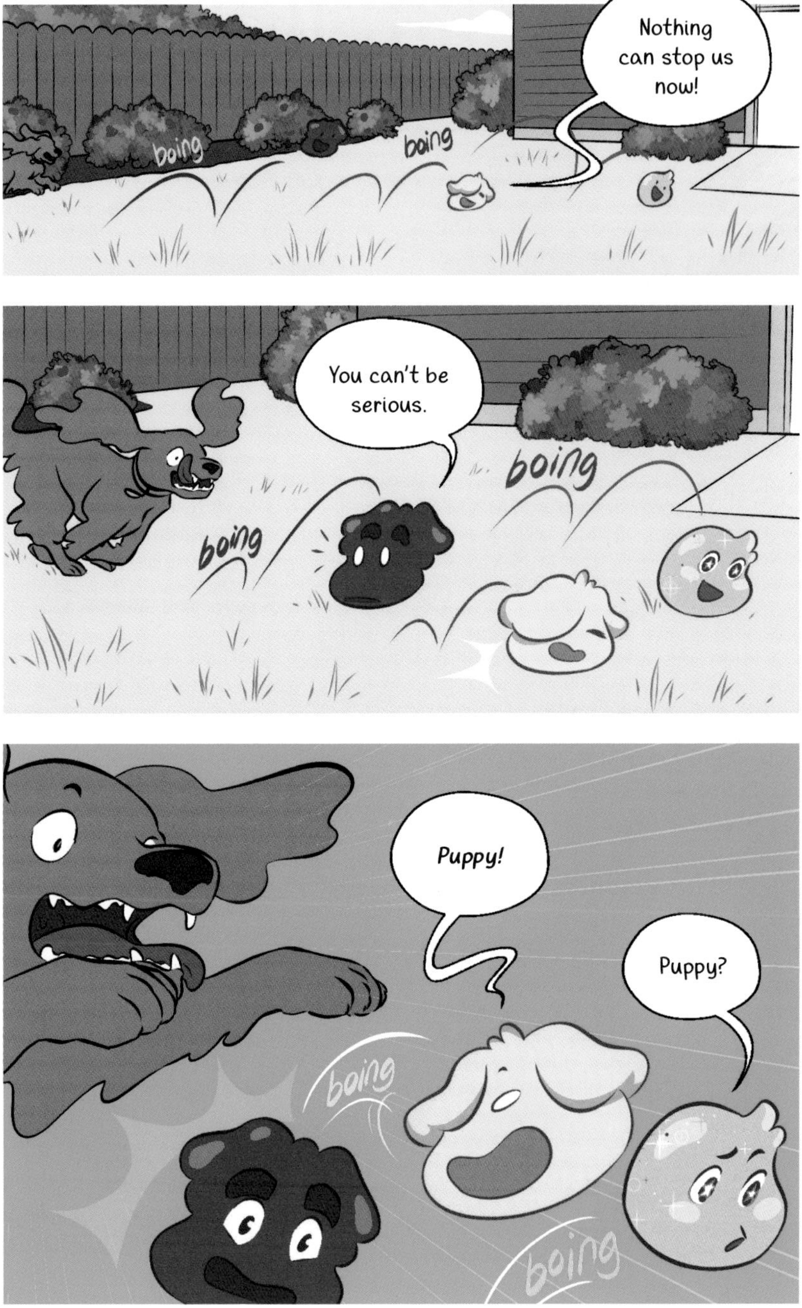
boing
boing
Nothing can stop us now!
You can't be serious.
boing
boing
Puppy!
Puppy?
boing
boing

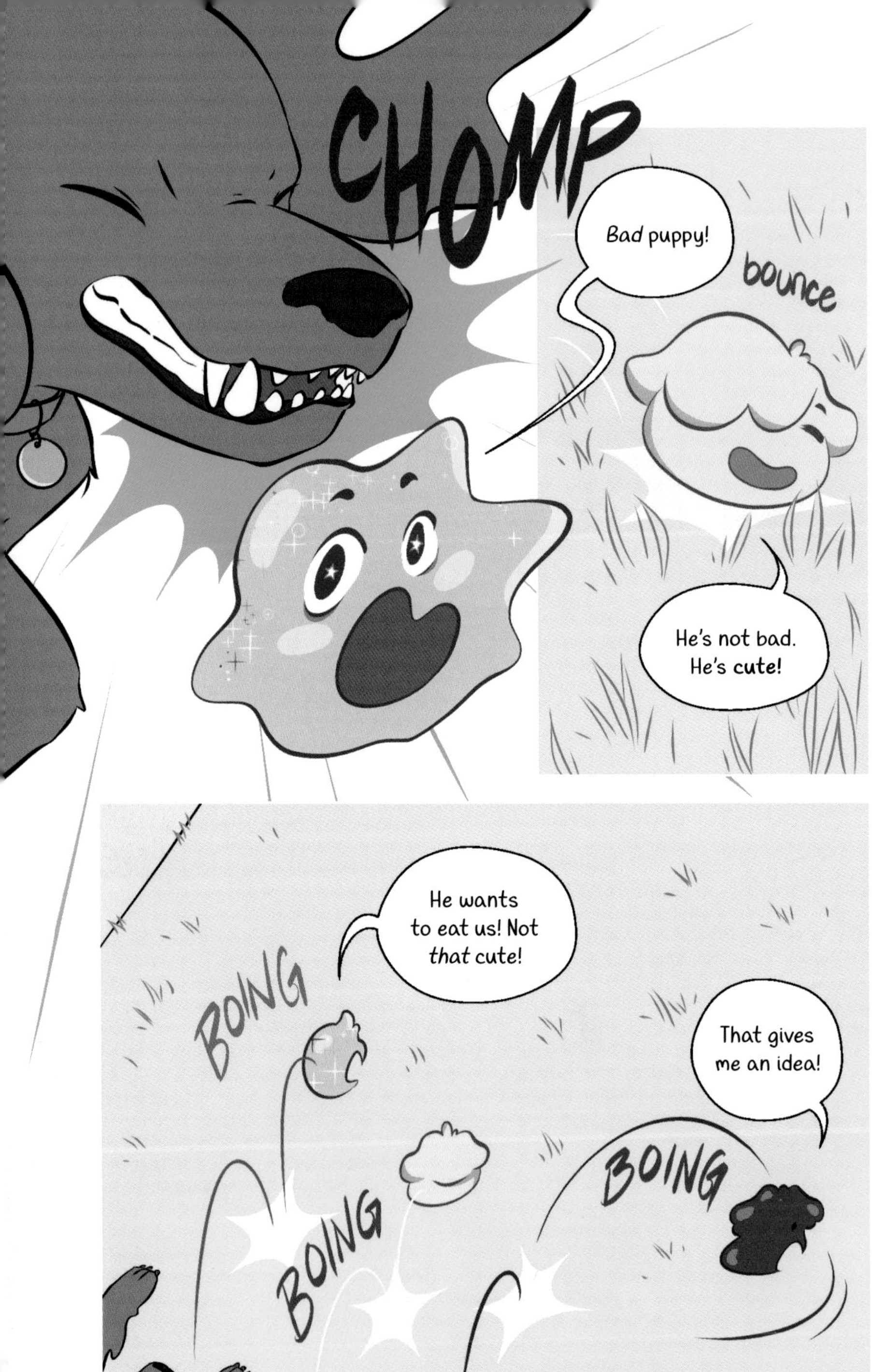
CHOMP
Bad puppy!
bounce
He's not bad. He's cute!
He wants to eat us! Not *that* cute!
BOING
That gives me an idea!
BOING
BOING

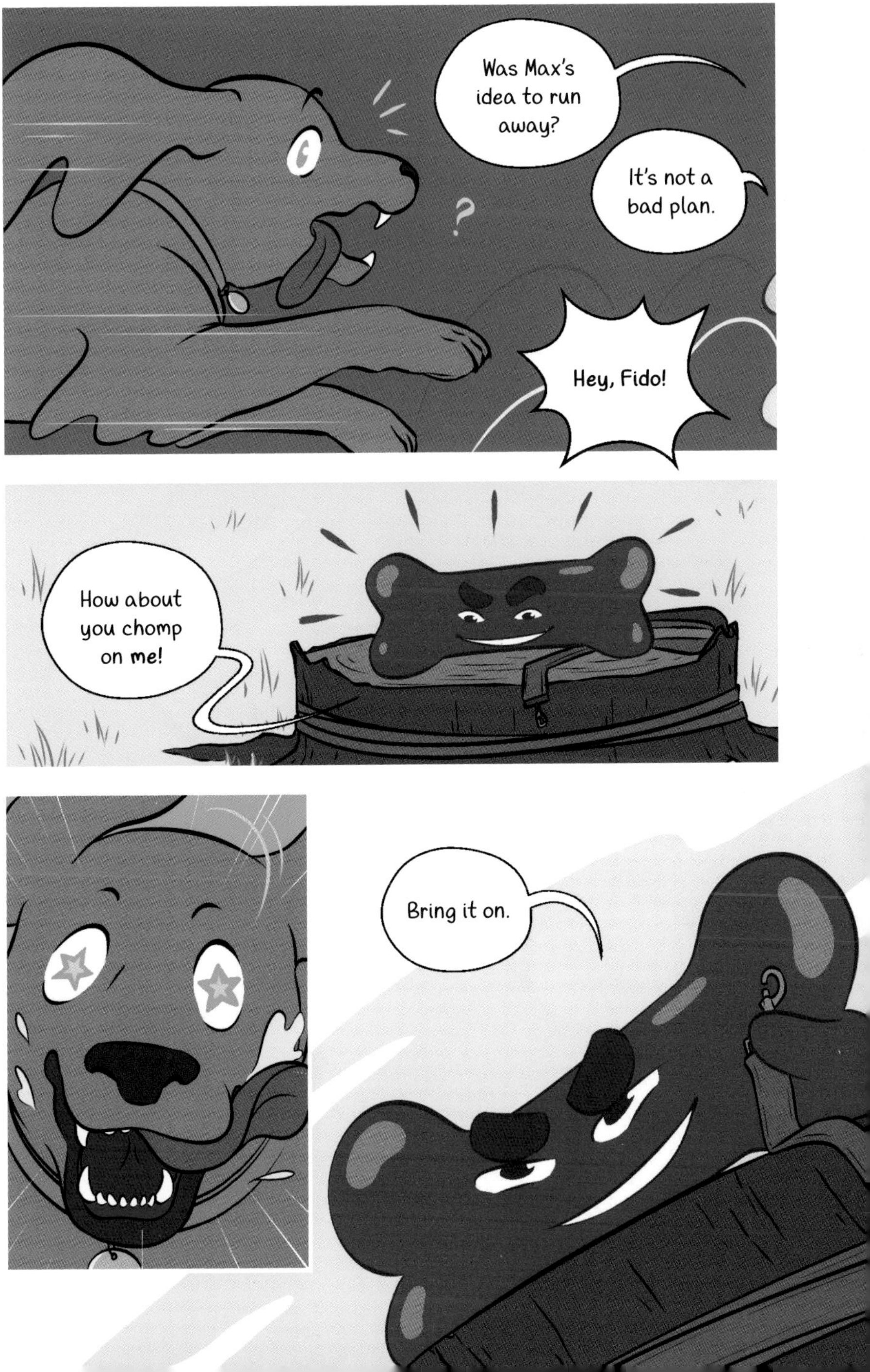
Was Max's idea to run away?
It's not a bad plan.
?
Hey, Fido!
How about you chomp on **me**!
Bring it on.

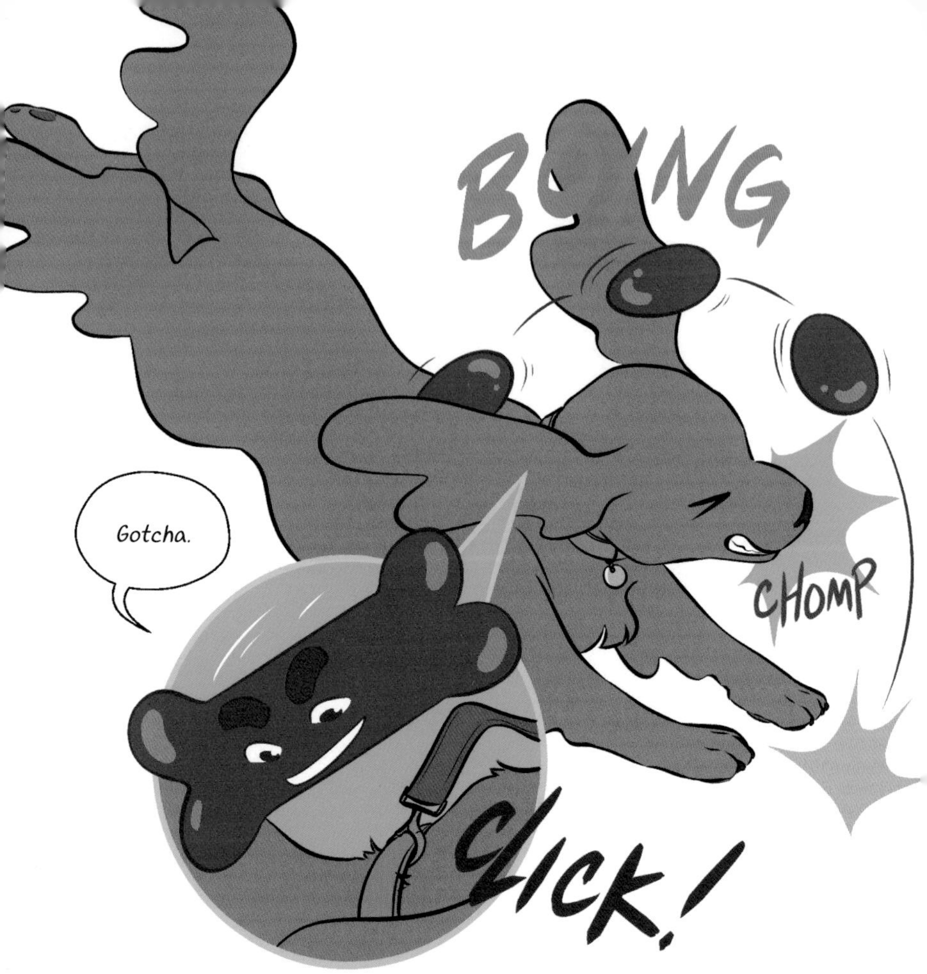
Gotcha.
CHOMP
CLICK!

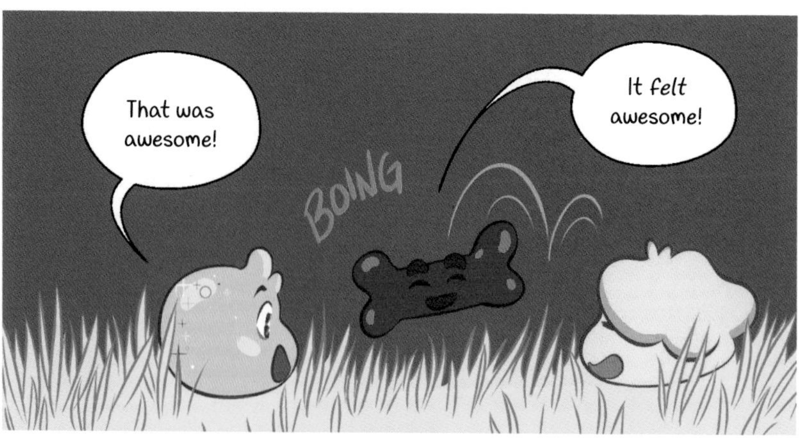
That was awesome!
BOING
It felt awesome!

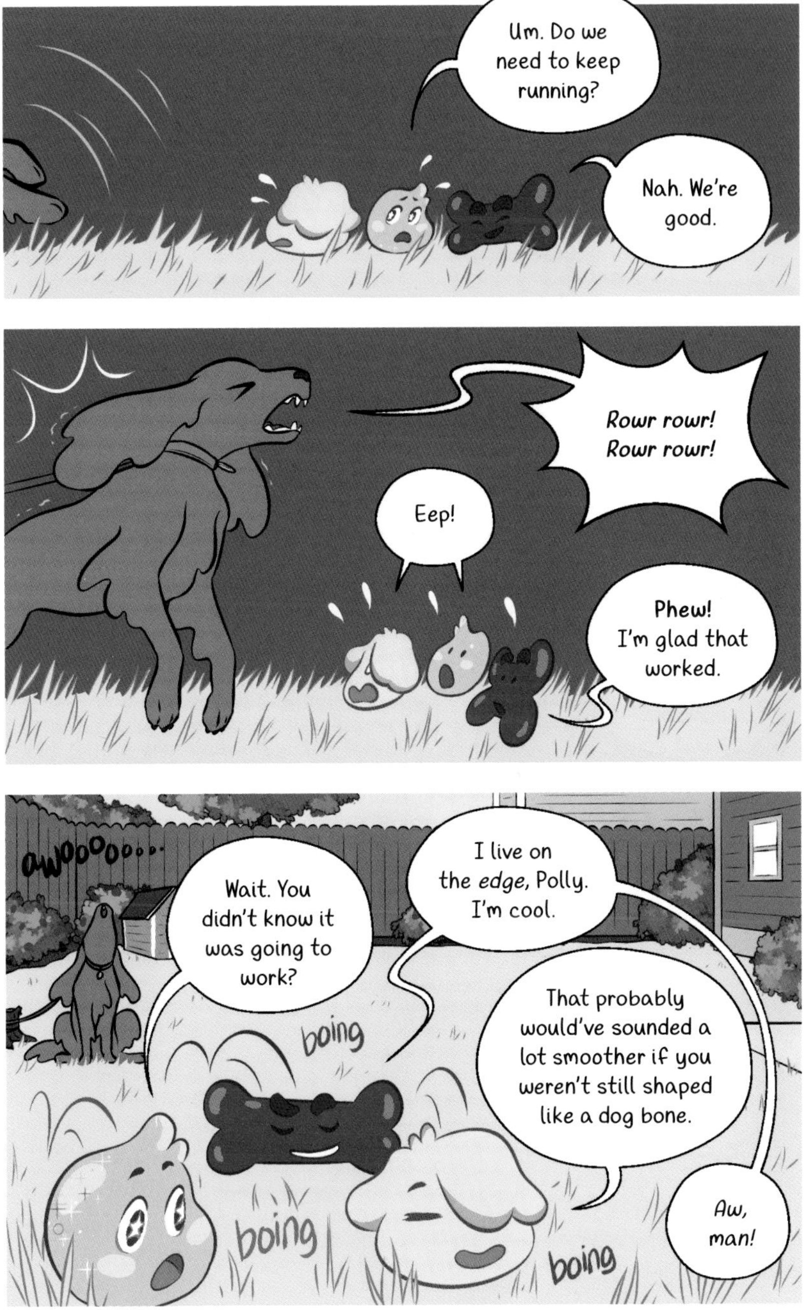
Um. Do we need to keep running?
Nah. We're good.
Rowr rowr! Rowr rowr!
Eep!
Phew! I'm glad that worked.
AWOOOOooo...
Wait. You didn't know it was going to work?
I live on the *edge*, Polly. I'm cool.
boing
That probably would've sounded a lot smoother if you weren't still shaped like a dog bone.
boing
boing
Aw, man!

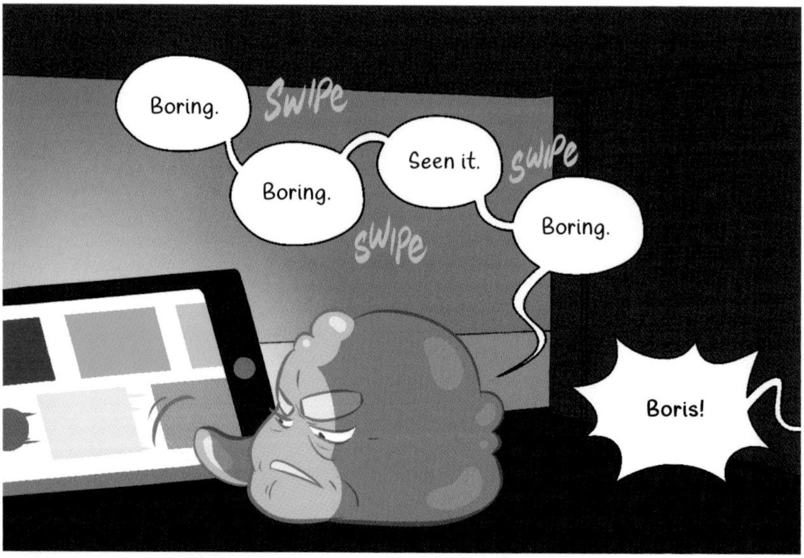
Boring.
SWIPE
Boring.
Seen it.
SWIPE
SWIPE
Boring.
Boris!

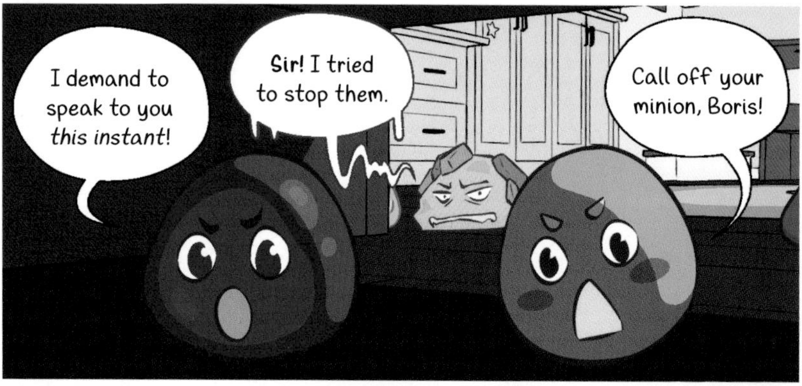
I demand to speak to you *this instant!*
Sir! I tried to stop them.
Call off your minion, Boris!

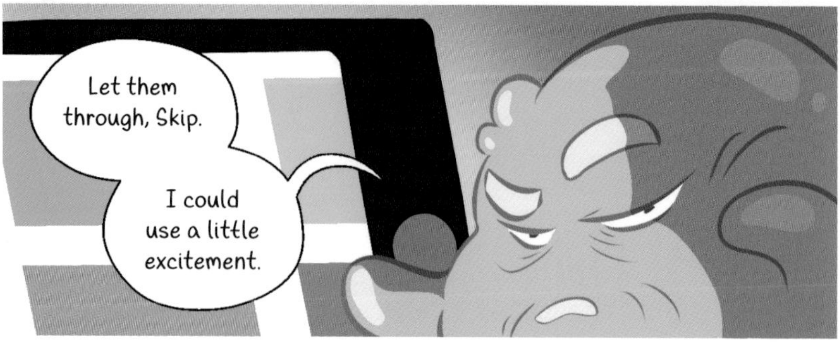
Let them through, Skip.
I could use a little excitement.

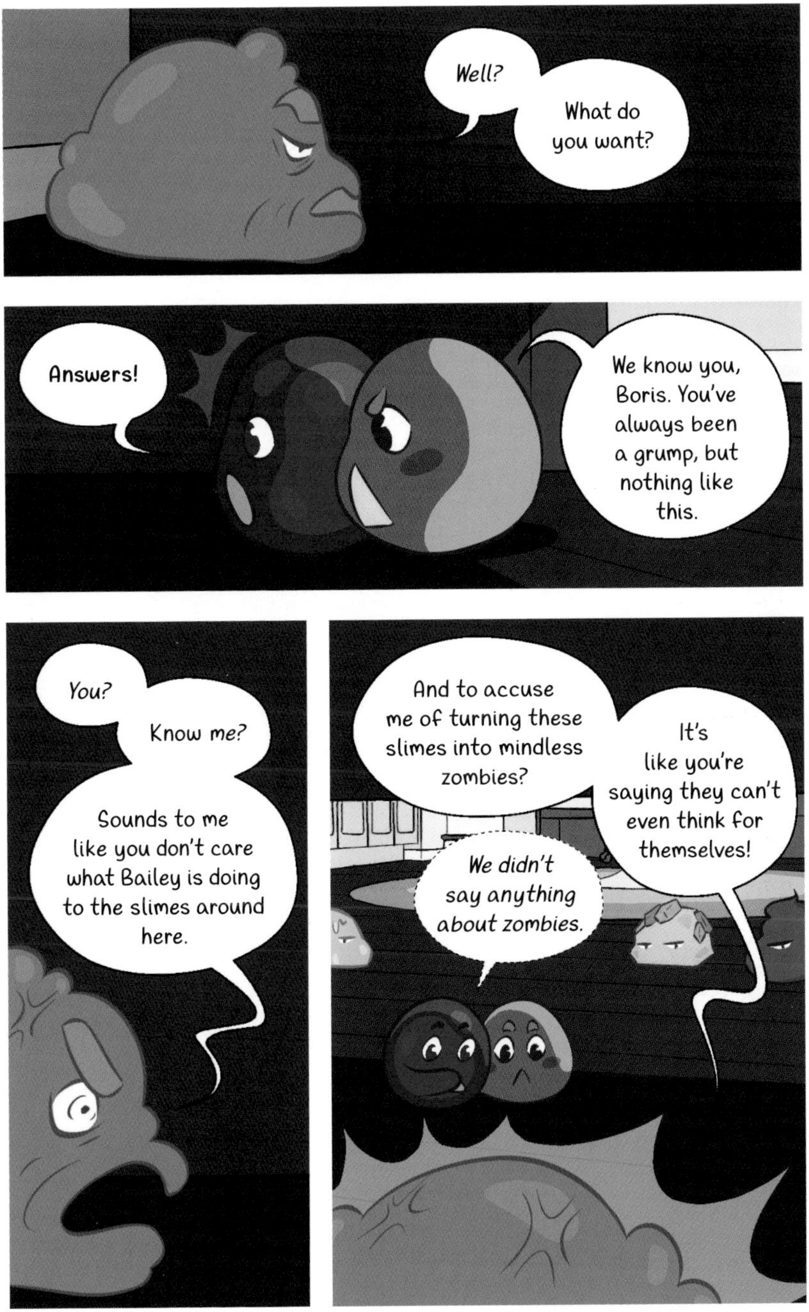
Well?
What do you want?
Answers!
We know you, Boris. You've always been a grump, but nothing like this.
You?
Know me?
Sounds to me like you don't care what Bailey is doing to the slimes around here.
And to accuse me of turning these slimes into mindless zombies?
It's like you're saying they can't even think for themselves!
We didn't say anything about zombies.

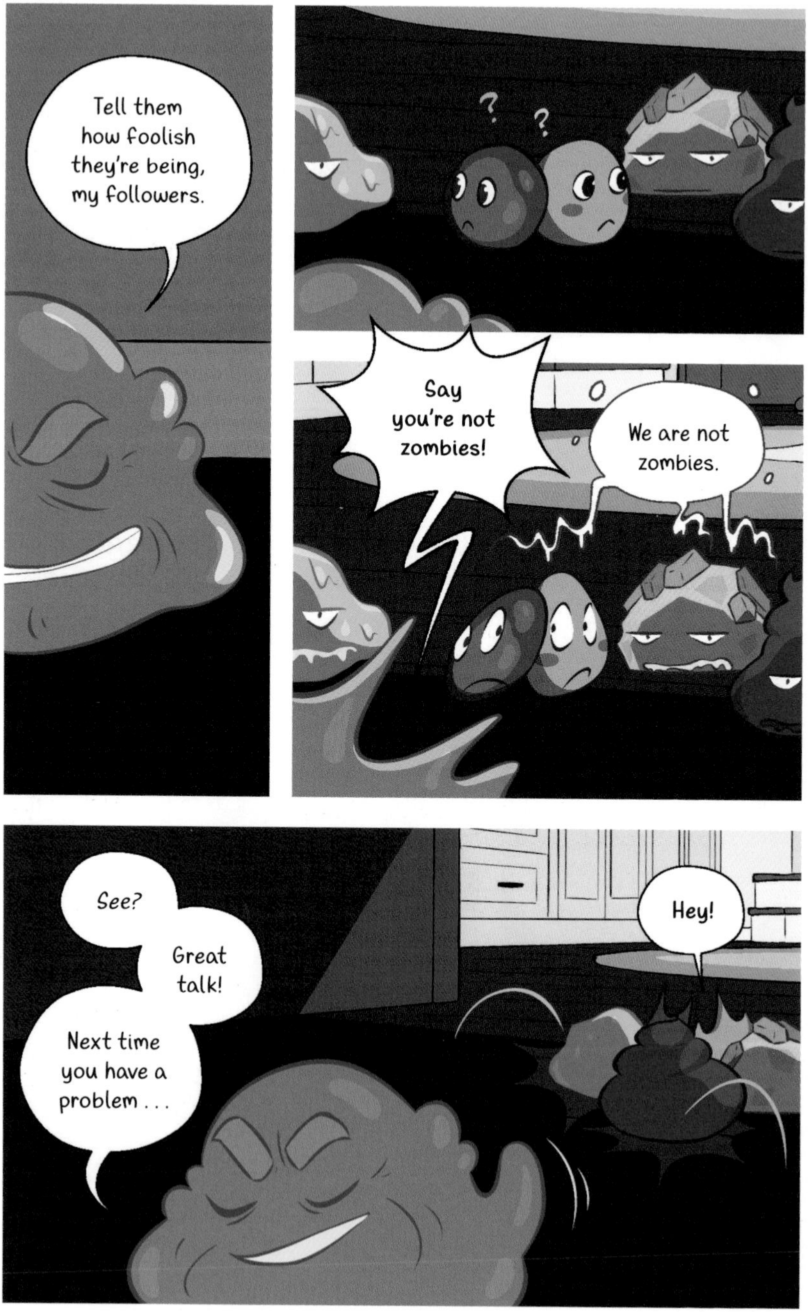
Tell them how foolish they're being, my followers.
Say you're not zombies!
We are not zombies.
See?
Great talk!
Next time you have a problem . . .
Hey!

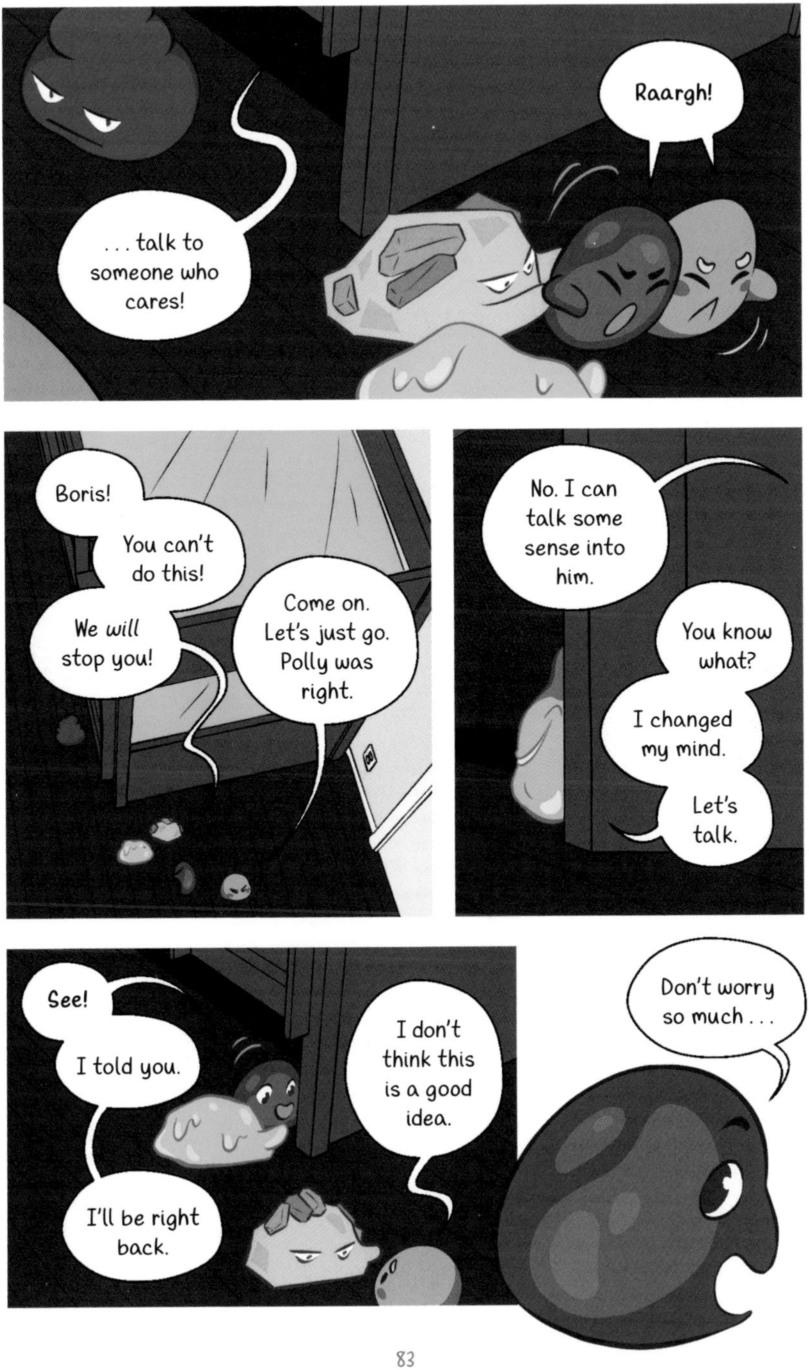
. . . talk to someone who cares!
Raargh!
Boris!
You can't do this!
We *will* stop you!
Come on. Let's just go. Polly was right.
No. I can talk some sense into him.
You know what?
I changed my mind.
Let's talk.
See!
I told you.
I'll be right back.
I don't think this is a good idea.
Don't worry so much . . .

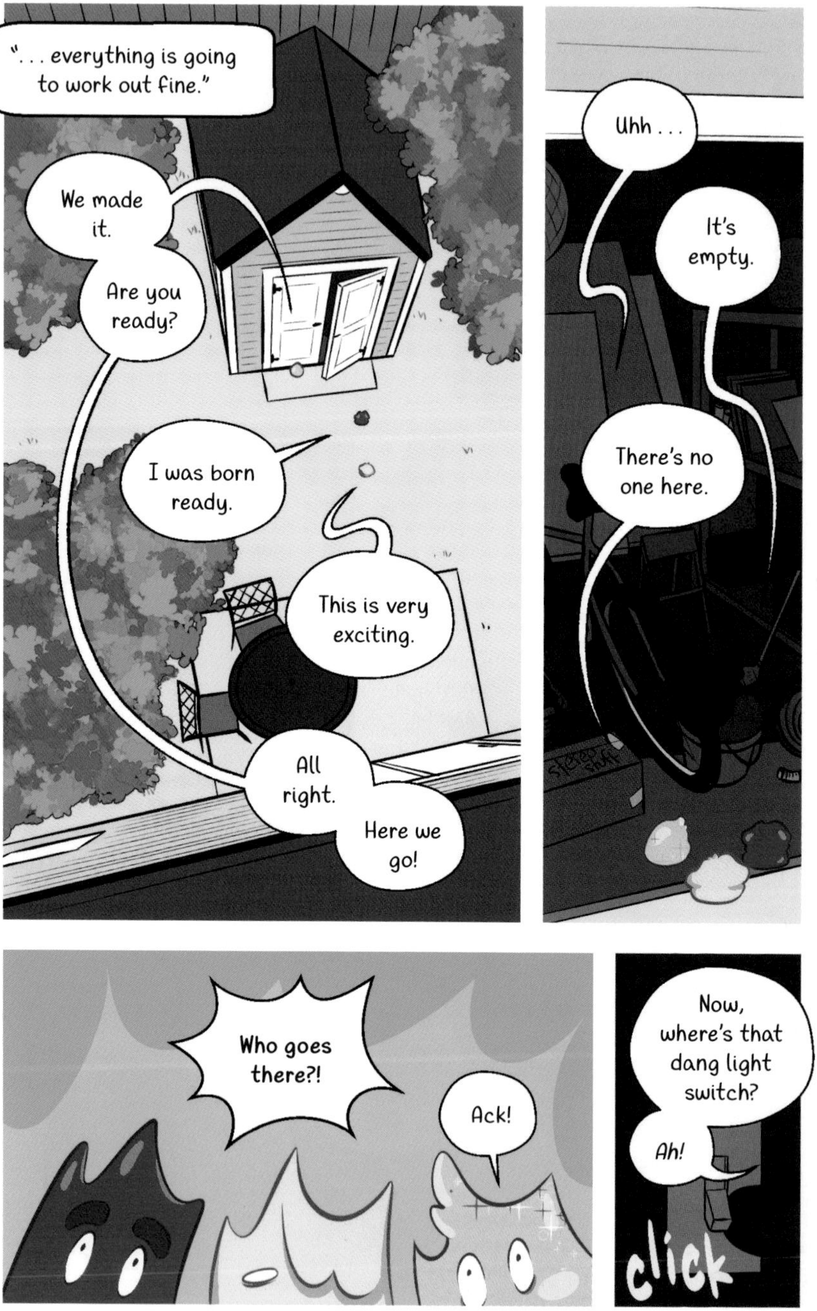
". . . everything is going to work out fine."
We made it.
Are you ready?
I was born ready.
This is very exciting.
All right.
Here we go!
Uhh . . .
It's empty.
There's no one here.
stereo stuff
Who goes there?!
Ack!
Now, where's that dang light switch?
Ah!
click

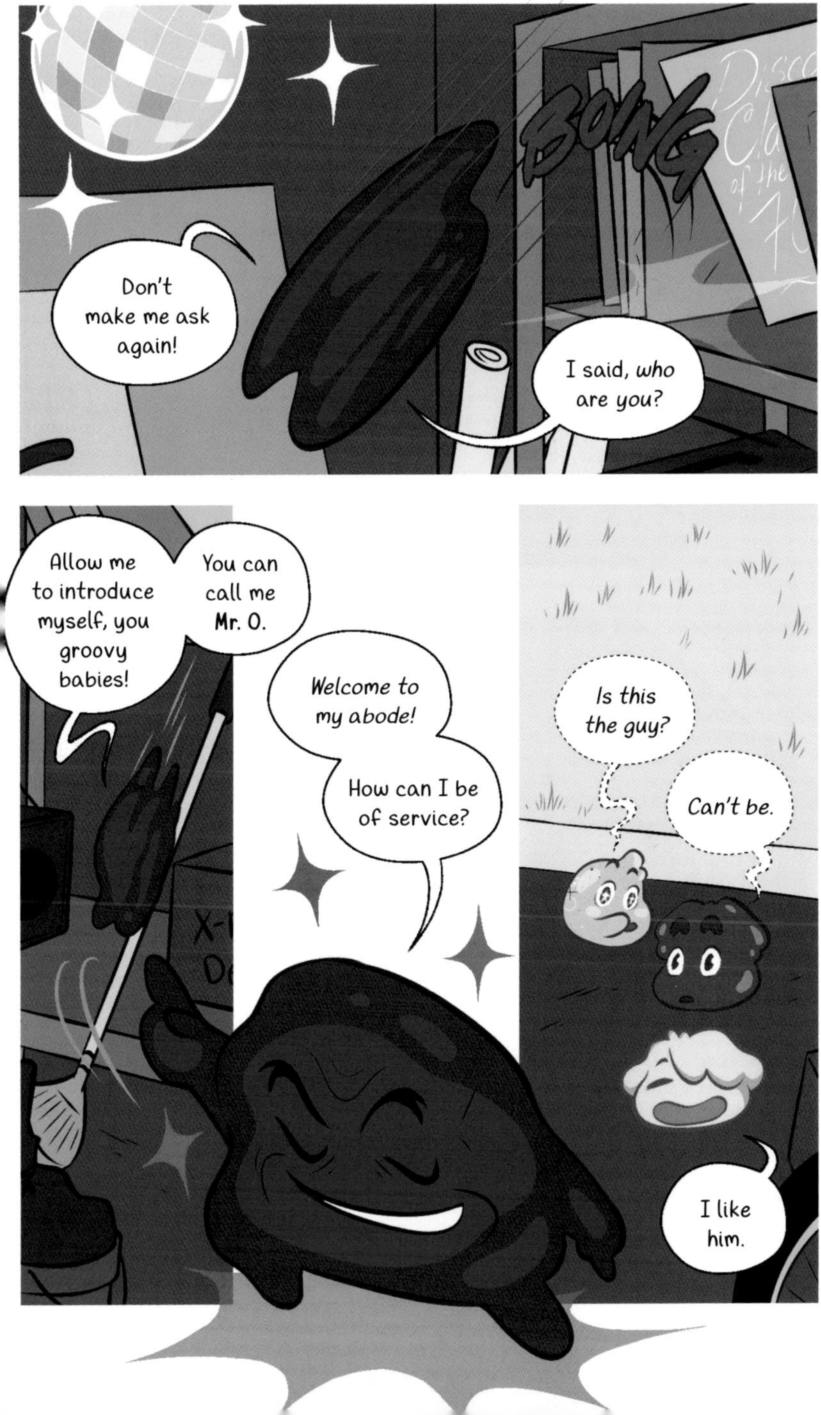
BOING
Don't make me ask again!
I said, *who* are you?
Allow me to introduce myself, you groovy babies!
You can call me **Mr. O.**
Welcome to my abode!
How can I be of service?
Is this the guy?
Can't be.
I like him.

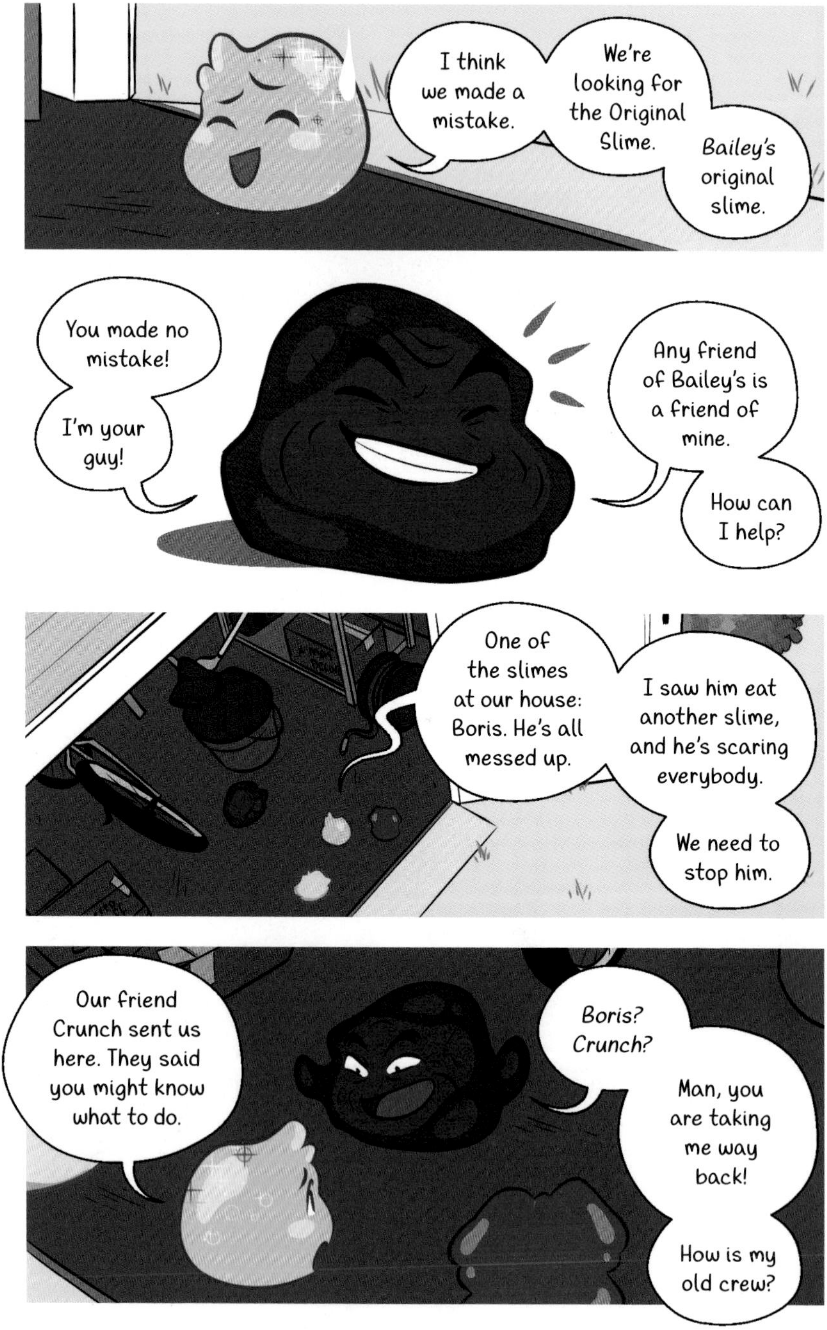

I think we made a mistake.
We're looking for the Original Slime.
Bailey's original slime.
You made no mistake!
I'm your guy!
Any friend of Bailey's is a friend of mine.
How can I help?
One of the slimes at our house: Boris. He's all messed up.
I saw him eat another slime, and he's scaring everybody.
We need to stop him.
Our friend Crunch sent us here. They said you might know what to do.
Boris? Crunch?
Man, you are taking me way back!
How is my old crew?

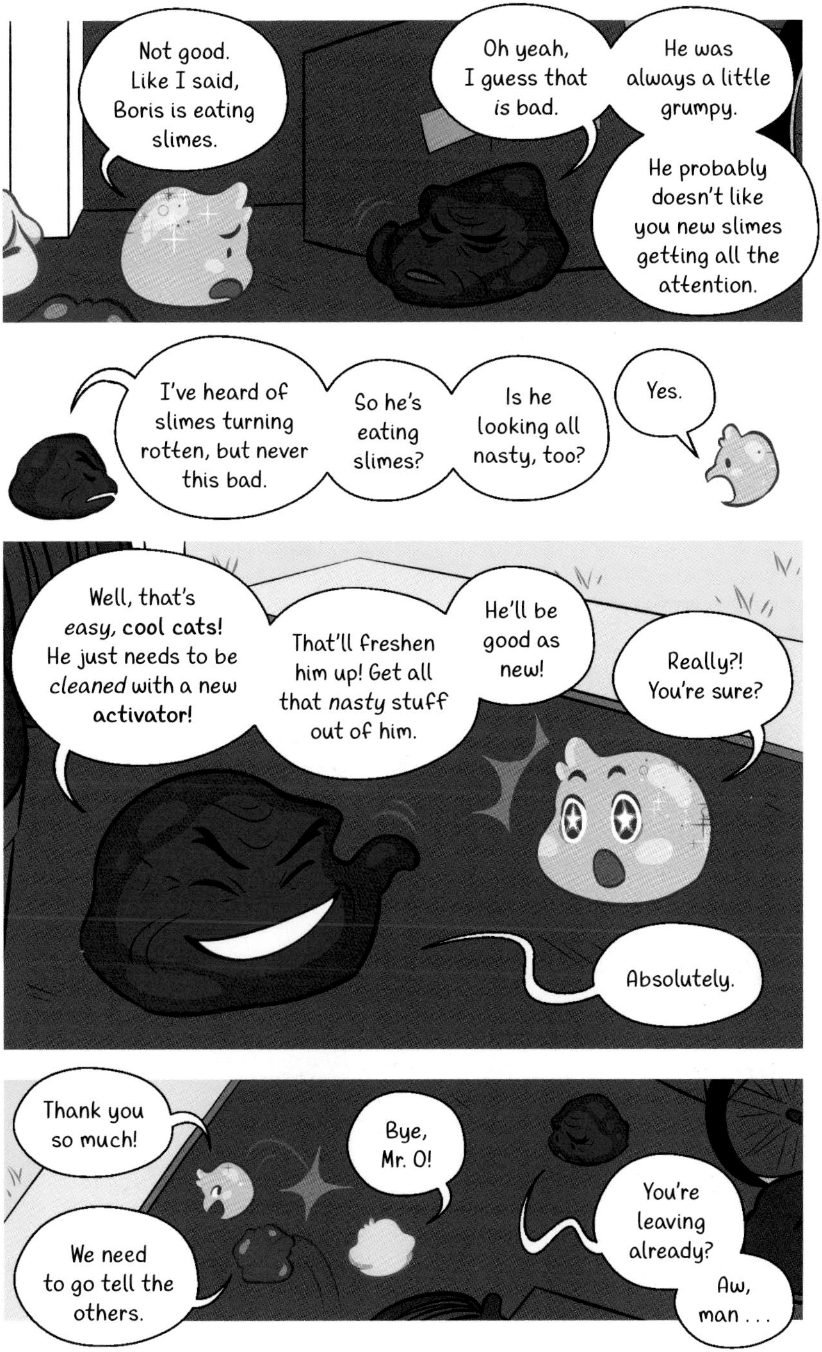
Not good. Like I said, Boris is eating slimes.
Oh yeah, I guess that *is* bad.
He was always a little grumpy.
He probably doesn't like you new slimes getting all the attention.
I've heard of slimes turning rotten, but never this bad.
So he's eating slimes?
Is he looking all nasty, too?
Yes.
Well, that's *easy,* **cool cats!** He just needs to be *cleaned* with a new **activator!**
That'll freshen him up! Get all that *nasty* stuff out of him.
He'll be good as new!
Really?! You're sure?
Absolutely.
Thank you so much!
We need to go tell the others.
Bye, Mr. O!
You're leaving already?
Aw, man . . .

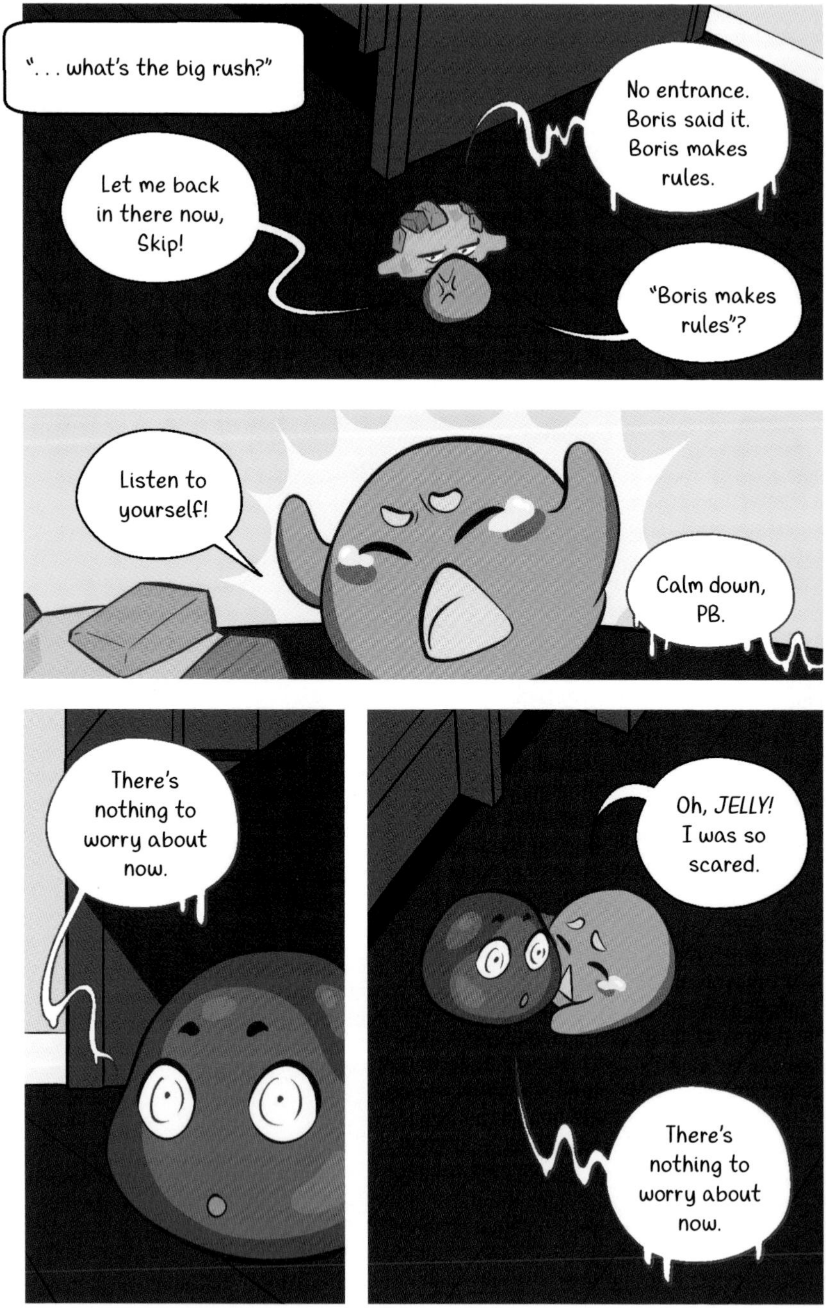
". . . what's the big rush?"
No entrance. Boris said it. Boris makes rules.
Let me back in there now, Skip!
"Boris makes rules"?
Listen to yourself!
Calm down, PB.
There's nothing to worry about now.
Oh, *JELLY!* I was so scared.
There's nothing to worry about now.

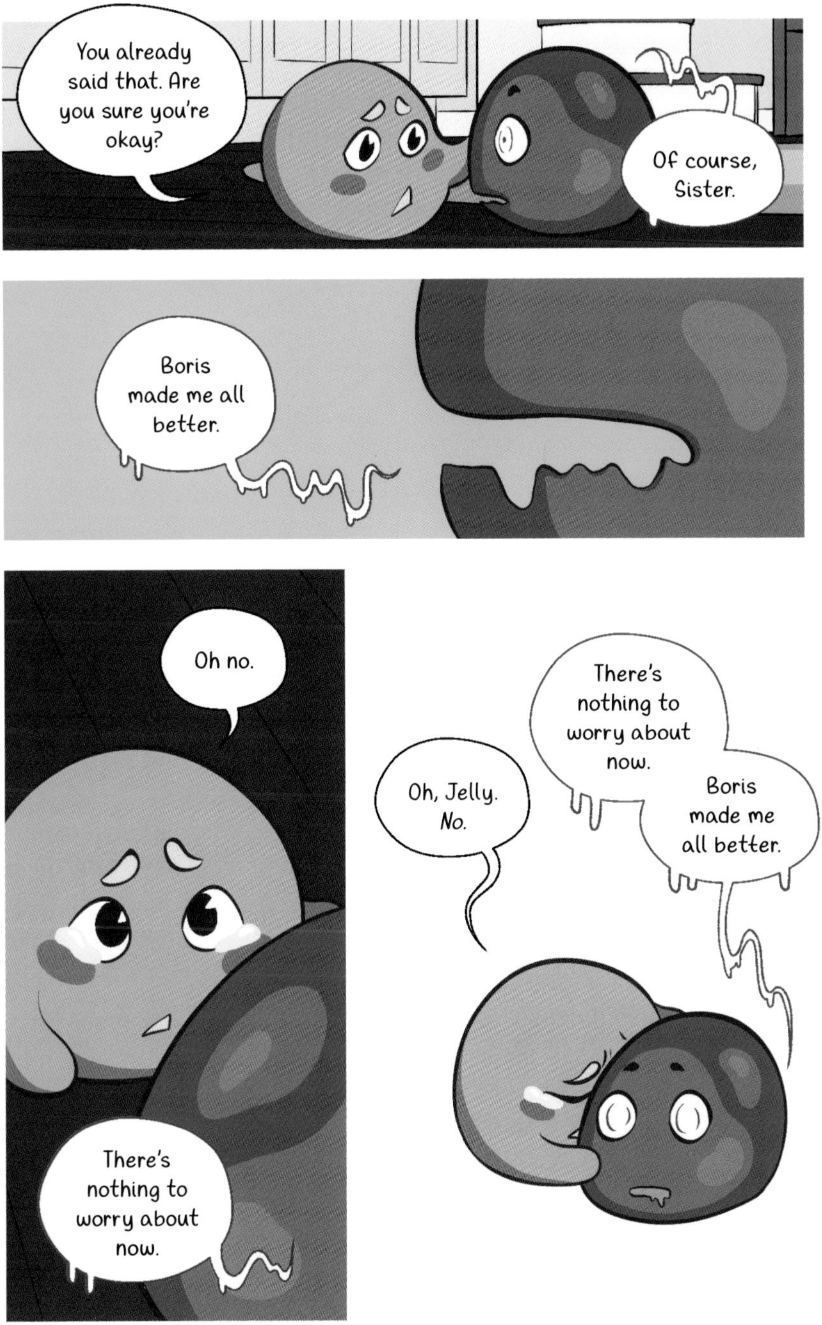

You already said that. Are you sure you're okay?
Of course, Sister.
Boris made me all better.
Oh no.
There's nothing to worry about now.
Oh, Jelly. No.
There's nothing to worry about now.
Boris made me all better.

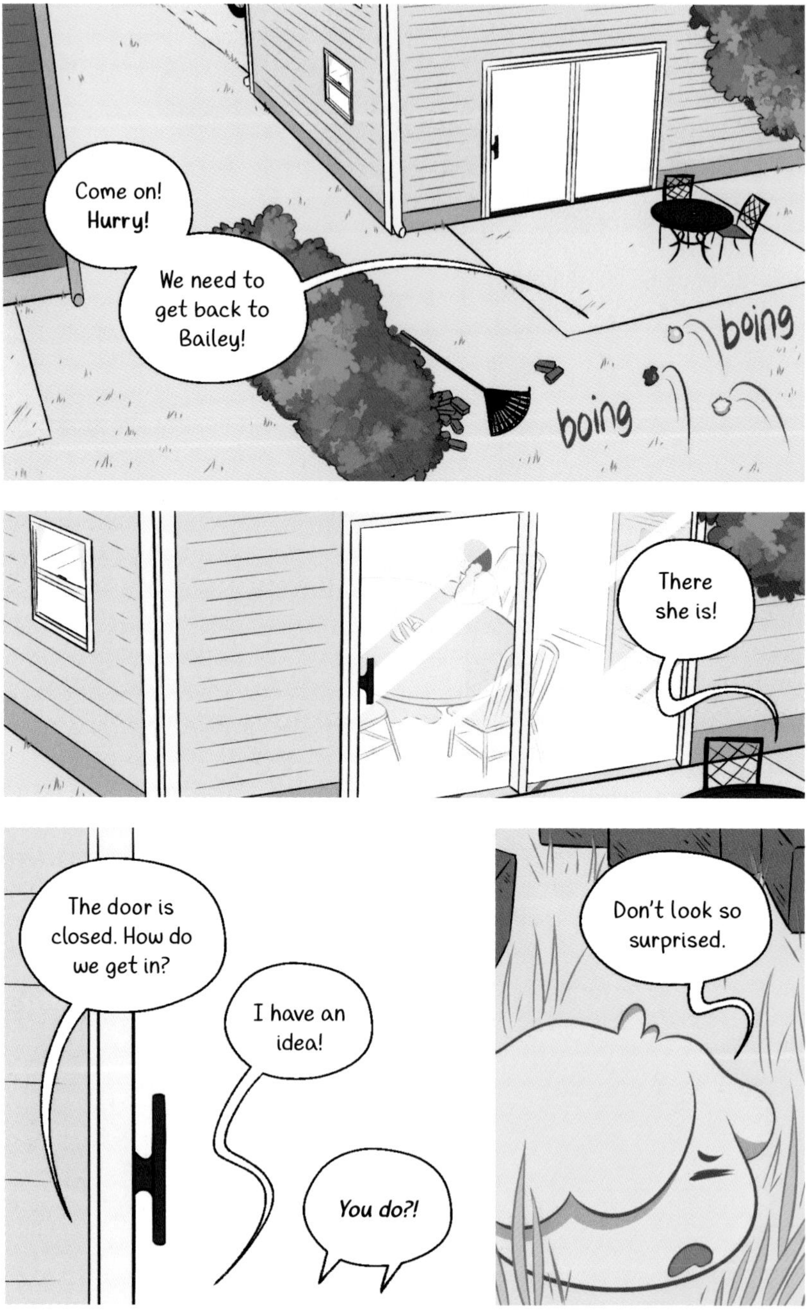
Come on! Hurry!
We need to get back to Bailey!
boing
boing
There she is!
The door is closed. How do we get in?
I have an idea!
You do?!
Don't look so surprised.

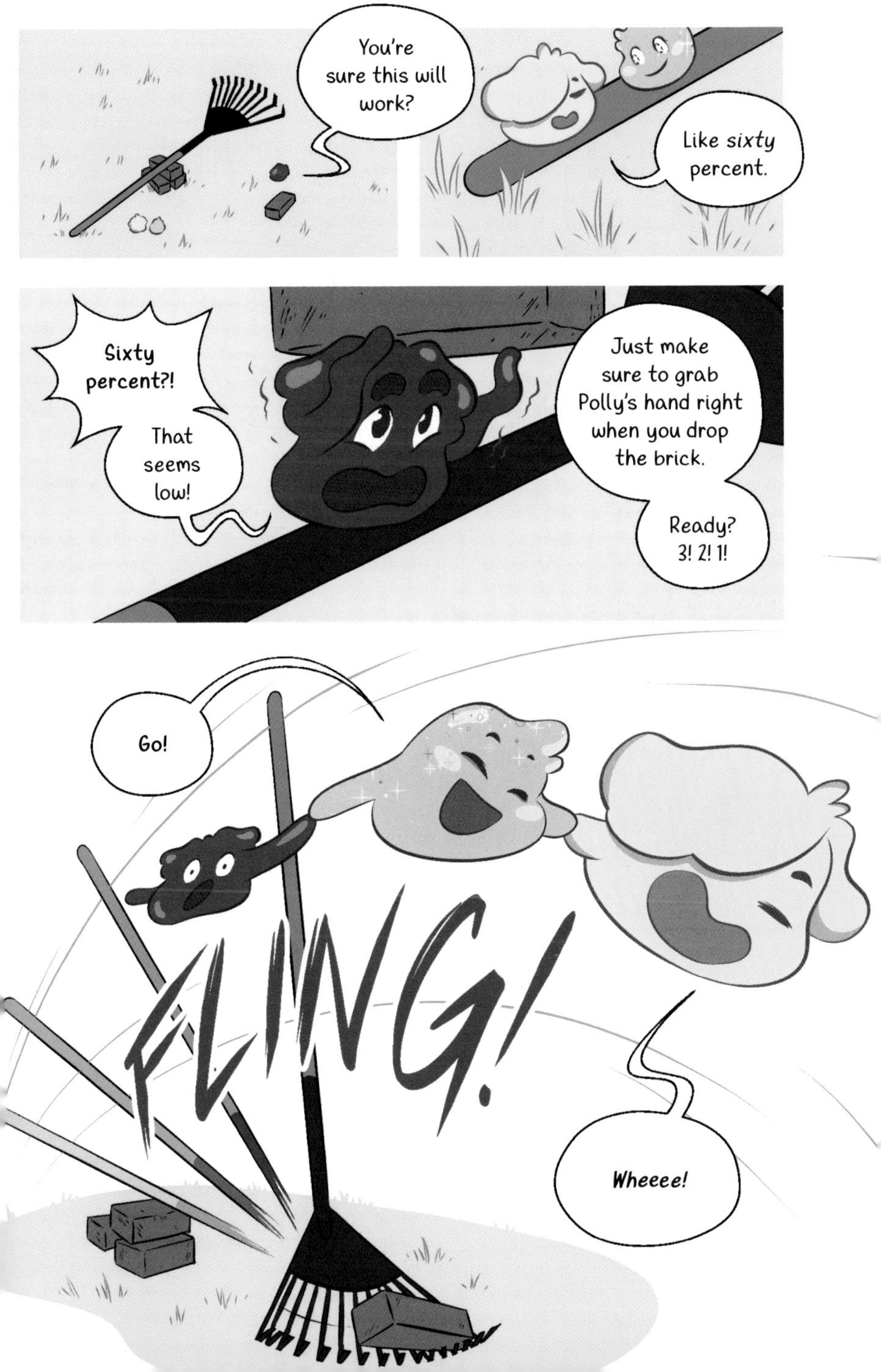
You're sure this will work?
Like *sixty* percent.
Sixty percent?!
That seems low!
Just make sure to grab Polly's hand right when you drop the brick.
Ready? 3! 2! 1!
Go!
FLING!
Wheeee!

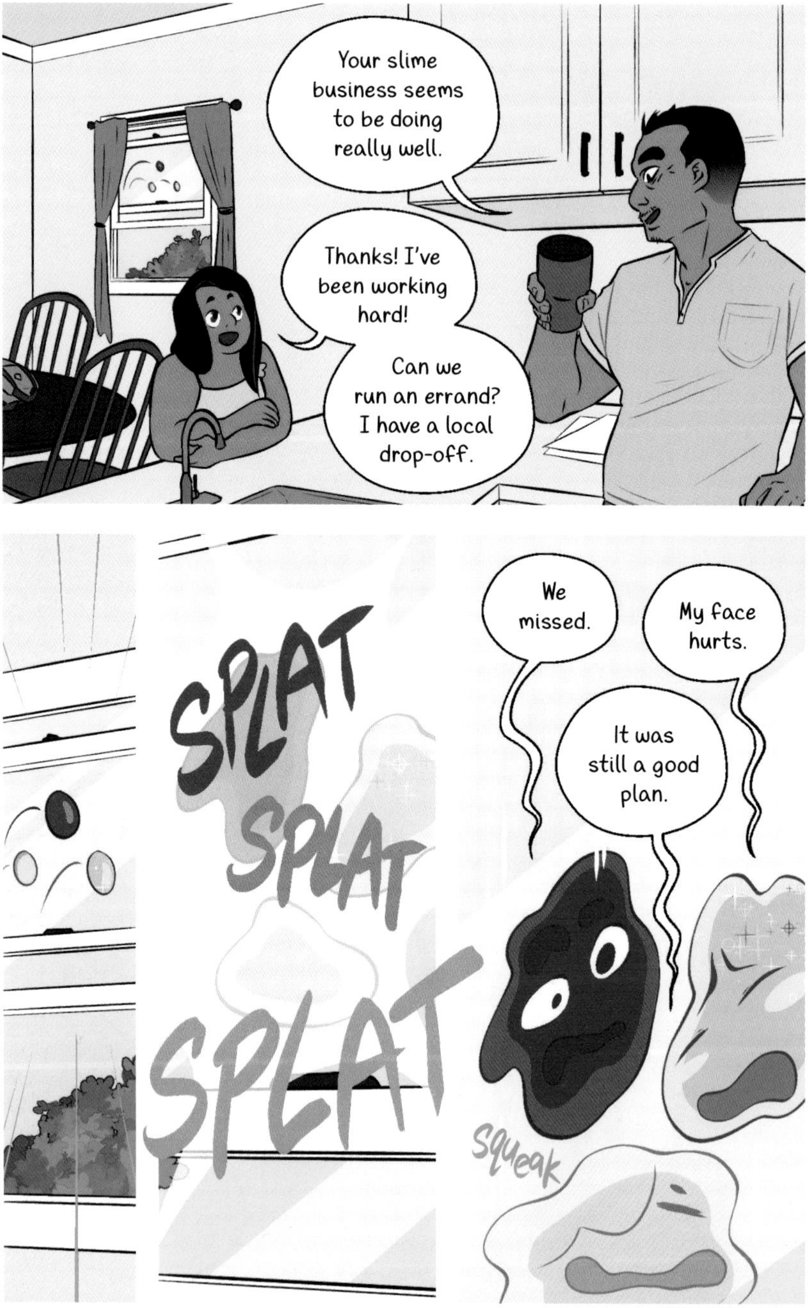
Your slime business seems to be doing really well.
Thanks! I've been working hard!
Can we run an errand? I have a local drop-off.
SPLAT
SPLAT
SPLAT
We missed.
My face hurts.
It was still a good plan.
squeak

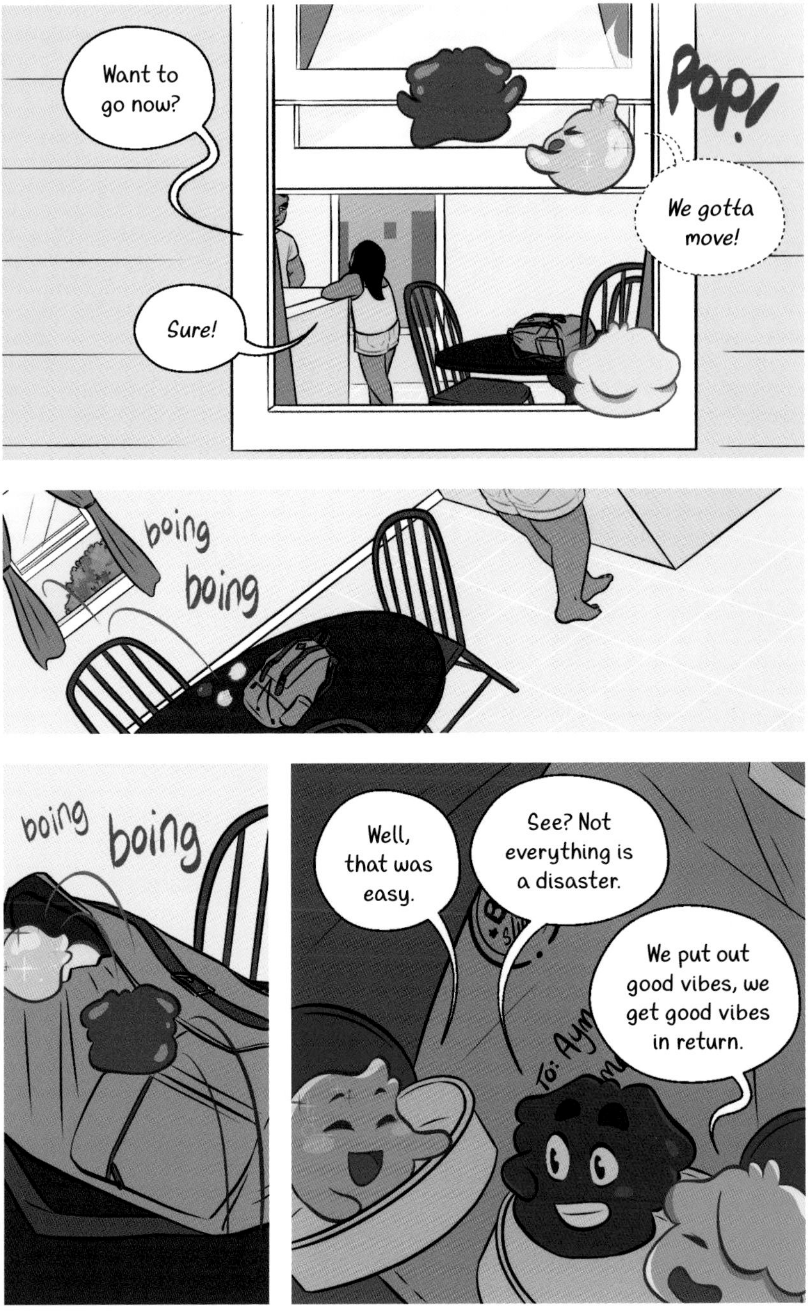
Want to go now?
POP!
We gotta move!
Sure!
boing
boing
boing
boing
Well, that was easy.
See? Not everything is a disaster.
We put out good vibes, we get good vibes in return.

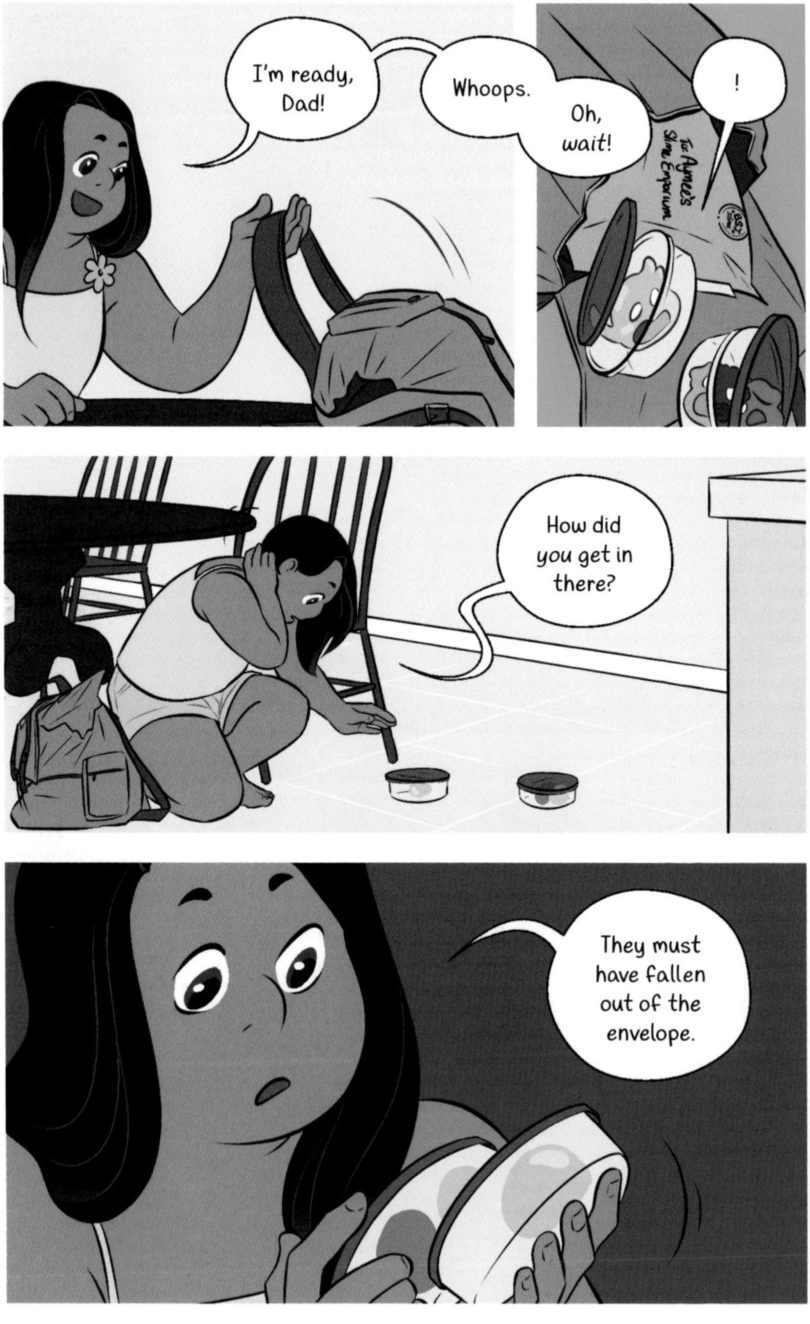
I'm ready, Dad!
Whoops.
Oh, wait!
To Aymee's Slime Emporium
!
How did you get in there?
They must have fallen out of the envelope.

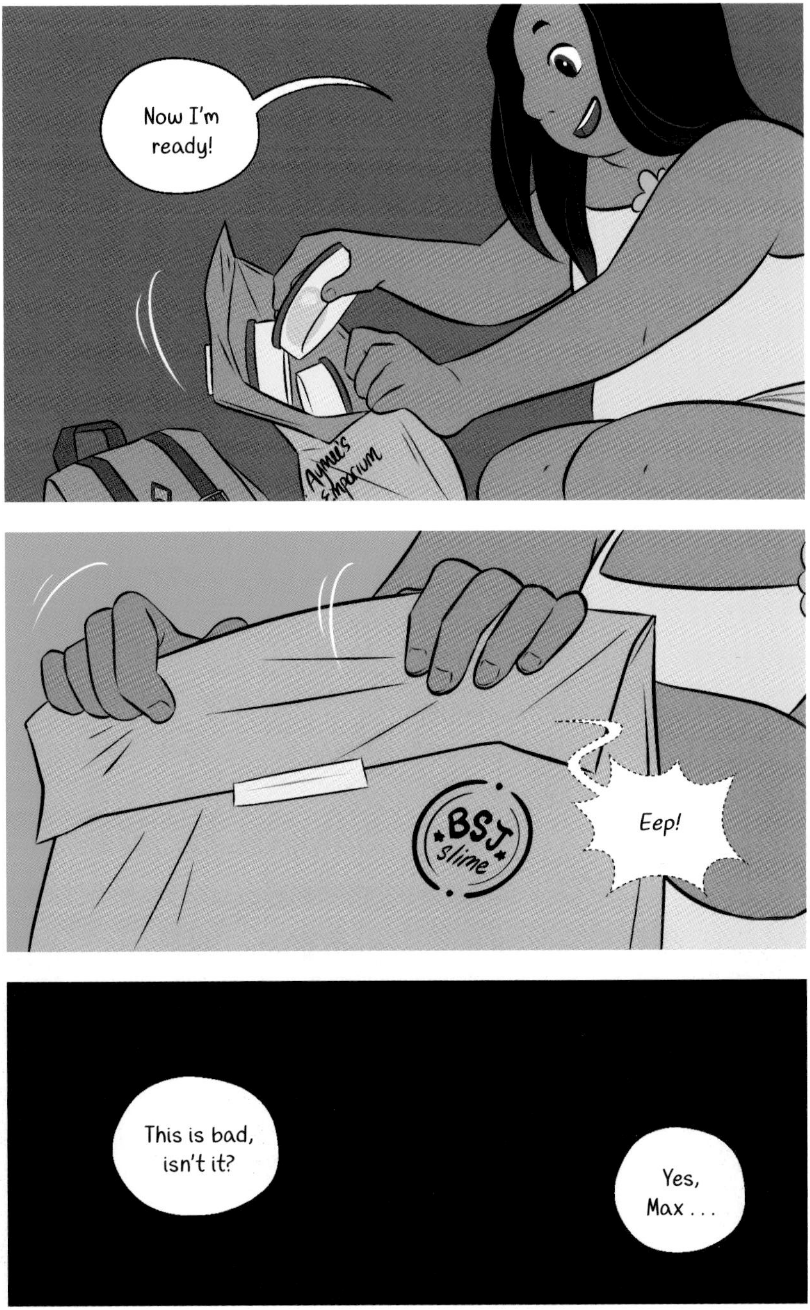
Now I'm ready!
Aymee's Emporium
BSJ slime
Eep!
This is bad, isn't it?
Yes, Max . . .

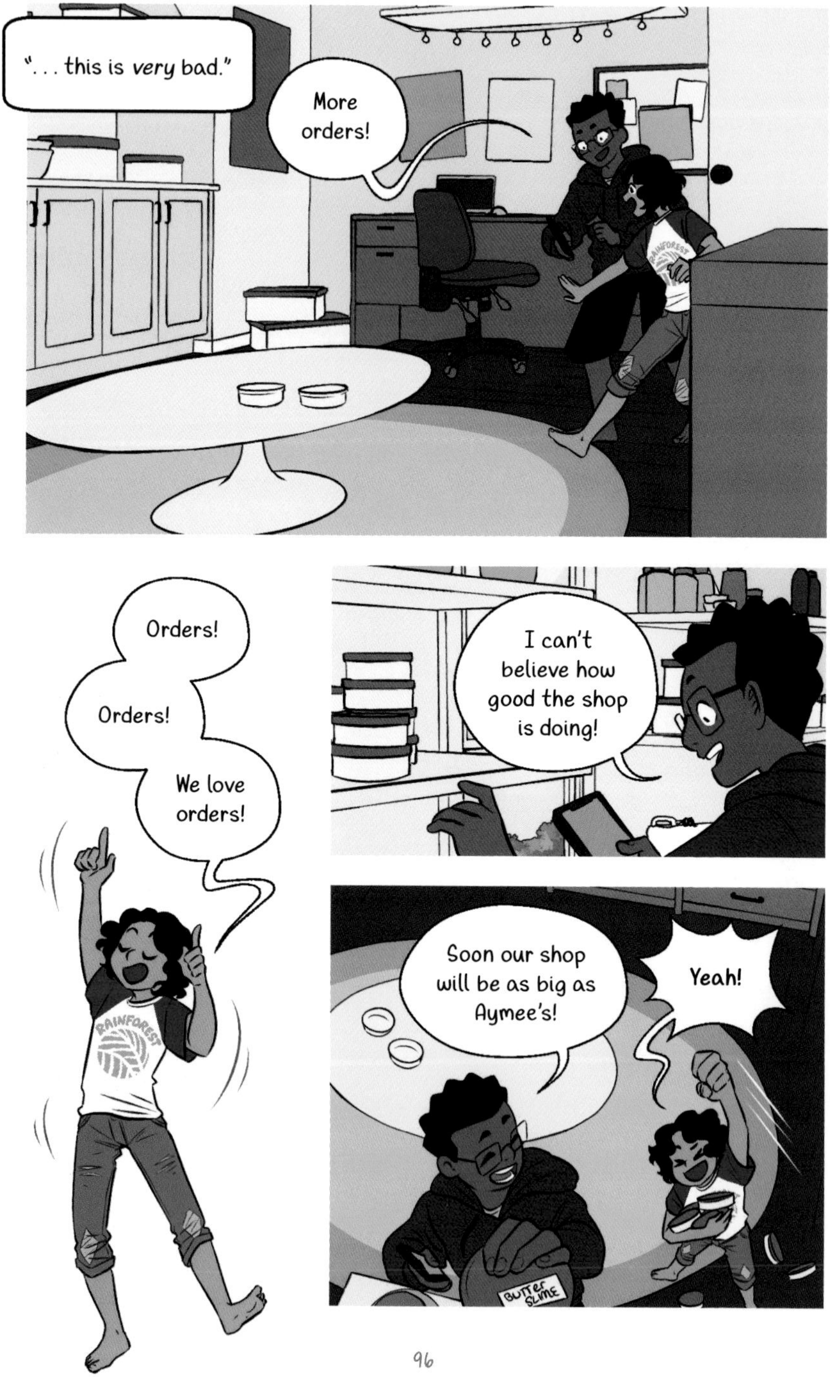
". . . this is *very* bad."
More orders!
Orders!
Orders!
We love orders!
I can't believe how good the shop is doing!
Soon our shop will be as big as Aymee's!
Yeah!
BUTTER SLIME

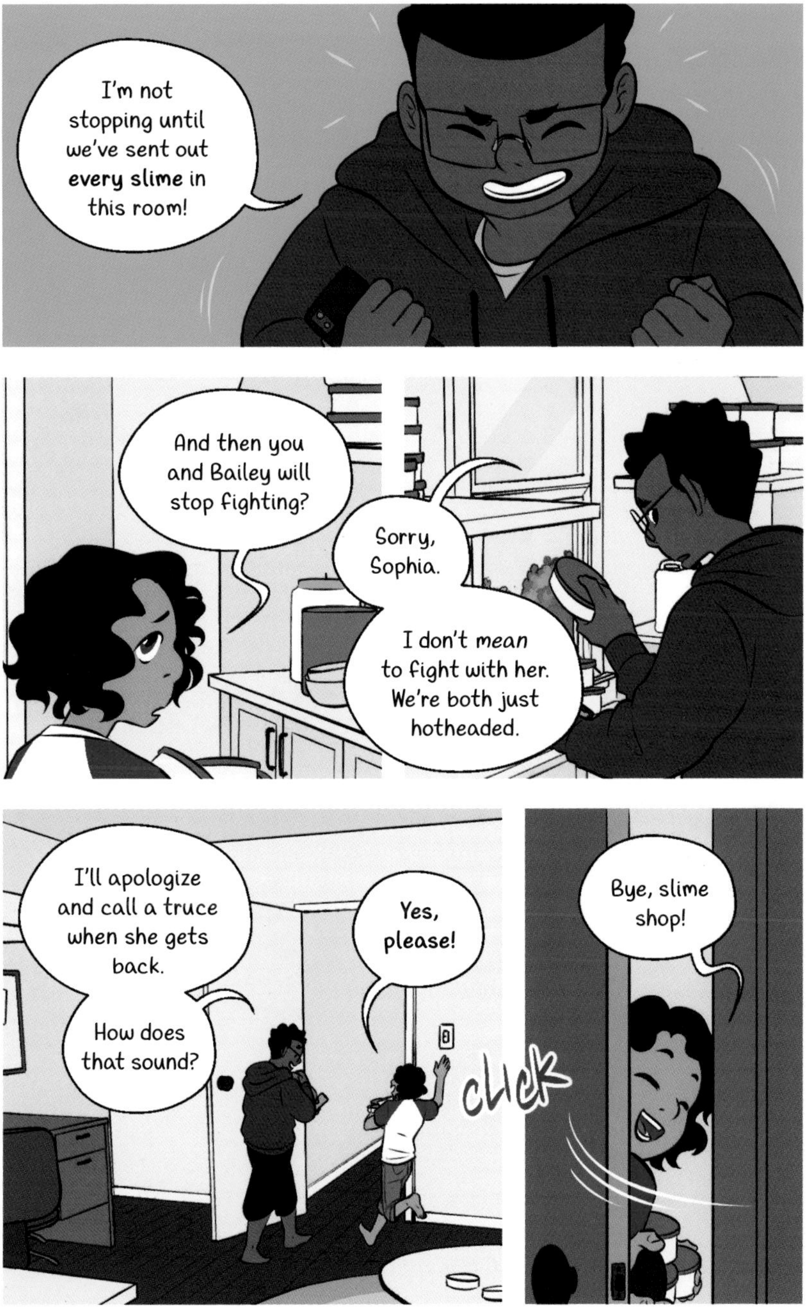
I'm not stopping until we've sent out **every slime** in this room!
And then you and Bailey will stop fighting?
Sorry, Sophia.
I don't *mean* to fight with her. We're both just hotheaded.
I'll apologize and call a truce when she gets back.
How does that sound?
Yes, please!
CLICK
Bye, slime shop!

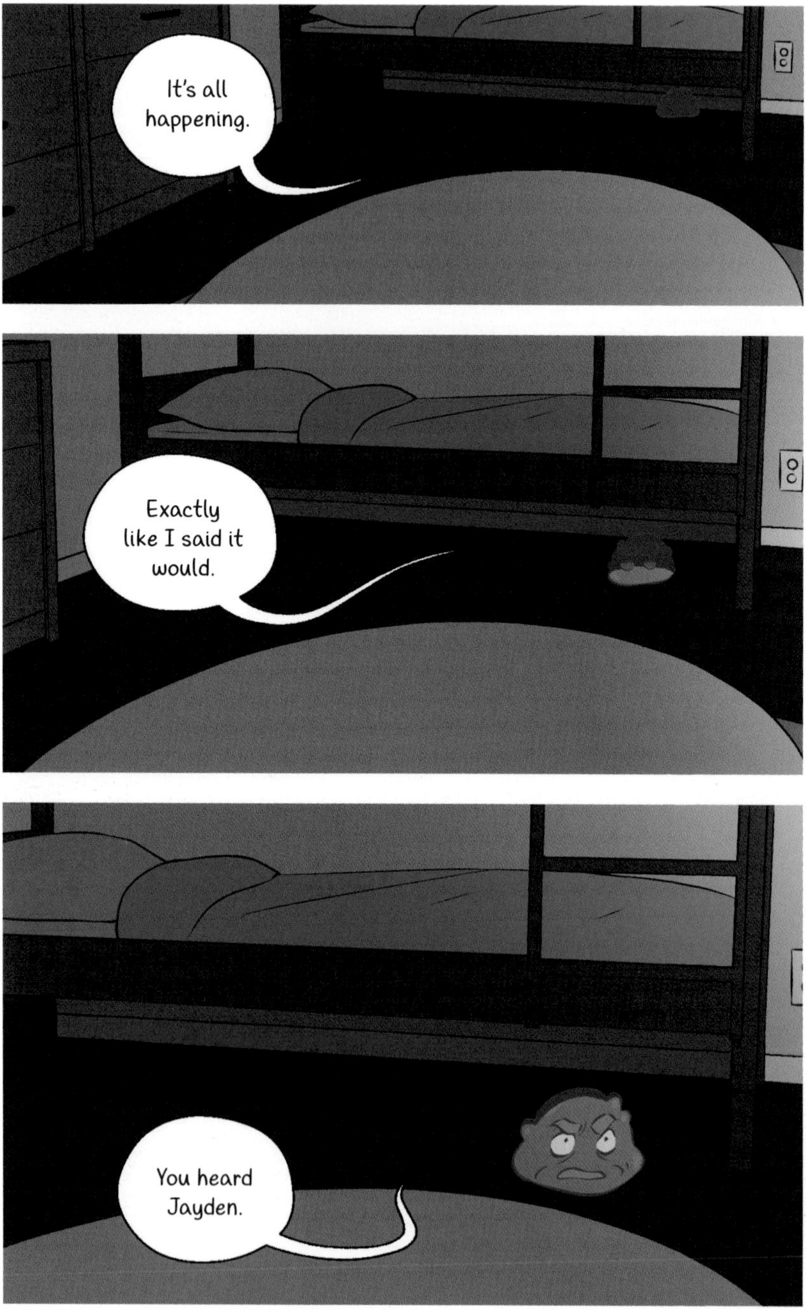
It's all happening.
Exactly like I said it would.
You heard Jayden.

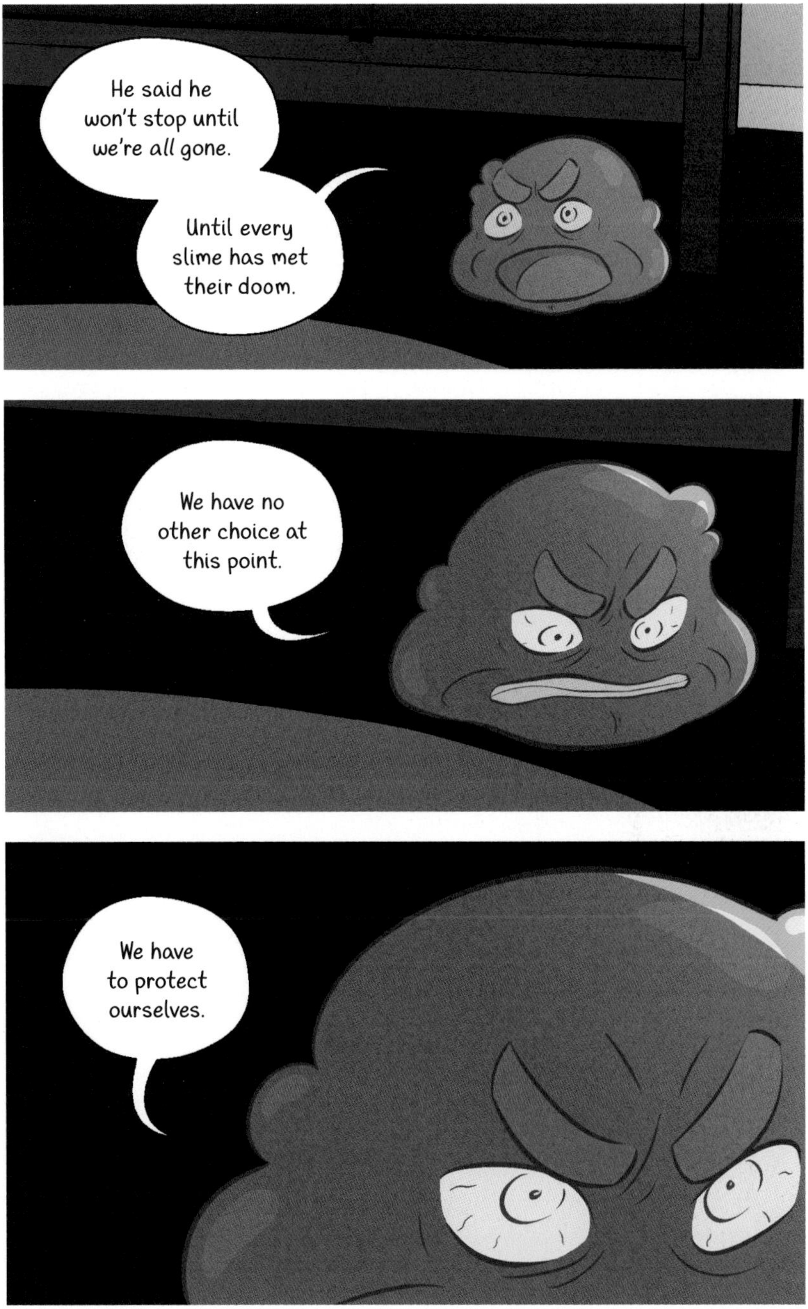
He said he won't stop until we're all gone.
Until every slime has met their doom.
We have no other choice at this point.
We have to protect ourselves.

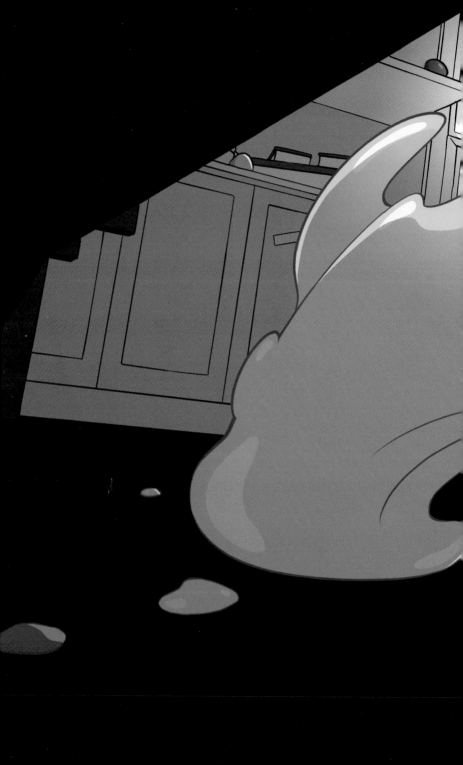

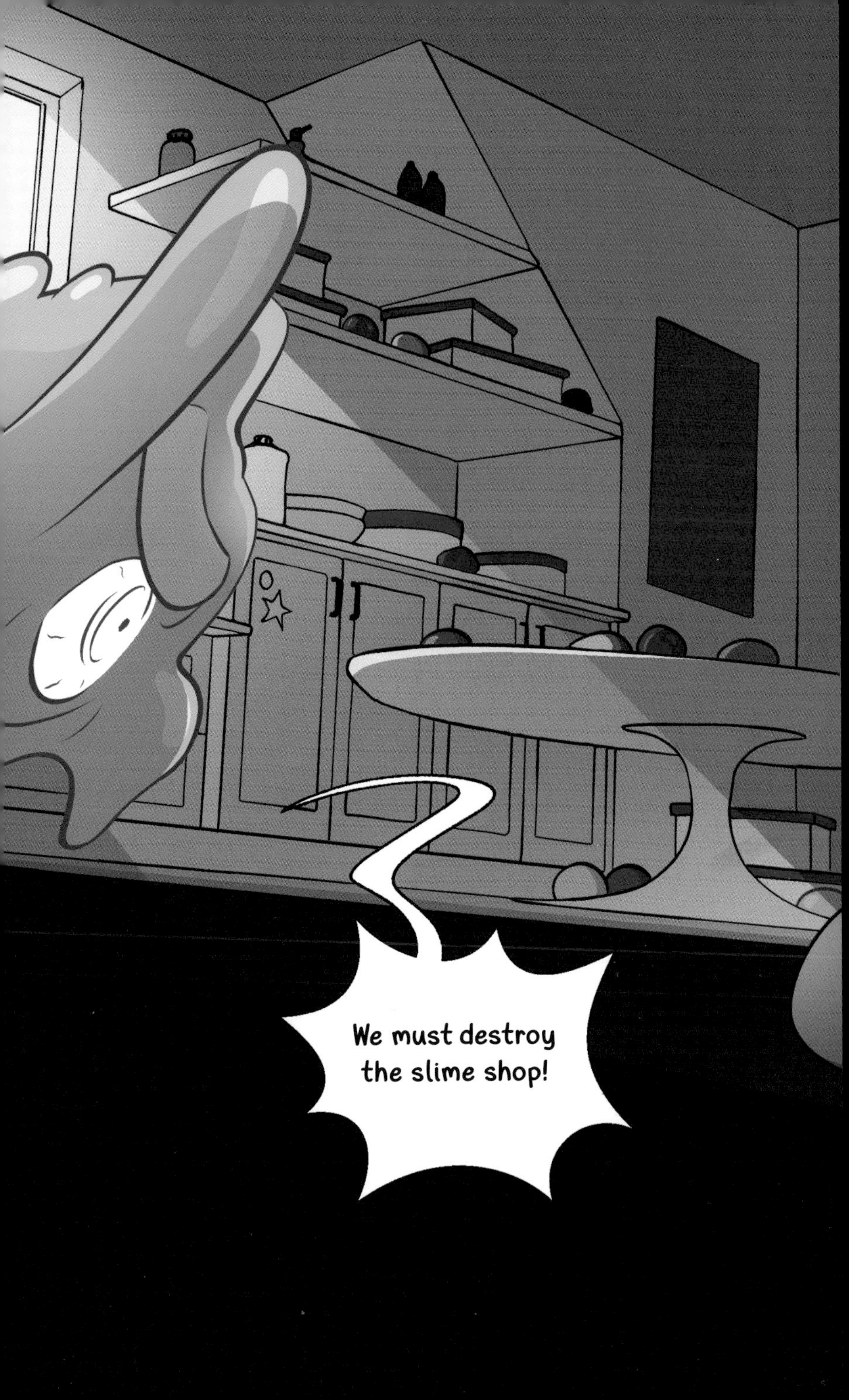
We must destroy
the slime shop!

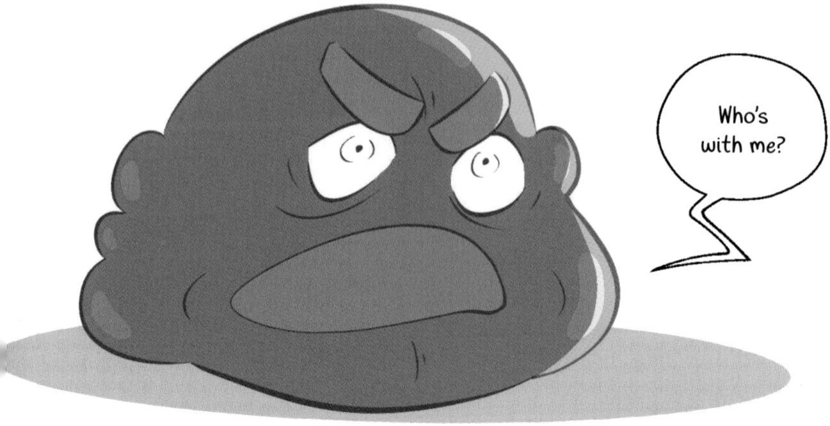
Who's with me?

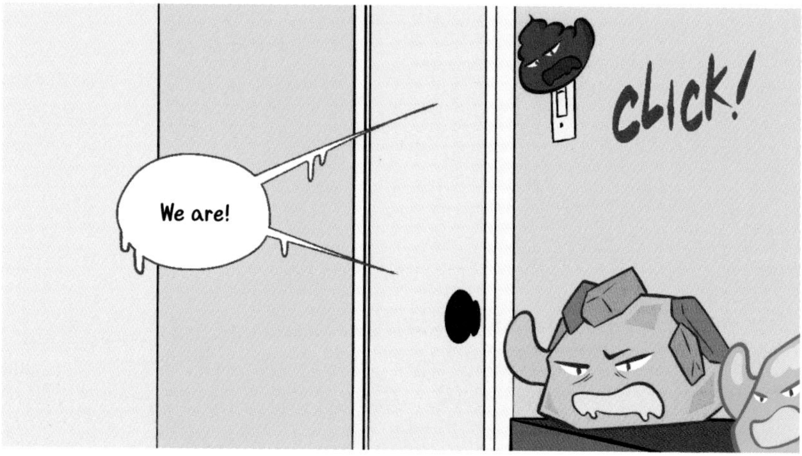
We are!
CLICK!

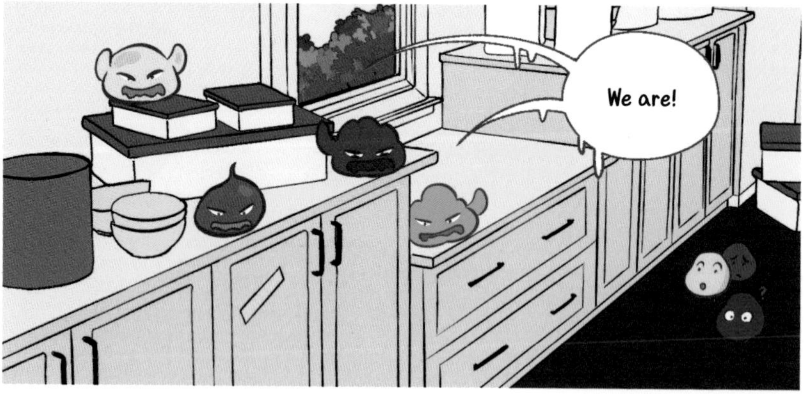
We are!

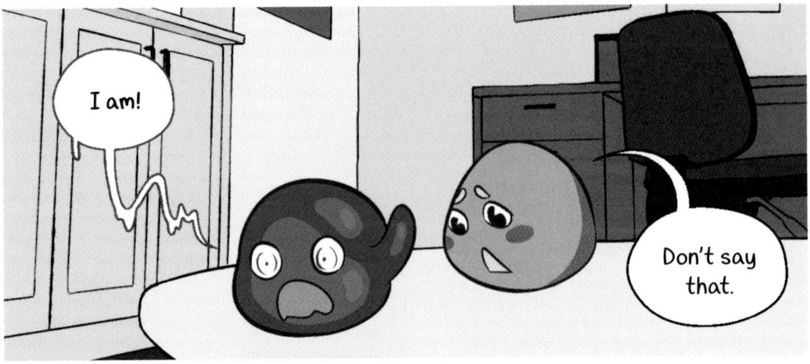
I am!
Don't say that.

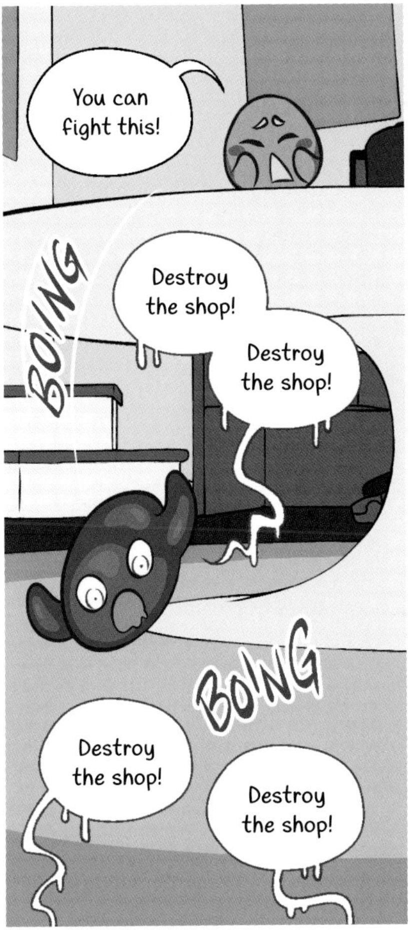
You can fight this!
BOING
Destroy the shop!
Destroy the shop!
BOING
Destroy the shop!
Destroy the shop!

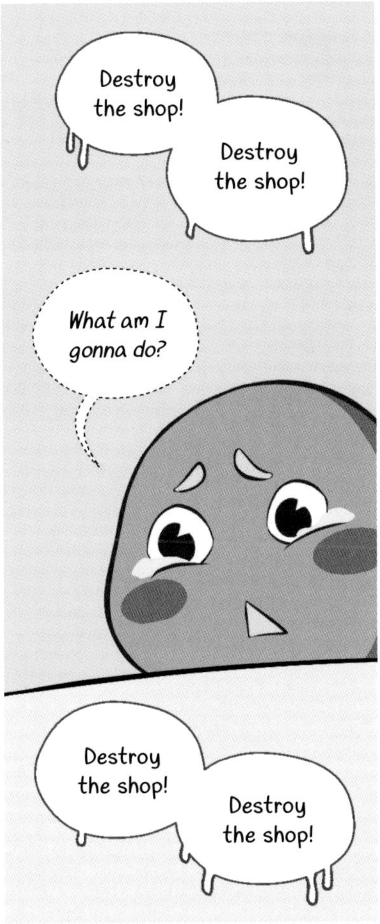
Destroy the shop!
Destroy the shop!
What am I gonna do?
Destroy the shop!
Destroy the shop!

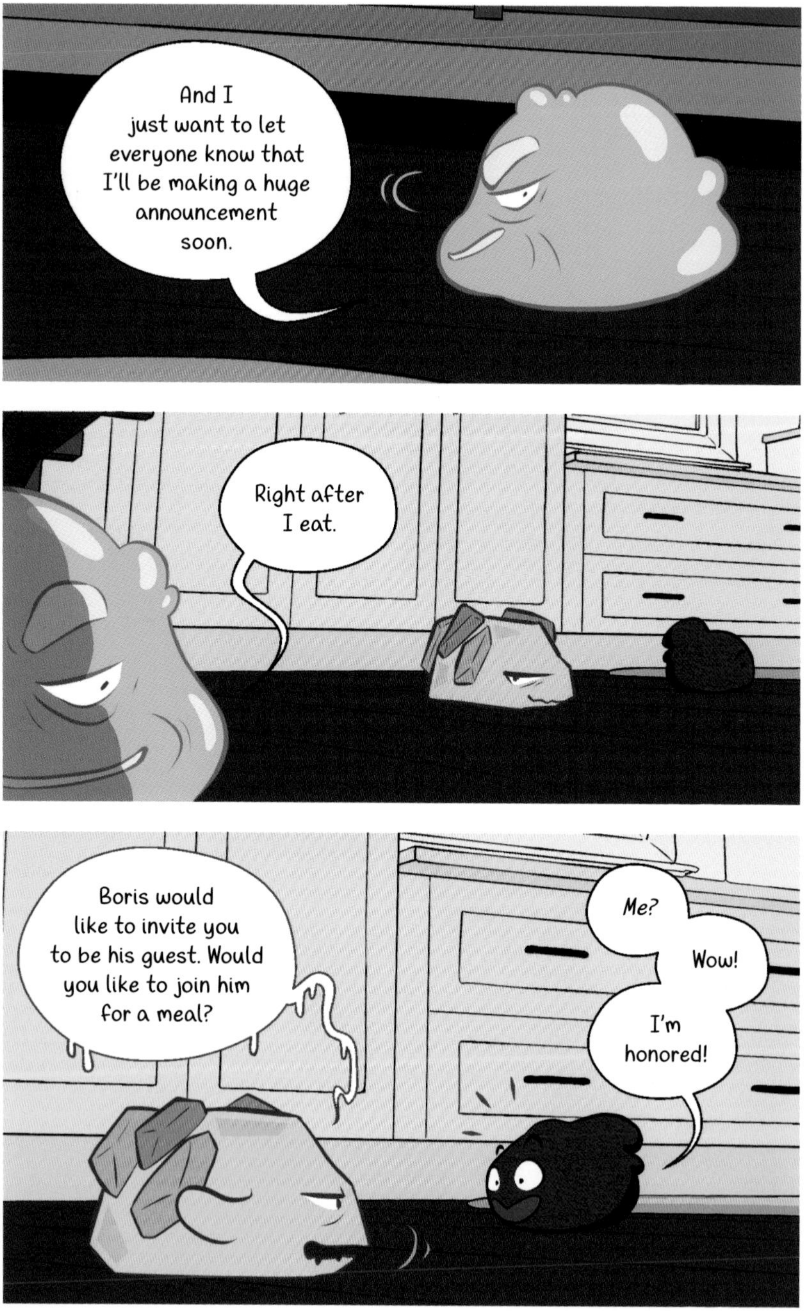
And I just want to let everyone know that I'll be making a huge announcement soon.
Right after I eat.
Boris would like to invite you to be his guest. Would you like to join him for a meal?
Me?
Wow!
I'm honored!

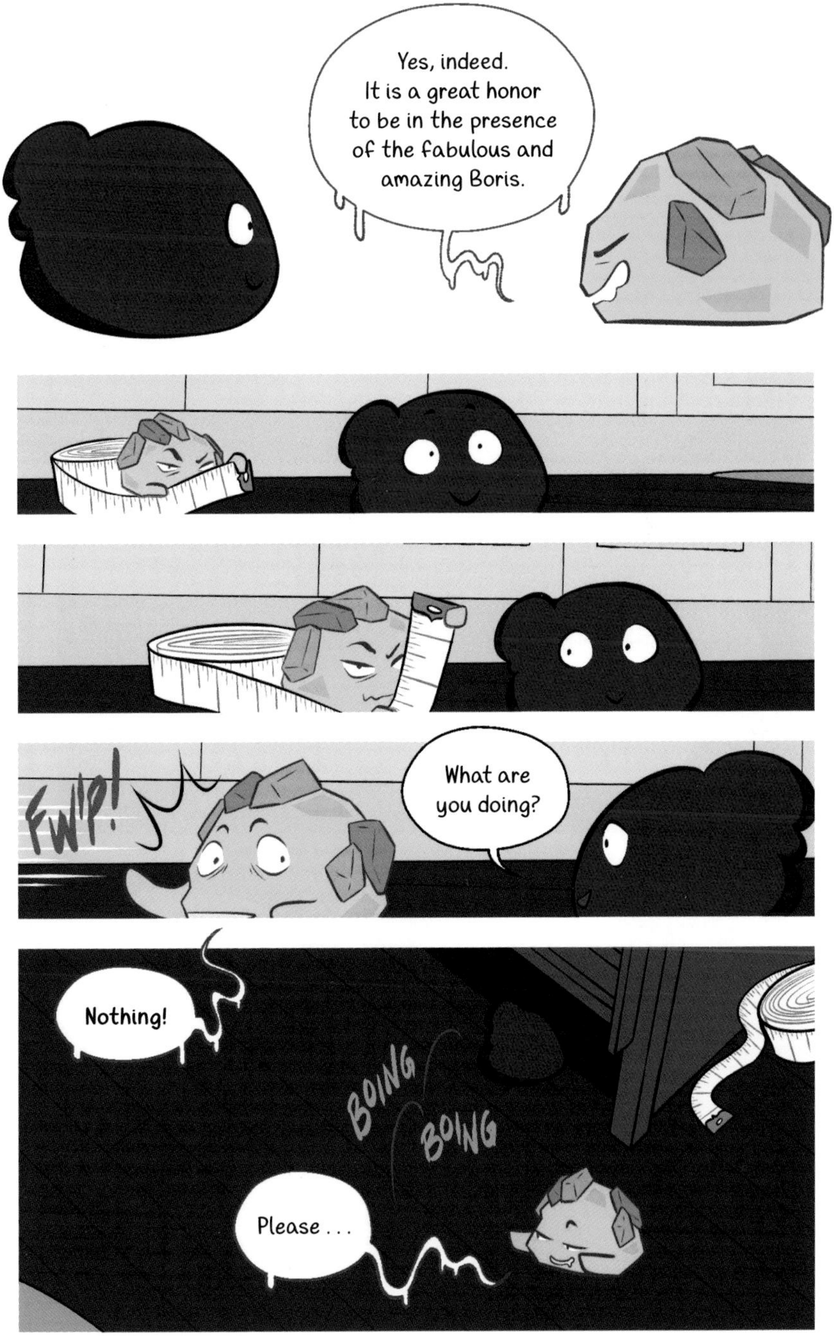
Yes, indeed.
It is a great honor
to be in the presence
of the fabulous and
amazing Boris.
FWIP!
What are
you doing?
Nothing!
BOING
BOING
Please . . .

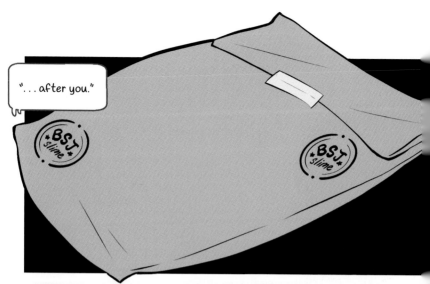

"...after you."

Nope.

She sealed that thing up *tight*.

We could always go with the flow.

See where we end up.

That's not a plan, Karma. That's not *anything*!

And if you haven't noticed, we can't "*see*" anything!

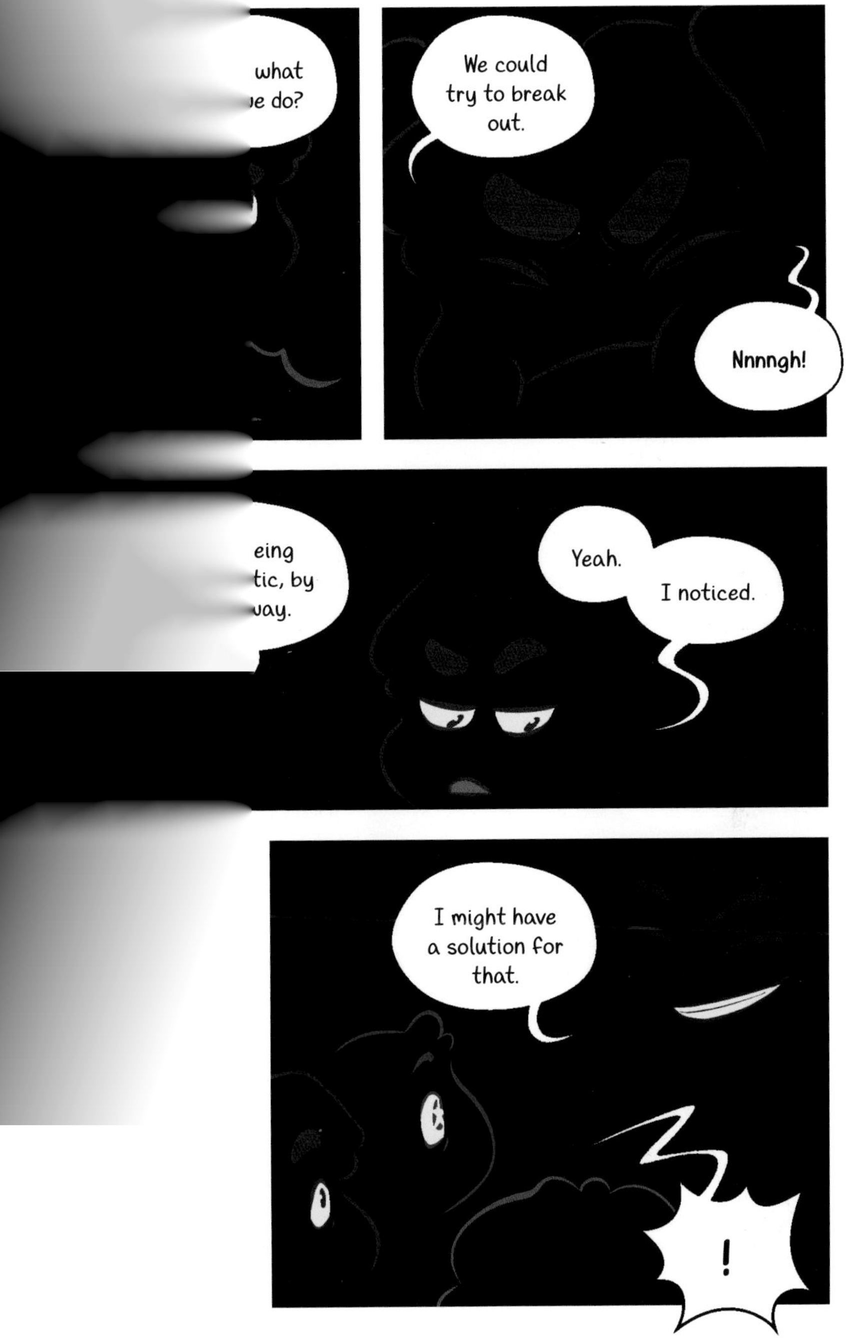
what
e do?
We could try to break out.
Nnnngh!
eing
tic, by
Yeah.
I noticed.
I might have a solution for that.
!

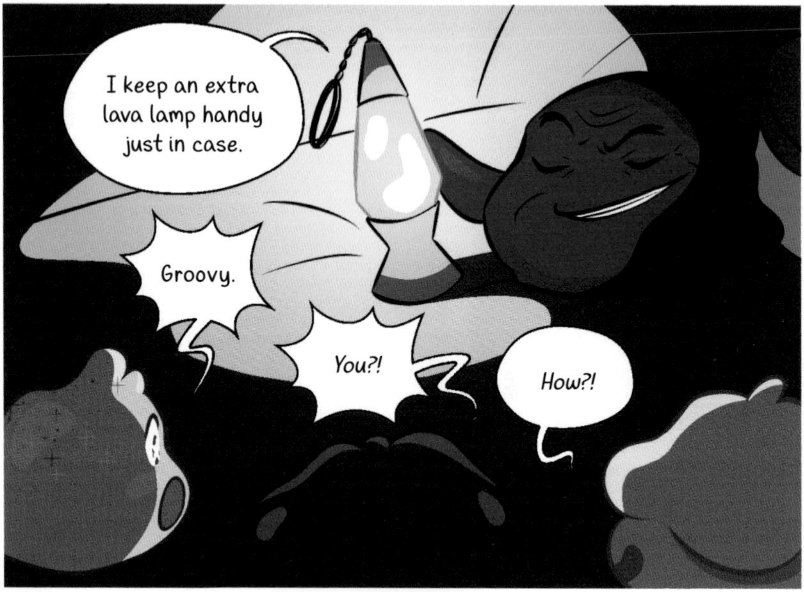
I keep an extra lava lamp handy just in case.
Groovy.
You?!
How?!

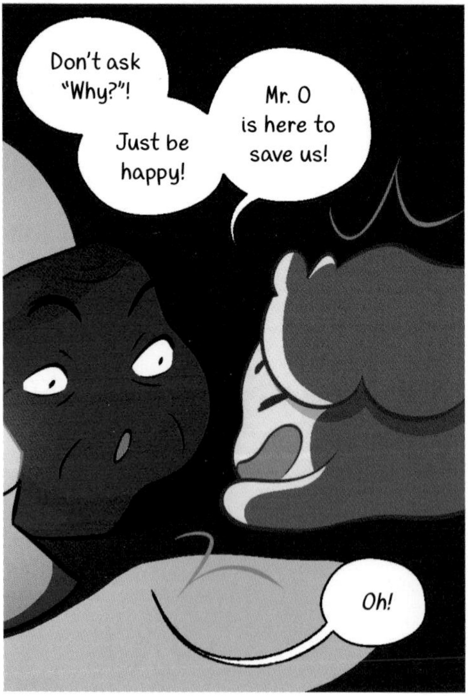
Don't ask "Why?"!
Just be happy!
Mr. O is here to save us!
Oh!

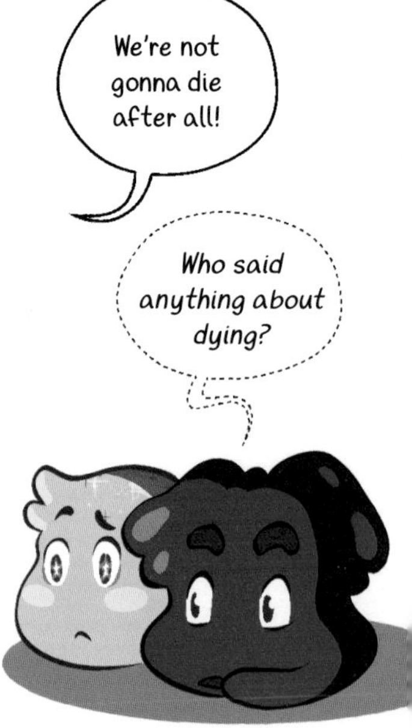
We're not gonna die after all!
Who said anything about dying?

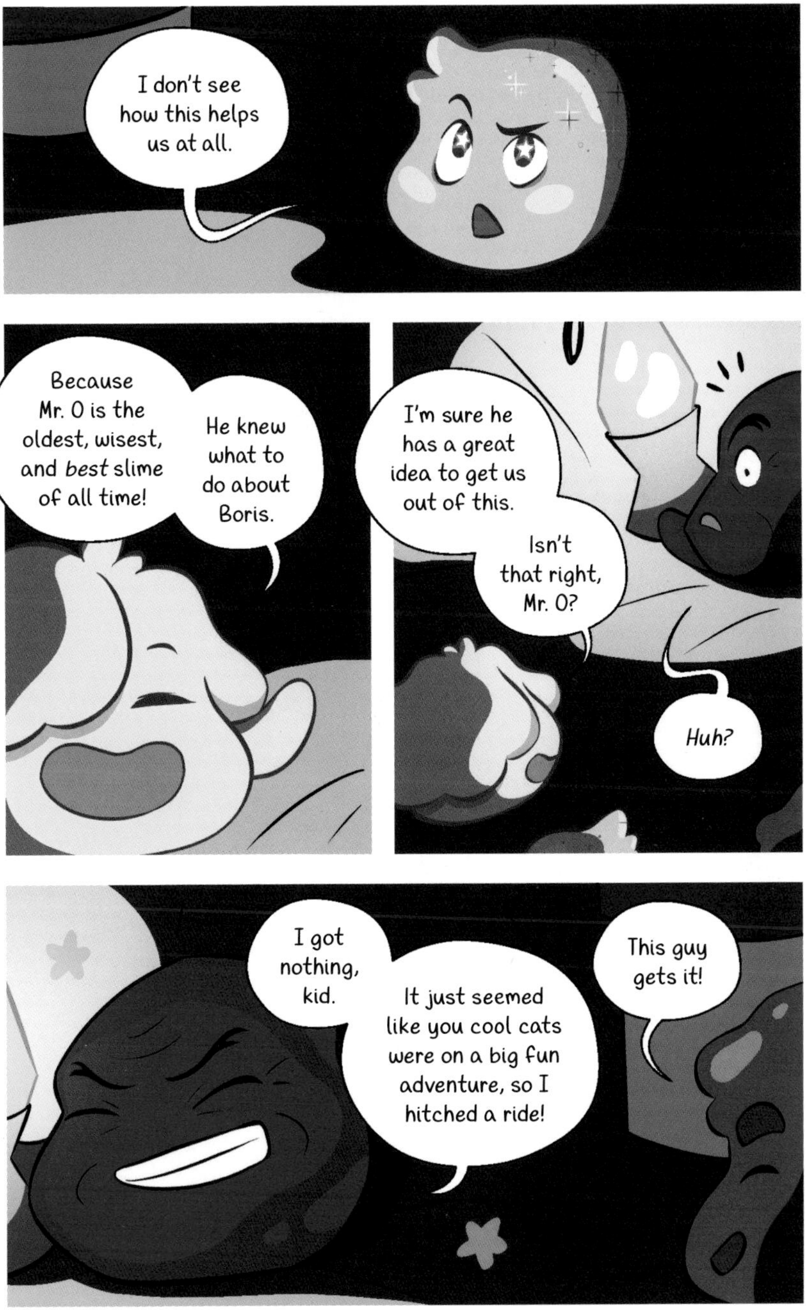
I don't see how this helps us at all.
Because Mr. O is the oldest, wisest, and *best* slime of all time!
He knew what to do about Boris.
I'm sure he has a great idea to get us out of this.
Isn't that right, Mr. O?
Huh?
I got nothing, kid.
It just seemed like you cool cats were on a big fun adventure, so I hitched a ride!
This guy gets it!

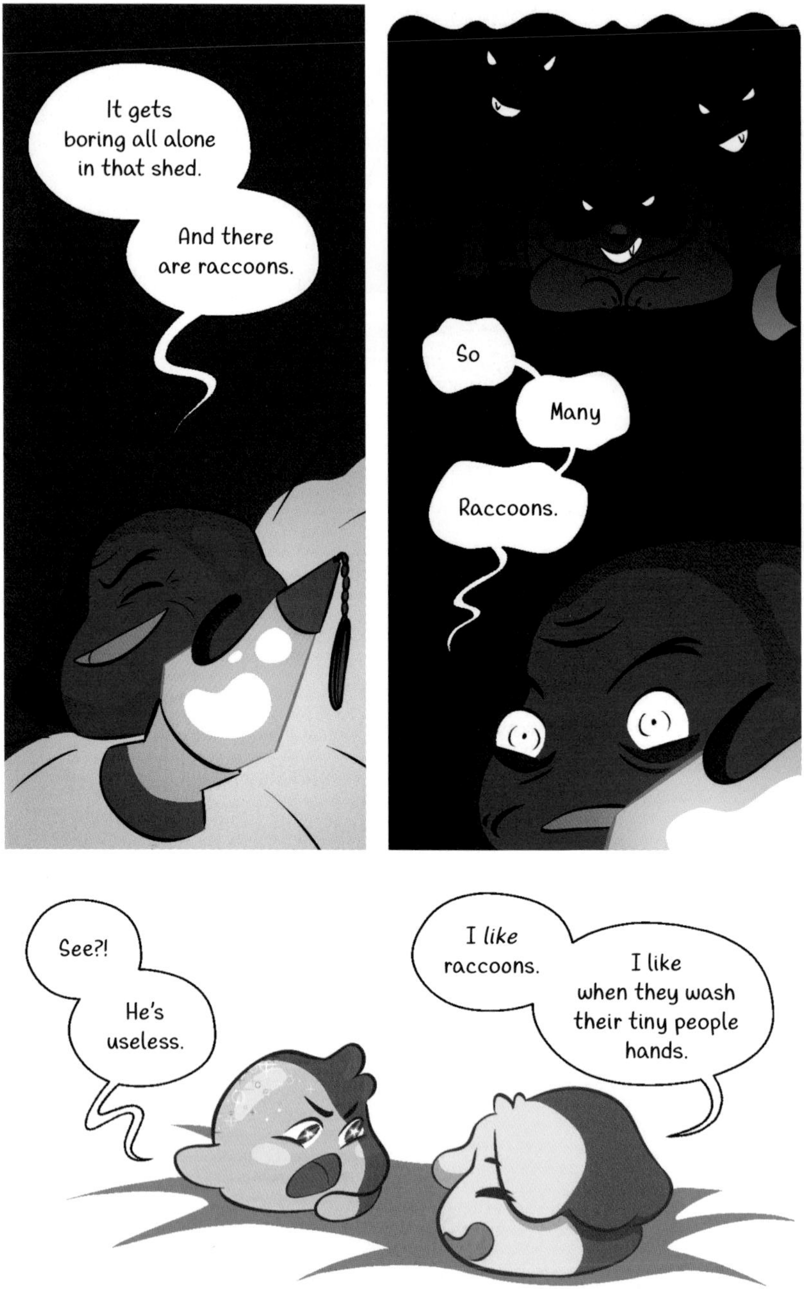
It gets boring all alone in that shed.
And there are raccoons.
So
Many
Raccoons.
See?!
He's useless.
I like raccoons.
I like when they wash their tiny people hands.

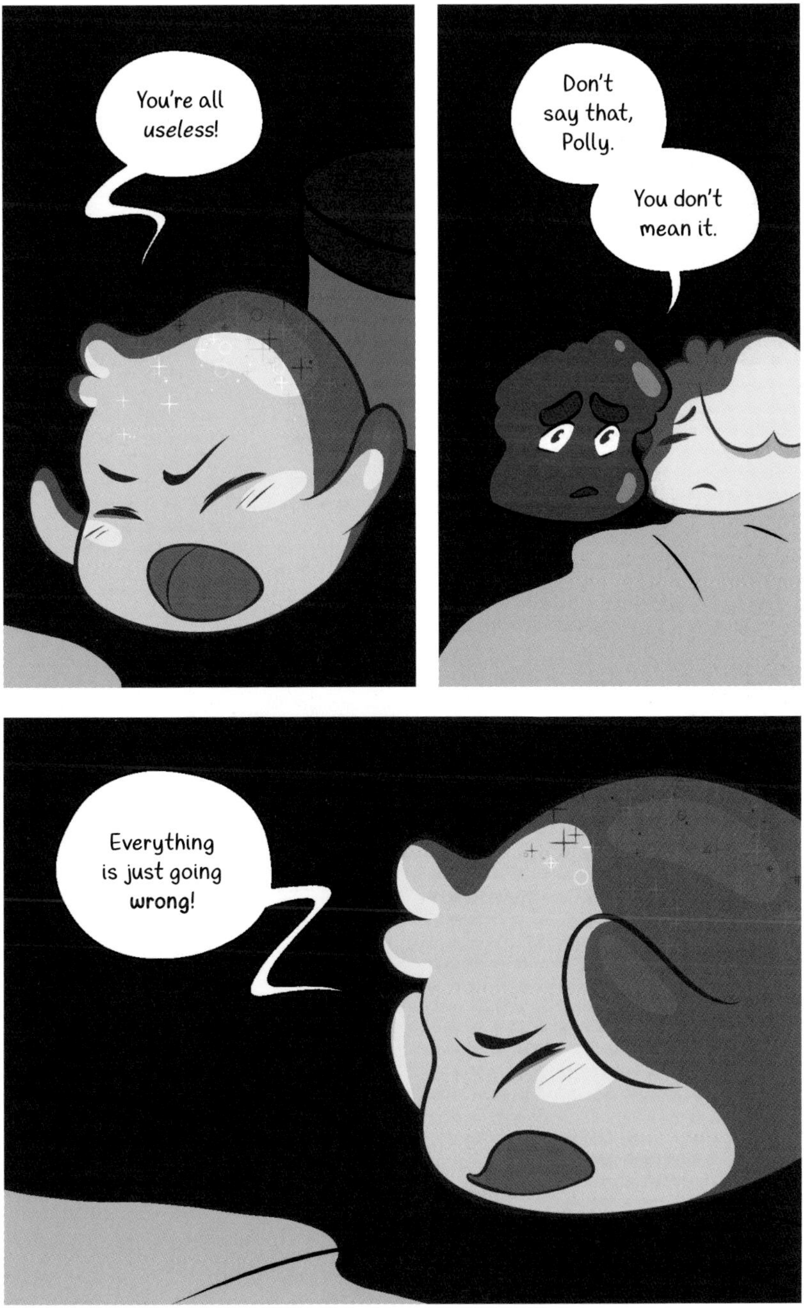
You're all *useless*!
Don't say that, Polly.
You don't mean it.
Everything is just going wrong!

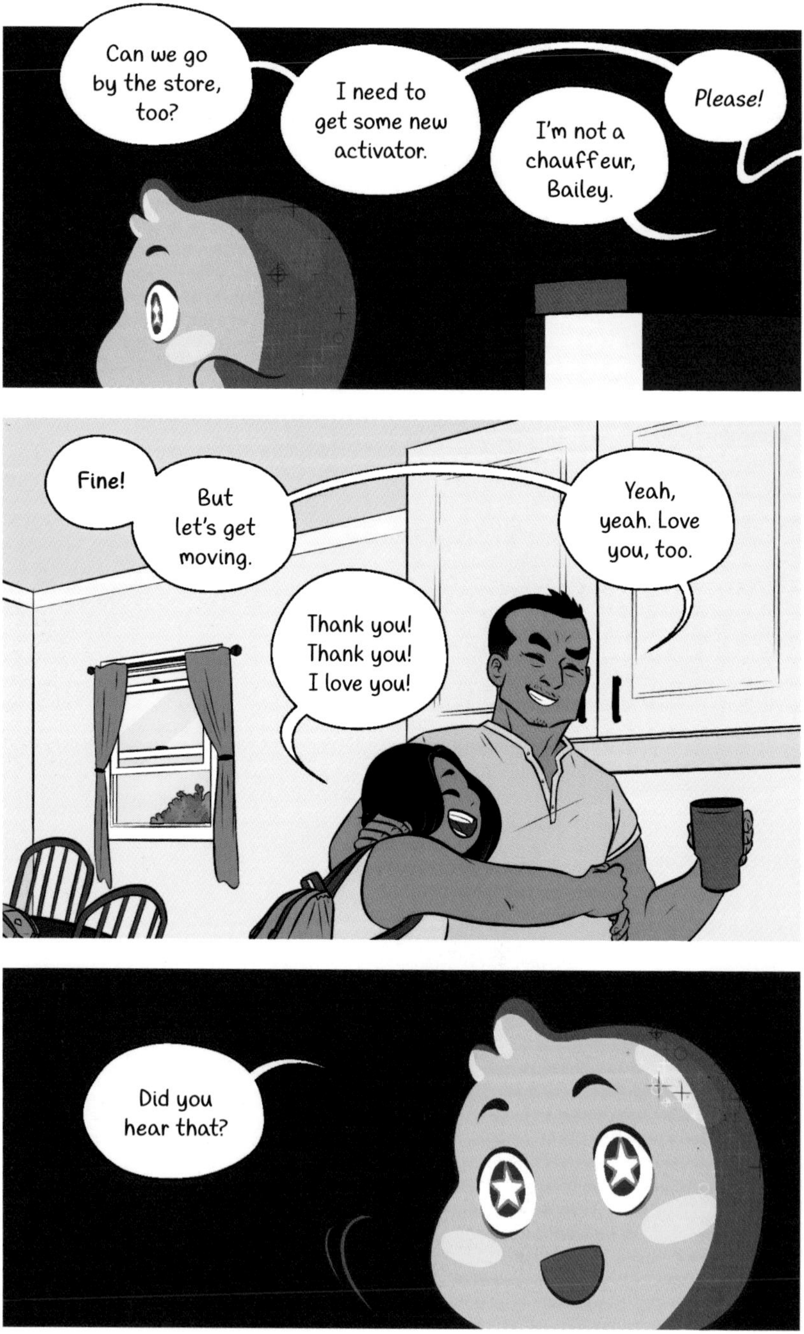
Can we go by the store, too?
I need to get some new activator.
I'm not a chauffeur, Bailey.
Please!
Fine!
But let's get moving.
Yeah, yeah. Love you, too.
Thank you! Thank you! I love you!
Did you hear that?

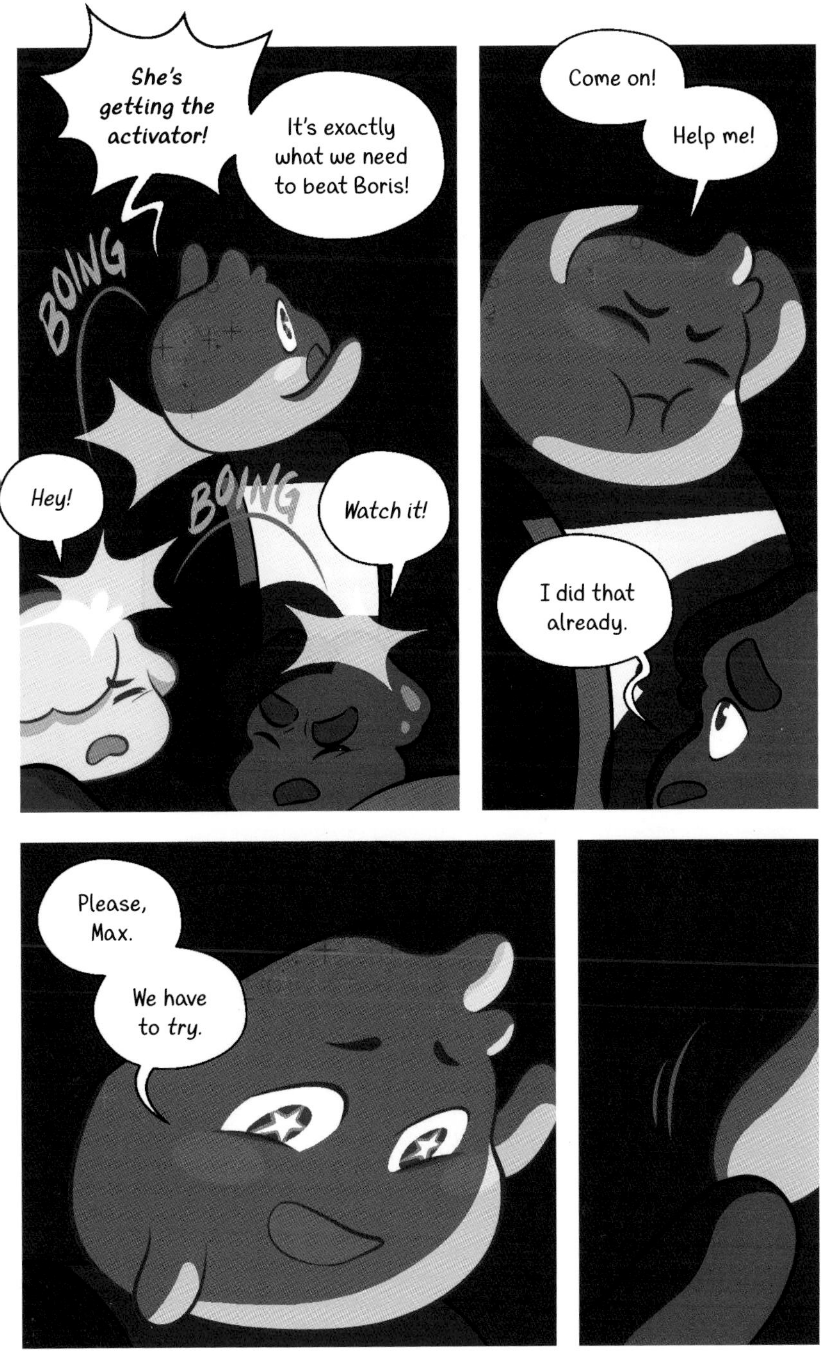
She's getting the activator!
It's exactly what we need to beat Boris!
BOING
Hey!
BOING
Watch it!
Come on!
Help me!
I did that already.
Please, Max.
We have to try.

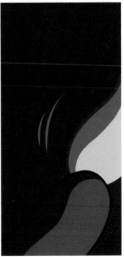

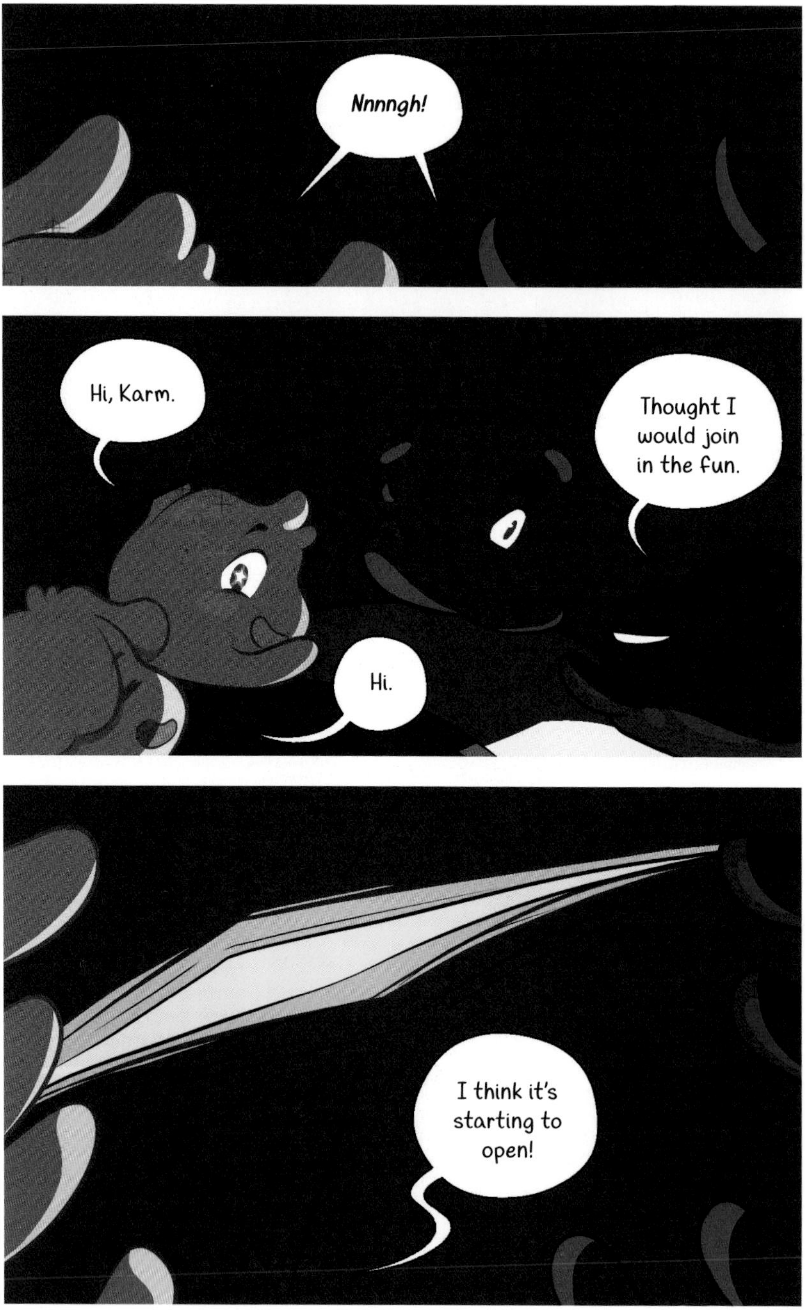
Nnnngh!
Hi, Karm.
Thought I would join in the fun.
Hi.
I think it's starting to open!

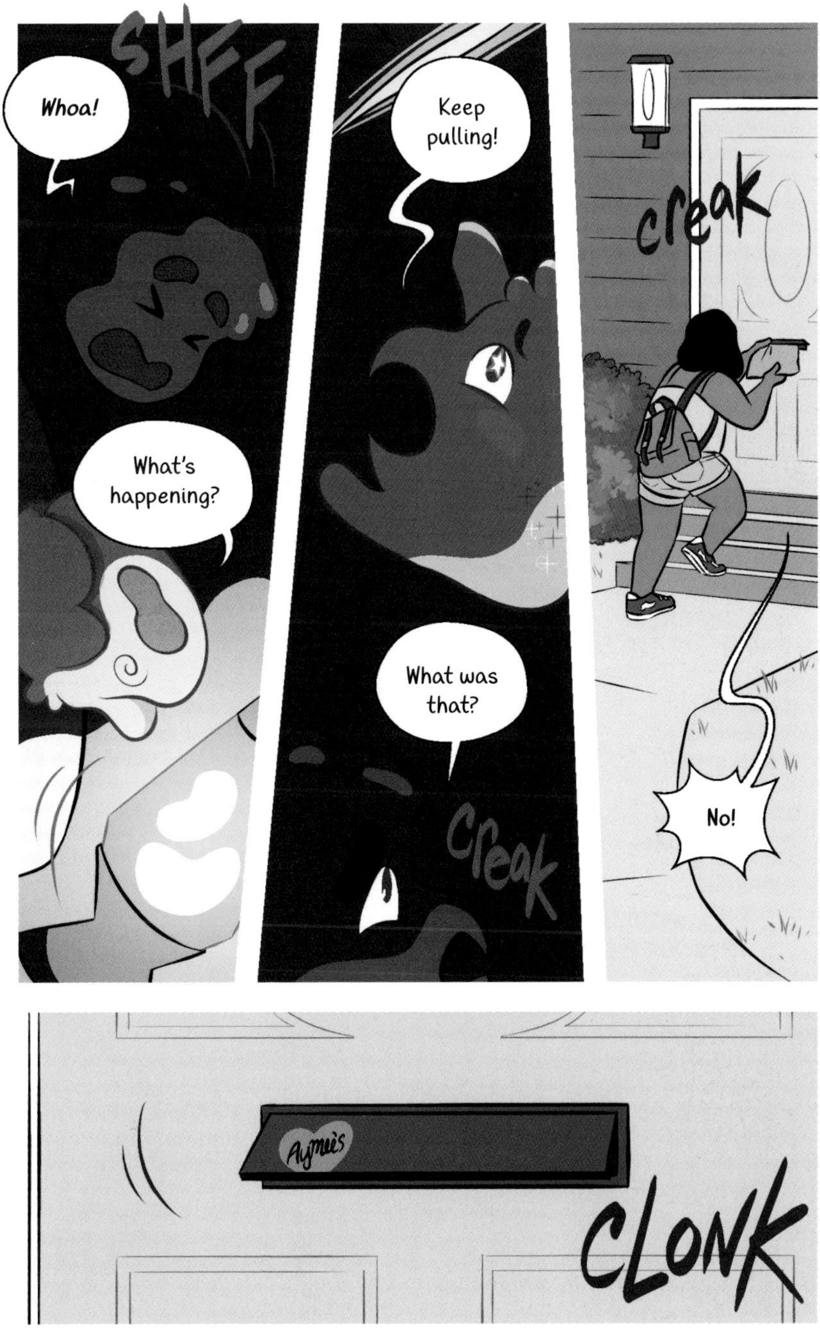
SHFF
Whoa!
What's happening?
Keep pulling!
What was that?
creak
creak
No!
Aymee's
CLONK

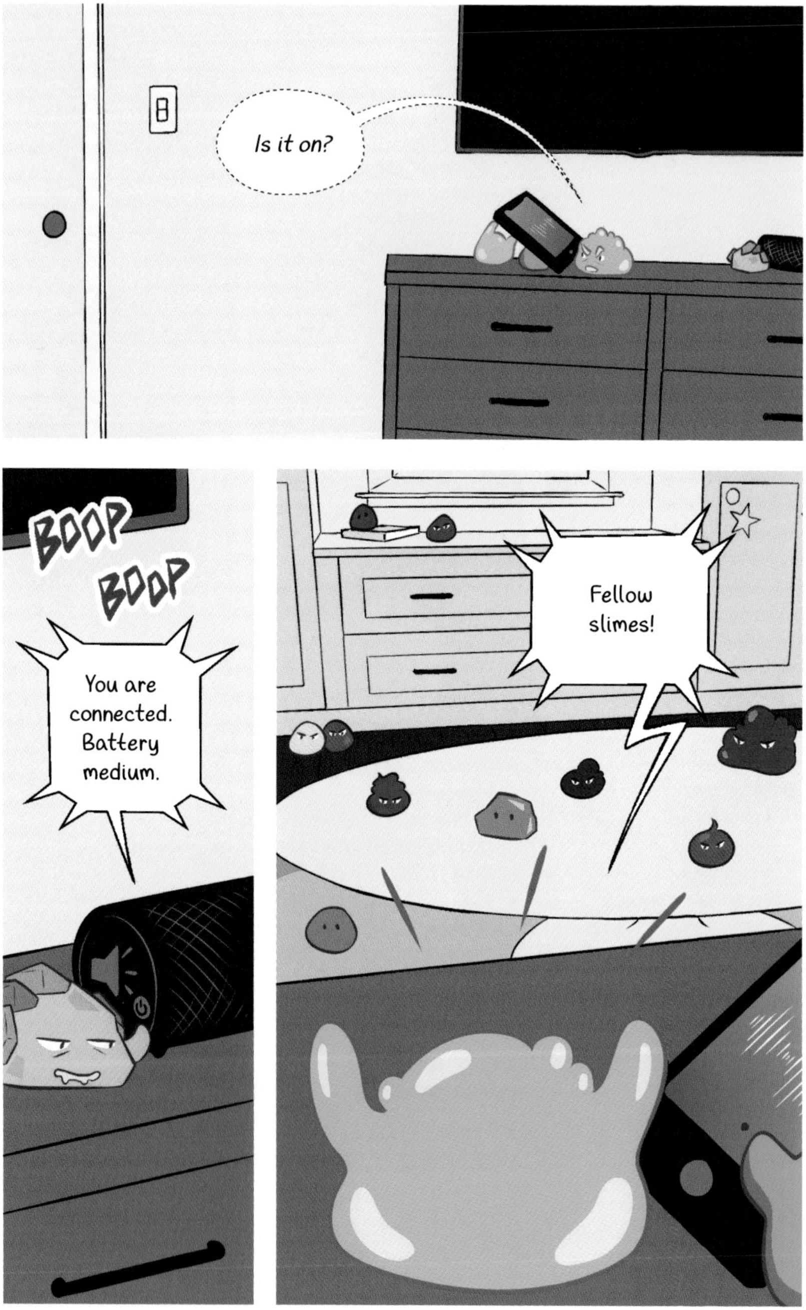
Is it on?
BOOP
BOOP
You are connected. Battery medium.
Fellow slimes!

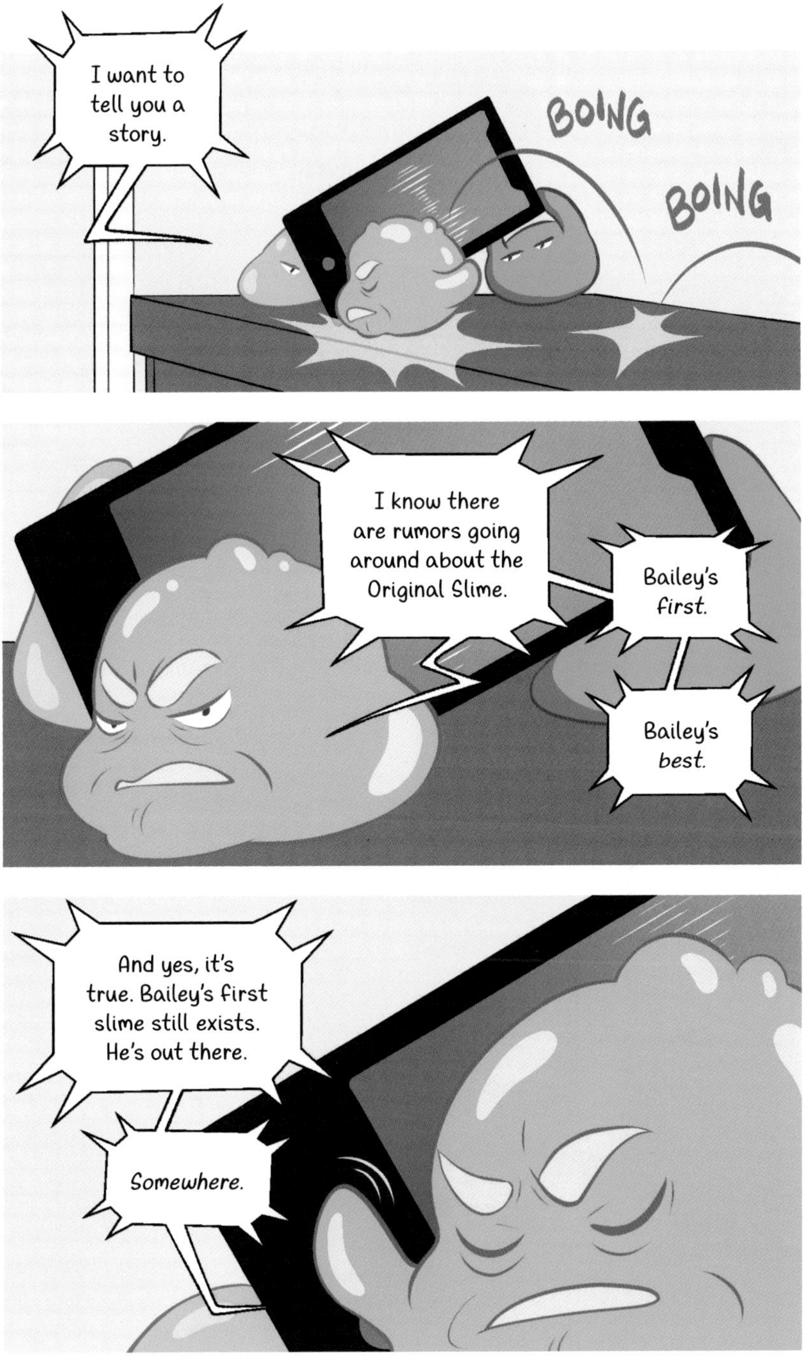
I want to tell you a story.
BOING
BOING
I know there are rumors going around about the Original Slime.
Bailey's *first.*
Bailey's *best.*
And yes, it's true. Bailey's first slime still exists. He's out there.
Somewhere.

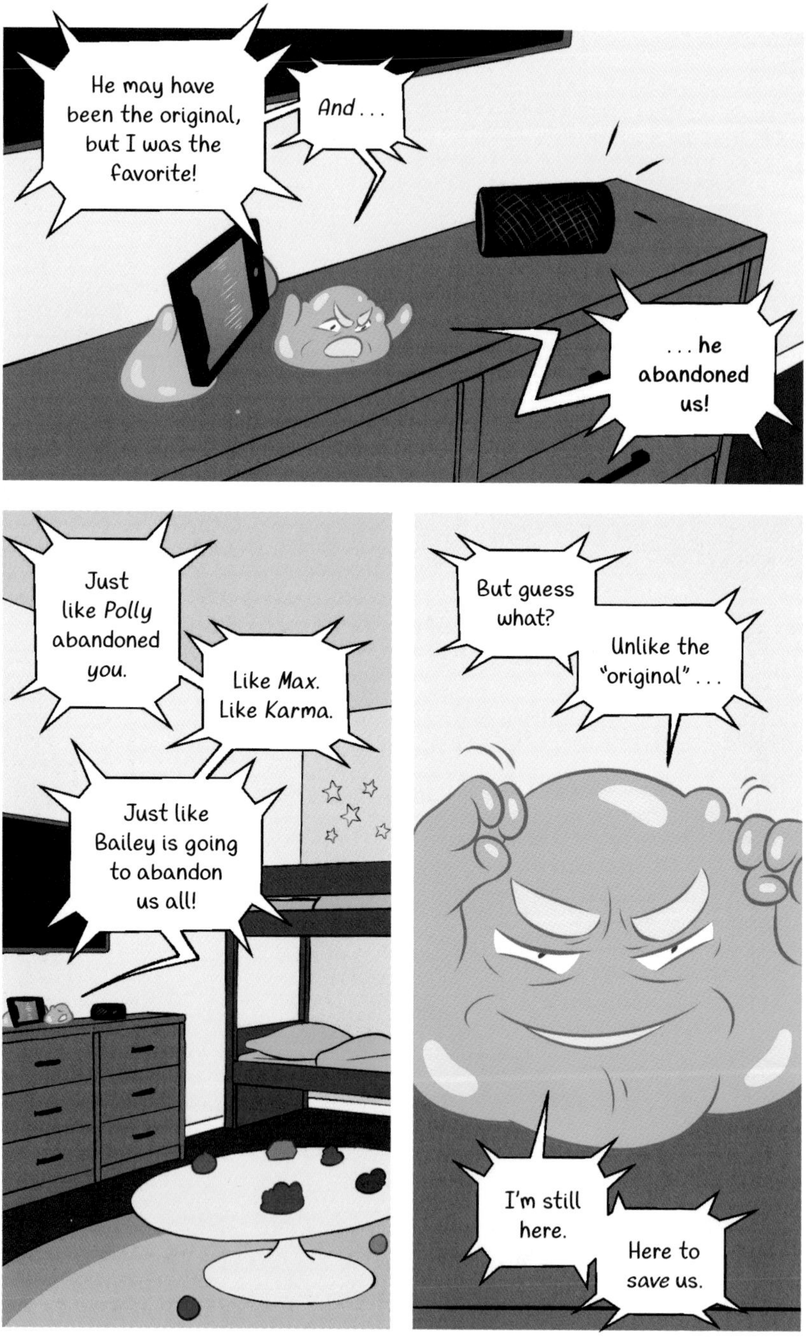
He may have been the original, but I was the favorite!
And . . .
. . . he abandoned us!
Just like *Polly* abandoned you.
Like *Max.* Like *Karma.*
Just like Bailey is going to abandon us all!
But guess what?
Unlike the "original" . . .
I'm still here.
Here to save us.

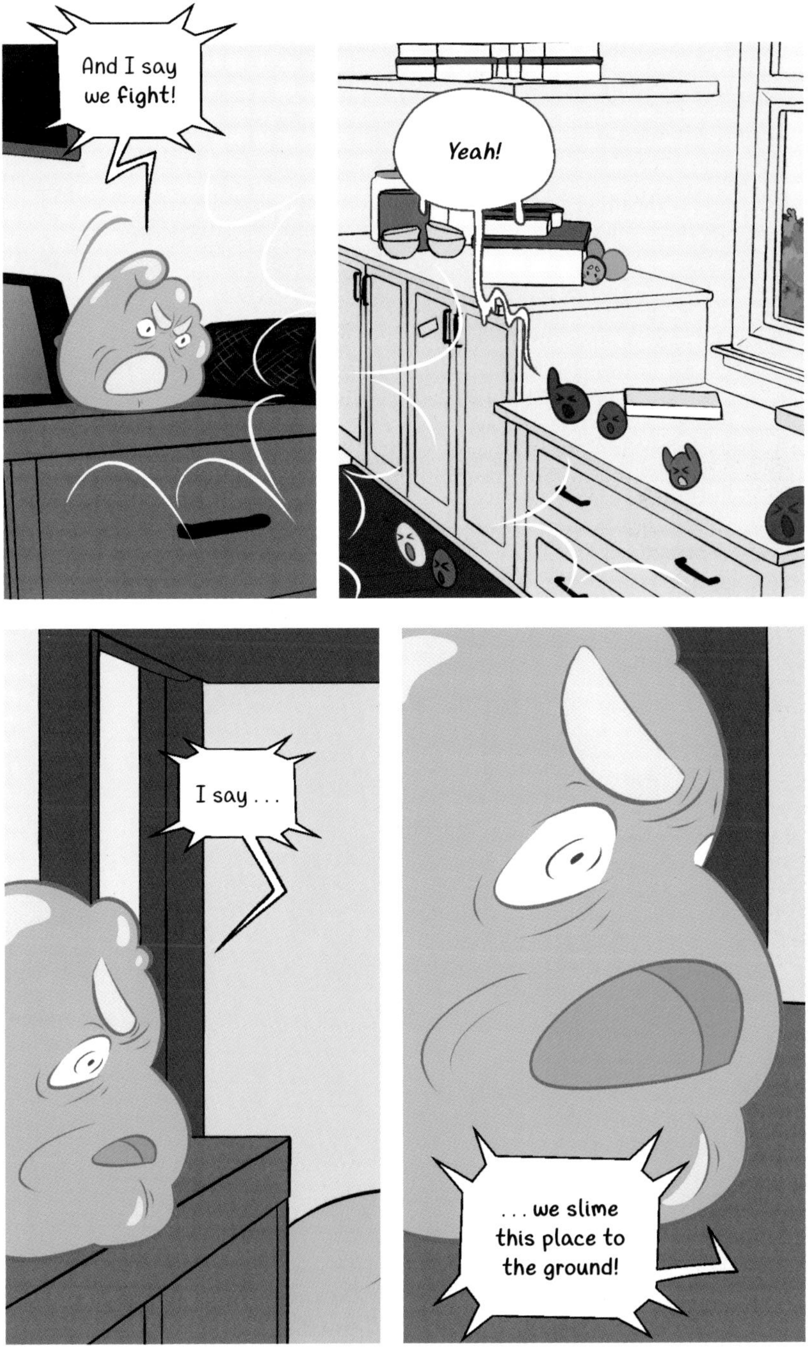
And I say we fight!
Yeah!
I say . . .
. . . we slime this place to the ground!

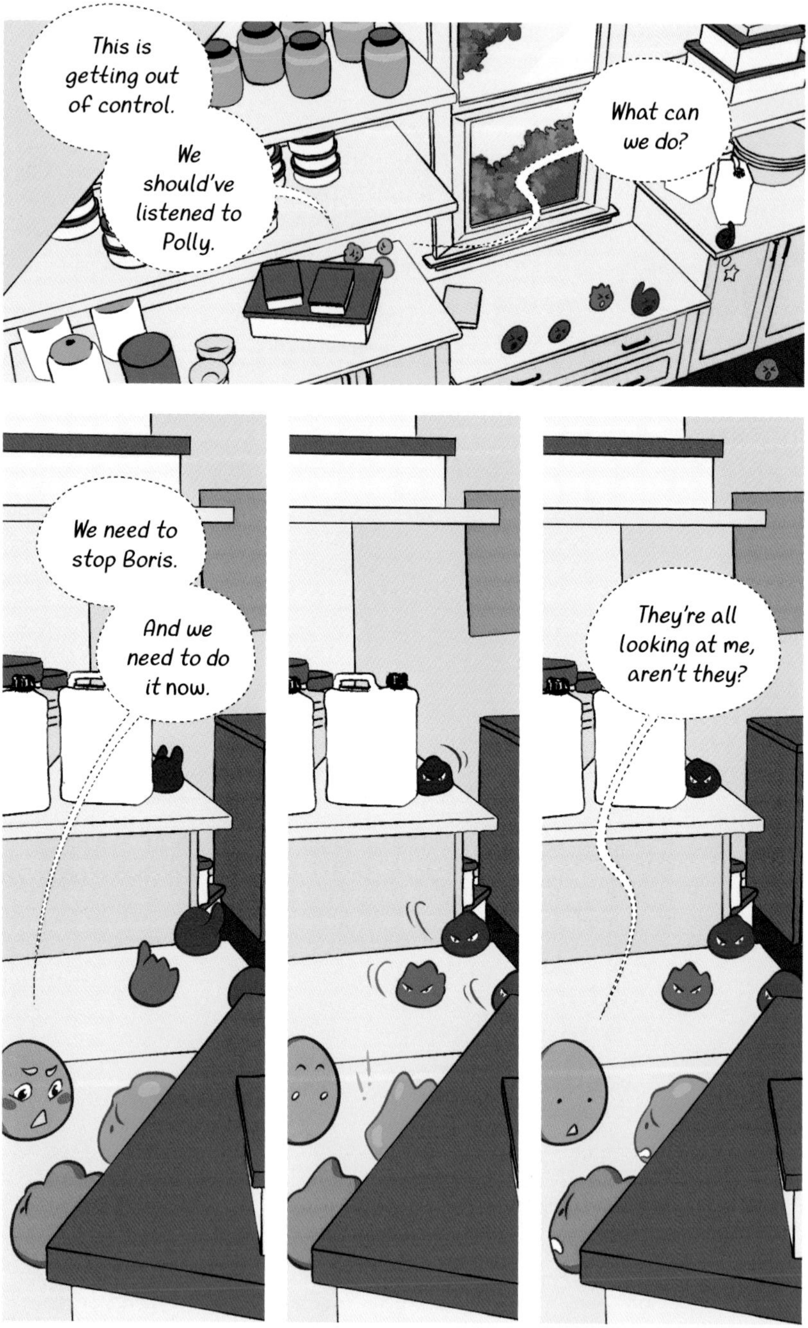
This is getting out of control.
We should've listened to Polly.
What can we do?
We need to stop Boris.
And we need to do it now.
They're all looking at me, aren't they?

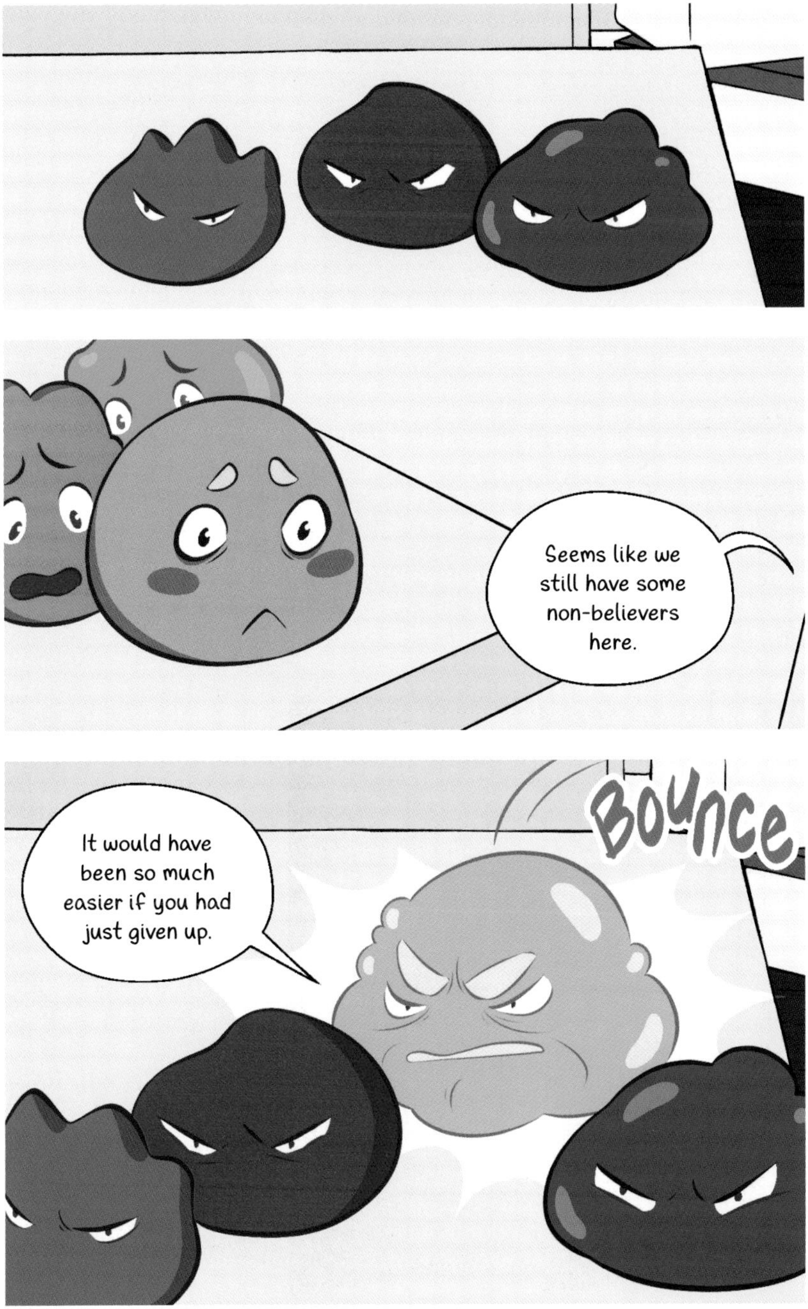
Seems like we still have some non-believers here.
It would have been so much easier if you had just given up.
BOUNCE

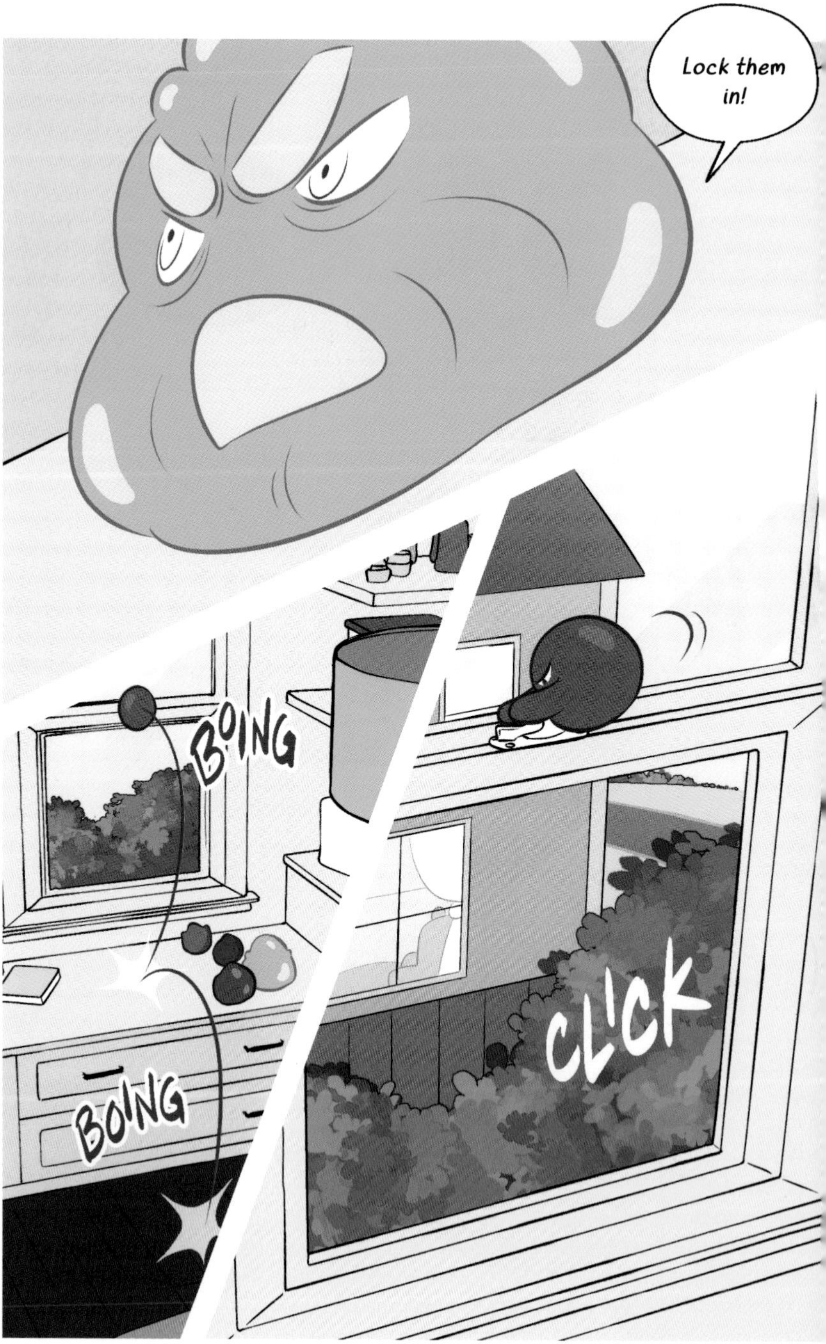
Lock them in!
BOING
BOING
CLICK

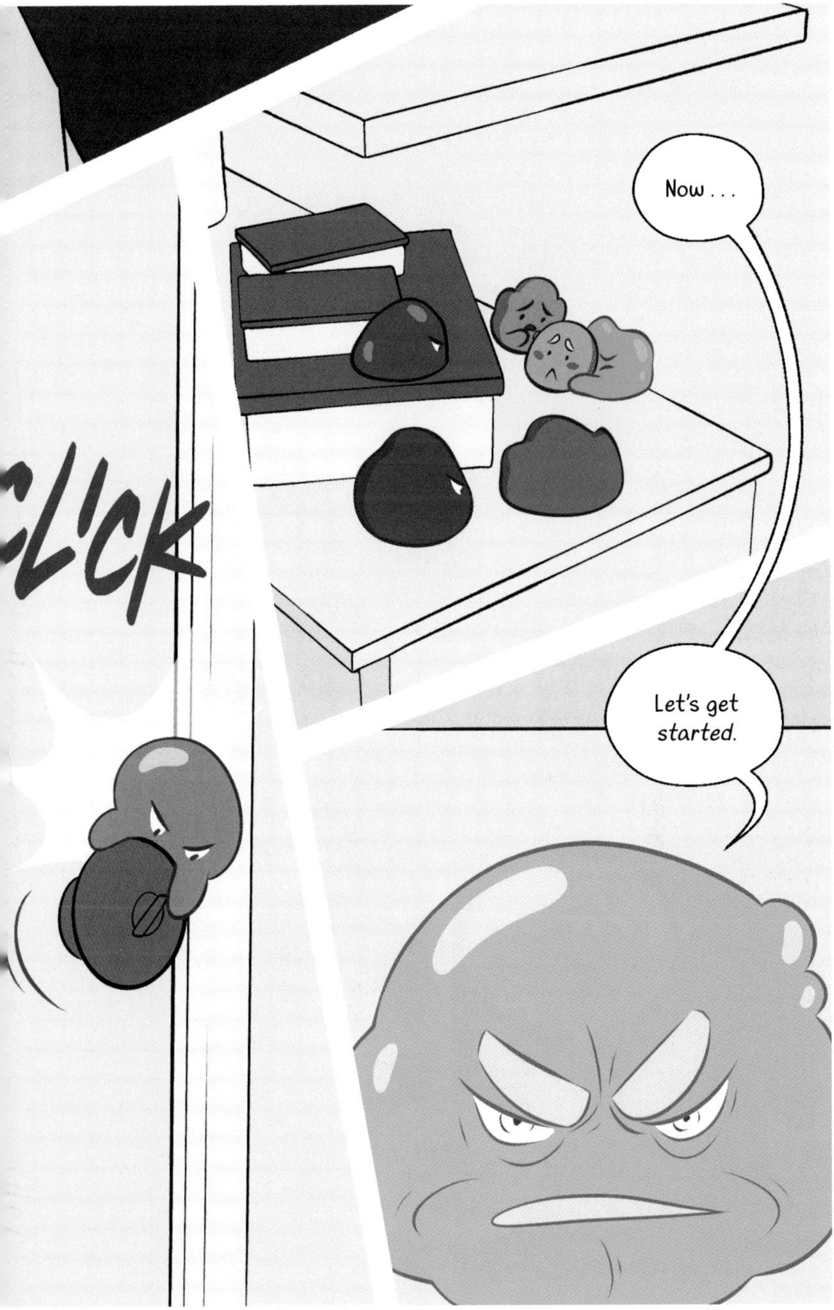
CLICK
Now . . .
Let's get started.

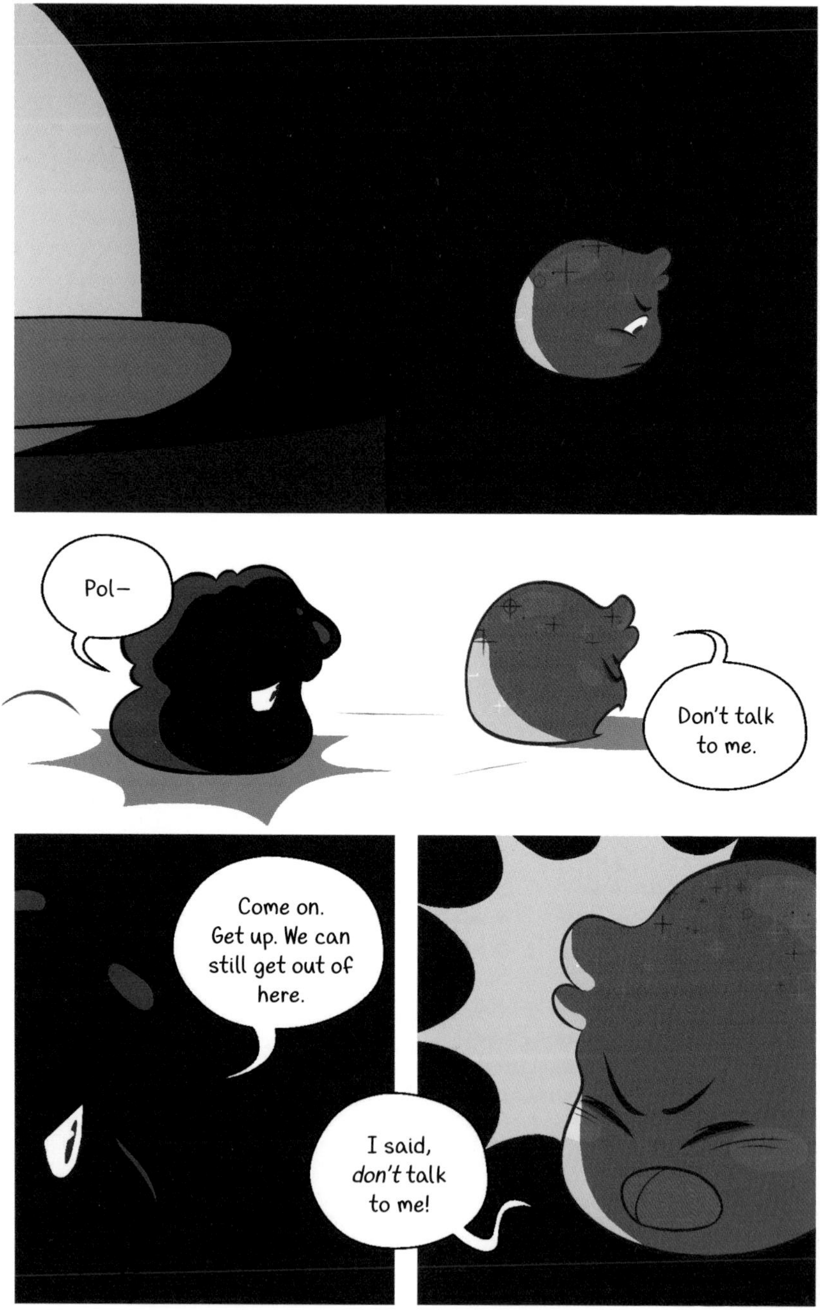
Pol–
Don't talk to me.
Come on. Get up. We can still get out of here.
I said, *don't* talk to me!

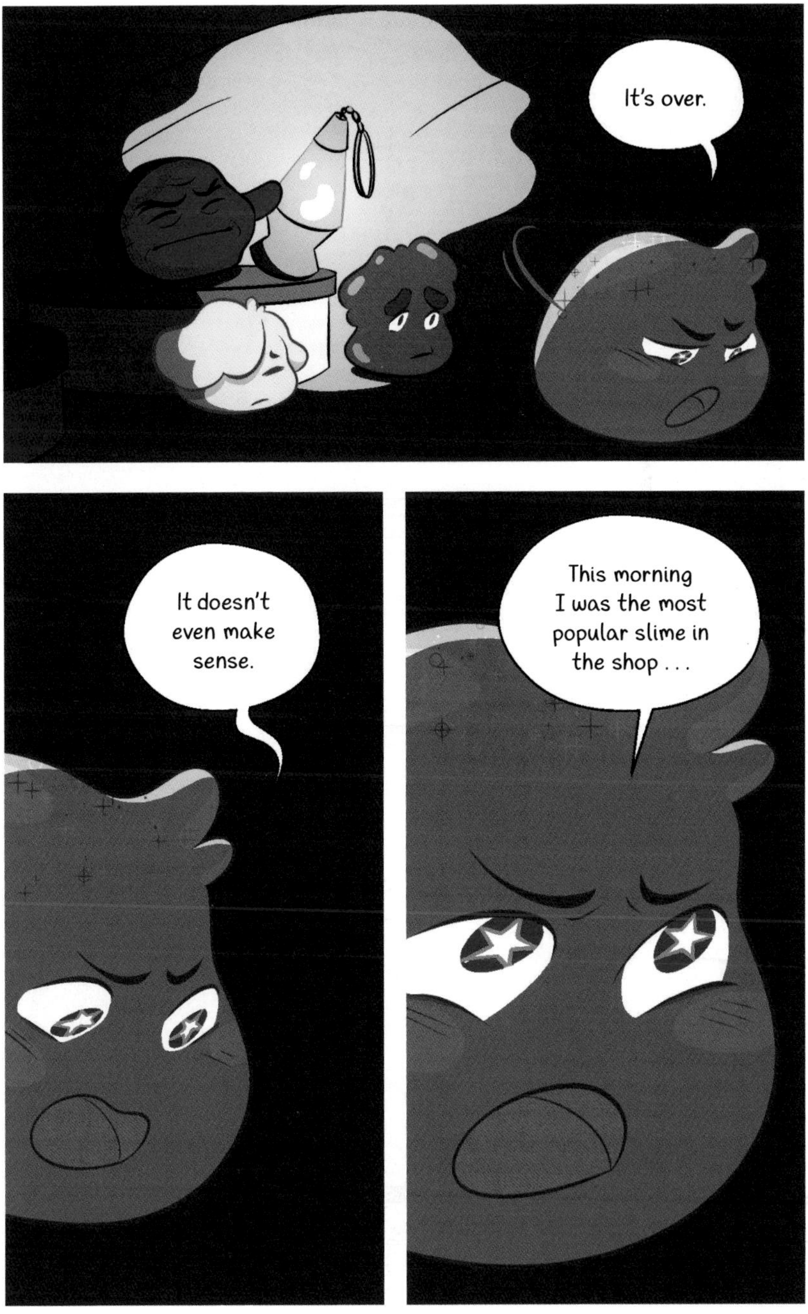
It's over.
It doesn't even make sense.
This morning I was the most popular slime in the shop . . .

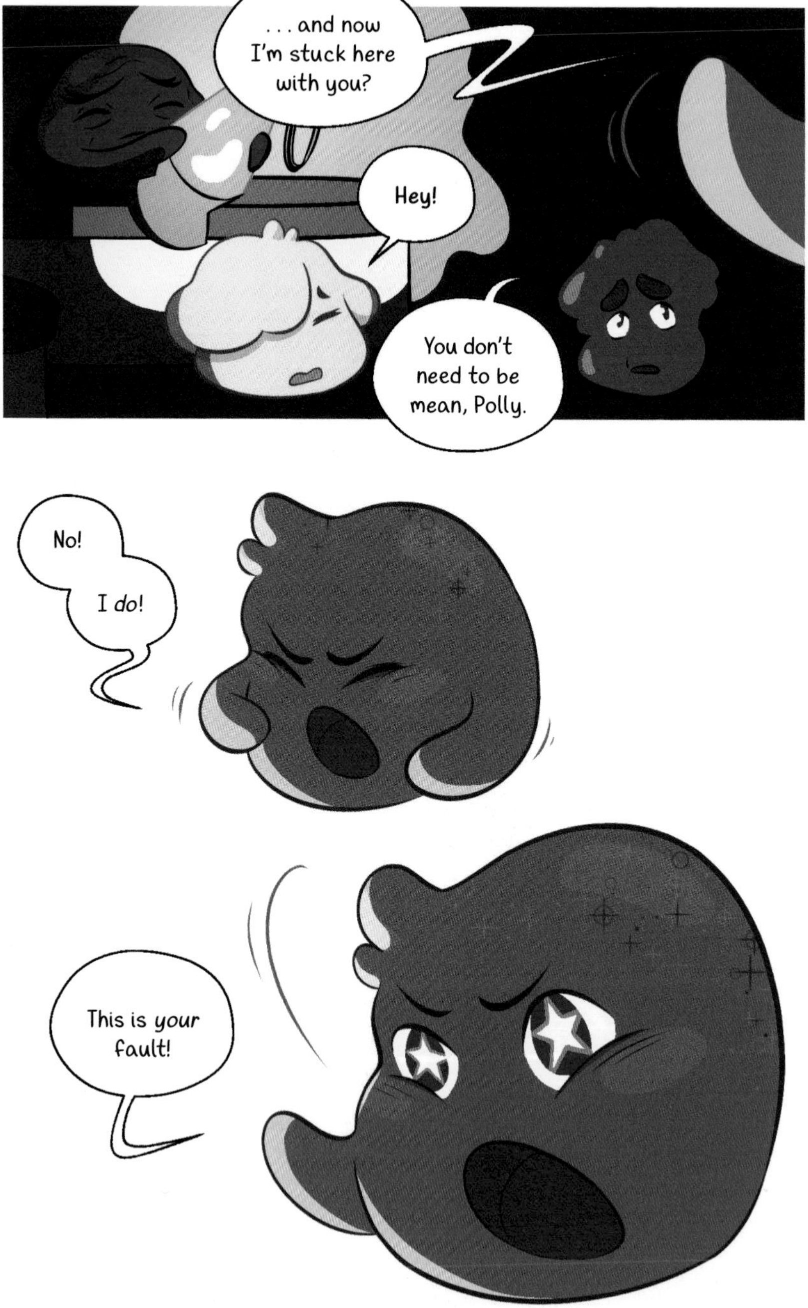
. . . and now I'm stuck here with you?
Hey!
You don't need to be mean, Polly.
No!
I *do*!
This is *your* fault!

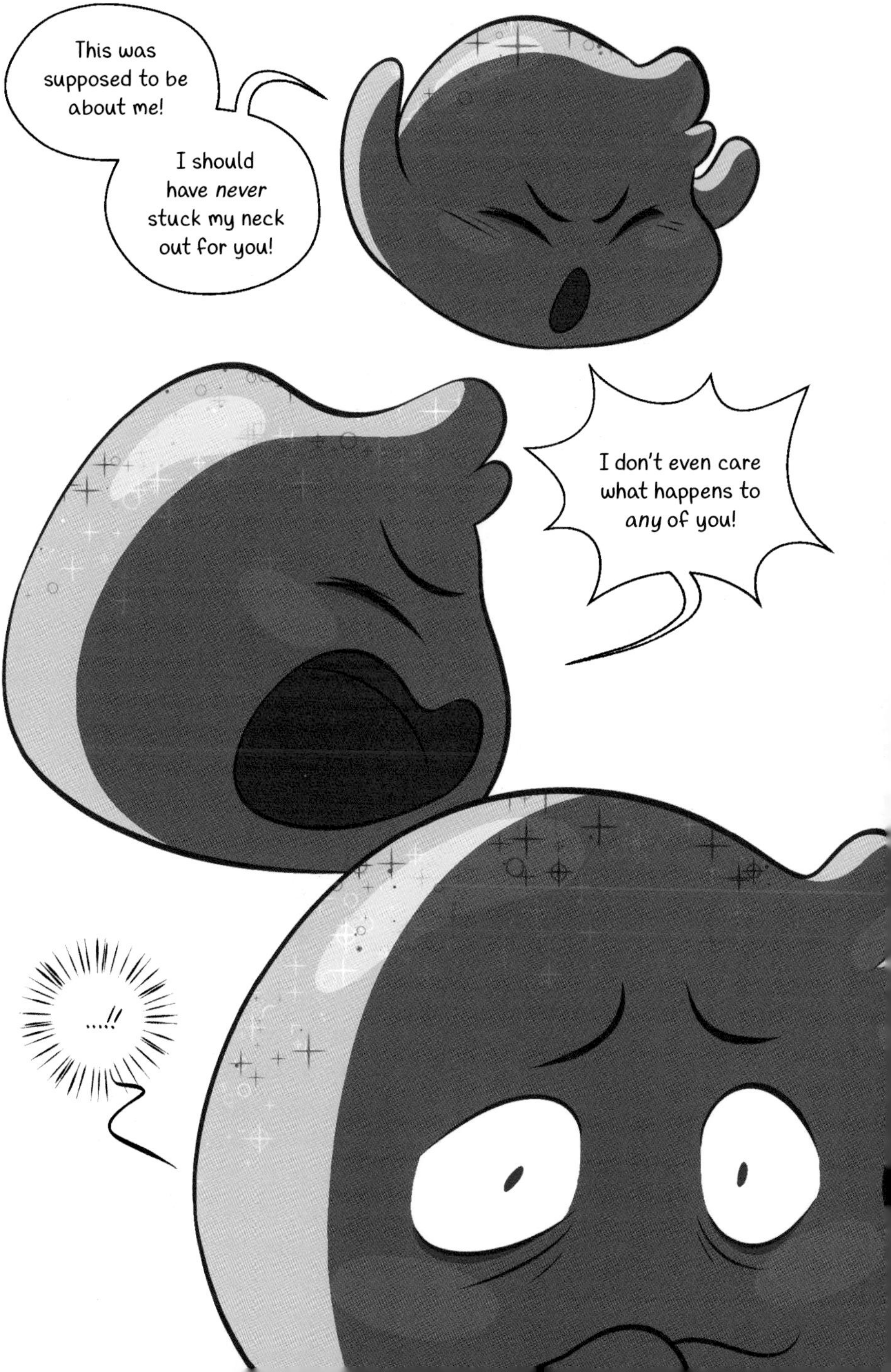
This was supposed to be about me!
I should have *never* stuck my neck out for you!
I don't even care what happens to *any* of you!
....!!

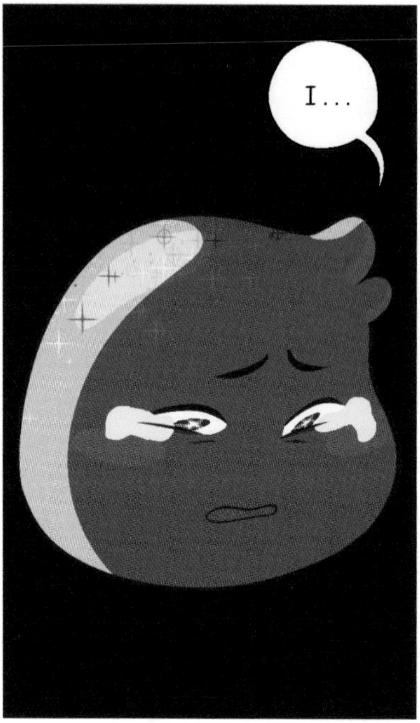
I...

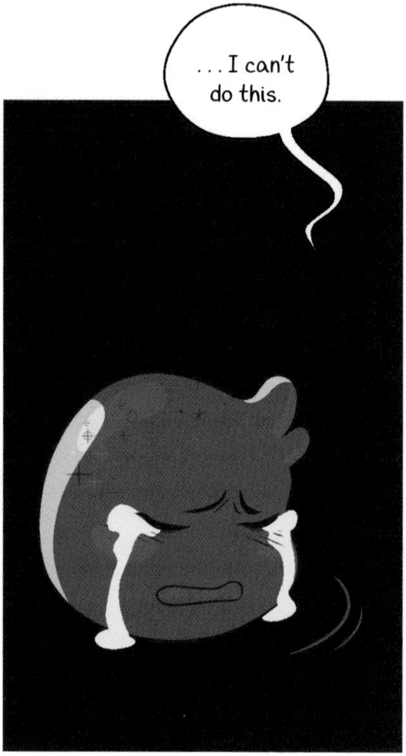
...I can't do this.

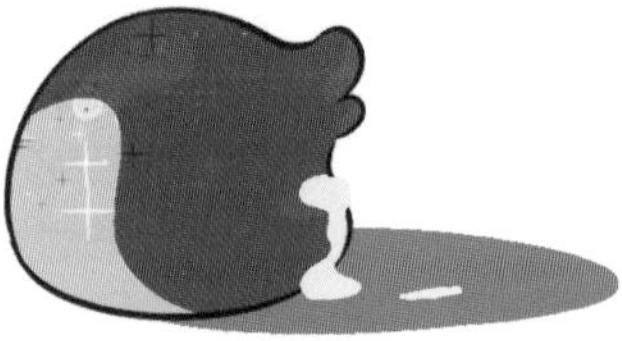

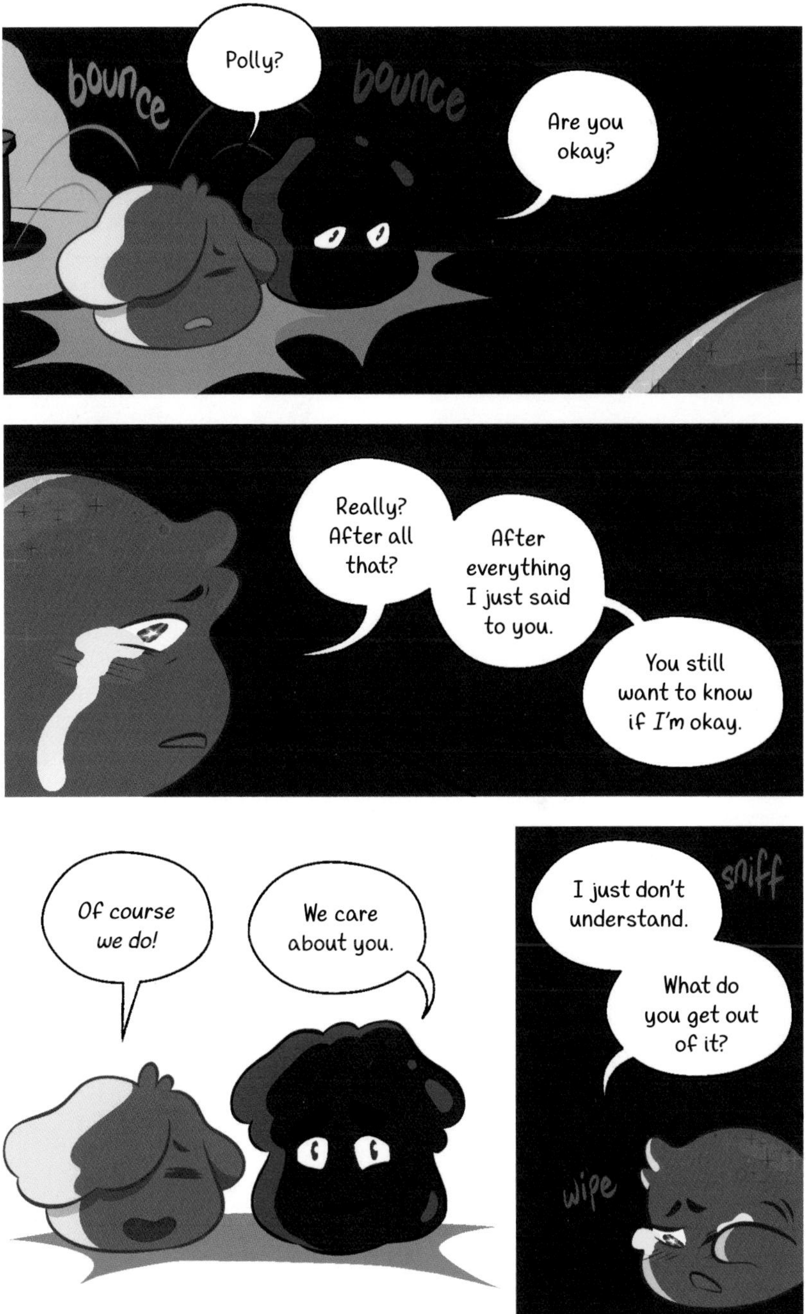
bounce
Polly?
bounce
Are you okay?
Really? After all that?
After everything I just said to you.
You still want to know if *I'm* okay.
Of course we do!
We care about you.
I just don't understand.
sniff
What do you get out of it?
wipe

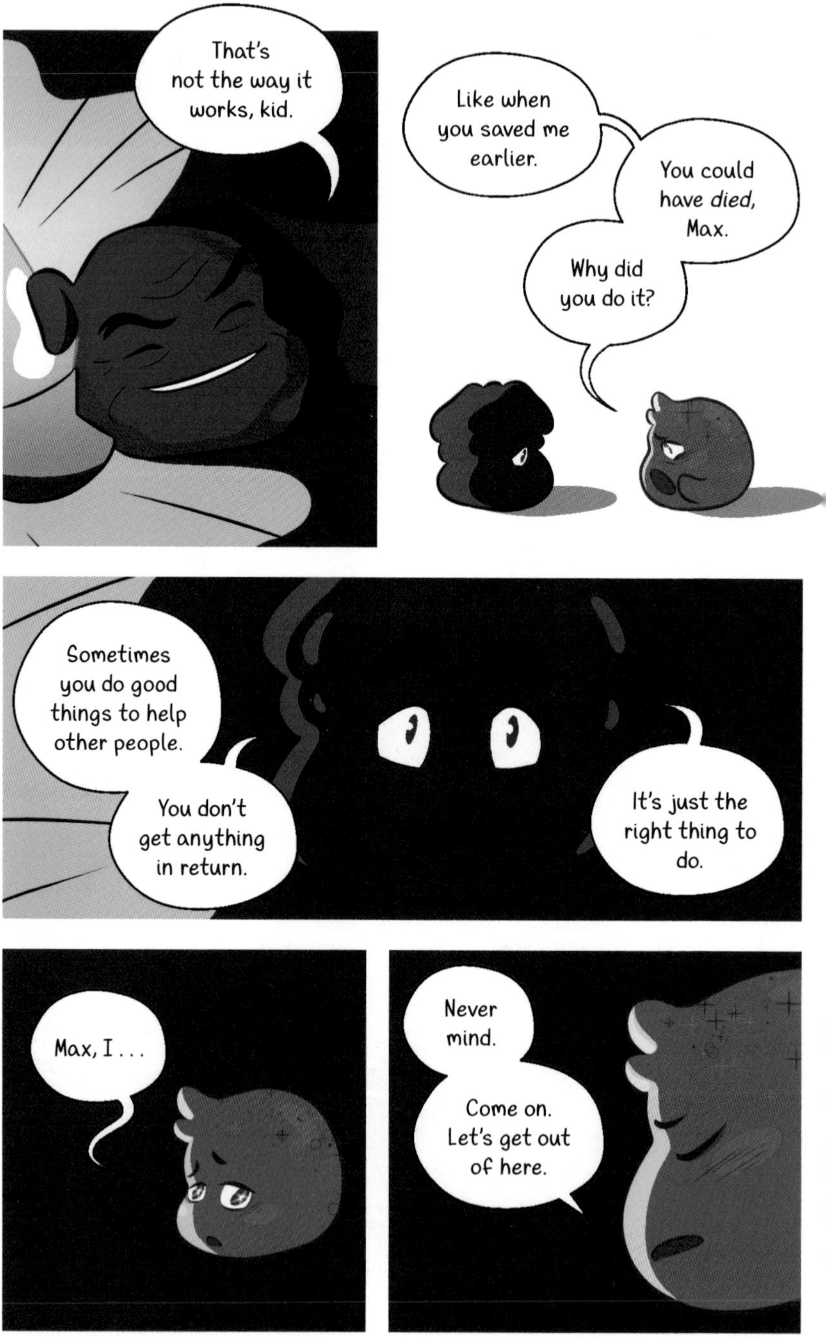
That's not the way it works, kid.
Like when you saved me earlier.
You could have *died*, Max.
Why did you do it?
Sometimes you do good things to help other people.
You don't get anything in return.
It's just the right thing to do.
Max, I . . .
Never mind.
Come on. Let's get out of here.

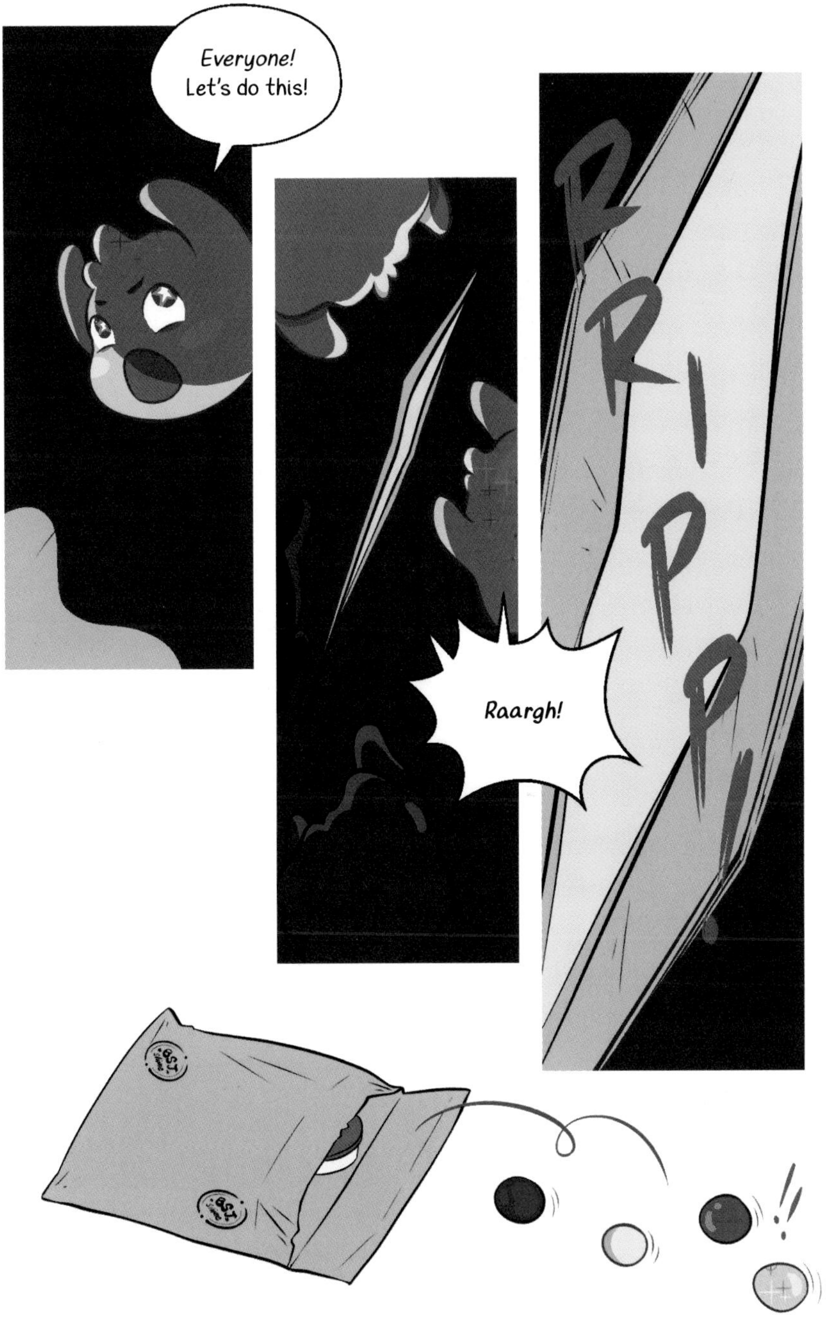
Everyone!
Let's do this!
RRIPPP!
Raargh!
!!

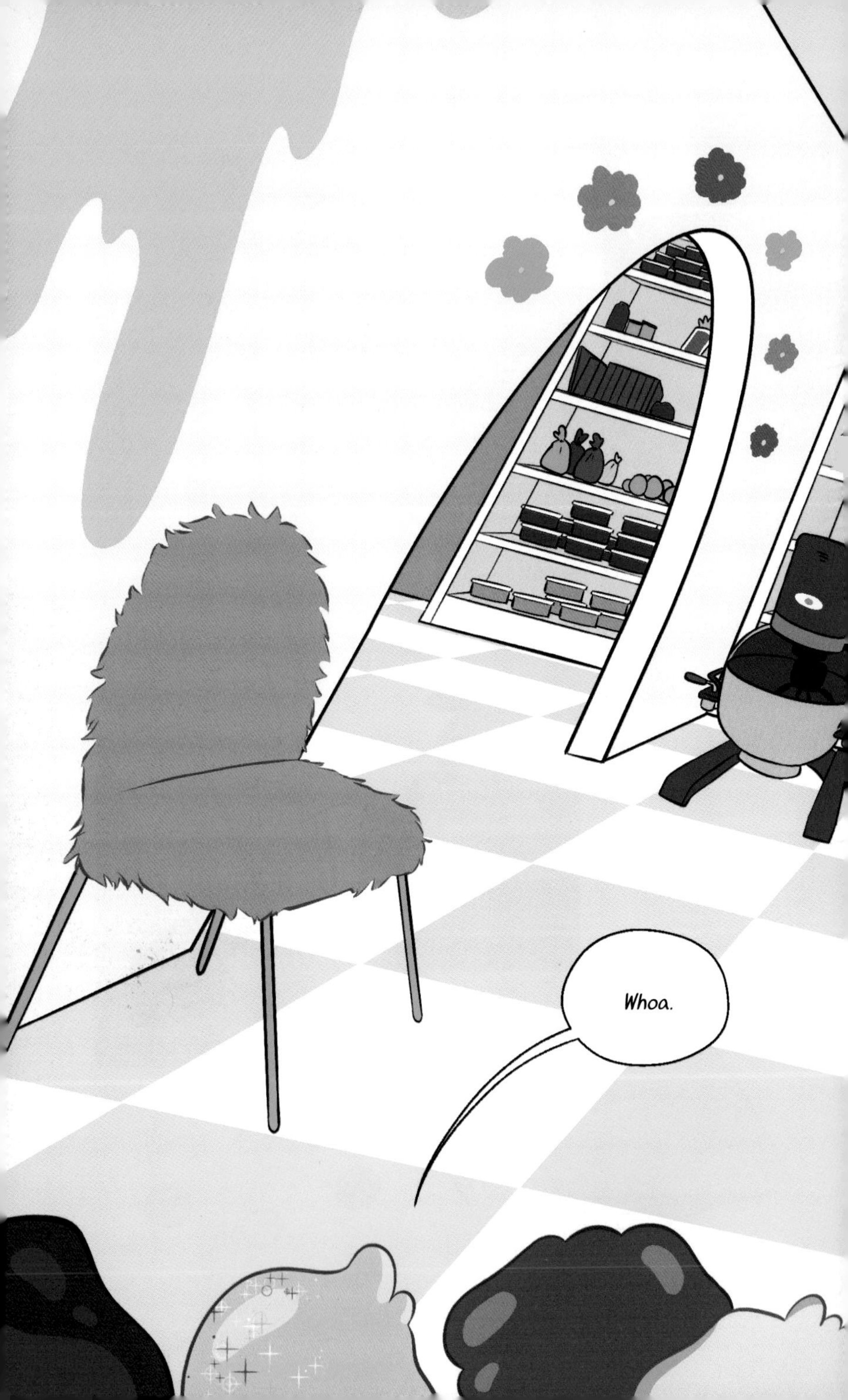
Whoa.

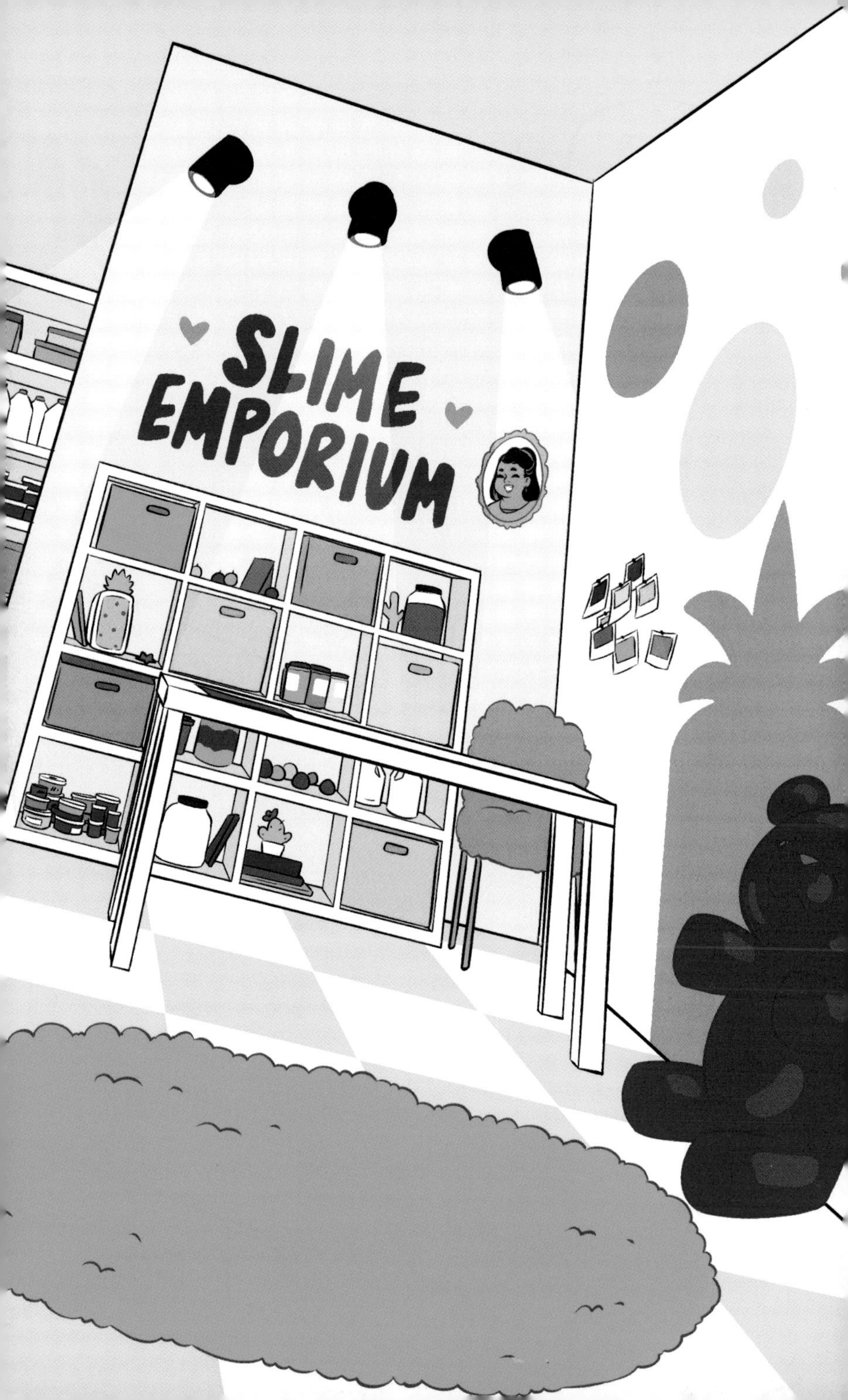
SLIME
EMPORIUM

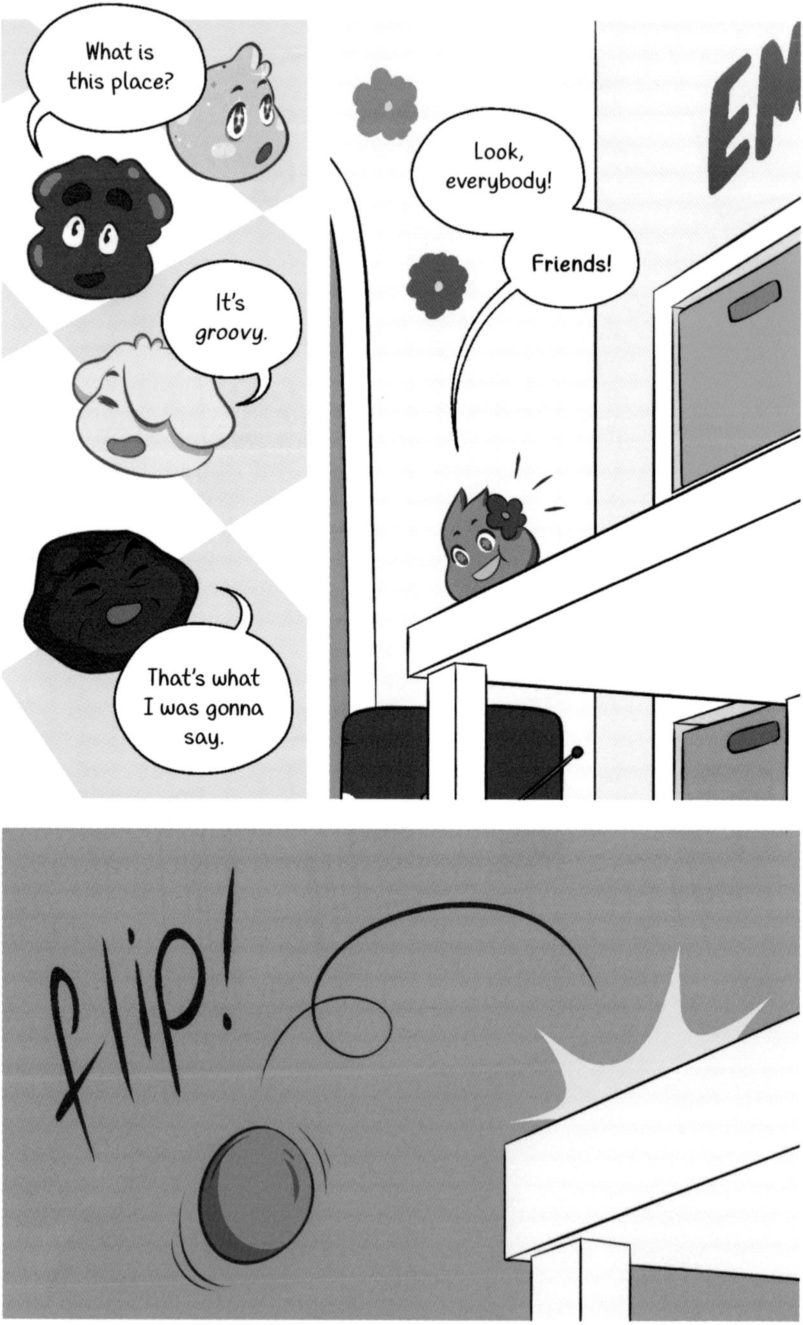
What is this place?
It's groovy.
That's what I was gonna say.
Look, everybody!
Friends!
flip!

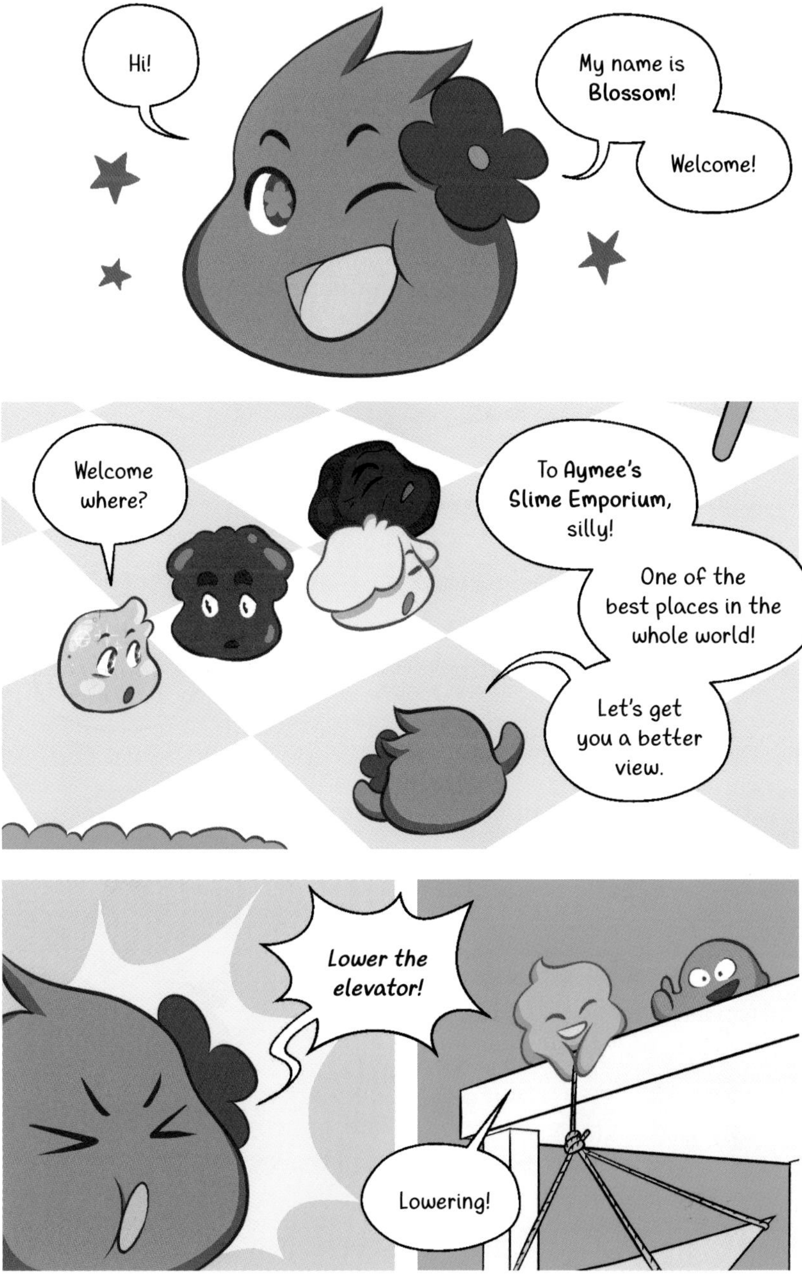
Hi!
My name is Blossom!
Welcome!
Welcome where?
To Aymee's Slime Emporium, silly!
One of the best places in the whole world!
Let's get you a better view.
Lower the elevator!
Lowering!

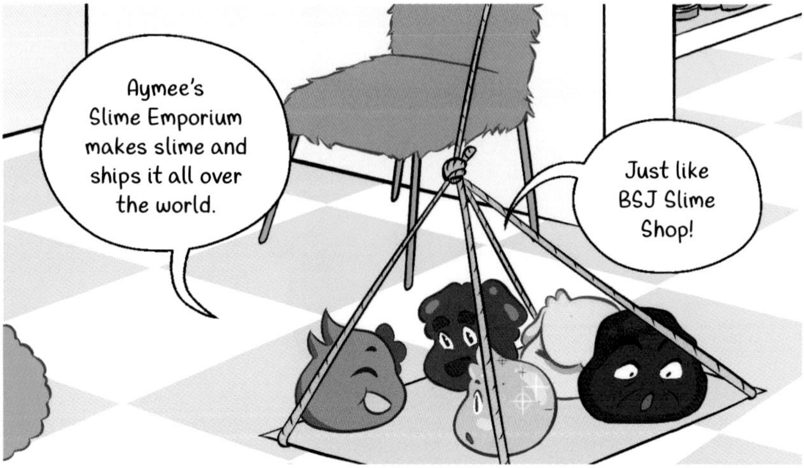
Aymee's Slime Emporium makes slime and ships it all over the world.
Just like BSJ Slime Shop!

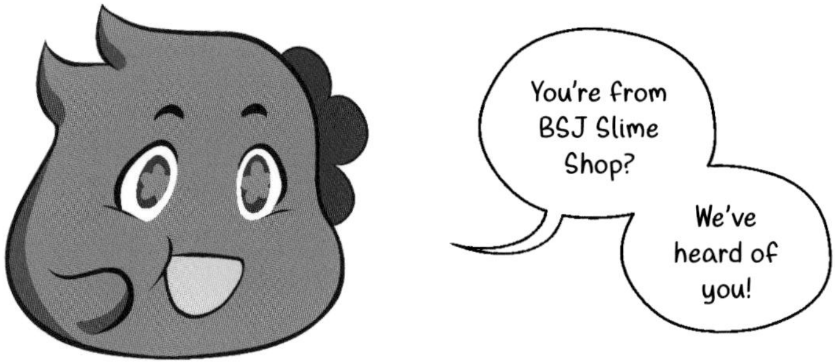
You're from BSJ Slime Shop?
We've heard of you!

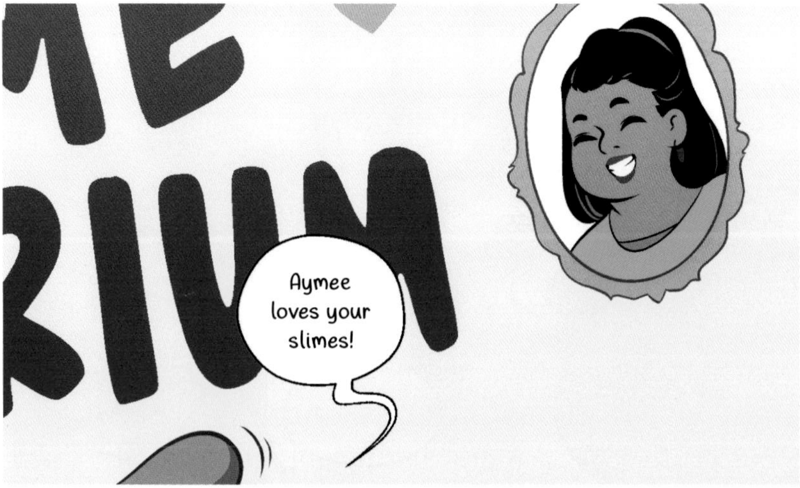
Aymee loves your slimes!

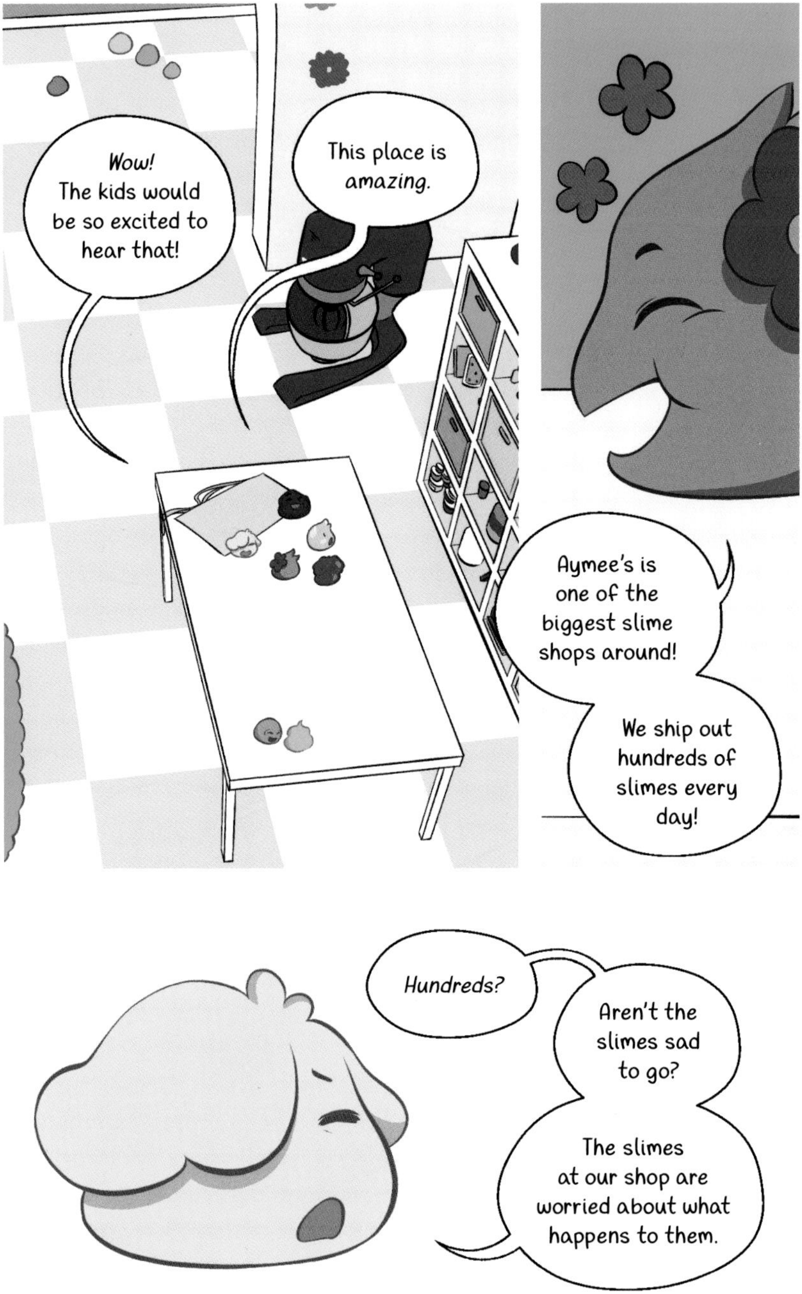
Wow!
The kids would be so excited to hear that!
This place is amazing.
Aymee's is one of the biggest slime shops around!
We ship out hundreds of slimes every day!
Hundreds?
Aren't the slimes sad to go?
The slimes at our shop are worried about what happens to them.

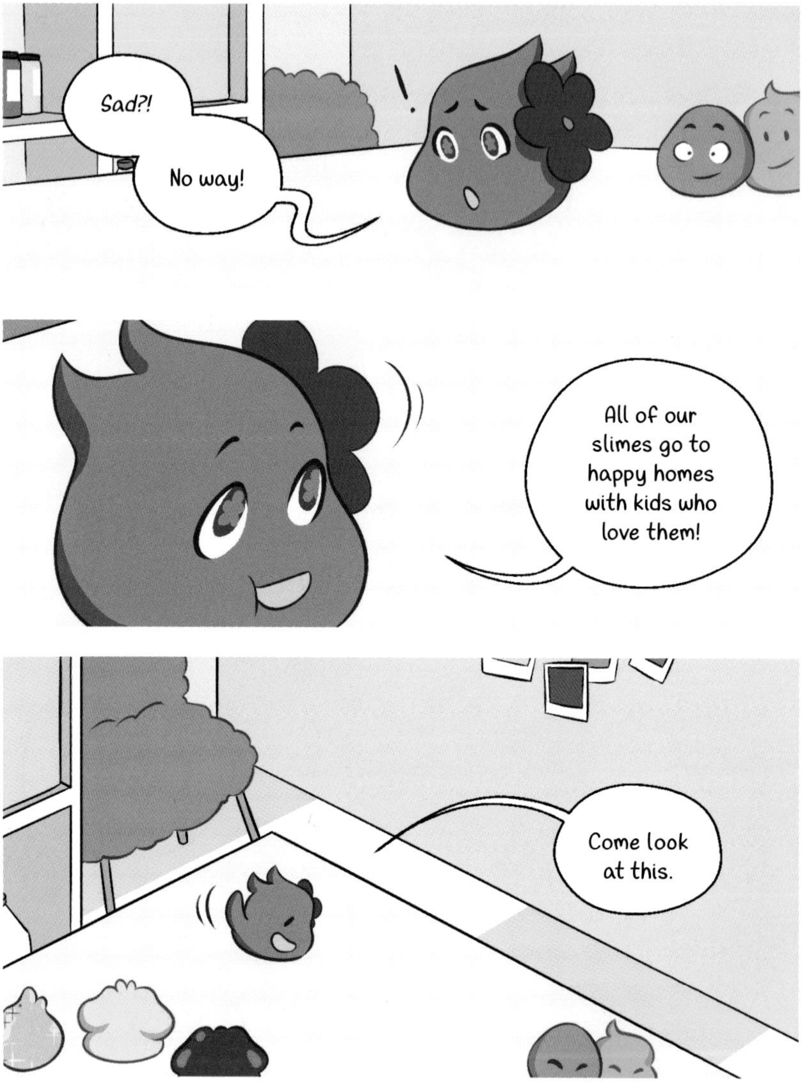
Sad?!
No way!
!
All of our slimes go to happy homes with kids who love them!
Come look at this.

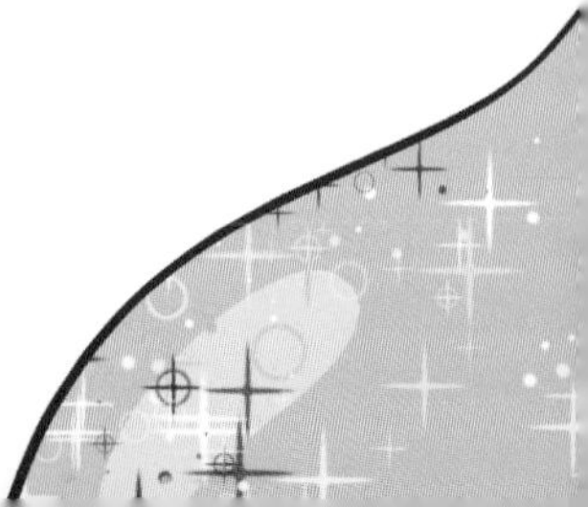

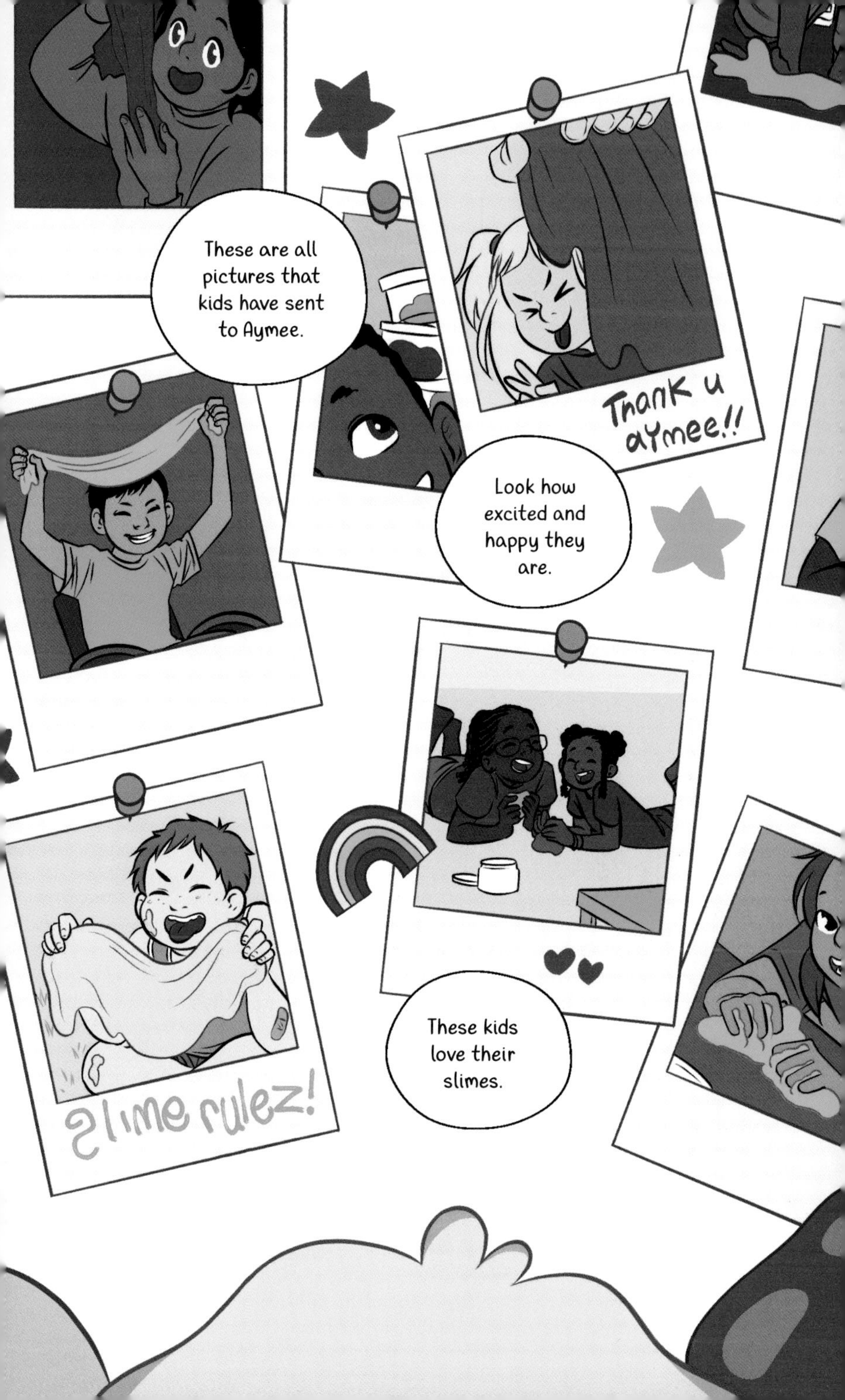
These are all pictures that kids have sent to Aymee.
Thank u aymee!!
Look how excited and happy they are.
slime rulez!
These kids love their slimes.

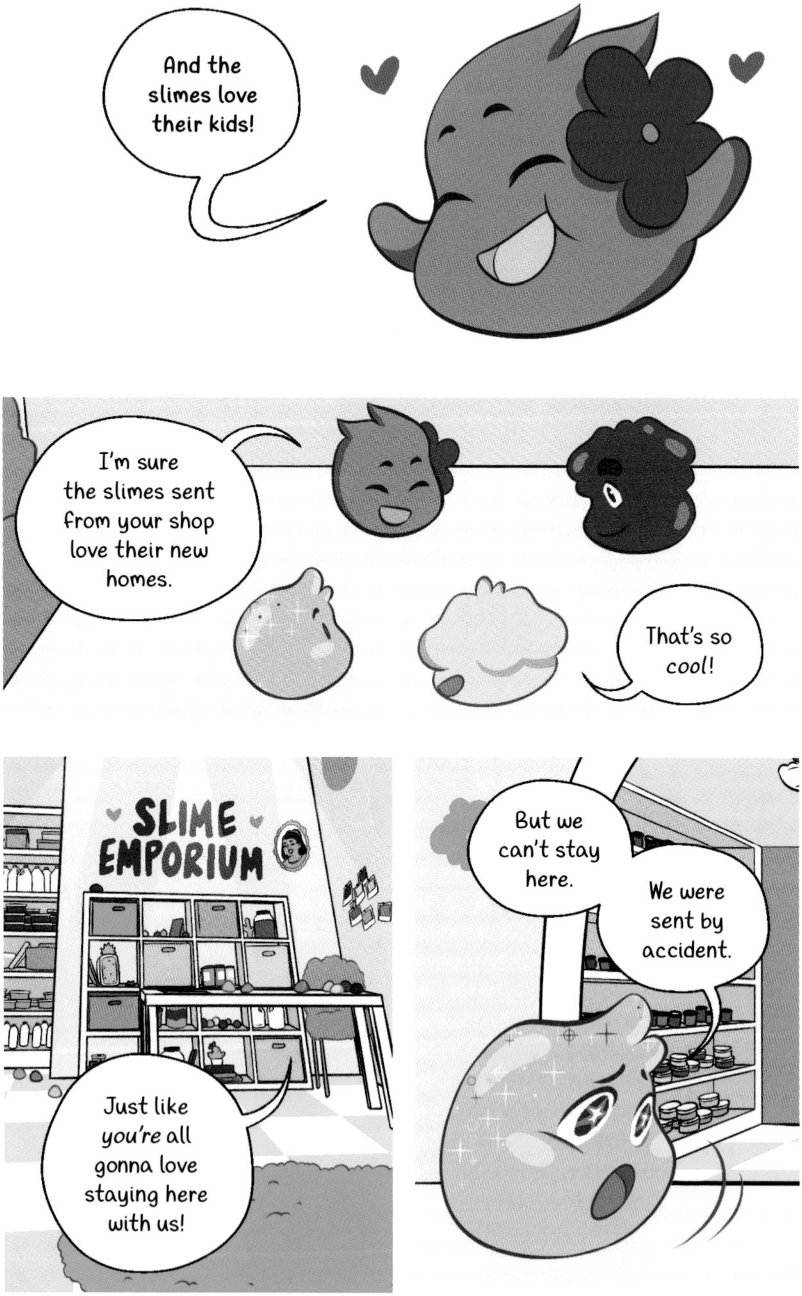

And the slimes love their kids!
I'm sure the slimes sent from your shop love their new homes.
That's so *cool*!
Just like *you're* all gonna love staying here with us!
But we can't stay here.
We were sent by accident.

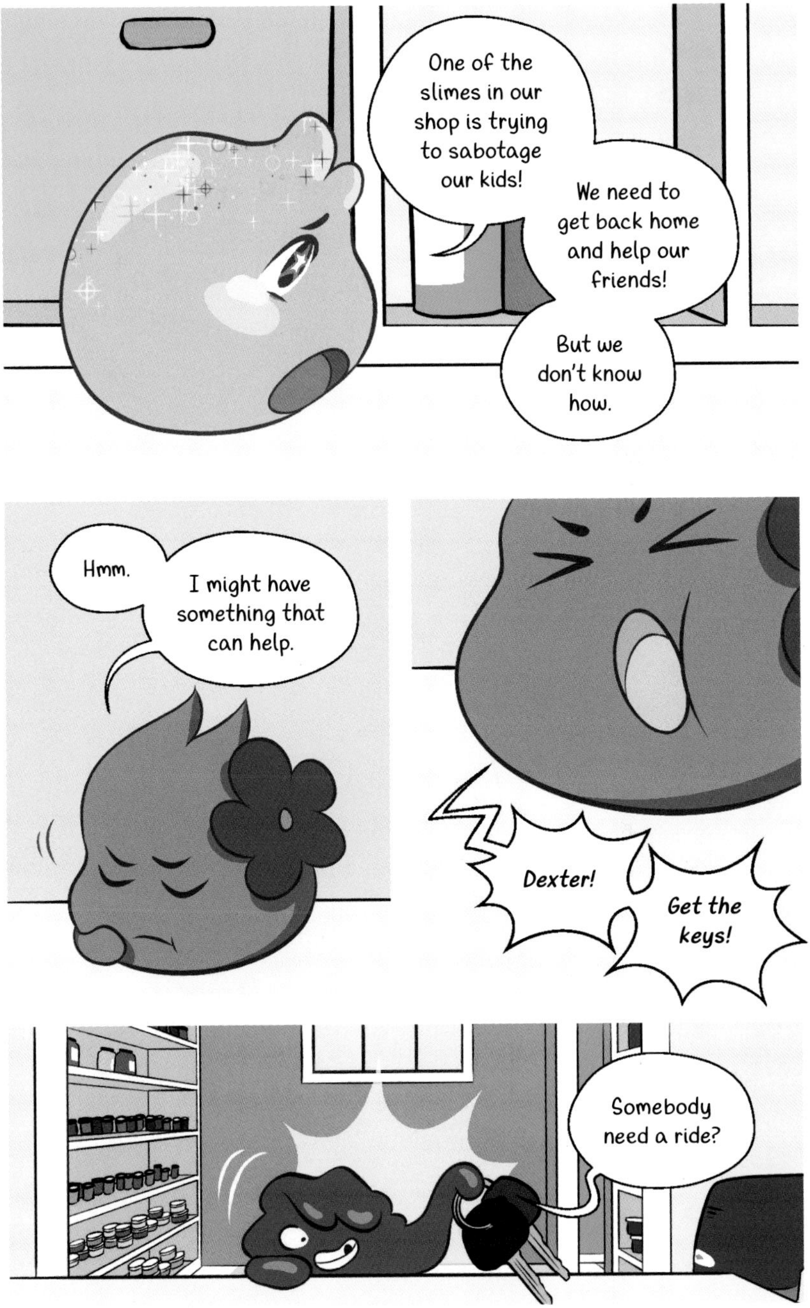
One of the slimes in our shop is trying to sabotage our kids!
We need to get back home and help our friends!
But we don't know how.
Hmm.
I might have something that can help.
Dexter!
Get the keys!
Somebody need a ride?

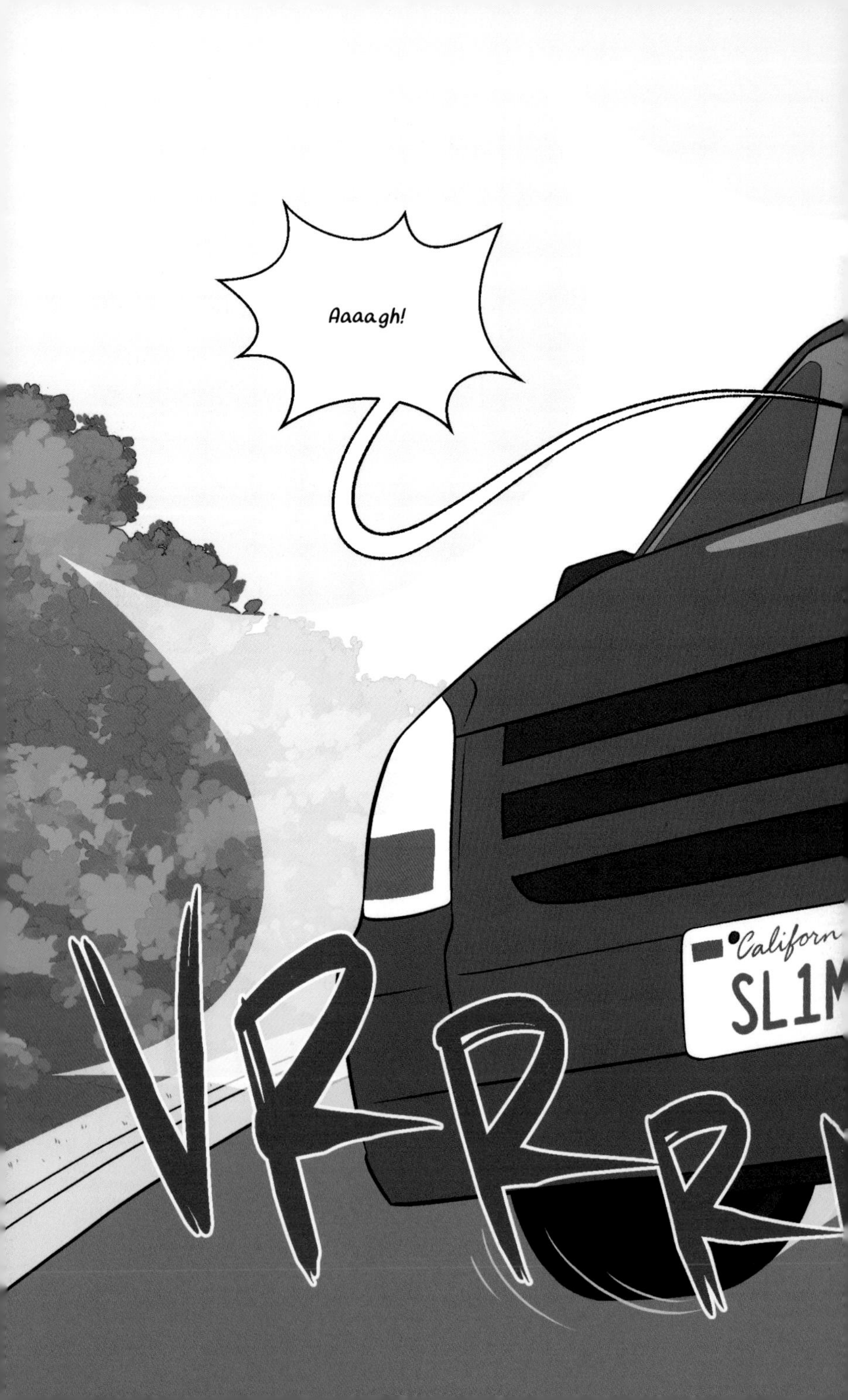
Aaaagh!
VRRR
Californ
SL1M

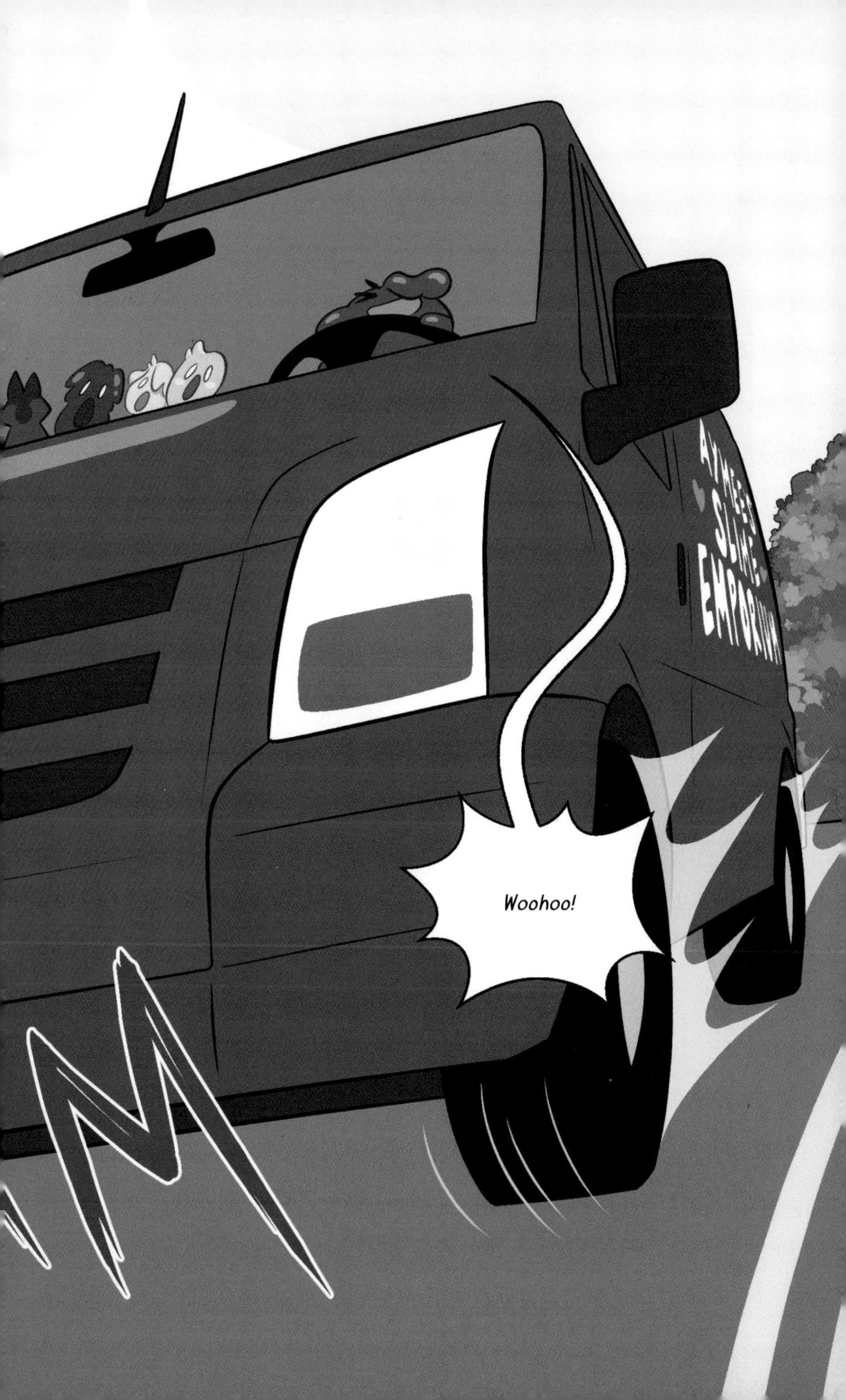
AYMEE'S SLIME EMPORIUM
Woohoo!

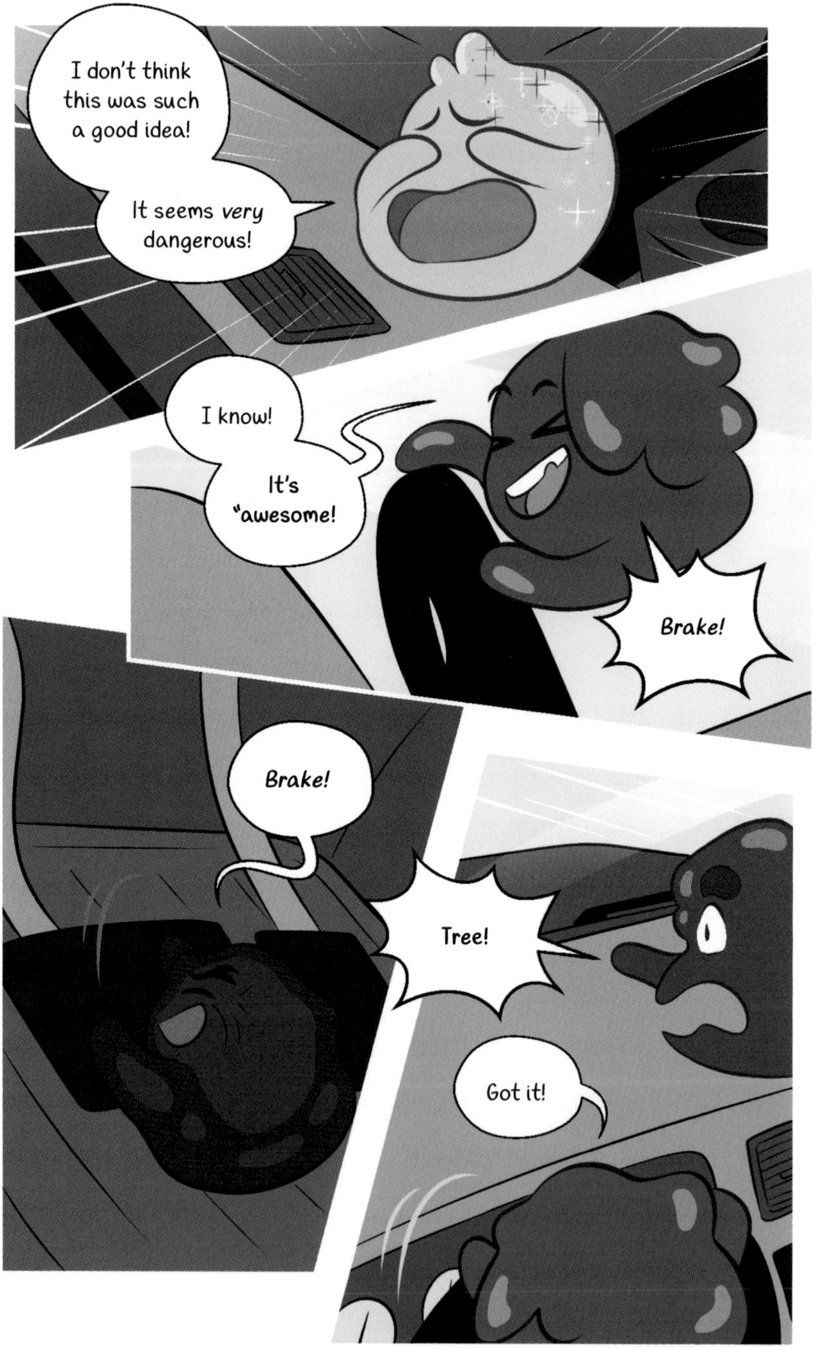
I don't think this was such a good idea!
It seems *very* dangerous!
I know!
It's "awesome!
Brake!
Brake!
Tree!
Got it!

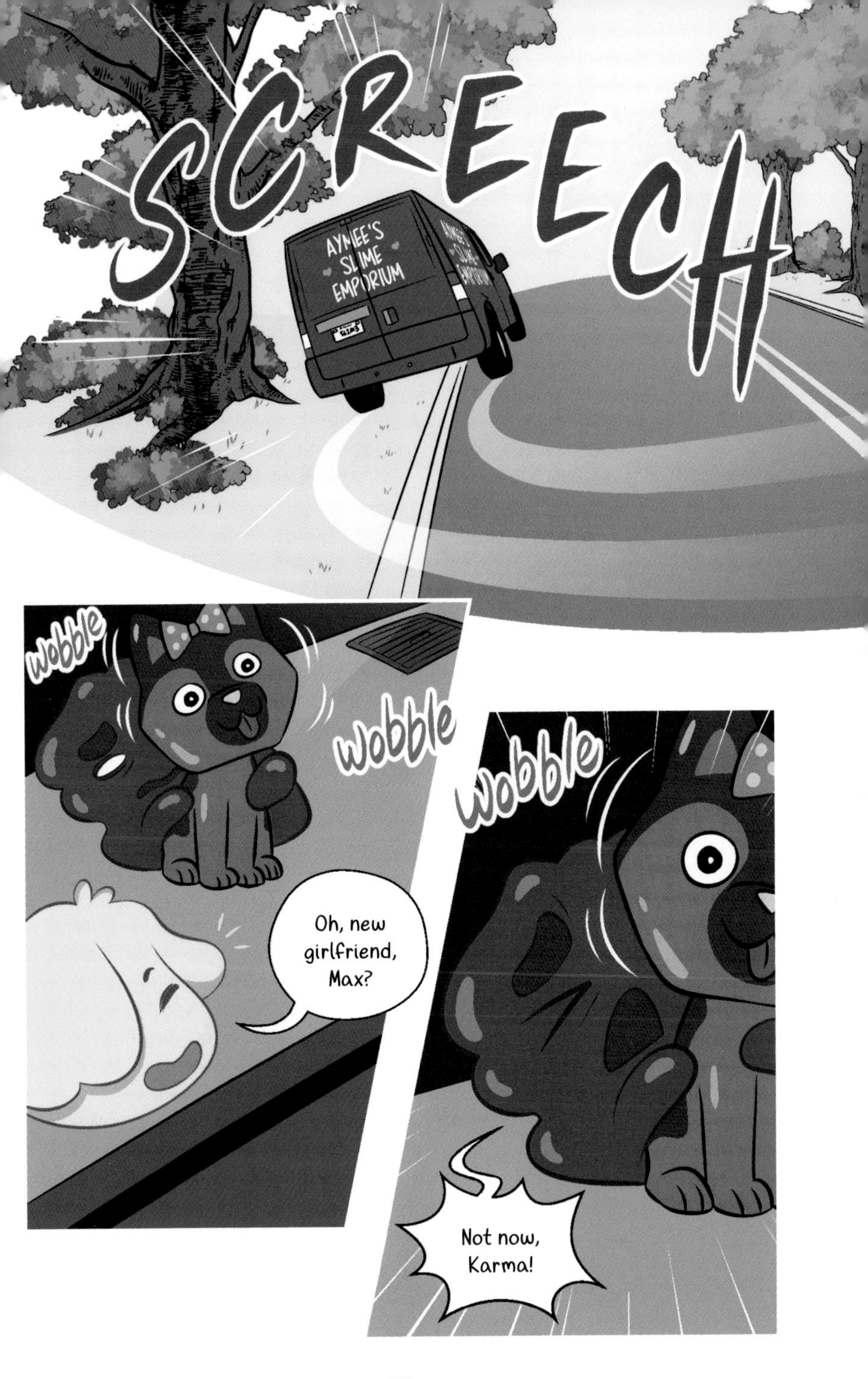
SCREECH
AYMEE'S SLIME EMPORIUM
AYMEE'S SLIME EMPORIUM
wobble
wobble
Oh, new girlfriend, Max?
wobble
Not now, Karma!

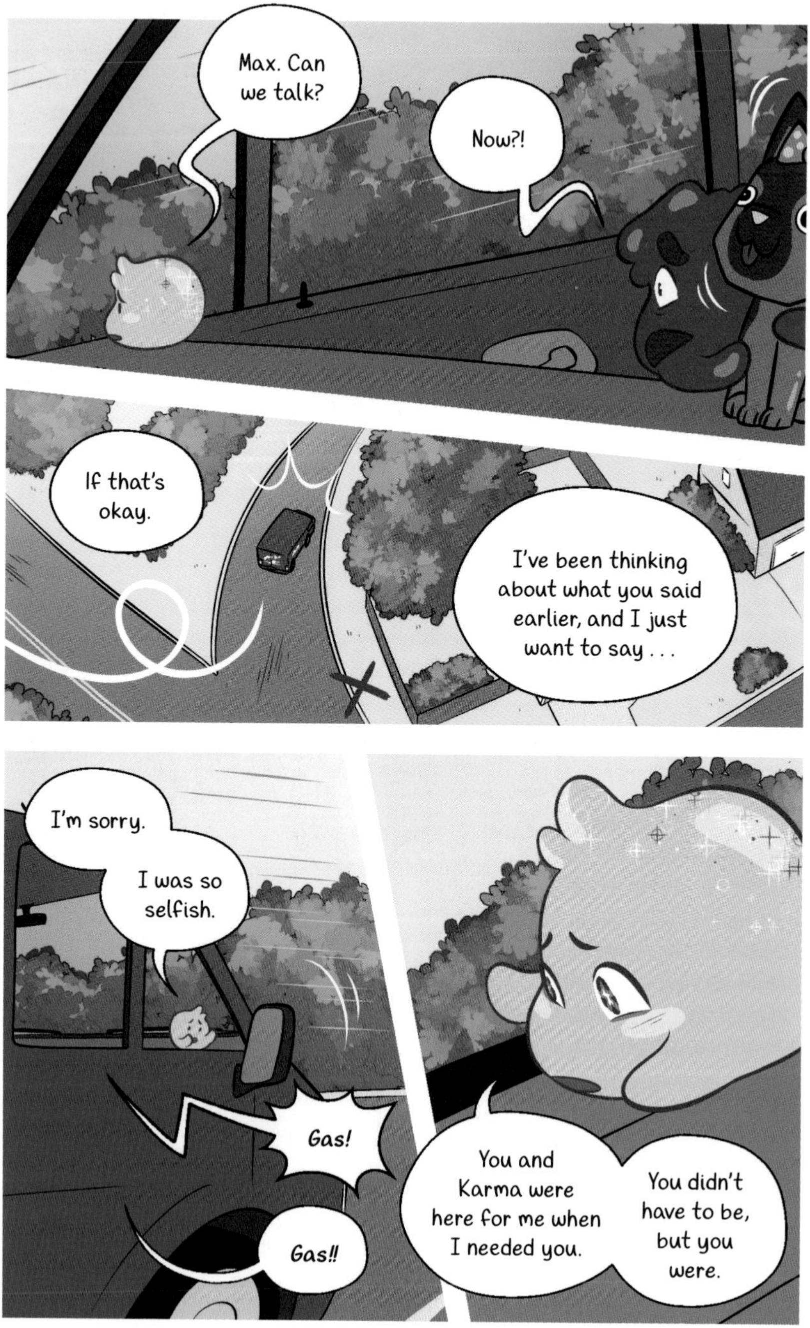
Max. Can we talk?
Now?!
If that's okay.
I've been thinking about what you said earlier, and I just want to say . . .
I'm sorry.
I was so selfish.
Gas!
Gas!!
You and Karma were here for me when I needed you.
You didn't have to be, but you were.

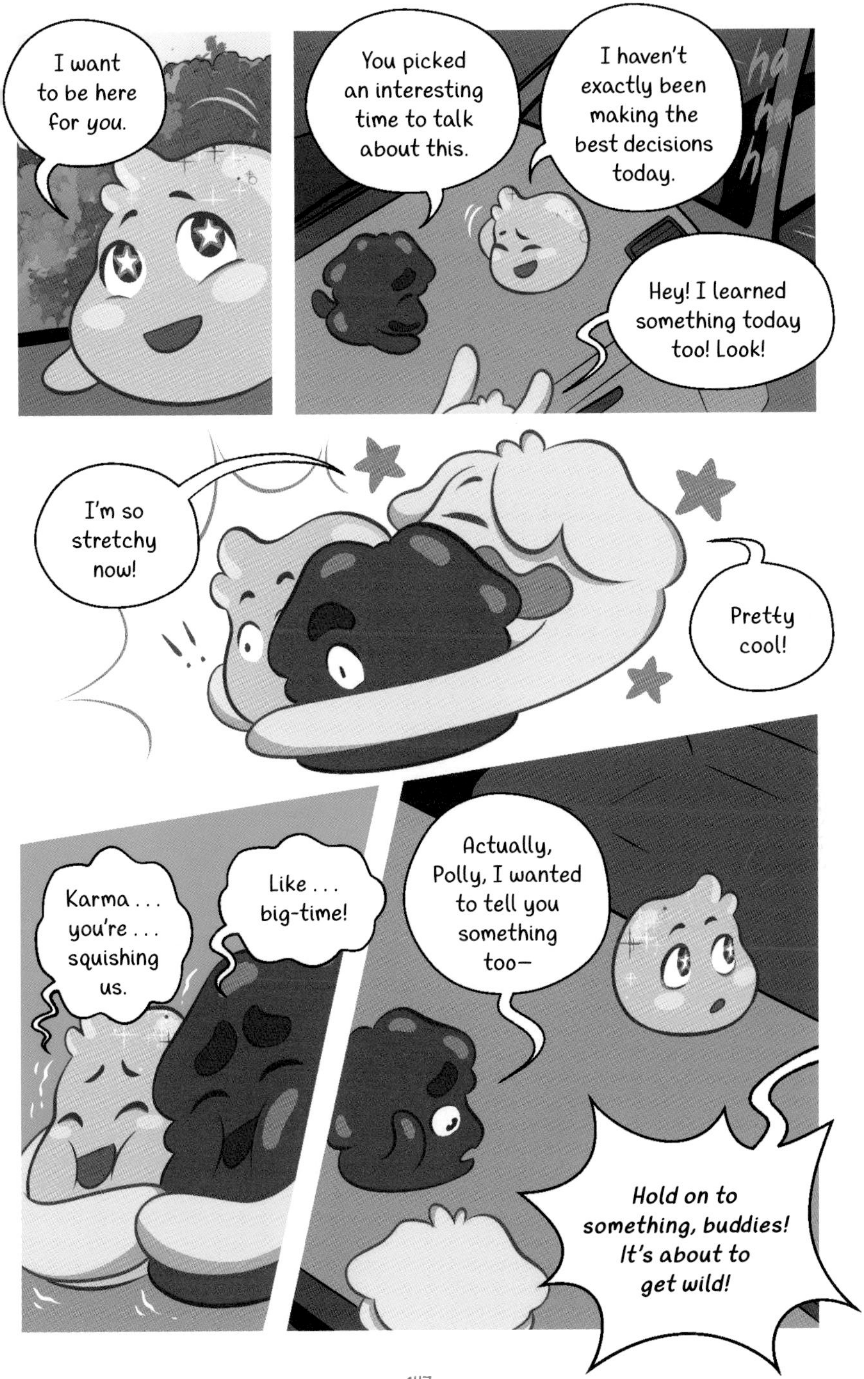
I want to be here for you.
You picked an interesting time to talk about this.
I haven't exactly been making the best decisions today.
ha ha ha
Hey! I learned something today too! Look!
I'm so stretchy now!
!!
Pretty cool!
Karma . . . you're . . . squishing us.
Like . . . big-time!
Actually, Polly, I wanted to tell you something too—
Hold on to something, buddies! It's about to get wild!

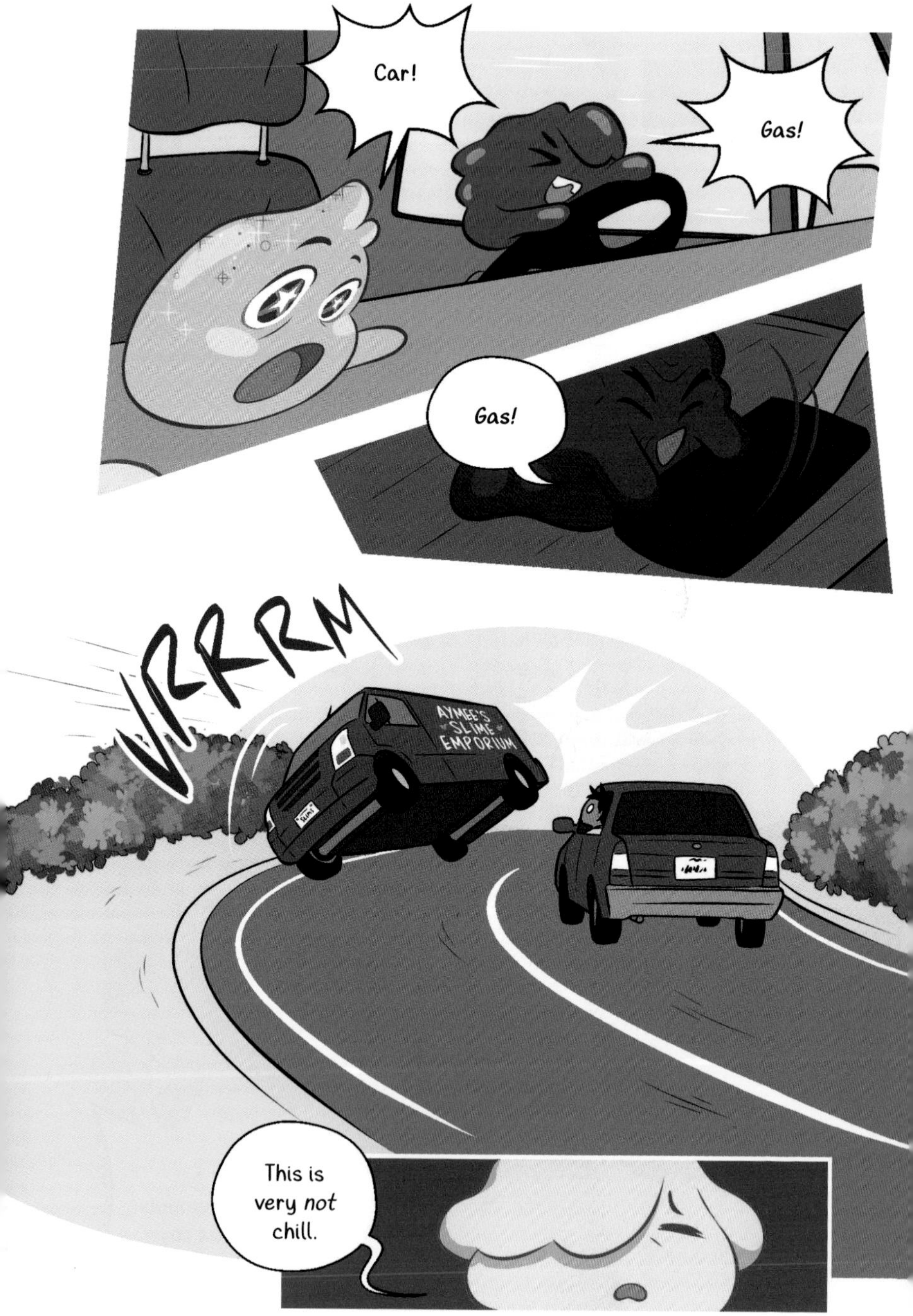
Car!
Gas!
Gas!
VRRRM
AYMEE'S SLIME EMPORIUM
This is very *not* chill.

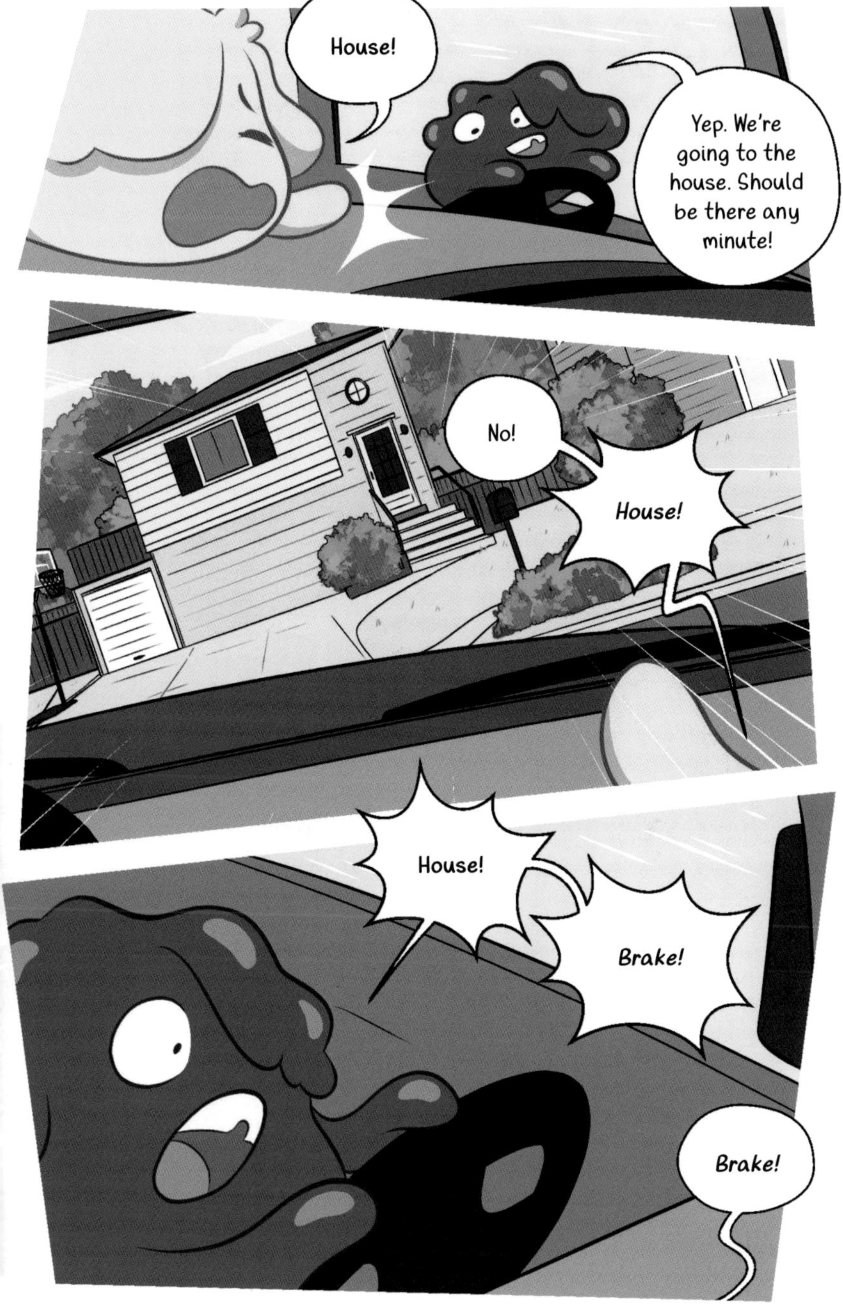
House!
Yep. We're going to the house. Should be there any minute!
No!
House!
House!
Brake!
Brake!

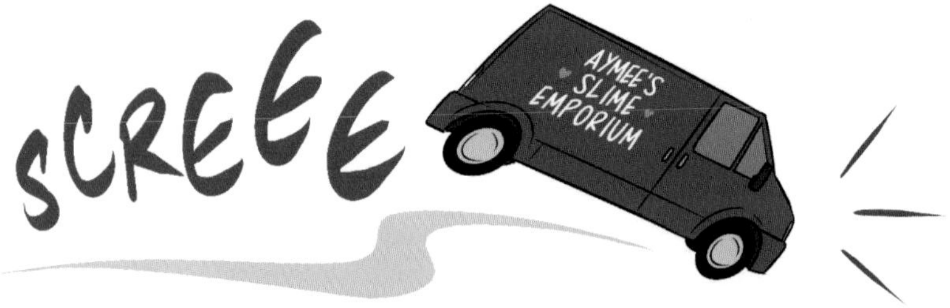
SCREEE
AYMEE'S SLIME EMPORIUM

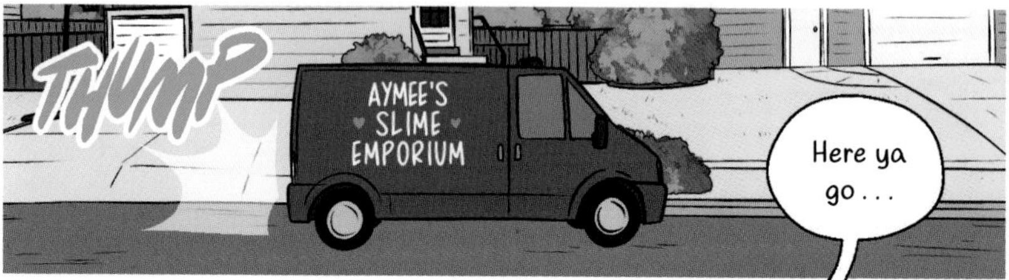
THUMP
AYMEE'S SLIME EMPORIUM
Here ya go . . .

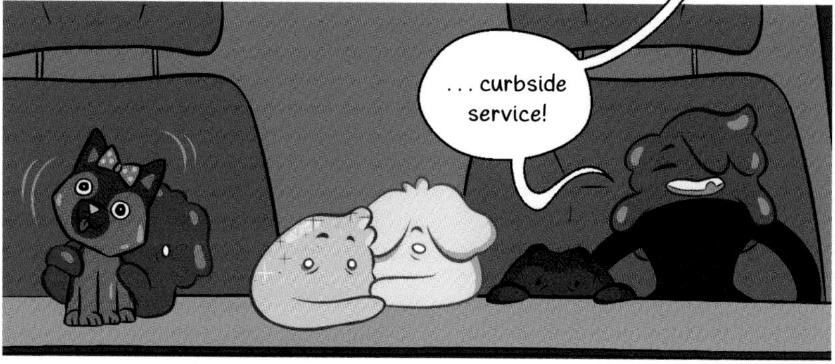
. . . curbside service!

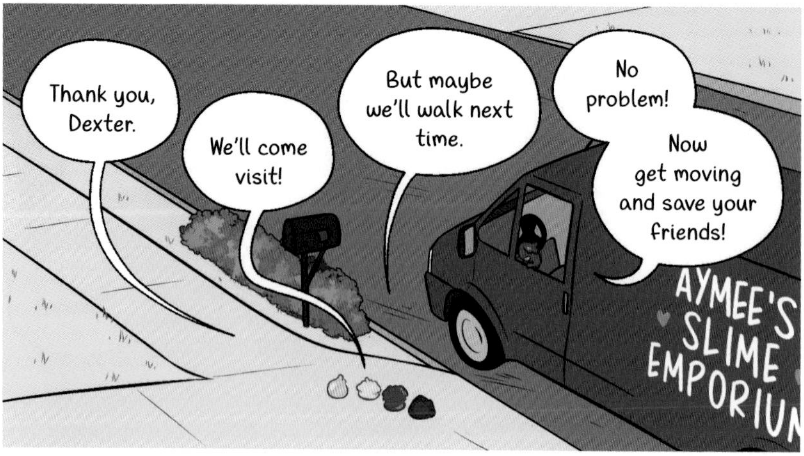
Thank you, Dexter.
We'll come visit!
But maybe we'll walk next time.
No problem!
Now get moving and save your friends!
AYMEE'S SLIME EMPORIUN

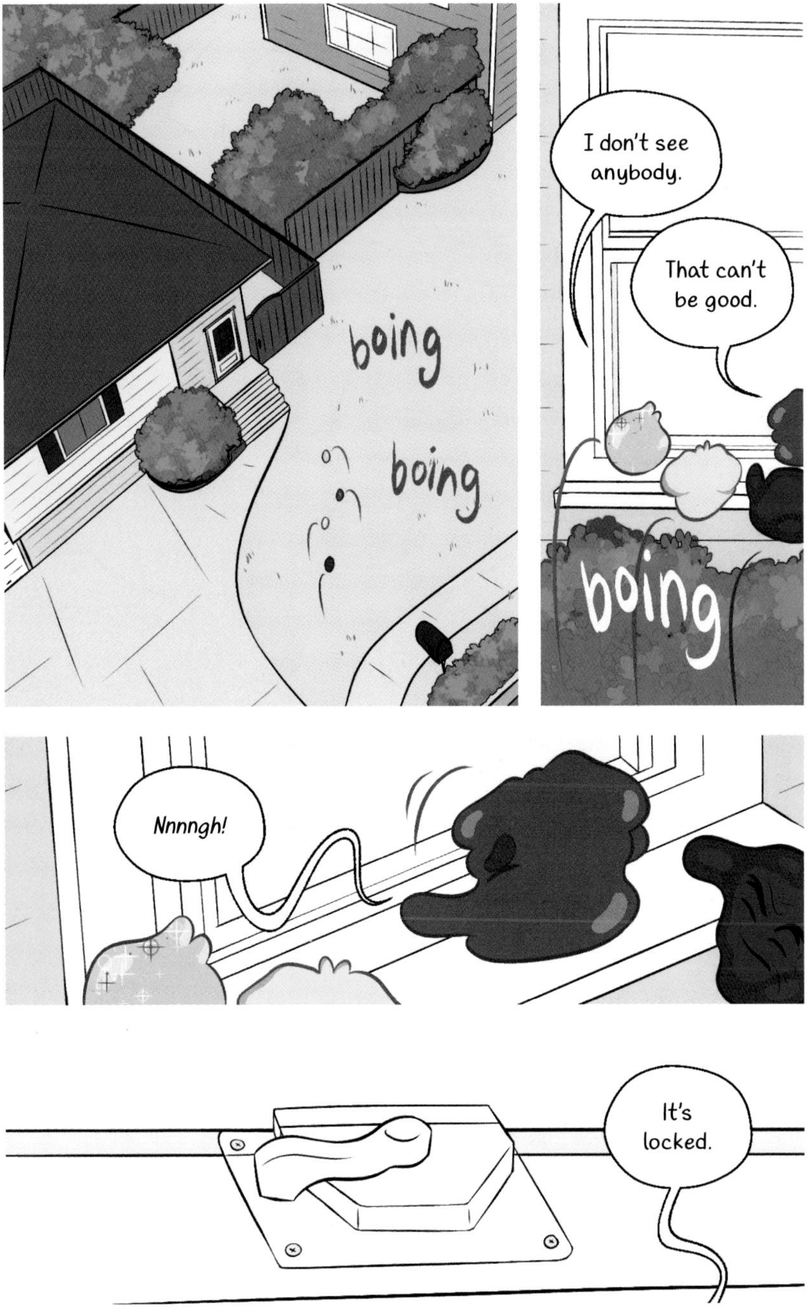
boing
boing
I don't see anybody.
That can't be good.
boing
Nnnngh!
It's locked.

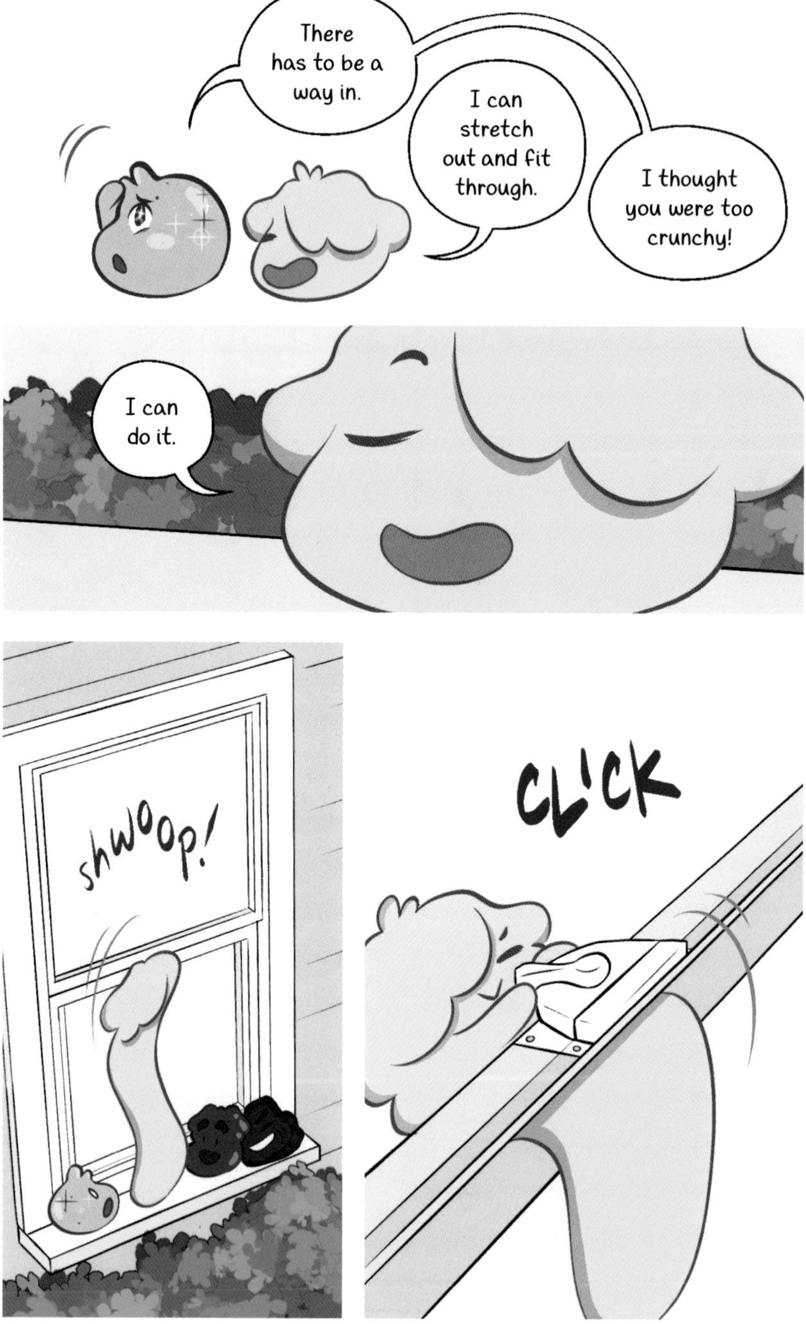
There has to be a way in.
I can stretch out and fit through.
I thought you were too crunchy!
I can do it.
shwoop!
CLICK

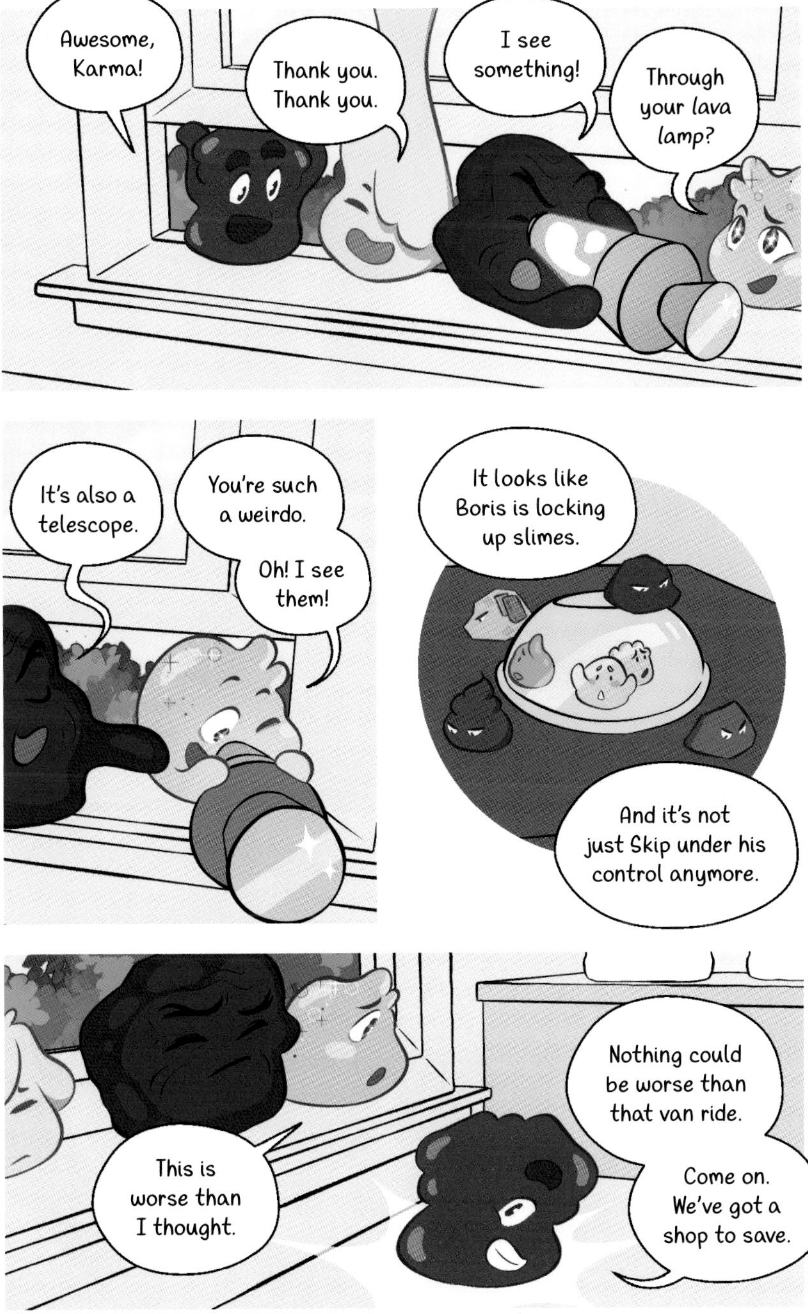
Awesome, Karma!
Thank you. Thank you.
I see something!
Through your lava lamp?
It's also a telescope.
You're such a weirdo.
Oh! I see them!
It looks like Boris is locking up slimes.
And it's not just Skip under his control anymore.
This is worse than I thought.
Nothing could be worse than that van ride.
Come on. We've got a shop to save.

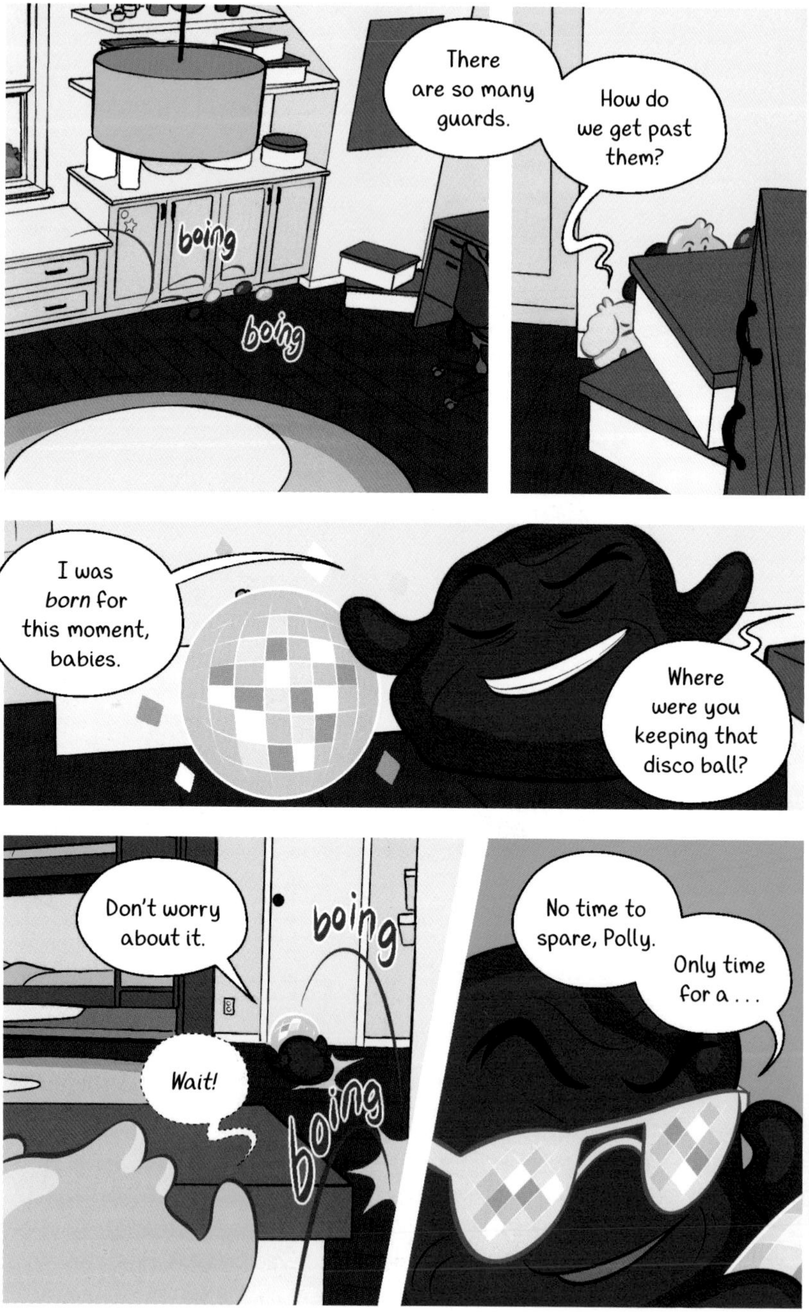
boing
boing
There are so many guards.
How do we get past them?
I was *born* for this moment, babies.
Where were you keeping that disco ball?
Don't worry about it.
boing
Wait!
boing
No time to spare, Polly.
Only time for a . . .

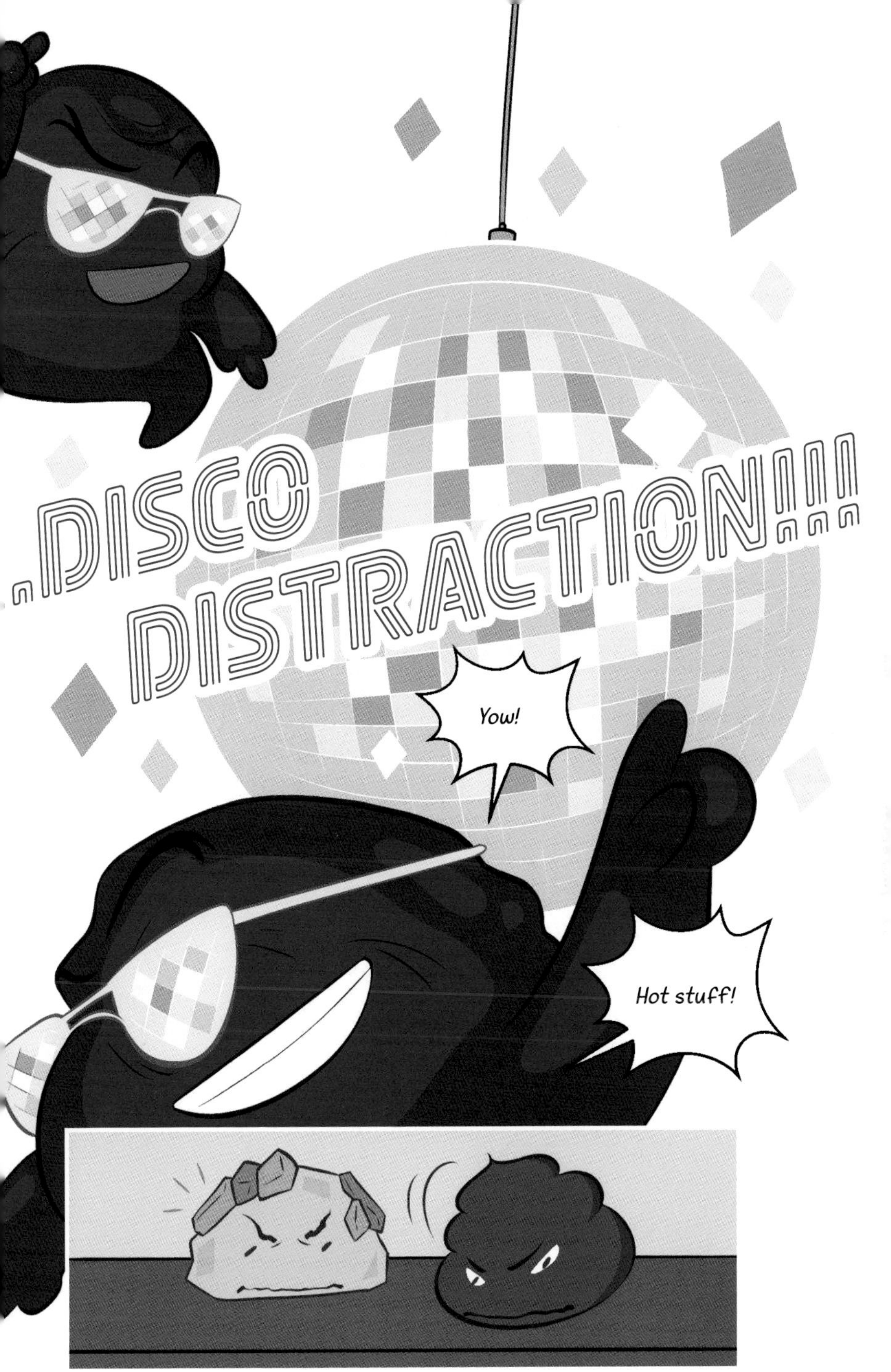
DISCO DISTRACTION!!!
You!
Hot stuff!

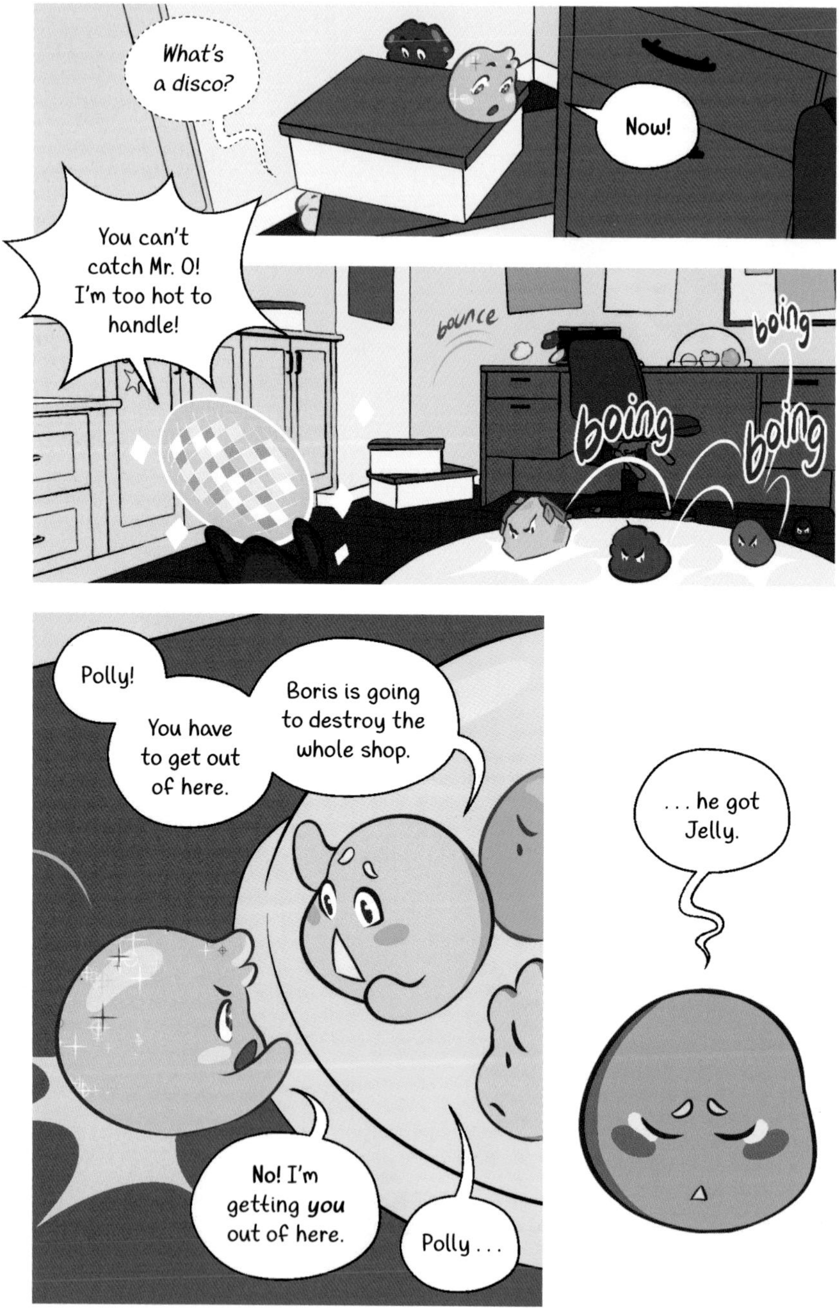
What's a disco?
Now!
You can't catch Mr. O! I'm too hot to handle!
bounce
boing
boing
boing
Polly!
You have to get out of here.
Boris is going to destroy the whole shop.
... he got Jelly.
No! I'm getting *you* out of here.
Polly . . .

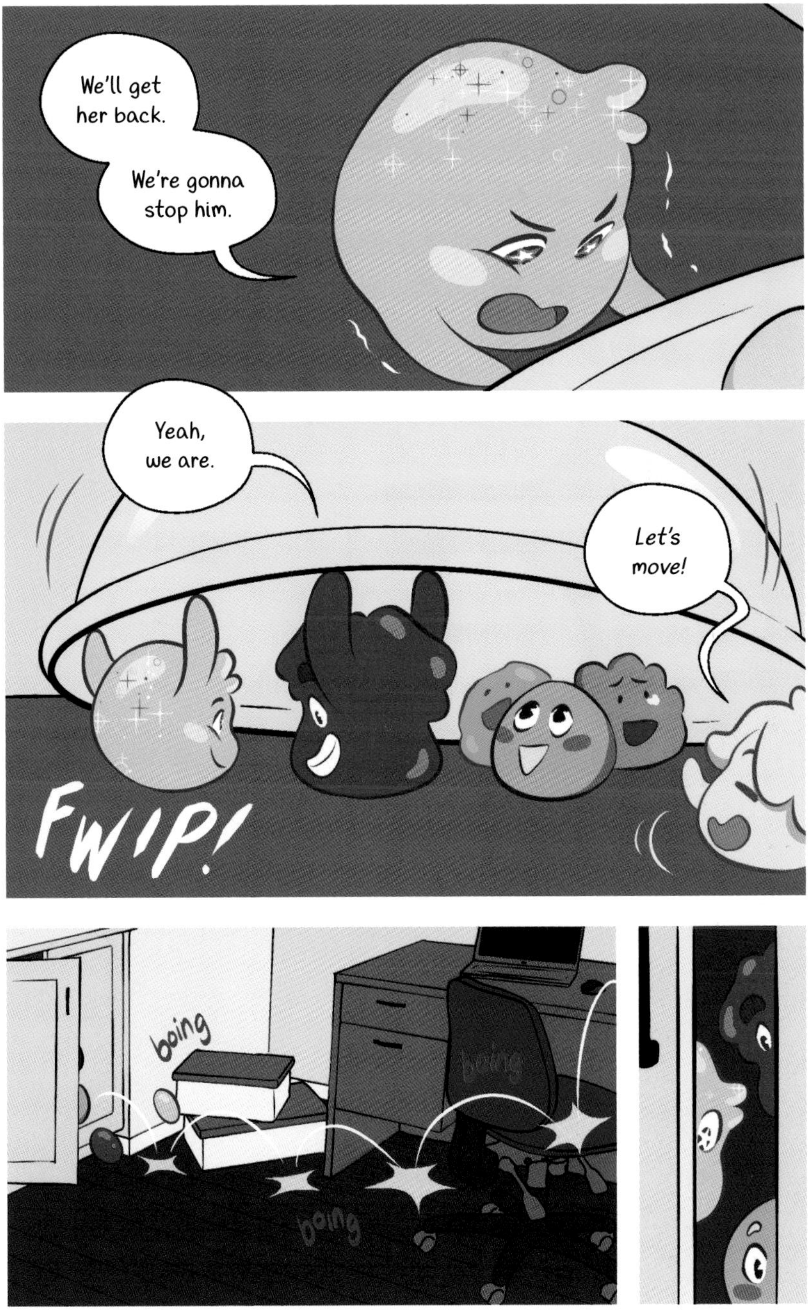
We'll get her back.
We're gonna stop him.
Yeah, we are.
Let's move!
FWIP!
boing
boing
boing

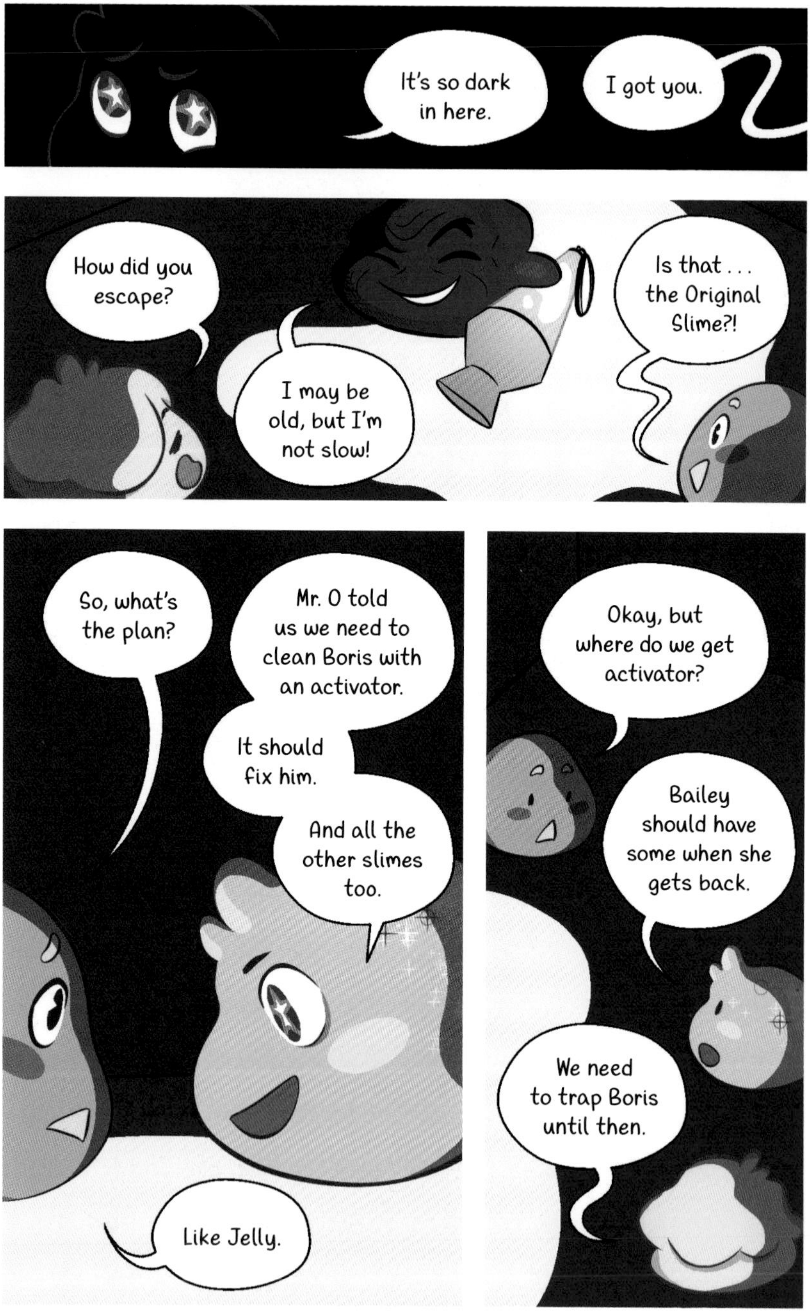
It's so dark in here.
I got you.
How did you escape?
I may be old, but I'm not slow!
Is that . . . the Original Slime?!
So, what's the plan?
Mr. O told us we need to clean Boris with an activator.
It should fix him.
And all the other slimes too.
Like Jelly.
Okay, but where do we get activator?
Bailey should have some when she gets back.
We need to trap Boris until then.

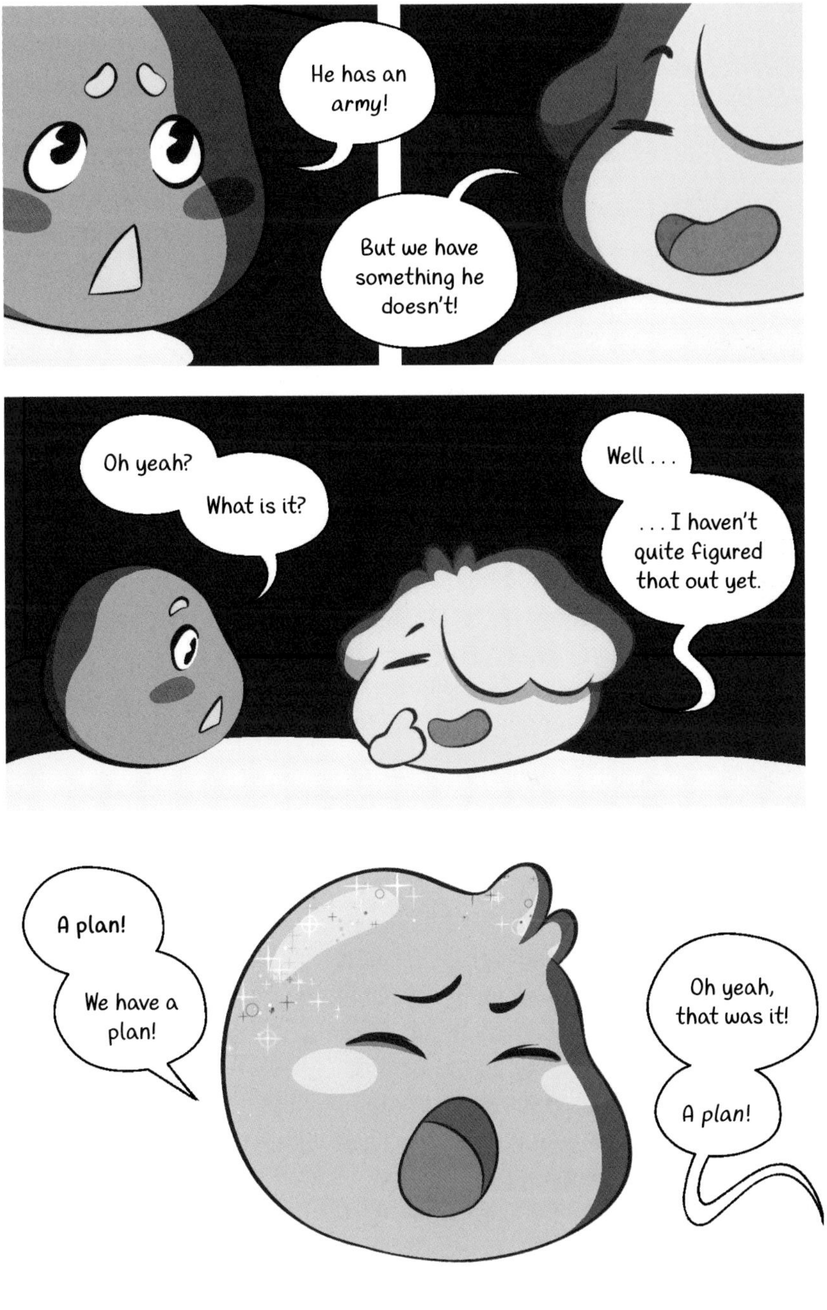
He has an army!
But we have something he doesn't!
Oh yeah?
What is it?
Well . . .
. . . I haven't quite figured that out yet.
A plan!
We have a plan!
Oh yeah, that was it!
A plan!

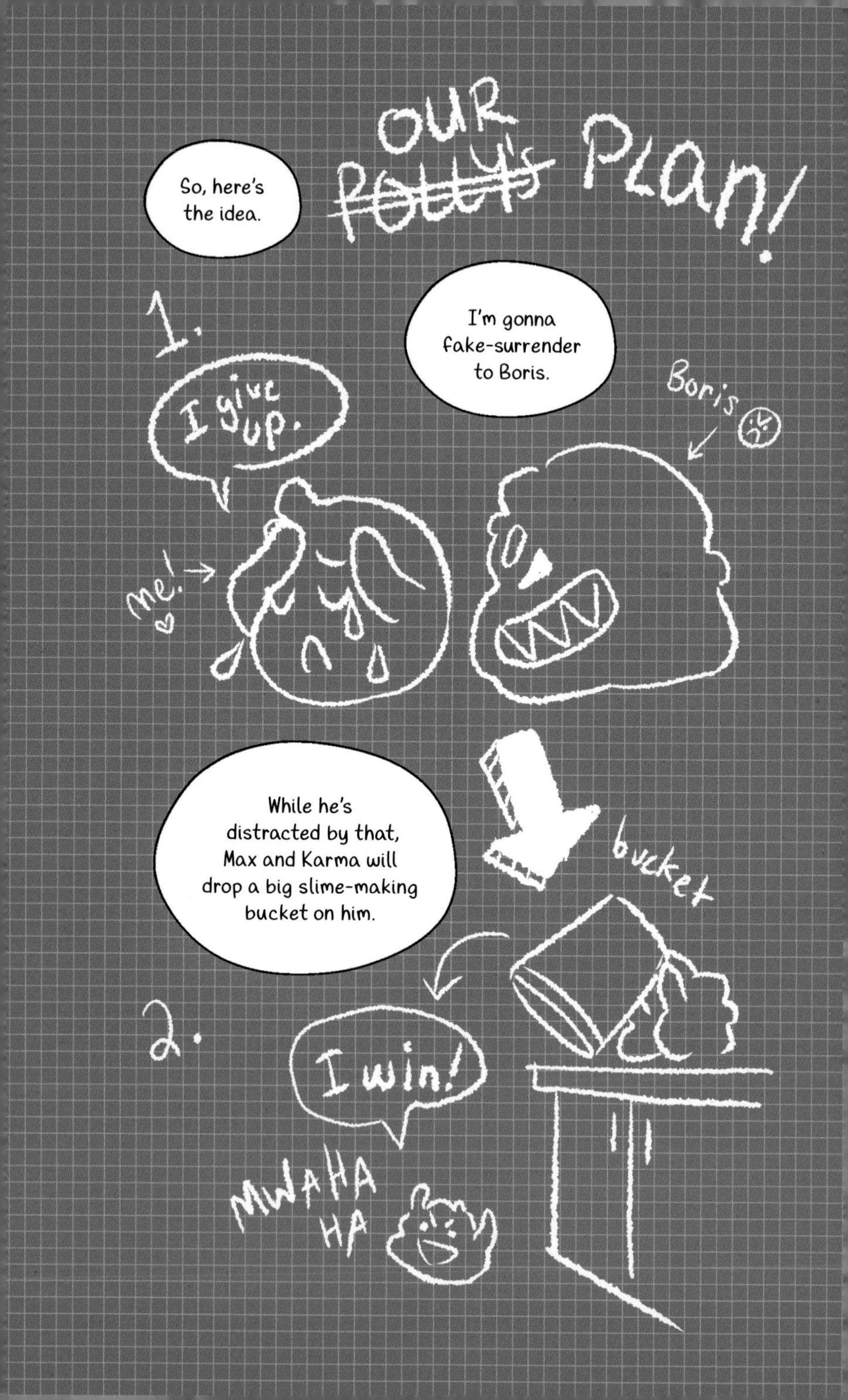
So, here's the idea.
OUR ~~POLLY's~~ PLAN!
1.
I'm gonna fake-surrender to Boris.
I give up.
Boris
me!
While he's distracted by that, Max and Karma will drop a big slime-making bucket on him.
bucket
2.
I win!
MWAHAHA HA

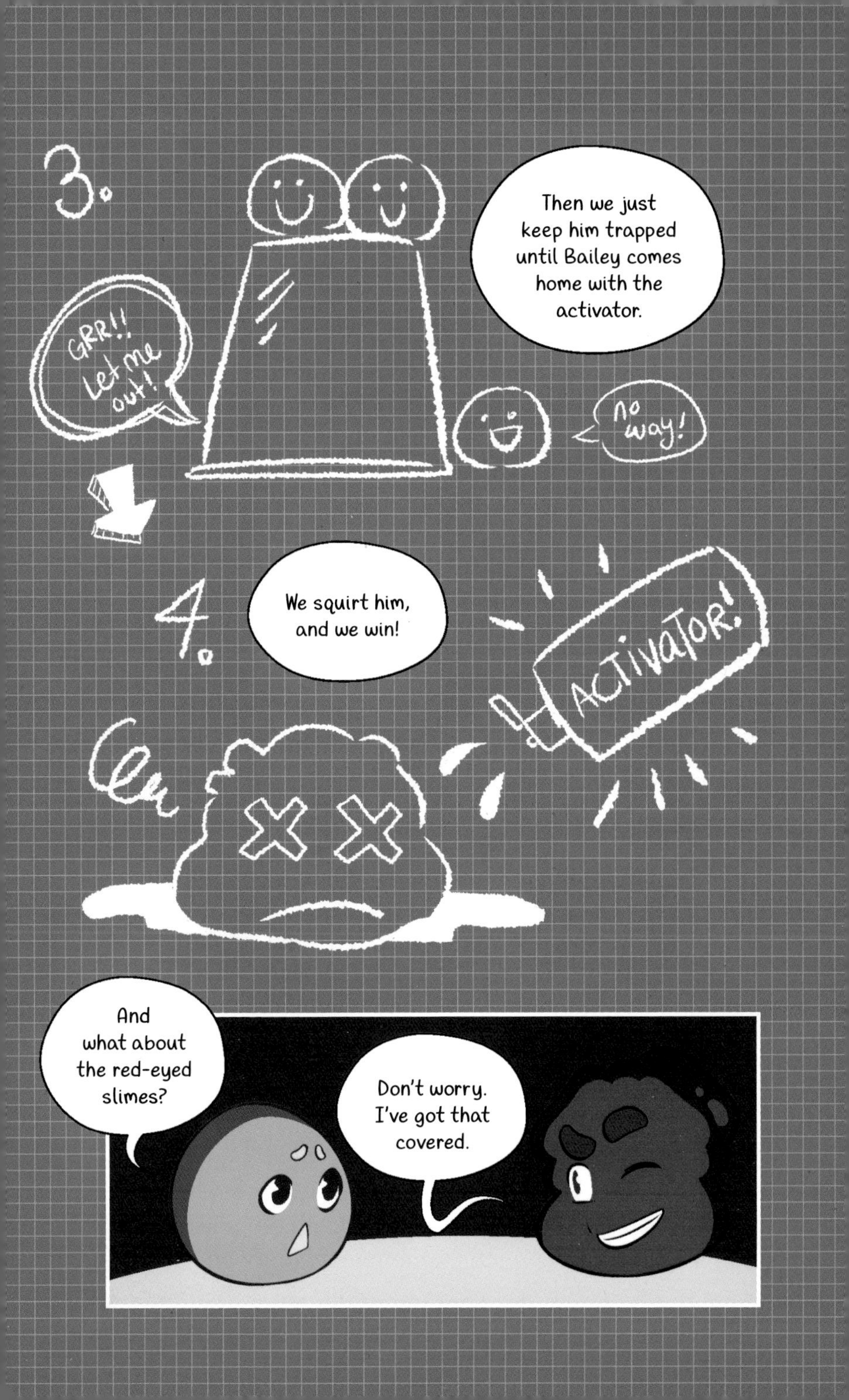
3.
Then we just keep him trapped until Bailey comes home with the activator.
GRR!! Let me out!
no way!
4.
We squirt him, and we win!
ACTIVATOR!
And what about the red-eyed slimes?
Don't worry. I've got that covered.

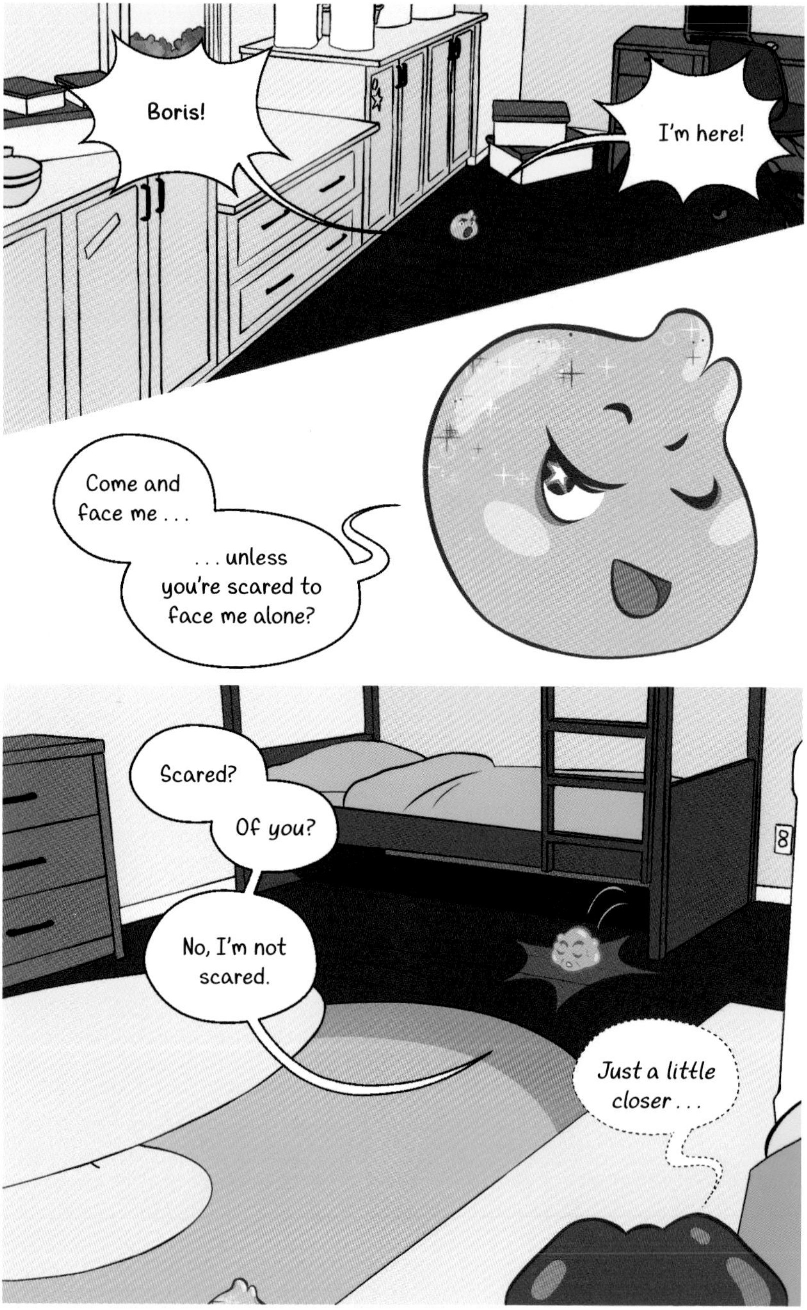
Boris!
I'm here!
Come and face me . . .
. . . unless you're scared to face me alone?
Scared?
Of you?
No, I'm not scared.
Just a little closer . . .

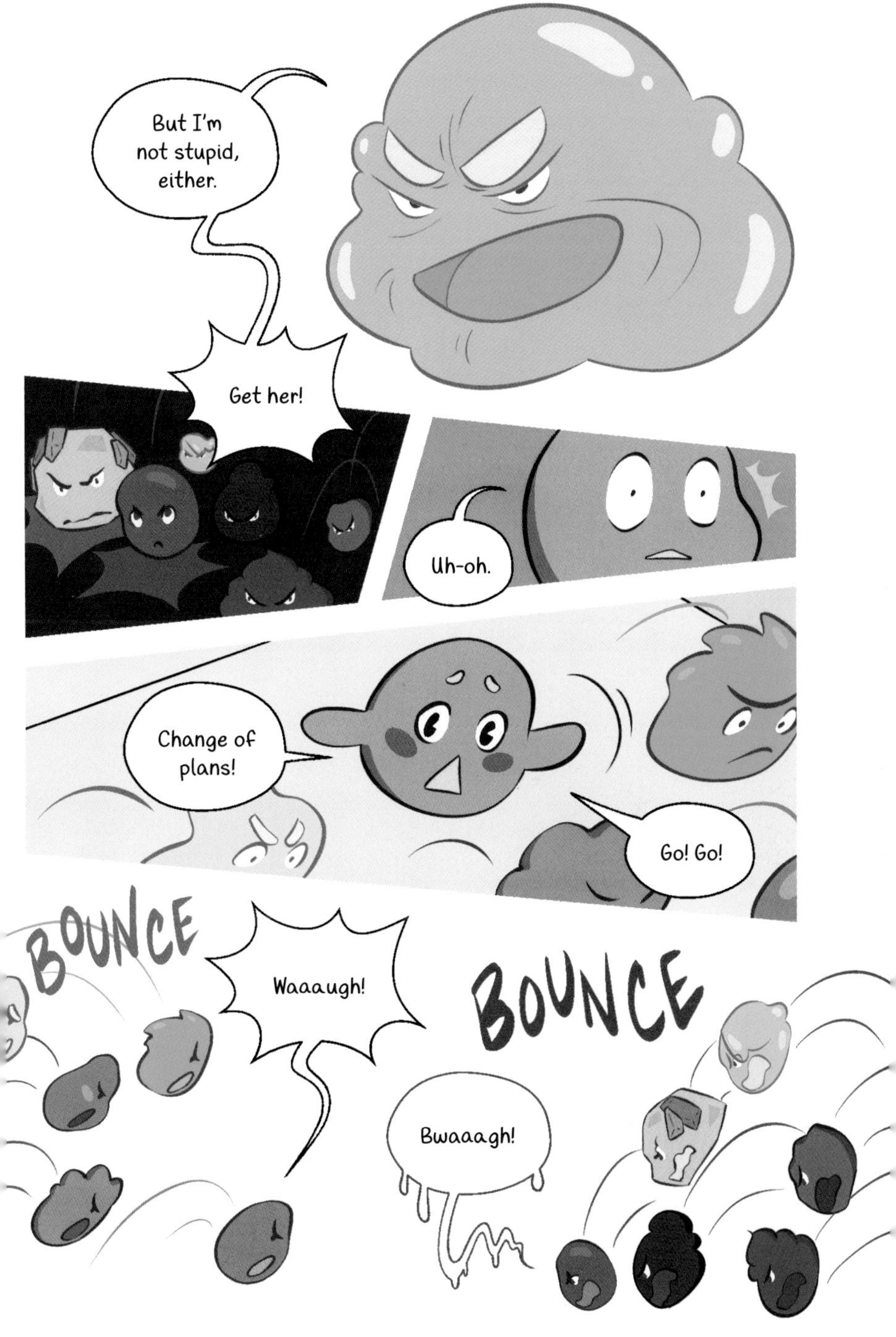
But I'm not stupid, either.
Get her!
Uh-oh.
Change of plans!
Go! Go!
BOUNCE
Waaaugh!
BOUNCE
Bwaaagh!

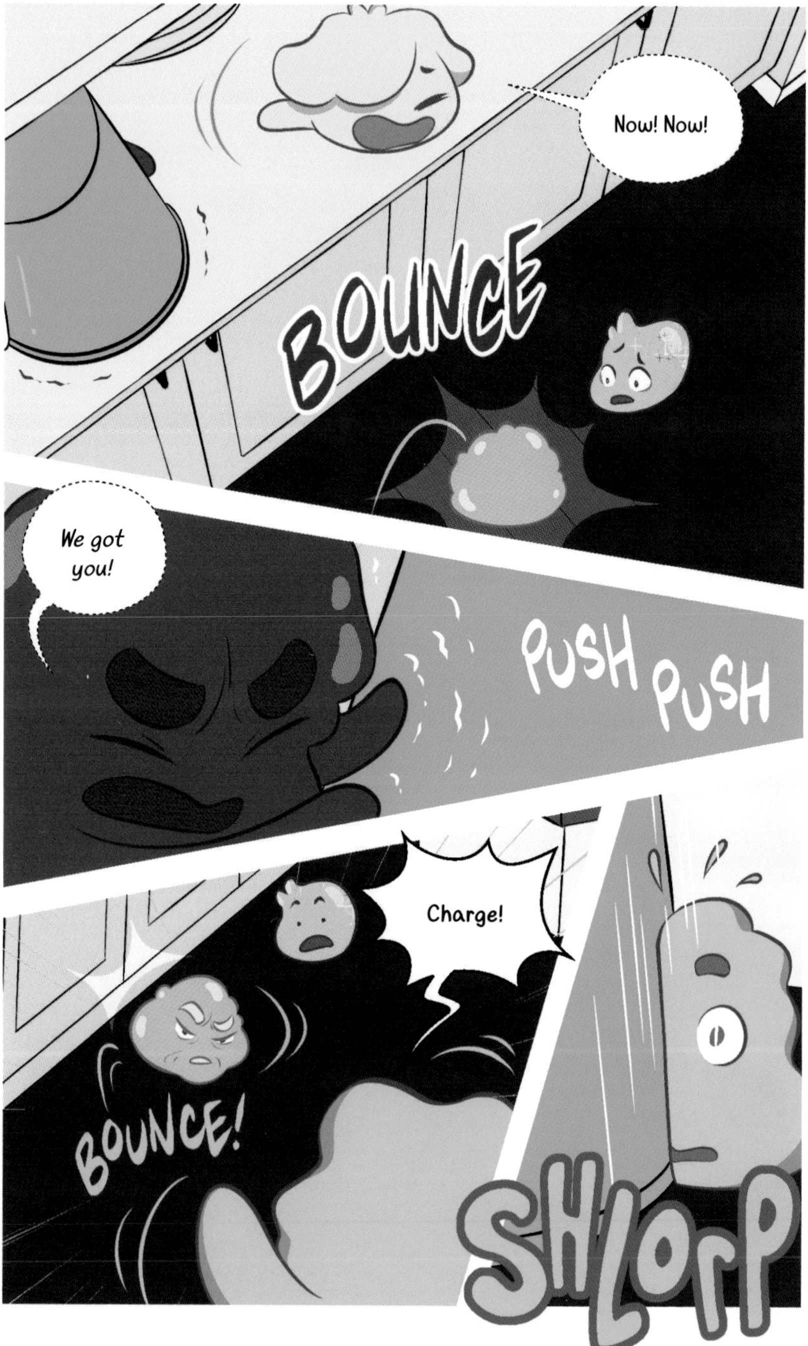
Now! Now!
BOUNCE
We got you!
PUSH PUSH
Charge!
BOUNCE!
SHLORP

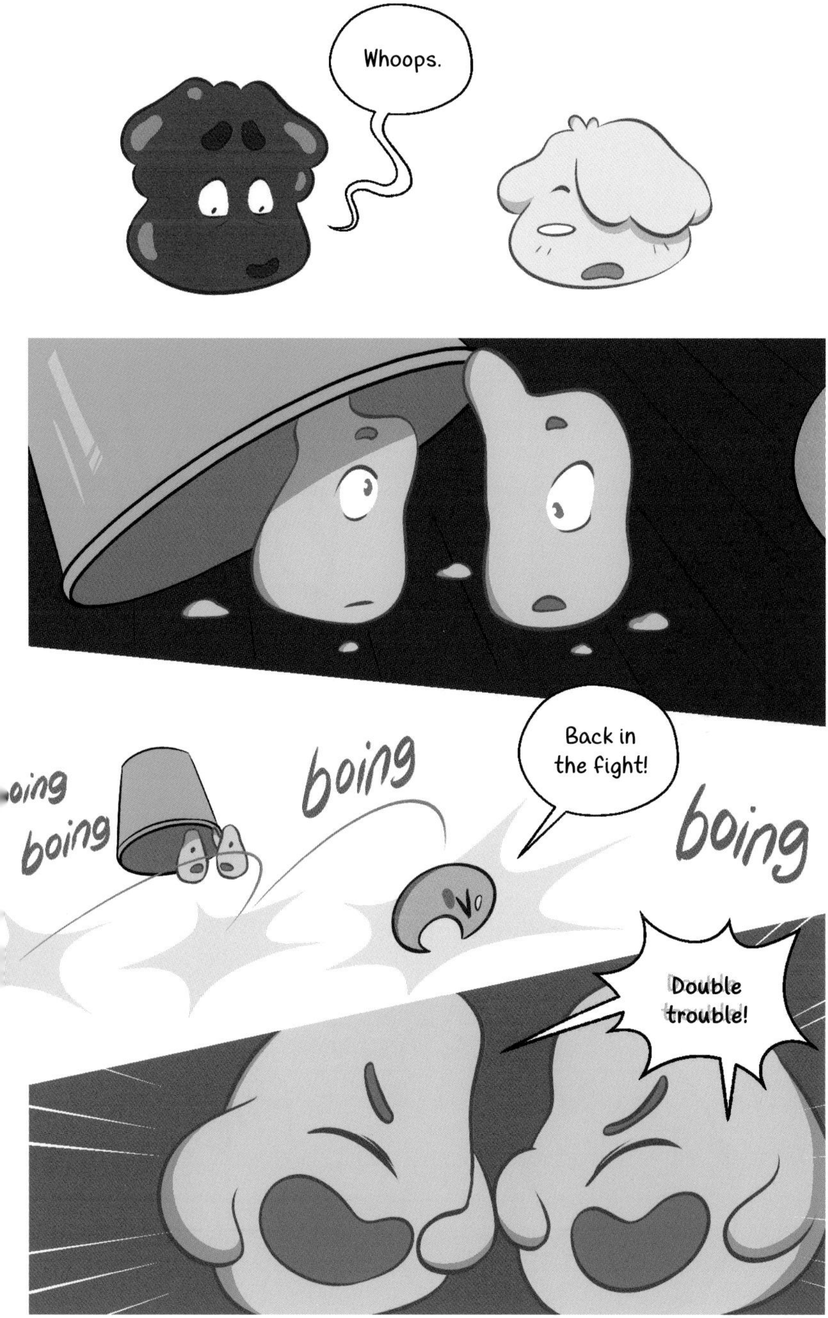
Whoops.
oing
boing
boing
Back in the fight!
boing
Double trouble!

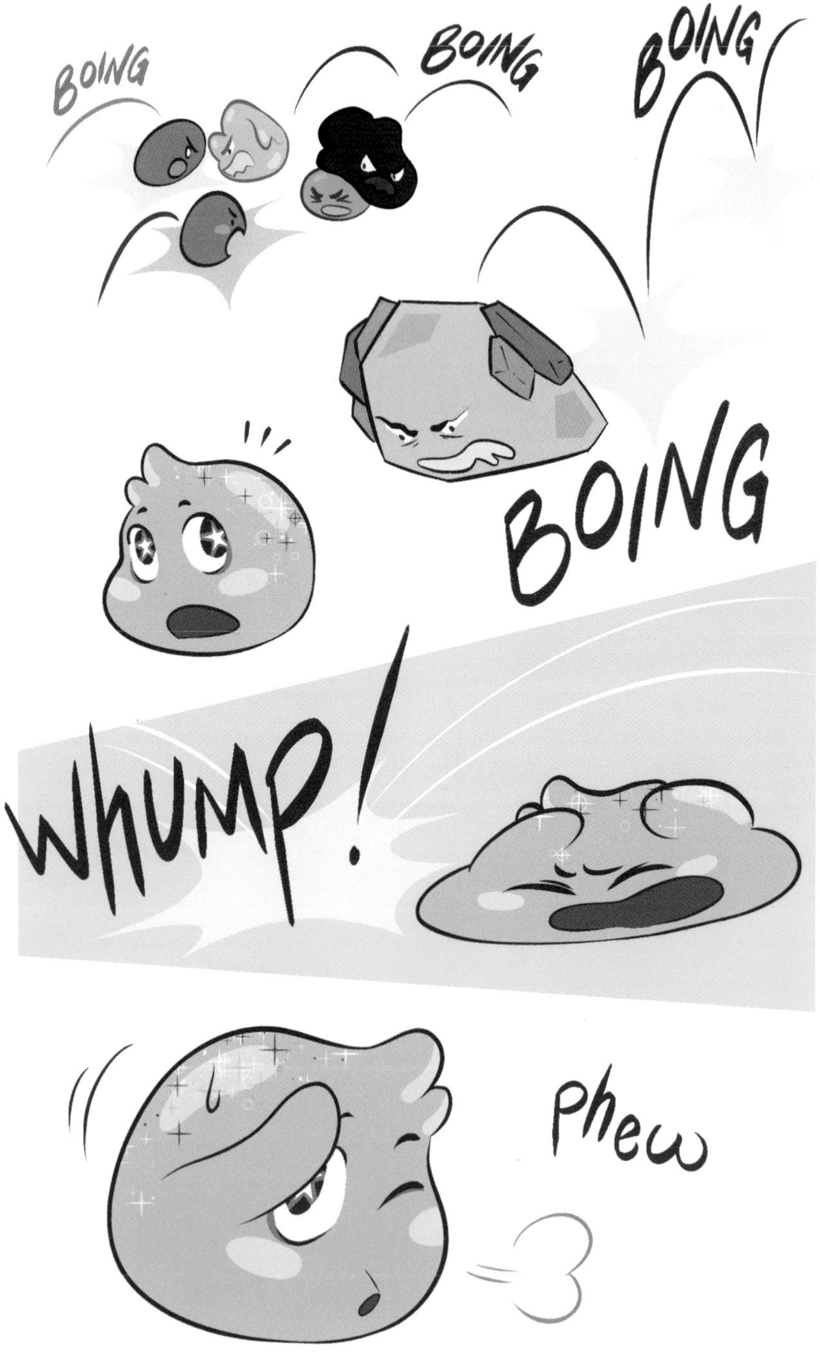
BOING
BOING
BOING
BOING
WHUMP!
Phew

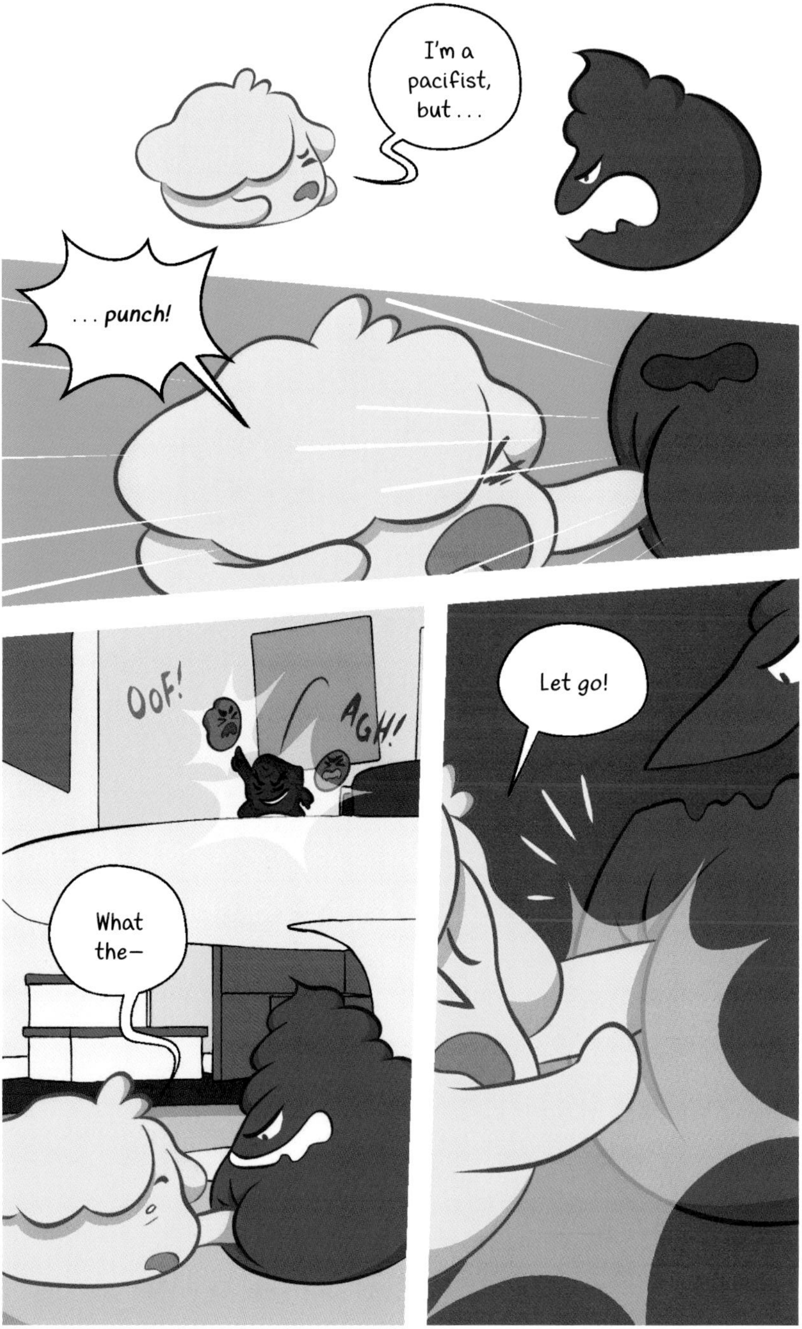
I'm a pacifist, but . . .
. . . punch!
OOF!
AGH!
What the—
Let go!

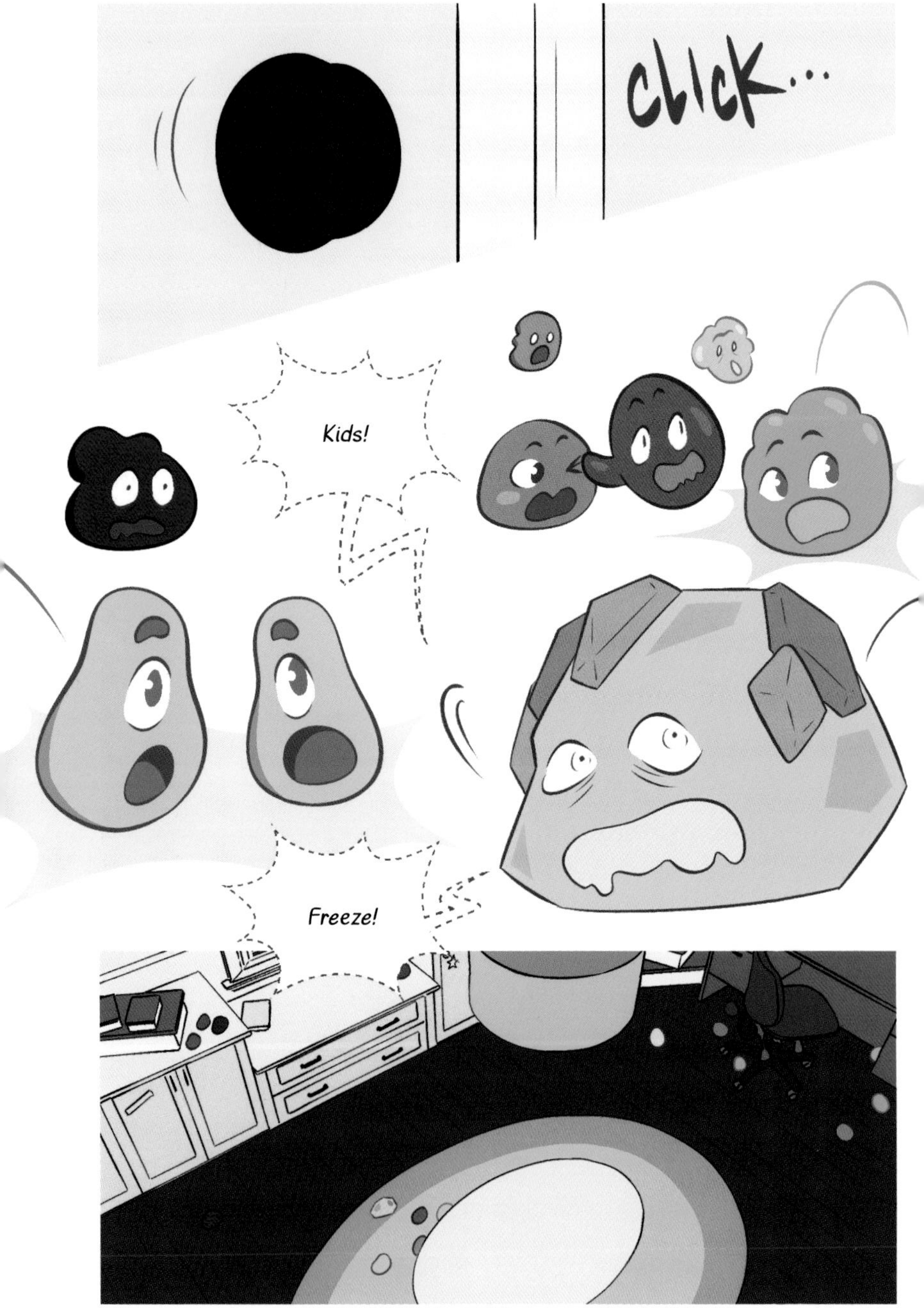
CLICK...
Kids!
Freeze!

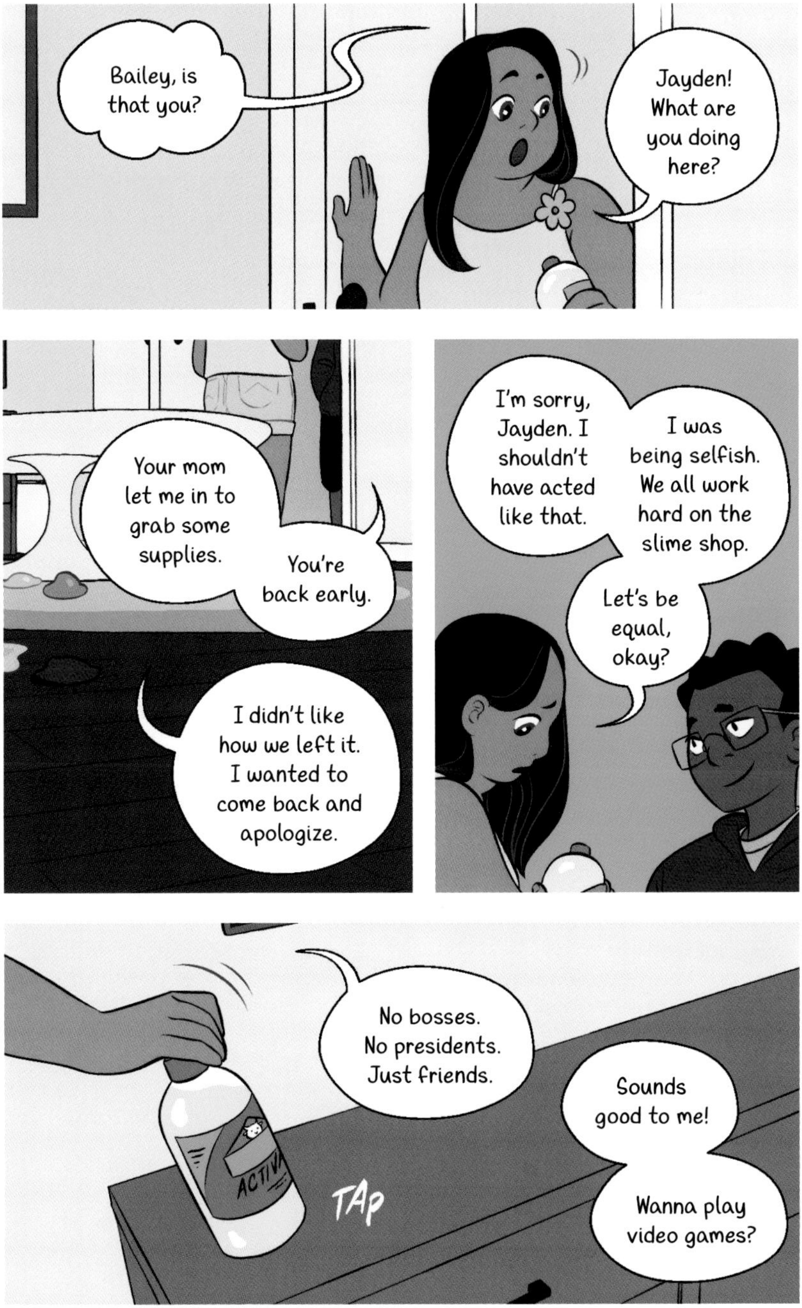
Bailey, is that you?
Jayden! What are you doing here?
Your mom let me in to grab some supplies.
You're back early.
I didn't like how we left it. I wanted to come back and apologize.
I'm sorry, Jayden. I shouldn't have acted like that.
I was being selfish. We all work hard on the slime shop.
Let's be equal, okay?
No bosses. No presidents. Just friends.
Sounds good to me!
Wanna play video games?
TAP

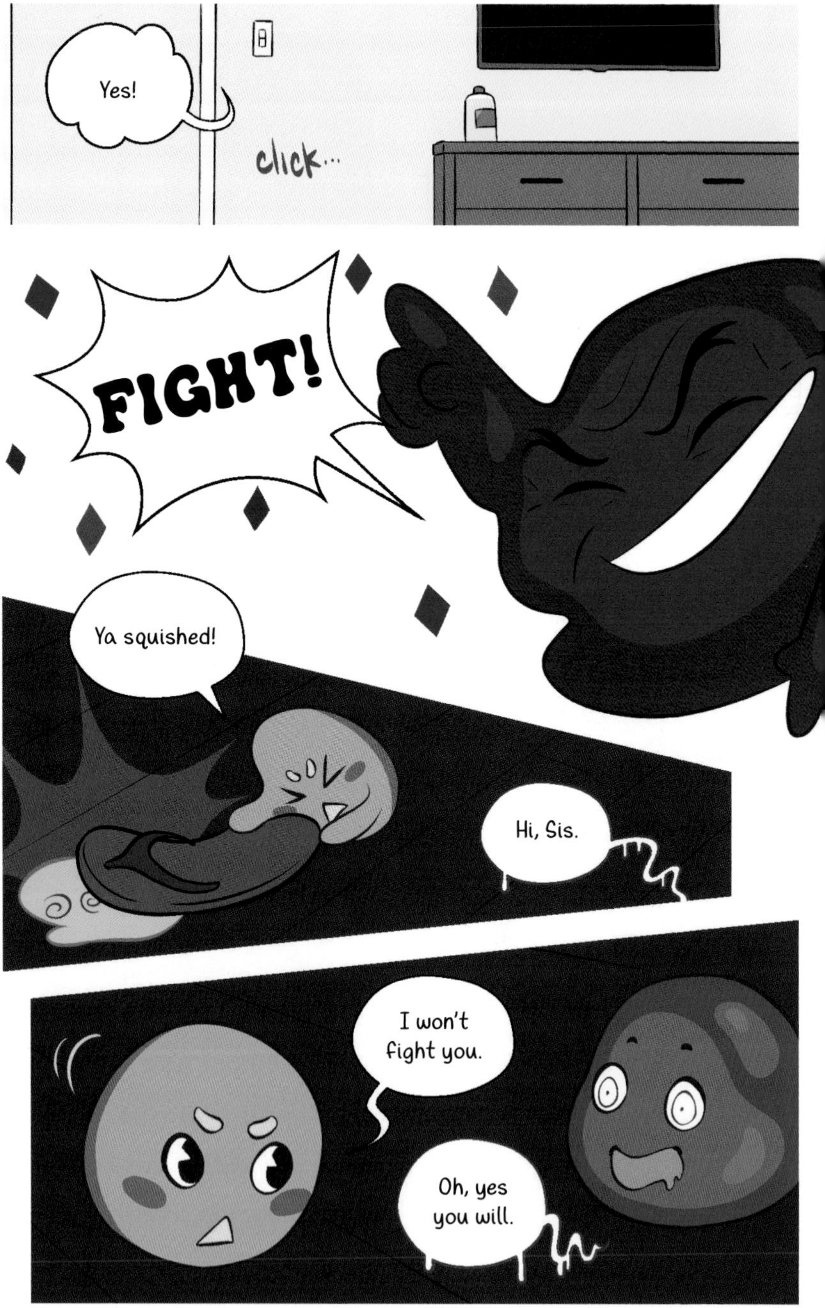
Yes!
click...
FIGHT!
Ya squished!
Hi, Sis.
I won't fight you.
Oh, yes you will.

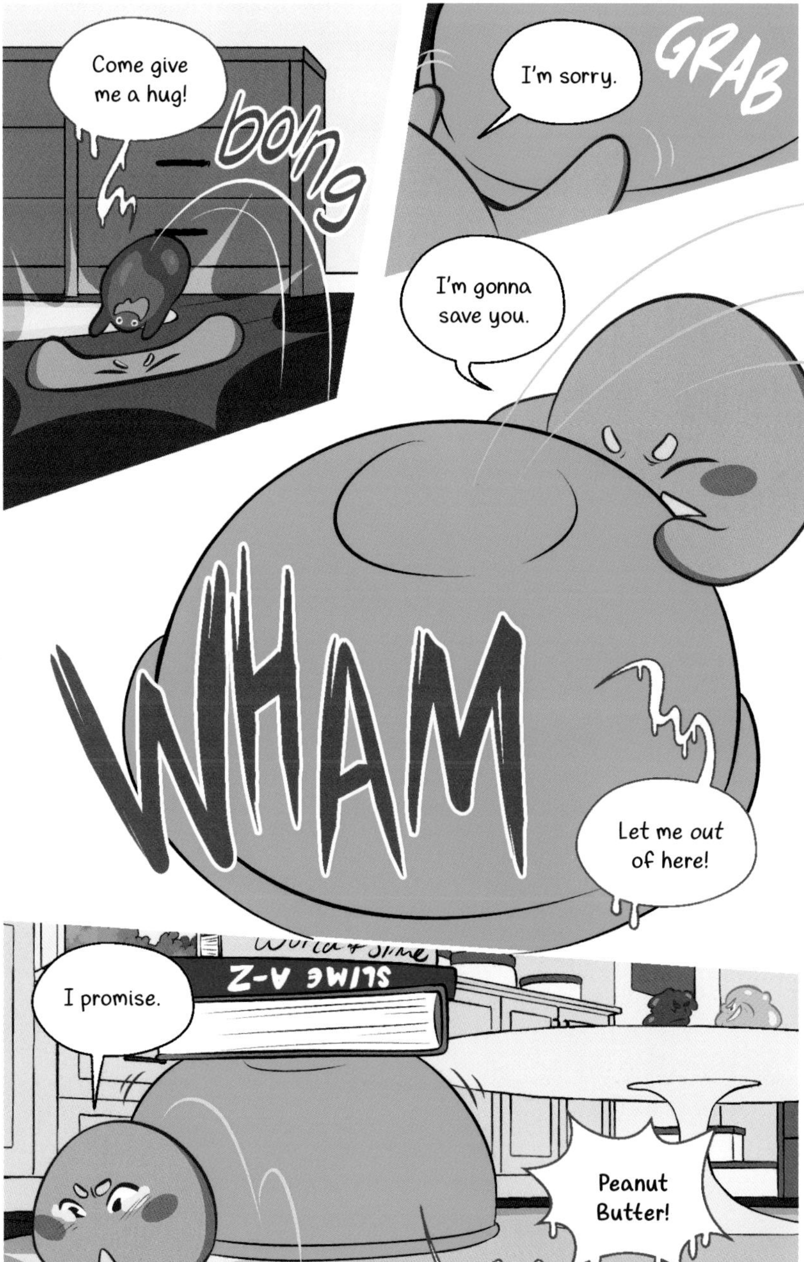
Come give me a hug!
boing
I'm sorry.
GRAB
I'm gonna save you.
WHAM
Let me out of here!
SLIME A-Z
I promise.
Peanut Butter!

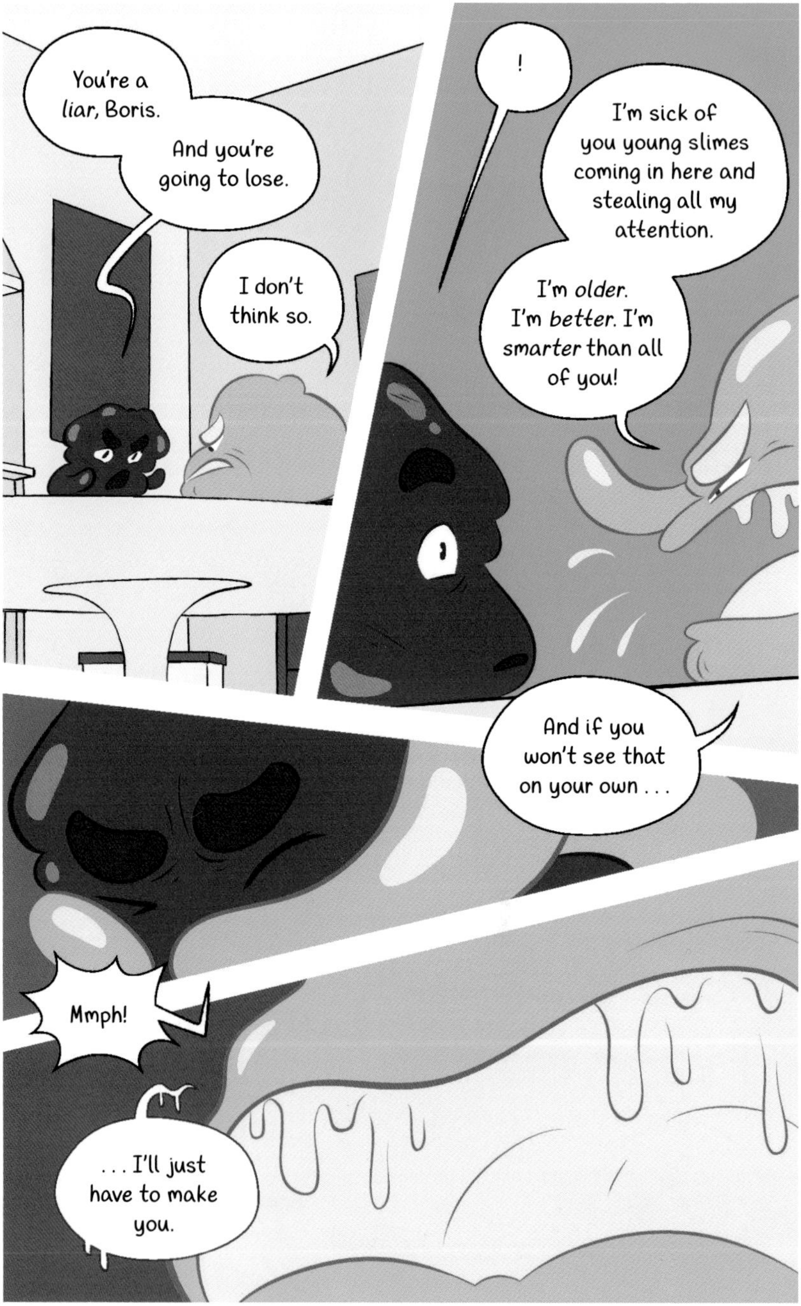
You're a liar, Boris.
And you're going to lose.
I don't think so.
!
I'm sick of you young slimes coming in here and stealing all my attention.
I'm *older*. I'm *better*. I'm *smarter* than all of you!
And if you won't see that on your own . . .
Mmph!
. . . I'll just have to make you.

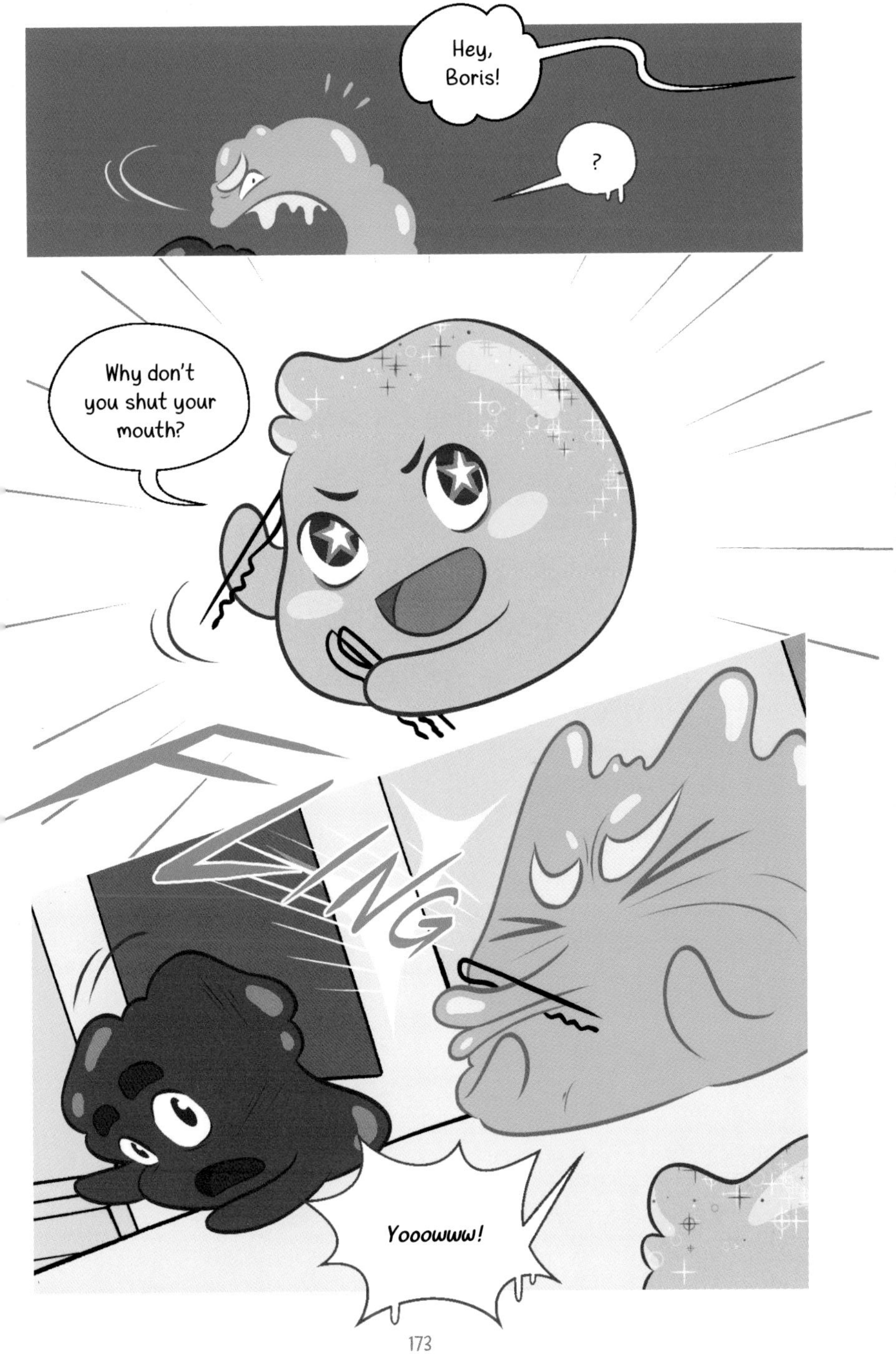
Hey, Boris!
?
Why don't you shut your mouth?
ZING
Yooowww!

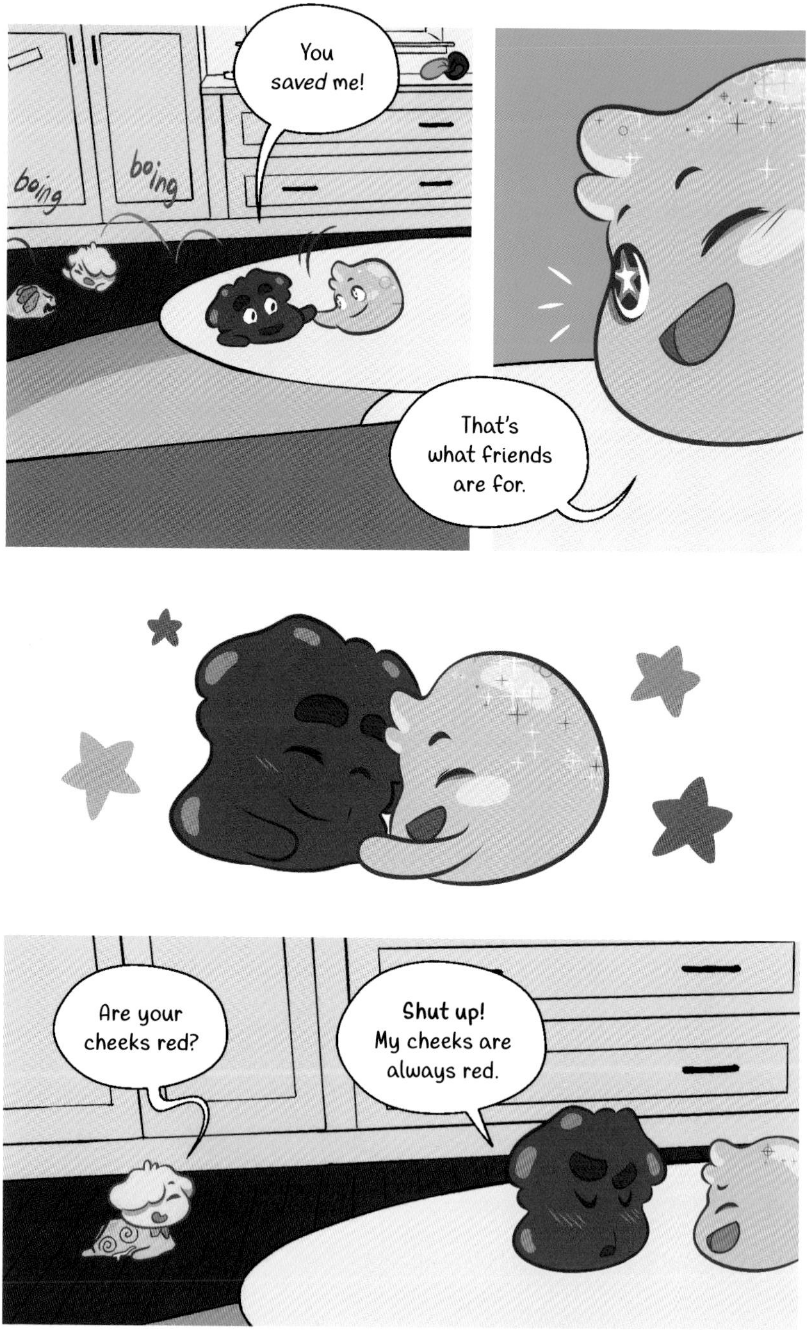
You saved me!
boing
boing
That's what friends are for.
Are your cheeks red?
Shut up!
My cheeks are always red.

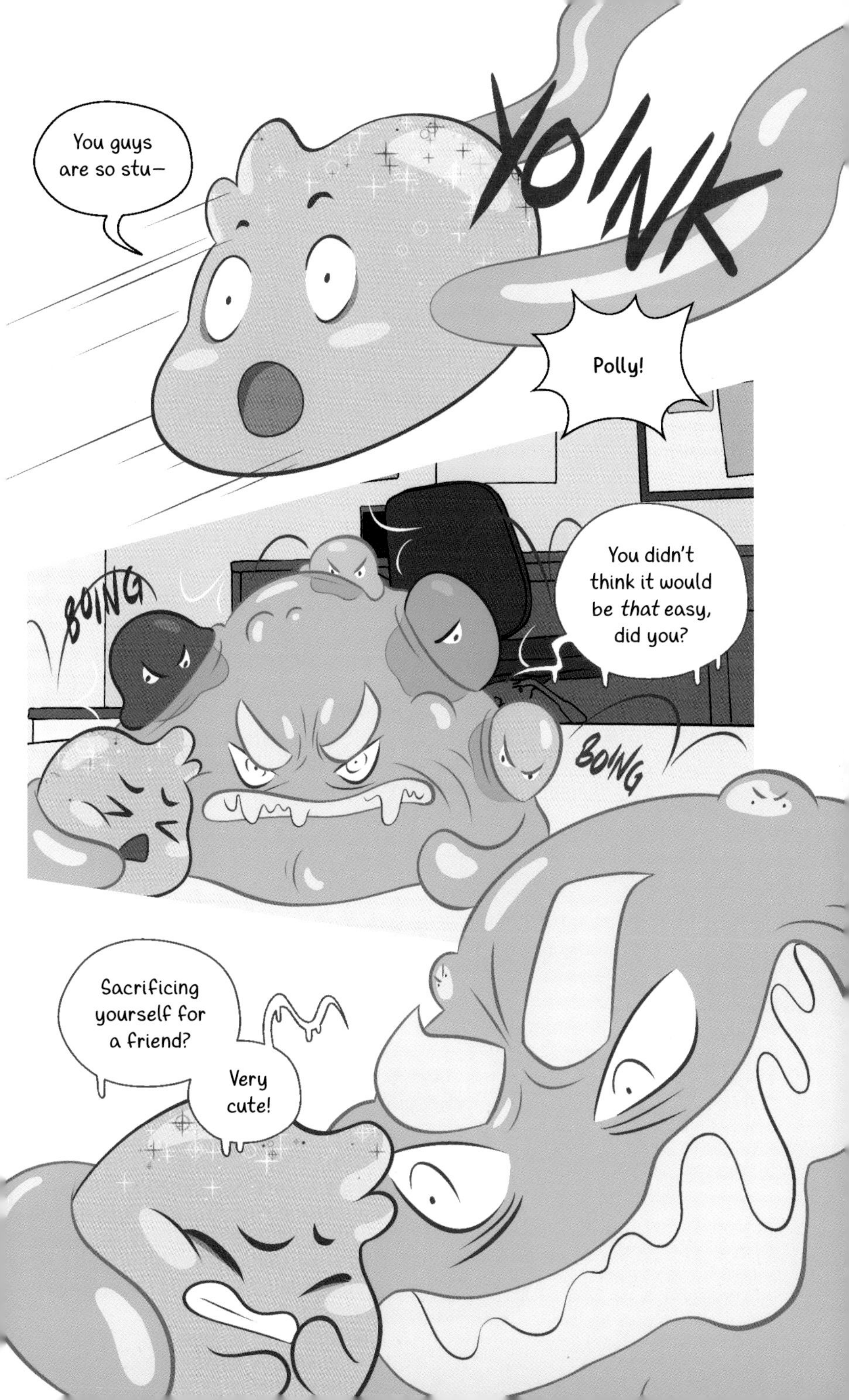
You guys are so stu—
YOINK
Polly!
BOING
You didn't think it would be *that* easy, did you?
BOING
Sacrificing yourself for a friend?
Very cute!

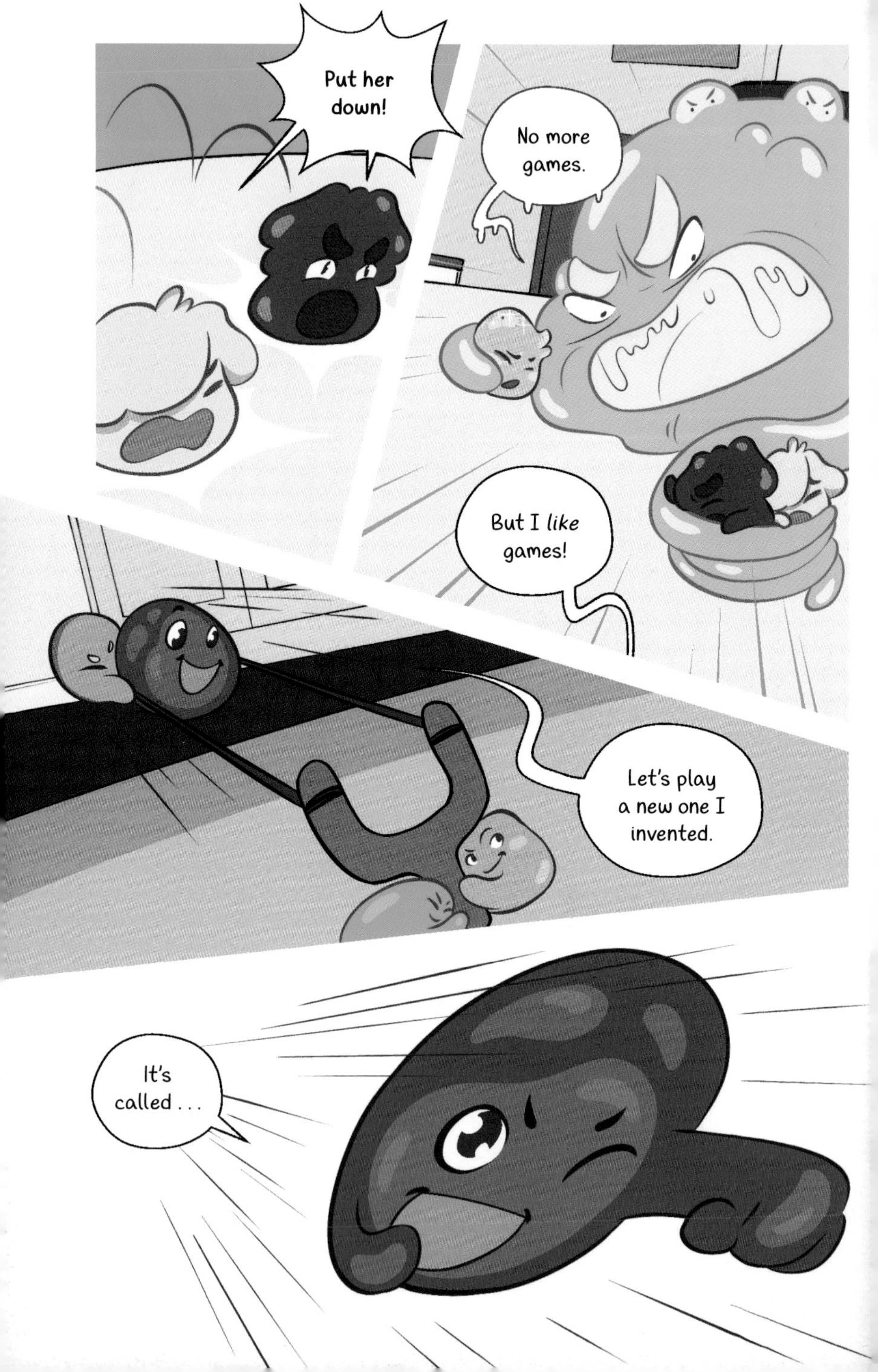
Put her down!
No more games.
But I *like* games!
Let's play a new one I invented.
It's called . . .

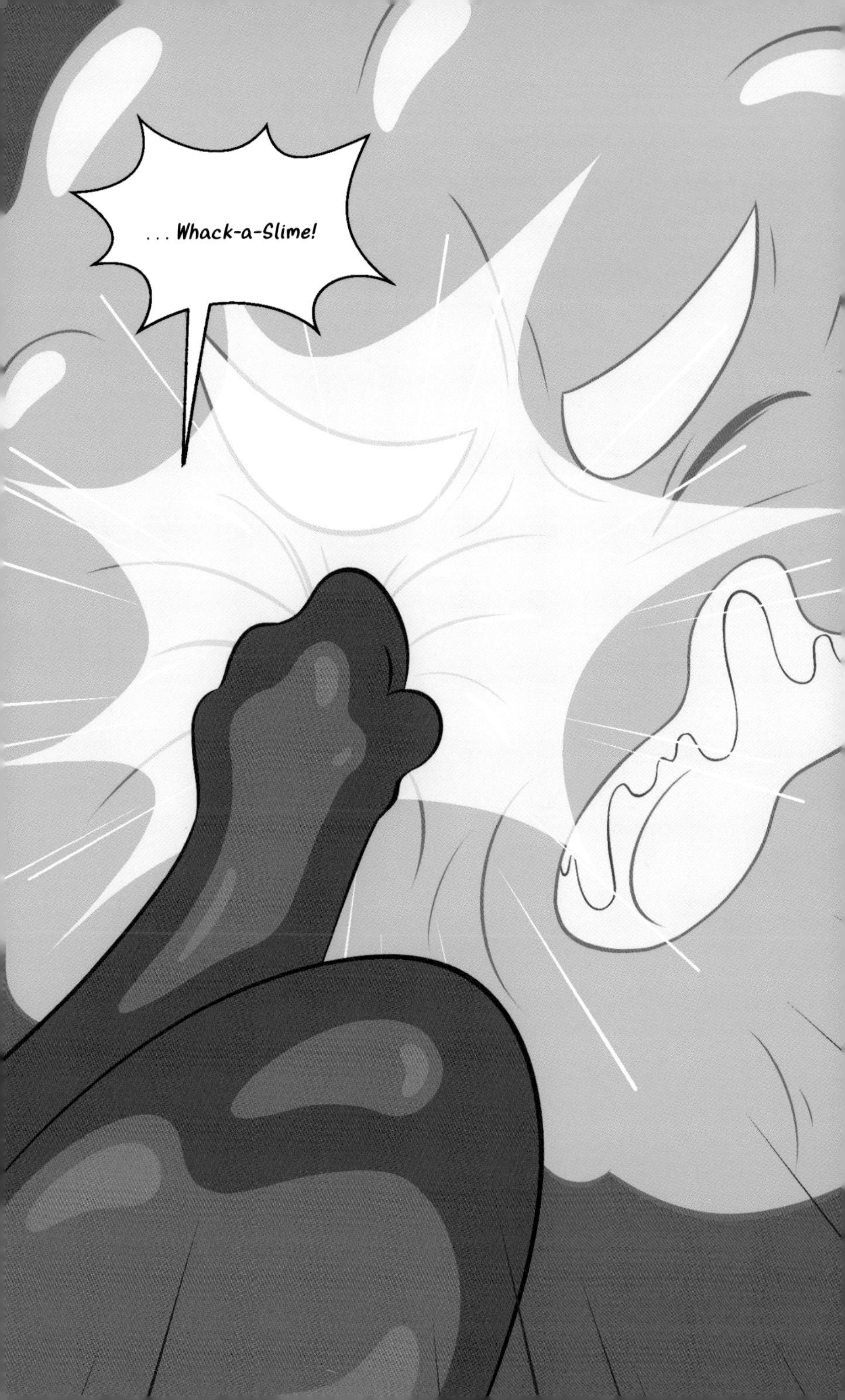
. . . Whack-a-Slime!

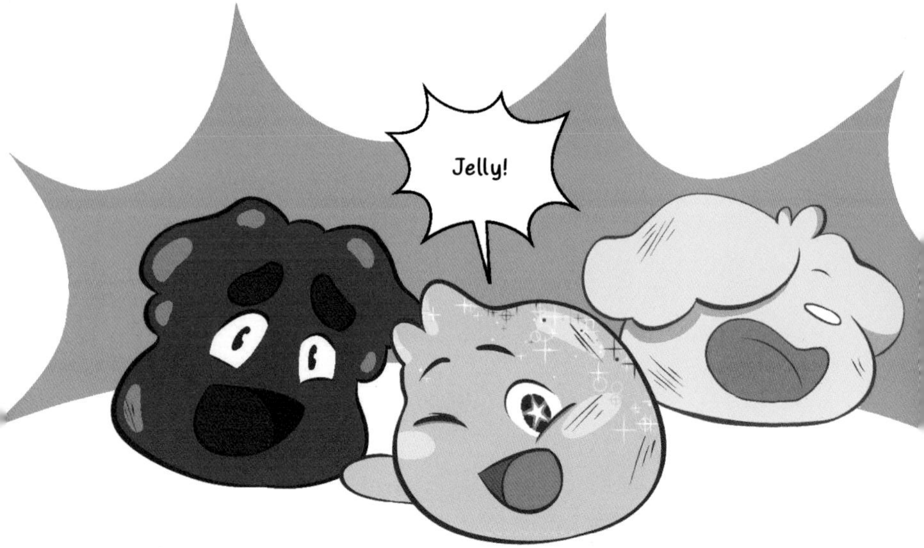
Jelly!

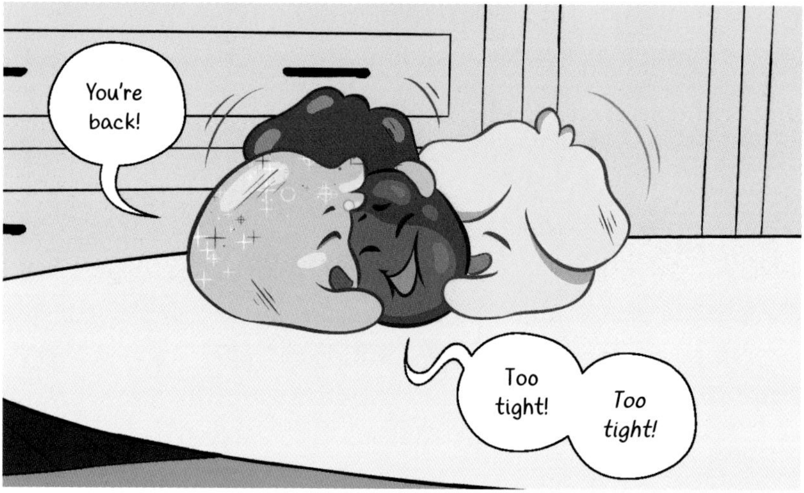
You're back!
Too tight!
Too tight!

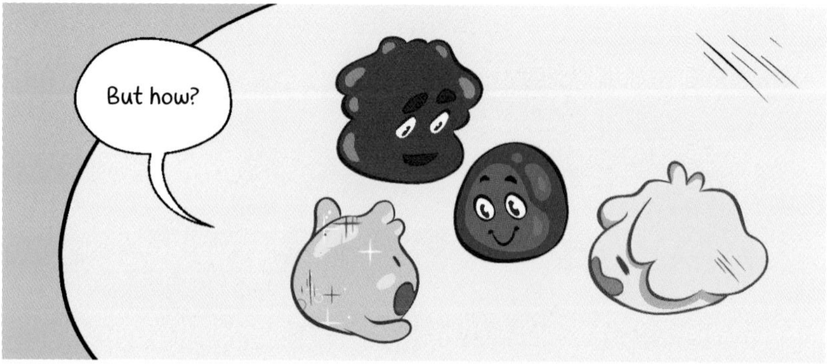
But how?

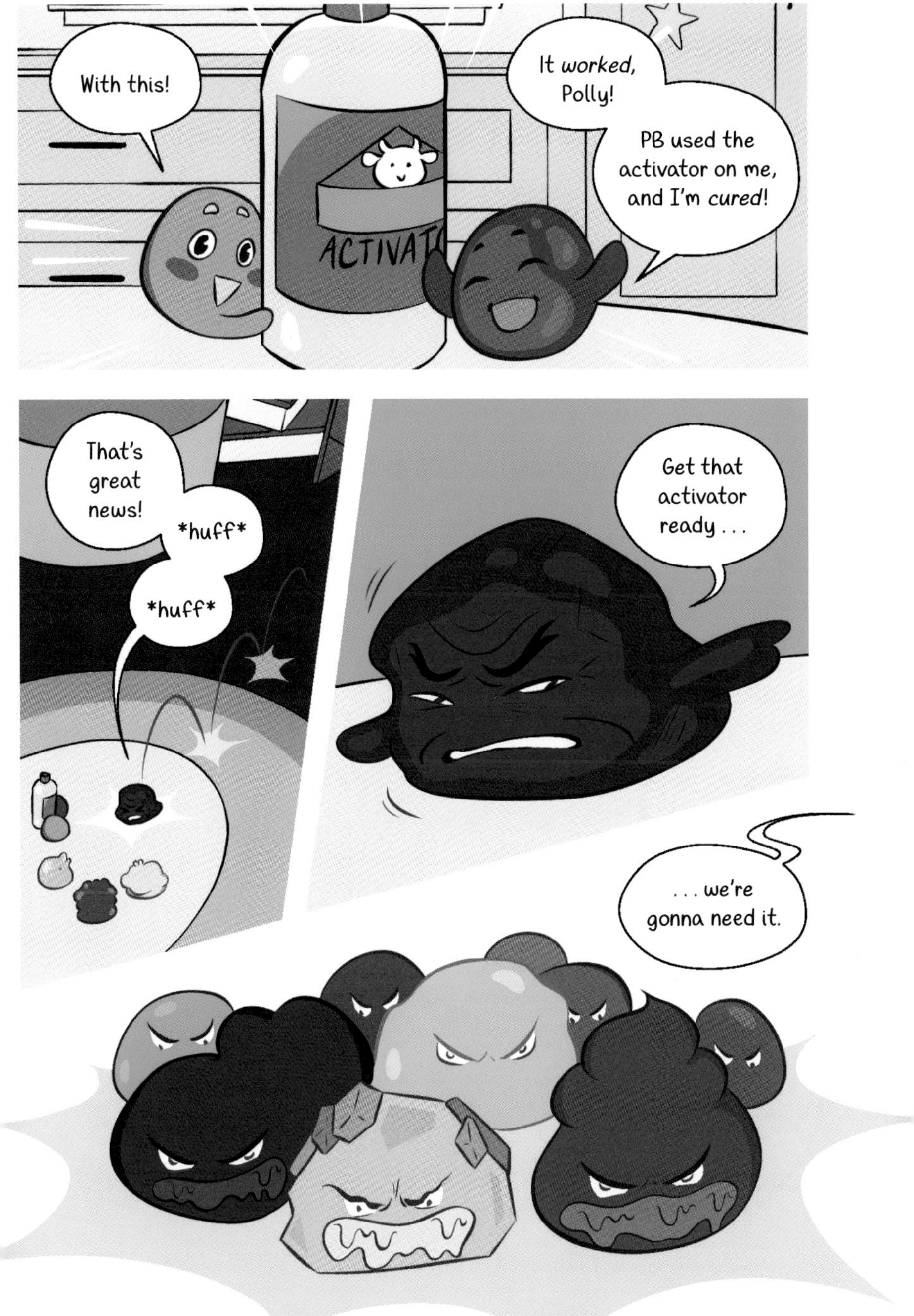
With this!
ACTIVAT
It worked, Polly!
PB used the activator on me, and I'm cured!
That's great news!
huff
huff
Get that activator ready . . .
. . . we're gonna need it.

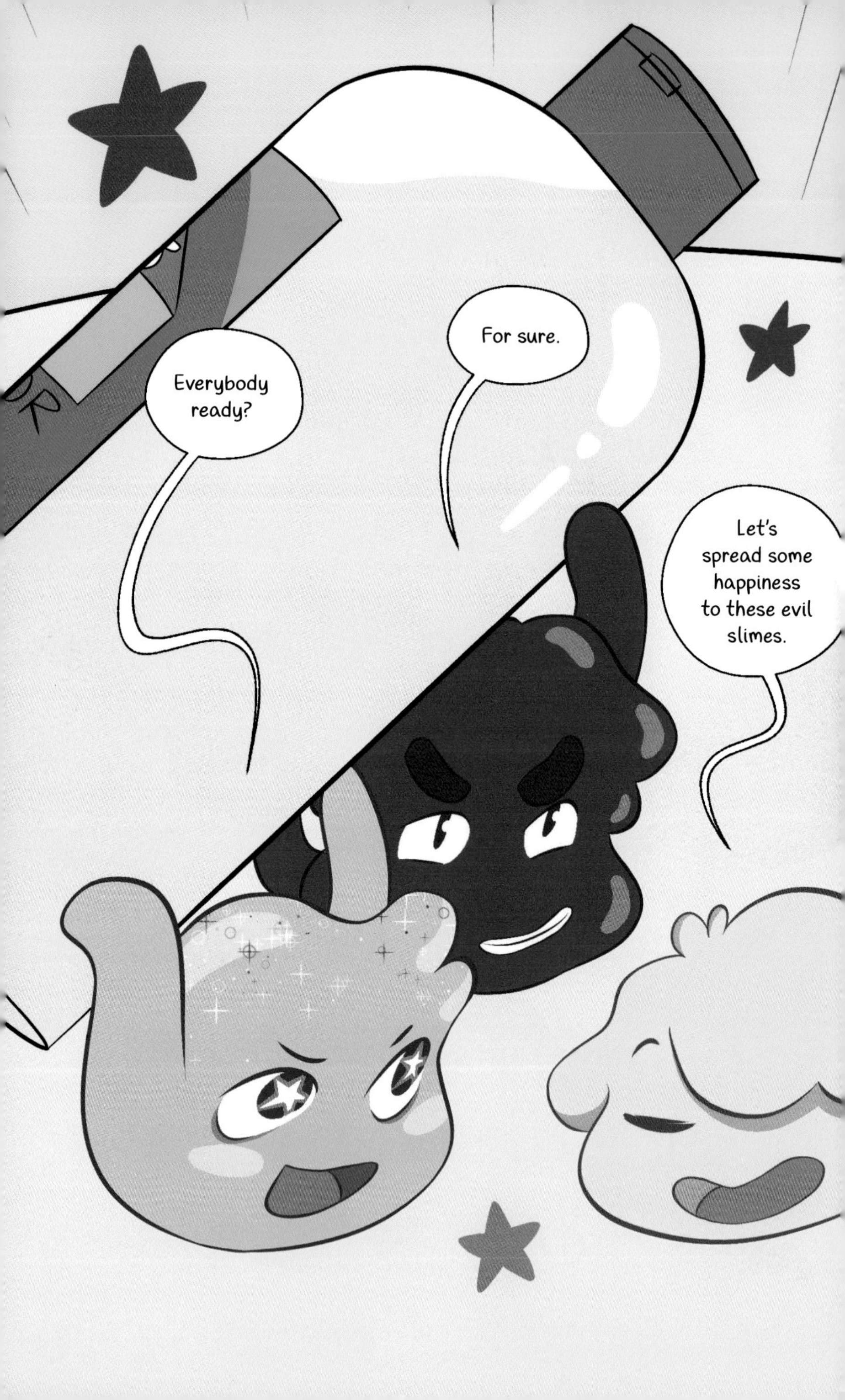
Everybody ready?
For sure.
Let's spread some happiness to these evil slimes.

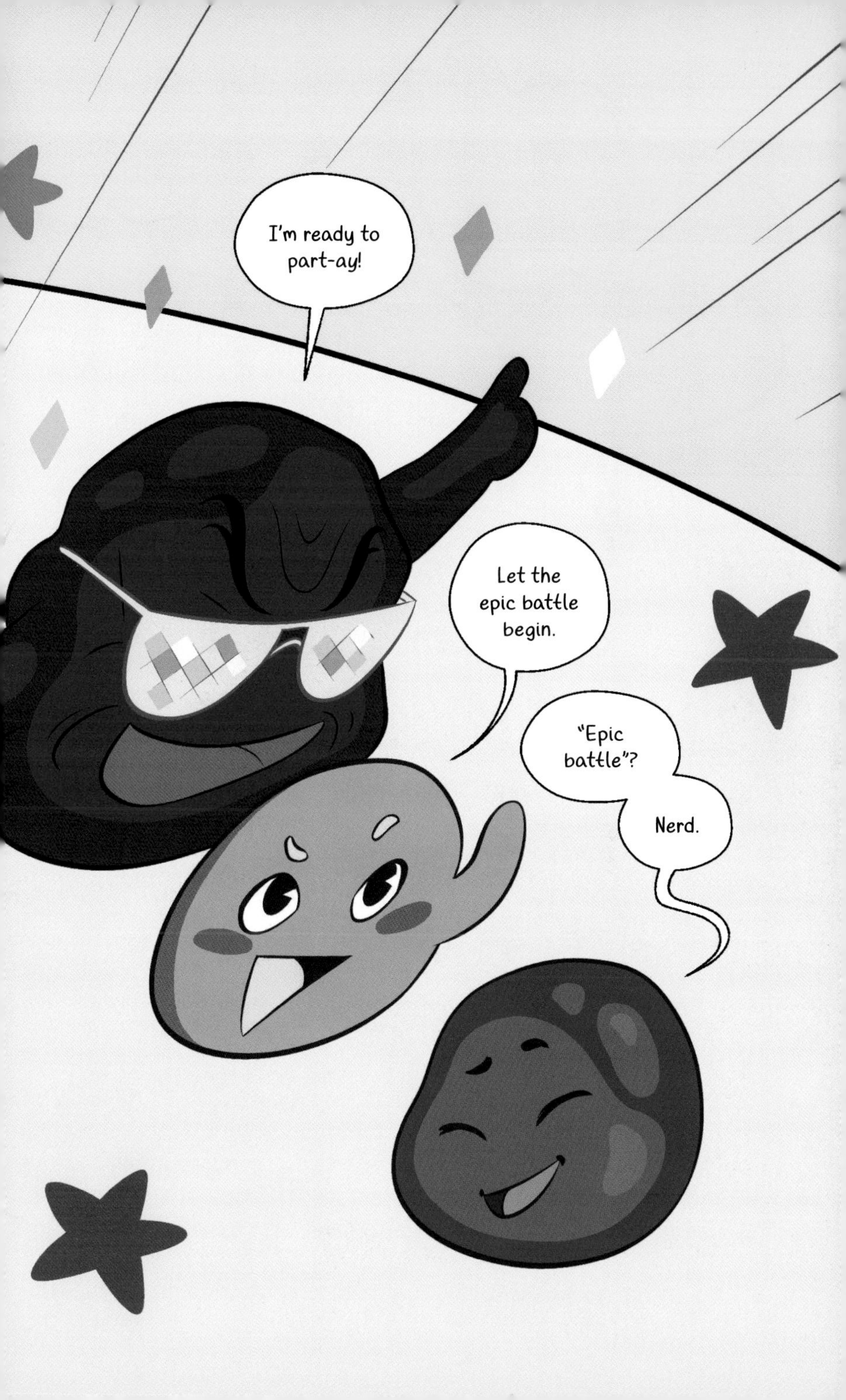
I'm ready to part-ay!
Let the epic battle begin.
"Epic battle"?
Nerd.

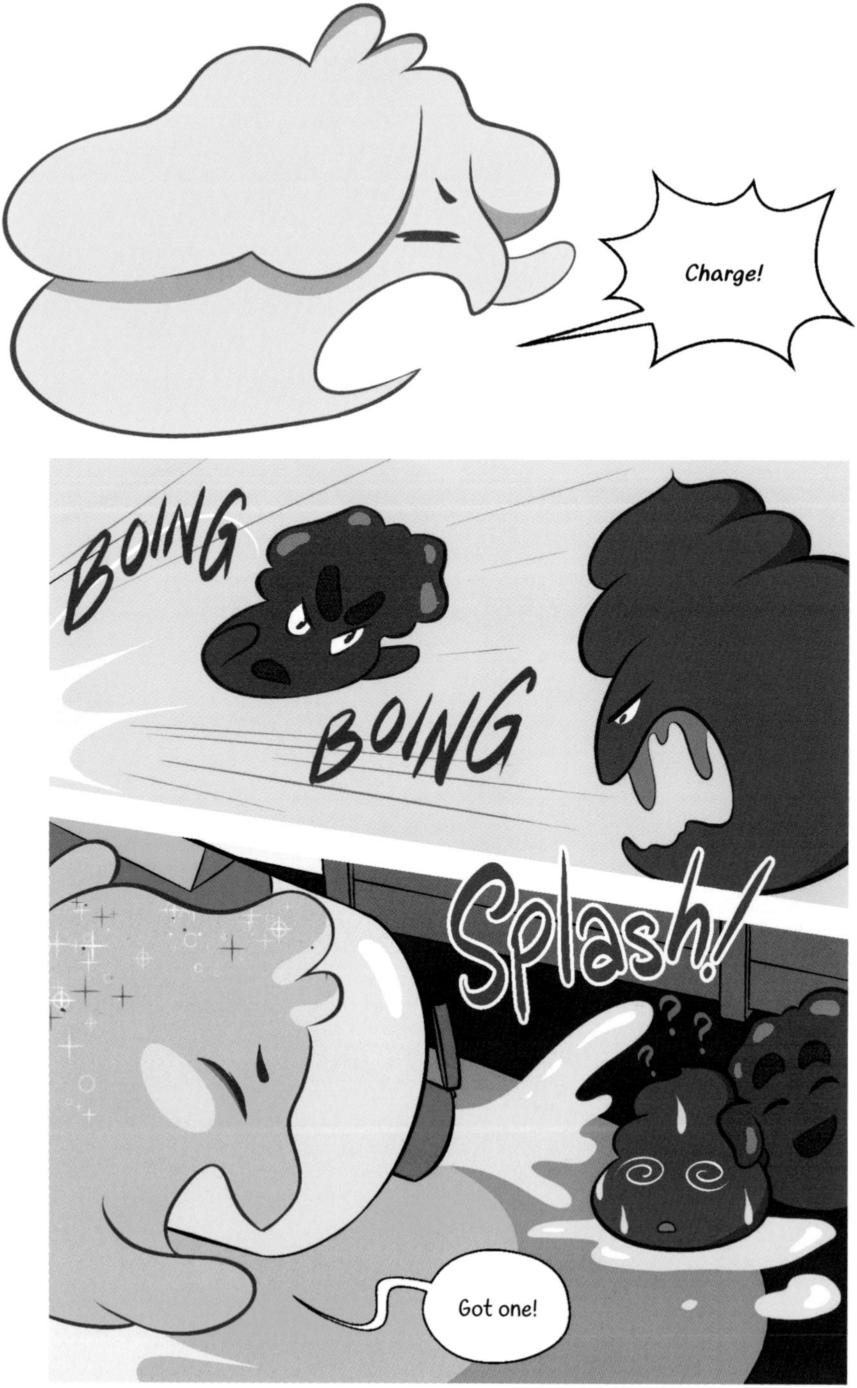
Charge!
BOING
BOING
Splash!
Got one!

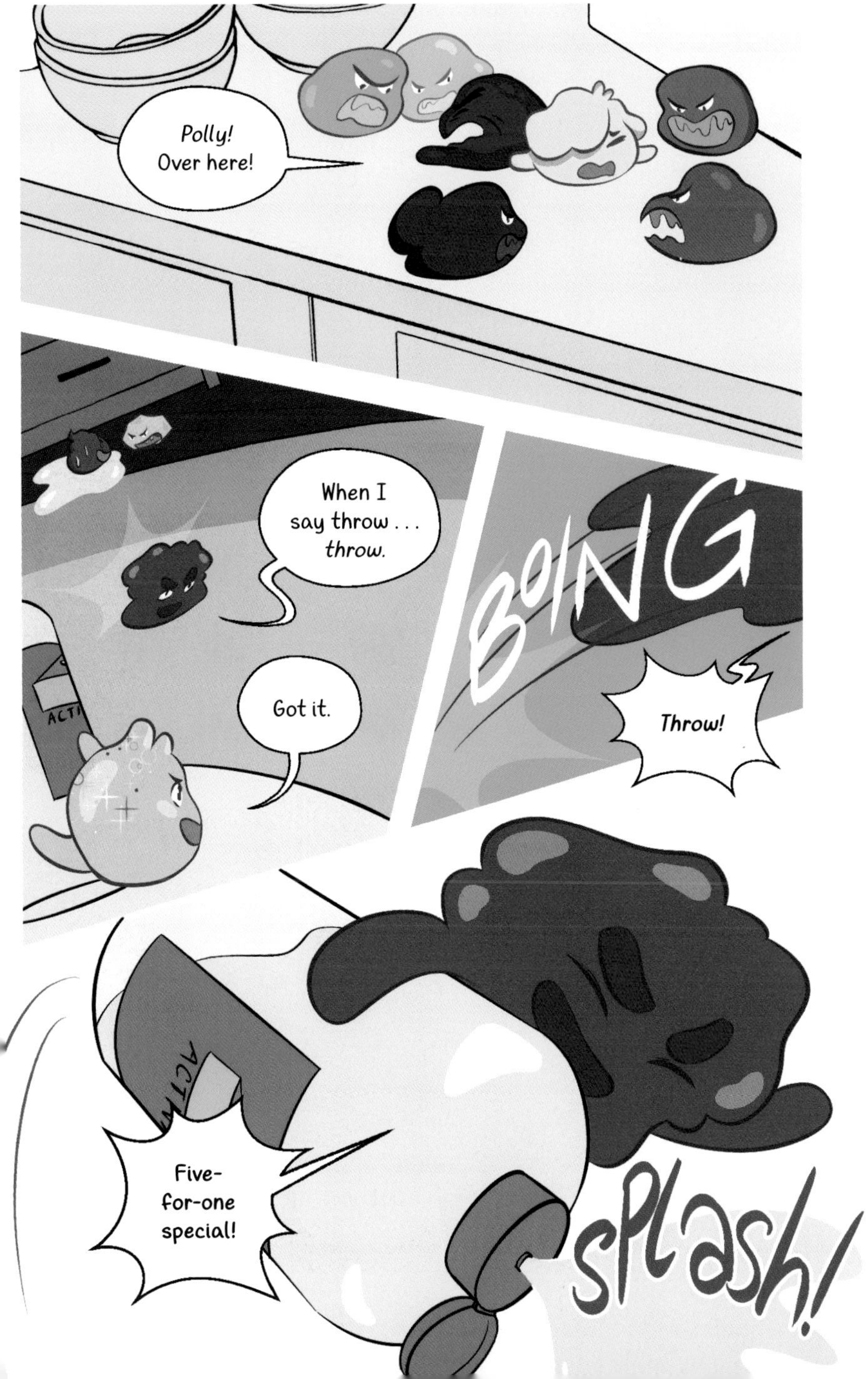
Polly!
Over here!
When I say throw . . . *throw.*
Got it.
BOING
Throw!
ACT
Five-for-one special!
SPLASH!

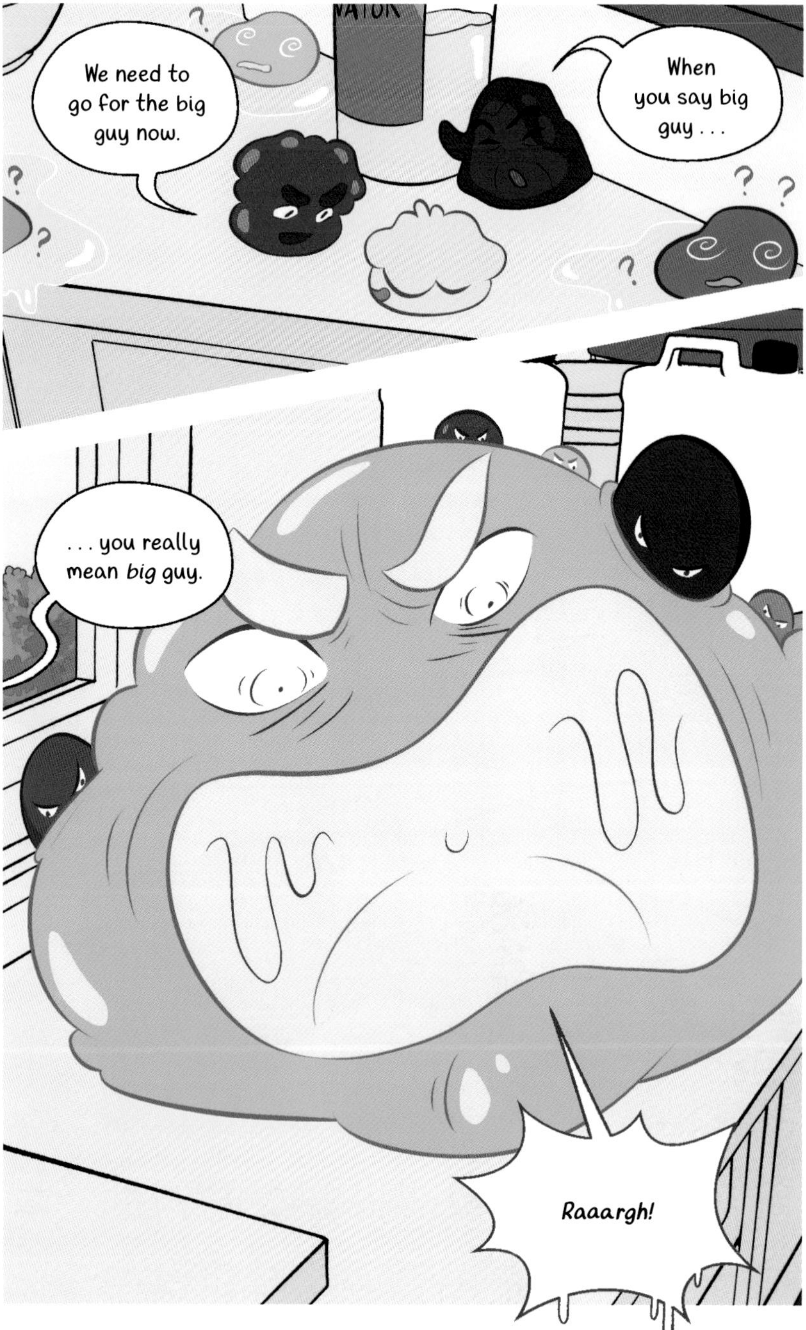
We need to go for the big guy now.
When you say big guy . . .
. . . you really mean *big* guy.
Raaargh!

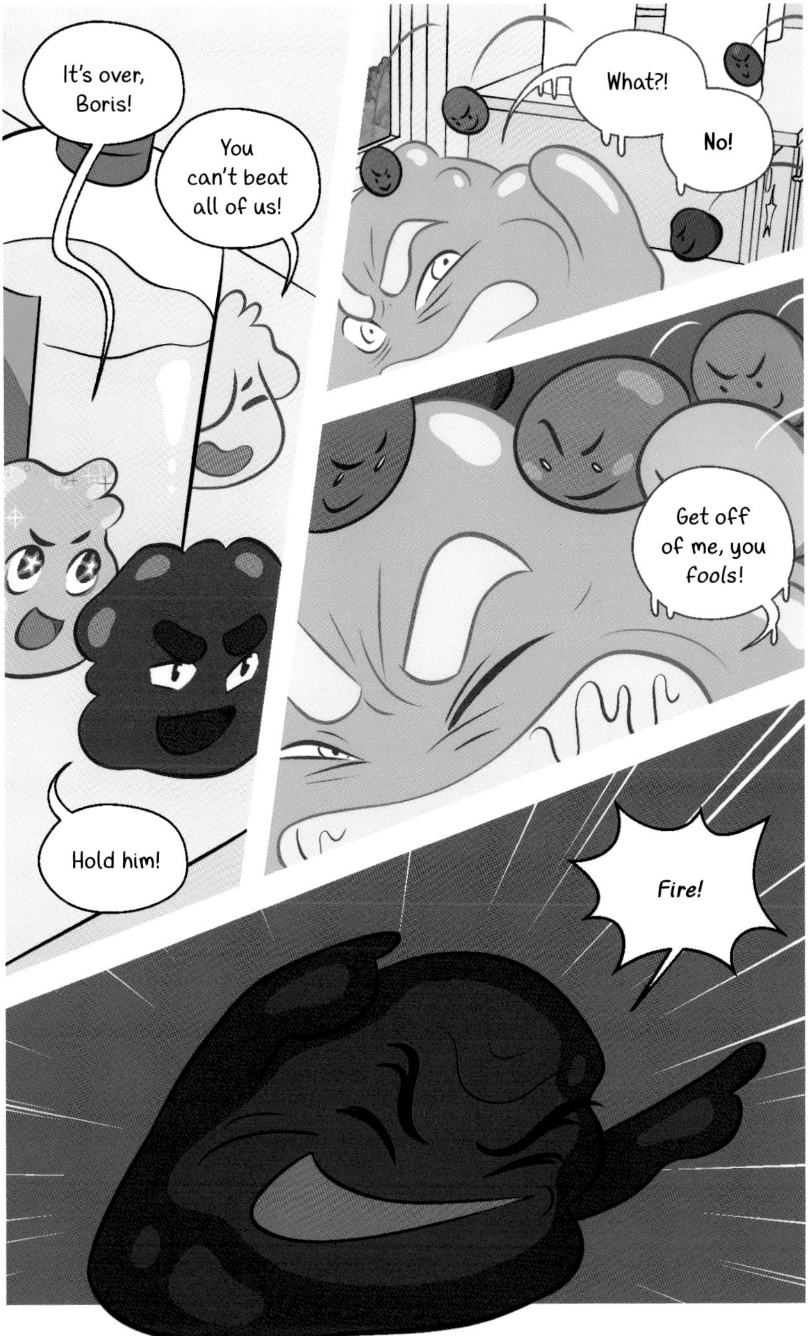
It's over, Boris!
You can't beat all of us!
Hold him!
What?!
No!
Get off of me, you fools!
Fire!

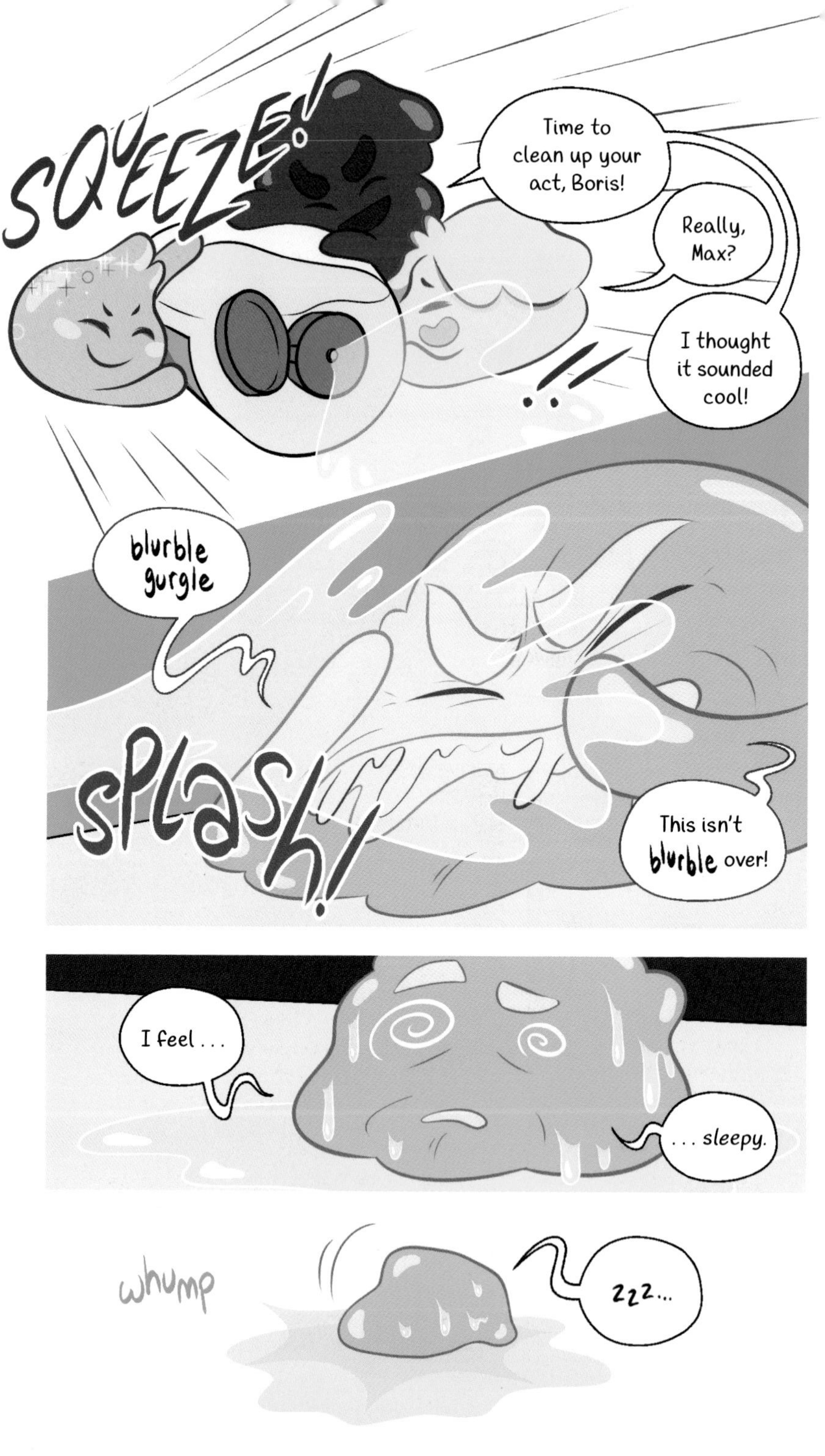
SQUEEZE!
Time to clean up your act, Boris!
Really, Max?
I thought it sounded cool!
blurble gurgle
SPLASH!
This isn't blurble over!
I feel . . .
. . . sleepy.
whump
zzz...

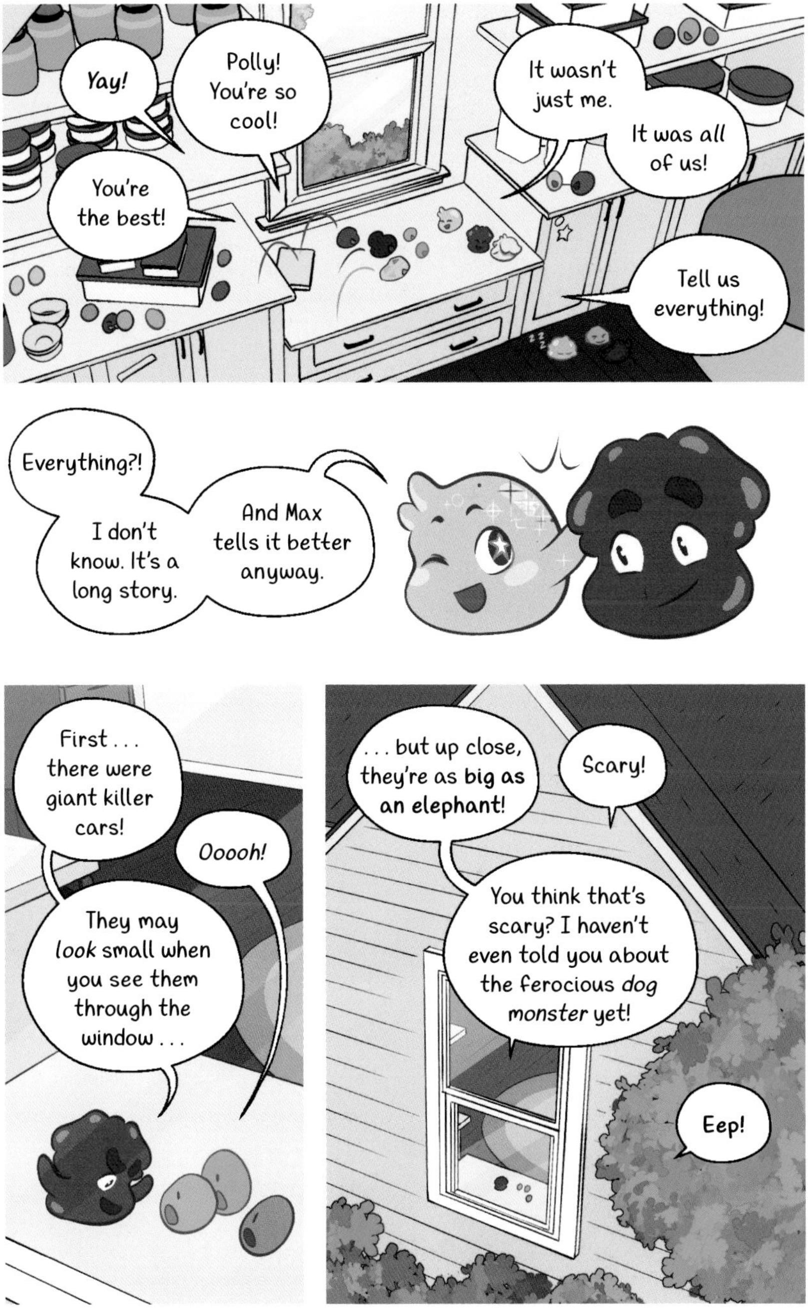
Yay!
Polly! You're so cool!
You're the best!
It wasn't just me.
It was all of us!
Tell us everything!
Everything?!
I don't know. It's a long story.
And Max tells it better anyway.
First . . . there were giant killer cars!
Ooooh!
They may *look* small when you see them through the window . . .
. . . but up close, they're as **big** as an elephant!
Scary!
You think that's scary? I haven't even told you about the ferocious *dog monster* yet!
Eep!

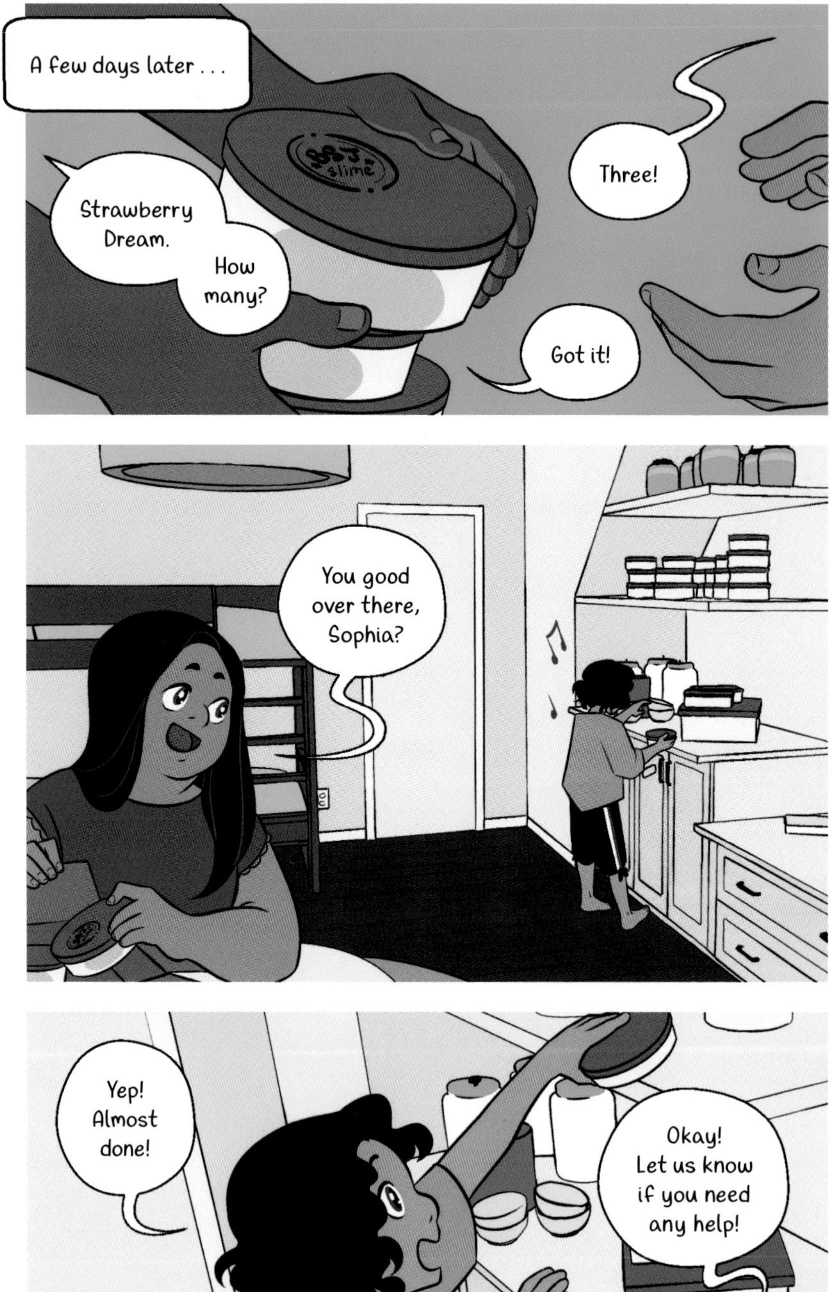
A few days later . . .
Strawberry Dream.
How many?
Three!
Got it!
You good over there, Sophia?
Yep! Almost done!
Okay! Let us know if you need any help!

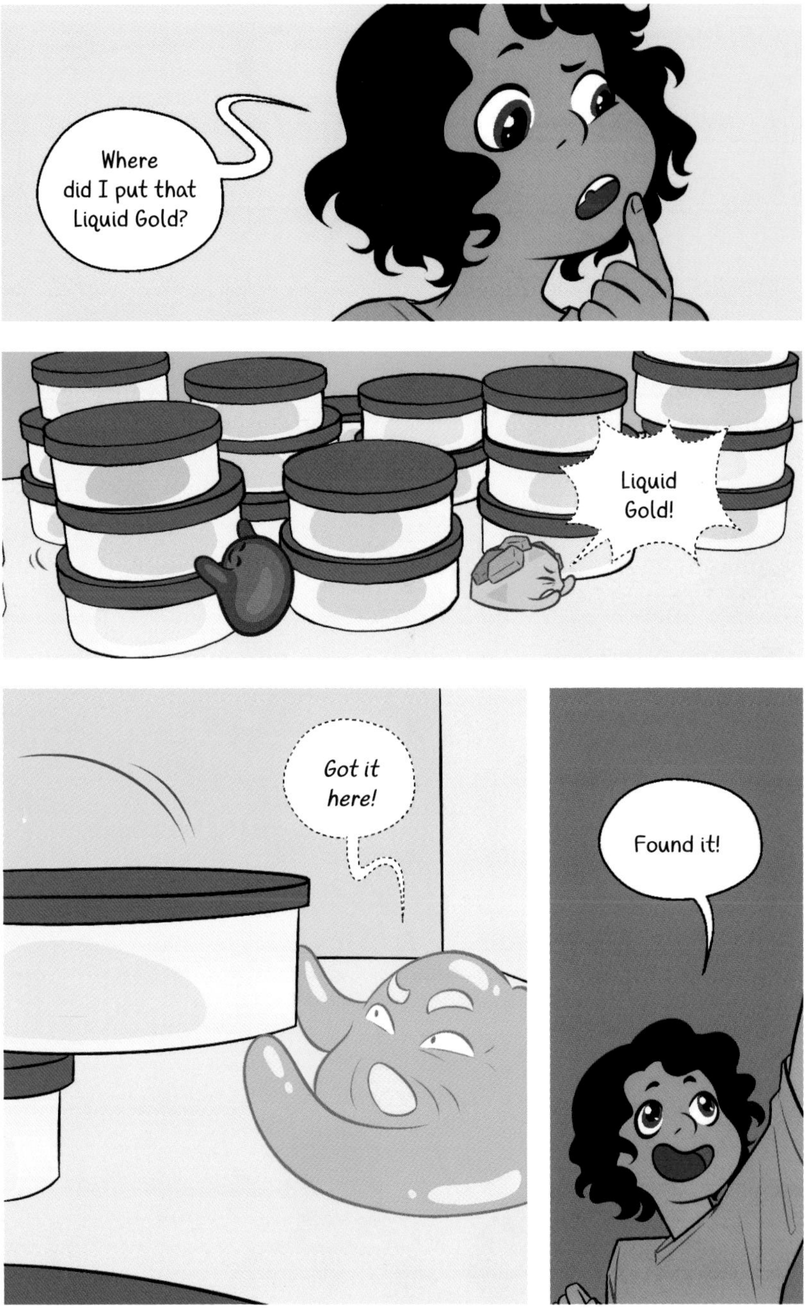
Where did I put that Liquid Gold?
Liquid Gold!
Got it here!
Found it!

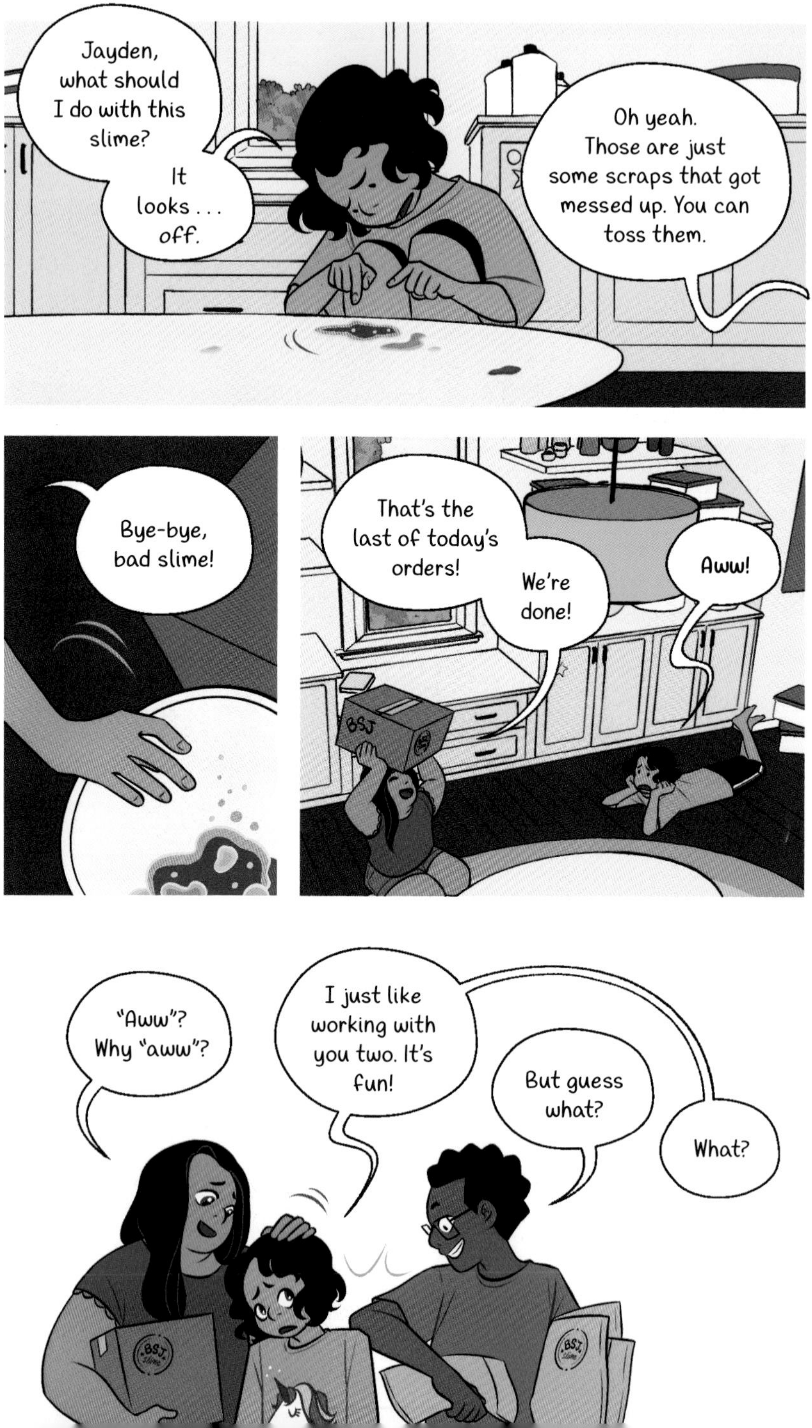
Jayden, what should I do with this slime?
It looks . . . off.
Oh yeah. Those are just some scraps that got messed up. You can toss them.
Bye-bye, bad slime!
That's the last of today's orders!
We're done!
Aww!
"Aww"? Why "aww"?
I just like working with you two. It's fun!
But guess what?
What?

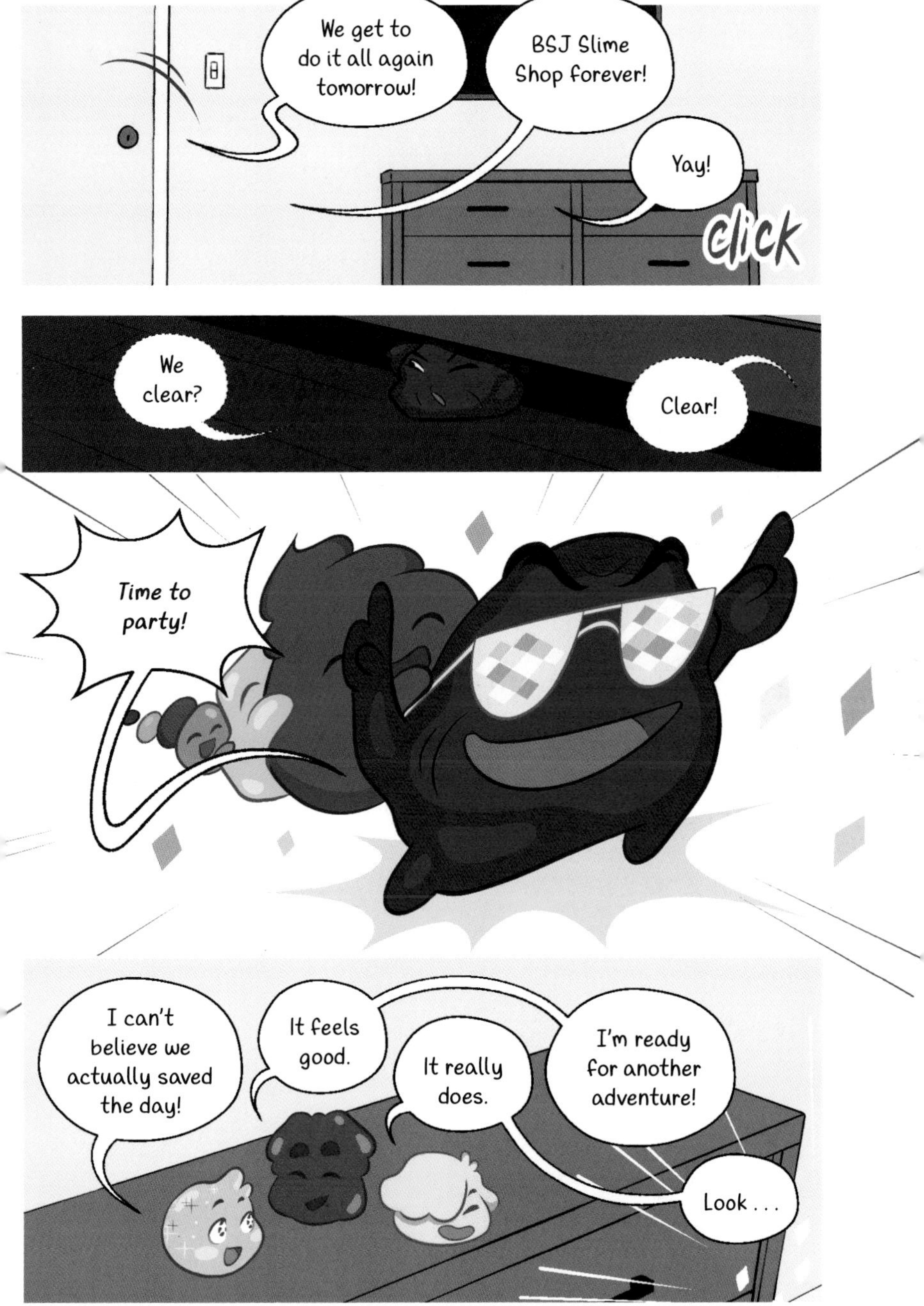
We get to do it all again tomorrow!
BSJ Slime Shop forever!
Yay!
click
We clear?
Clear!
Time to party!
I can't believe we actually saved the day!
It feels good.
It really does.
I'm ready for another adventure!
Look . . .

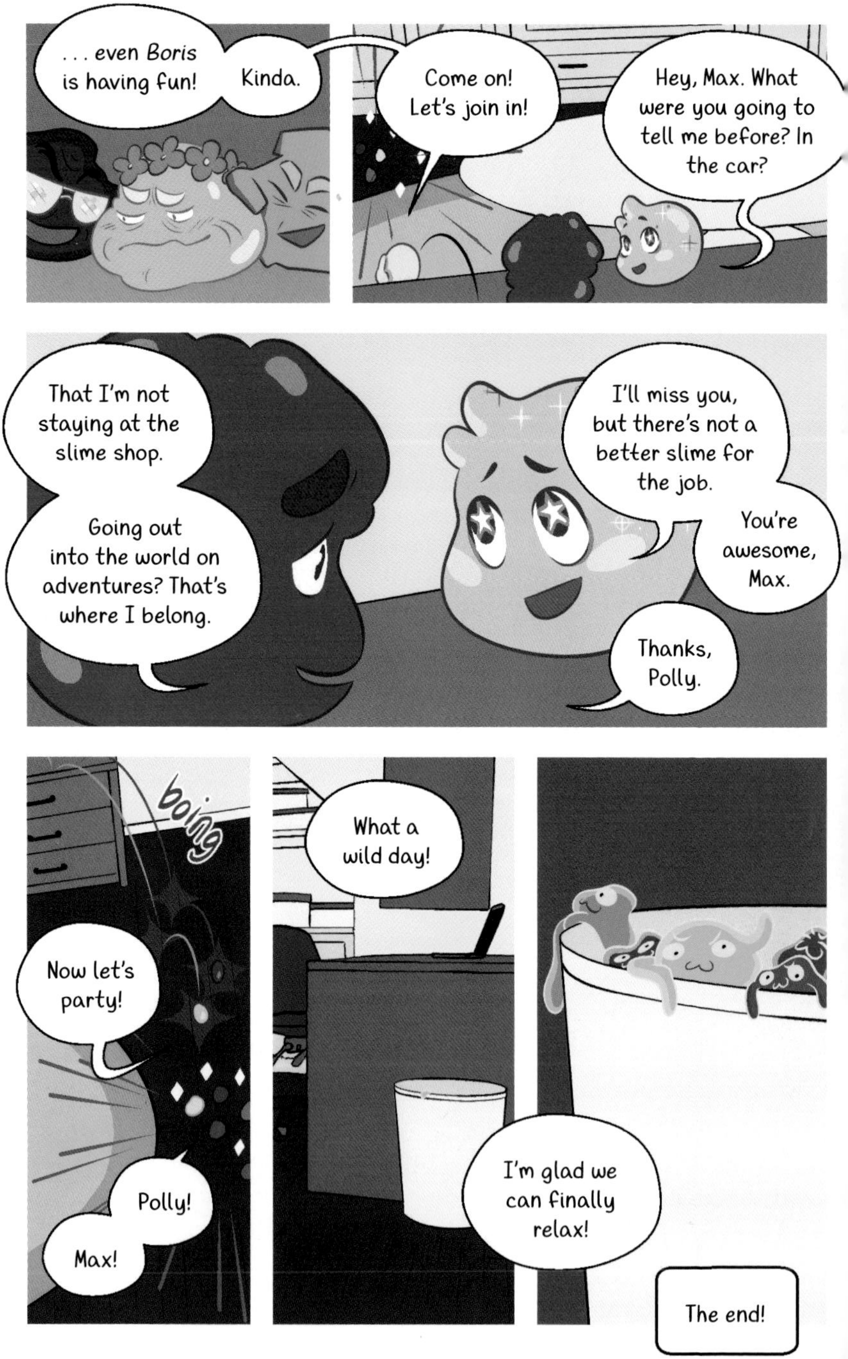

. . . even Boris is having fun!
Kinda.
Come on! Let's join in!
Hey, Max. What were you going to tell me before? In the car?
That I'm not staying at the slime shop.
Going out into the world on adventures? That's where I belong.
I'll miss you, but there's not a better slime for the job.
You're awesome, Max.
Thanks, Polly.
boing
Now let's party!
Polly!
Max!
What a wild day!
I'm glad we can finally relax!
The end!

SLIME RECIPES

Be sure to ask an adult for help!

CLEAR SLIME

Ingredients:

8 oz. nontoxic white craft glue

1 cup of activator (recipes can be found online or you can buy slime activator)

2-3 drops of food coloring (optional)

1/2 tsp of skin safe fragrance oil (optional)

Glitter (optional)

Fake sprinkles (optional)

Tools:

Medium bowl

Stir stick

Instructions:

1. Pour all 8 oz. of the white craft glue into the medium bowl.

    Note: If you want to color your slime or give it a scent, now is the time to do so!

    For color, add in 2-3 drops of food coloring of your choice.

For a lovely scent, mix in 1/2 tsp of skin safe fragrance oil of your choice.

2. Add 1 tbsp of activator at a time (for a total of 4 tbsp) and stir thoroughly, slowly pouring the activator in as you stir. Once the slime starts to unstick from the bowl, start kneading it with your hands. This will help distribute the activator through the slime.

   Note: Clear slime is much stringier than opaque slime and will require more kneading. Continuously knead until smooth. After all the kneading and mixing, air bubbles get trapped in the slime and will make it look cloudy instead of clear.

3. Your slime should feel dense. If it is too runny, feel free to knead in an additional 1-2 tbsp of activator. Because it will need to sit for a few days, you want to make sure your slime is thick so that it doesn't melt too much.

4. Let your slime sit for least 4-7 days. It will turn clear, as the air bubbles will rise and disappear on their own.

5. Your slime is now ready! Feel free to add glitter or fake sprinkles for fun, and enjoy!

CLOUD SLIME

Ingredients:

8 oz. nontoxic white craft glue

2 cups of activator (recipes can be found online or you can buy slime activator)

1/2 cup dry instant snow

2-3 drops of food coloring (optional)

1/2 tsp of skin safe fragrance oil (optional)

5 cups room temperature water

Glitter (optional)

Fake sprinkles (optional)

Tools:

Large bowl

Medium bowl

Small bowl

Stir stick

Instructions:

1. Pour all 8 oz. of the white craft glue into the large bowl.

   Note: If you want to color your slime or give it a scent, now is the time to do so!

   For color, add in 2-3 drops of food coloring of your choice.

   For a lovely scent, mix in 1/2 tsp of skin safe fragrance oil of your choice.

2. Time to start activating your slime! Start by adding 1 tbsp of activator at a time. Make sure to stir for about 15 seconds between each tbsp before adding another to ensure the activator is mixed in thoroughly. Don't worry, it's normal for the slime to look very stringy as you activate it!

   Keep adding 1 tbsp at a time as you stir. You will use 4 tbsps in total for these first couple of steps. Keep activator nearby because we will need it again in a few steps.

3. At this point your slime should start to unstick from the sides of the bowl. This is good! It means the slime is coming together. Take the slime out and start kneading it with your hands. This will ensure the activator is distributed throughout and will help smooth out any activator lumps.
4. Put the slime to the side for now and get a medium bowl. Add a 1/2 cup of dry instant snow.
5. Take 1 tbsp of dry instant snow from your medium bowl and add it to a small bowl.
6. Add 5 cups of room temperature water to the medium bowl and use your hand to lightly stir it. You'll be able to watch as it grows before your eyes!
7. Now that the wet instant snow is ready, take 1 cup at a time and mix it thoroughly into the slime base in the large bowl.

   Note: 9 cups of wet instant snow will be needed. Do NOT add all 9 cups at once.
8. After a few cups of wet snow, you will notice that the slime has started to melt. This is normal! To bring it back to a firmer consistency, mix in 1 tbsp of activator at a time. You will need a total of 4 tbsps for this.
9. Continue mixing in 1 cup of wet snow at a time. Repeat the previous activator step as needed, alternating between adding wet snow and activator.

   Note: Activator should only be added after every 2 or 3 cups of wet snow.
10. Take the 1 tbsp of dry instant snow set aside in the small bowl and stir it into the slime. This will help absorb moisture and perfect your cloud slime for some amazing DRIZZLES!
11. Feel free to add glitter or sprinkles. This step is optional.
12. CONGRATULATIONS! YOU DID IT! Your cloud slime is complete. Give yourself a pat on the back because this is the hardest type of slime to make!

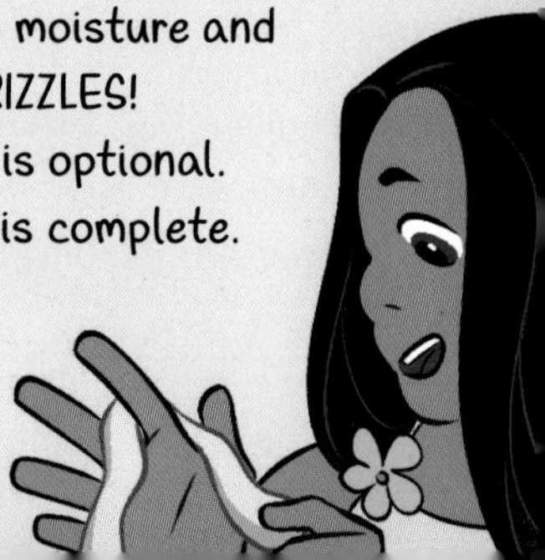

DIY CLAY KIT SLIME

Ingredients:

8 oz. nontoxic white craft glue
1 cup of activator (recipes can be found online or you can buy slime activator)
Soft air-dry clay
Silicone molds (optional)
2-3 drops of food coloring (optional)
1 tsp of acrylic paint (optional)
1/2 tsp of skin safe fragrance oil (optional)

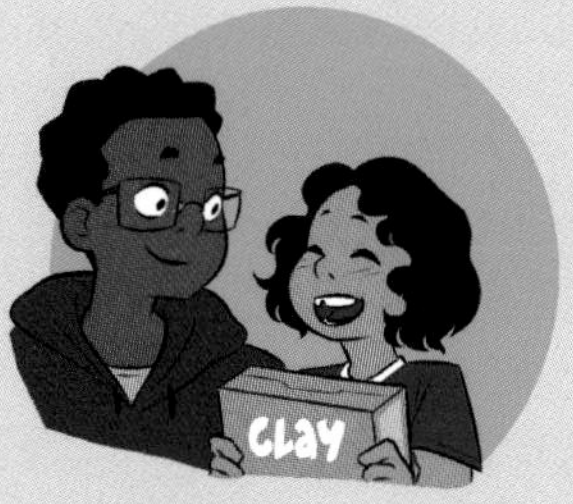
CLAY

Tools:

Medium bowl
Stir stick

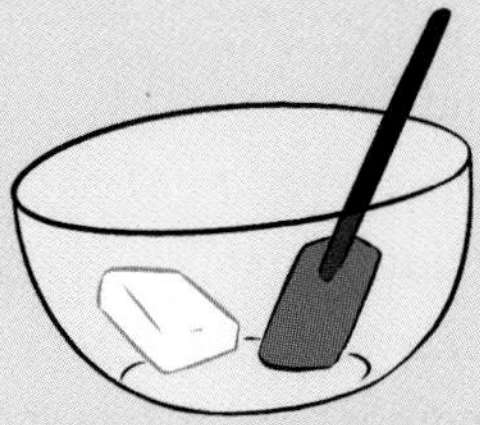

Instructions:

Slime Base

1. Pour all 8 oz. of the white craft glue into the medium bowl.
   Note: If you want to color your slime or give it a scent, now is the time to do so!
   For color, add in either 2-3 drops of food coloring or 1 tsp of acrylic paint in the color of your choice.
   For a lovely scent, mix in 1/2 tsp of skin safe fragrance oil of your choice.
2. Add 1 tbsp of activator at a time (for a total of 4 tbsp) and stir thoroughly, slowly pouring the activator in as you stir. Once the slime starts to unstick from the bowl, start kneading it with your hands. This will help distribute the activator through the slime.

If the slime feels stringy, the activator still needs to be distributed evenly. Continue to knead until smooth.

If the slime is too runny, feel free to knead in an additional 1-2 tbsp of activator. This is optional depending on desired consistency.

3. Your slime base is ready!

Clay Creation

4. When making your clay pieces, soft air-dry clay is the best type of clay to use. There are many types of silicone molds that you can find online or in stores, but you can also shape your creations by hand. It's completely up to you! You can stick with white or use different colors to help personalize your clay, or you can paint on details with acrylic paint.

Note: Some of my favorite creations are dessert-shaped, like donuts, cakes, and ice cream! The list of things you can make is endless, so get creative!

5. Once your clay pieces are complete, you're ready to mix them into your slime. How do you know when it's mixed in well?

When you mix the clay in, it'll break down into soft chunks! It'll feel nice to mix in as the clay breaks down. It's satisfying! You keep kneading and mixing until all the clay chunks have dissolved into the slime. You'll know it's fully mixed when you have a smooth, buttery texture.

DIY clay kits are some of the most popular slimes to play with.

CAST OF CHARACTERS

Polly

Polly is the most popular slime in the slime shop, but sometimes that popularity goes to her head.

Karma

Karma is a crunchy hippie slime who likes to go with the flow, even if it gets her in trouble sometimes.

Max

Max is an aspiring rapper slime who pretends to be tough and cool, but on the inside, he's a softy.

Boris is the grumpiest slime in the house. He doesn't like the slime shop and will do anything he can to destroy it!

Boris

Skip

Skip is a nervous and paranoid slime. He's not a bad slime, but he's easily tricked!

Peanut Butter

Jelly

Peanut Butter and Jelly are two sister slimes who have each other's backs and finish each other's sentences.

Original Slime

Mr. O, the Original Slime, is the oldest and most mysterious slime around!

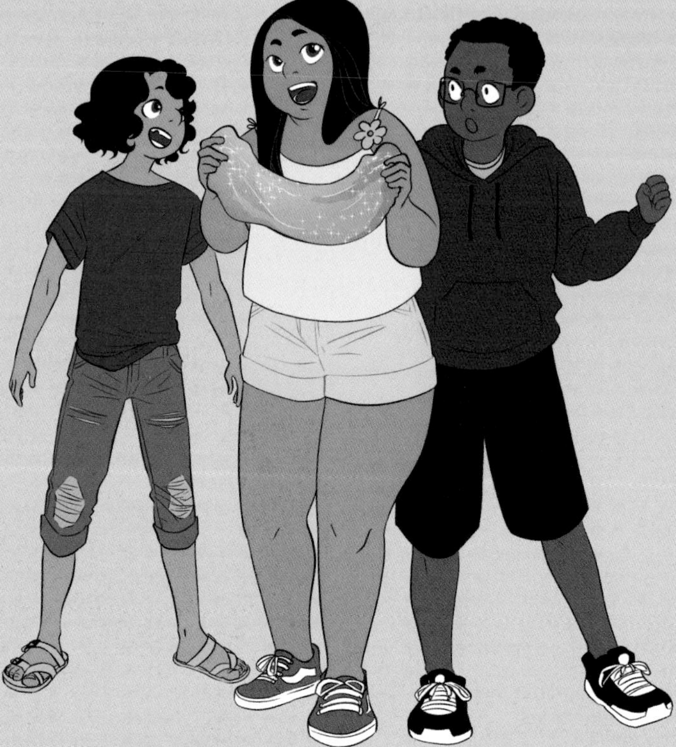

Sophia, Bailey, and Jayden

Humans! Bailey and Sophia are sisters and Jayden is their best friend. Together they run the BSJ Slime Shop.

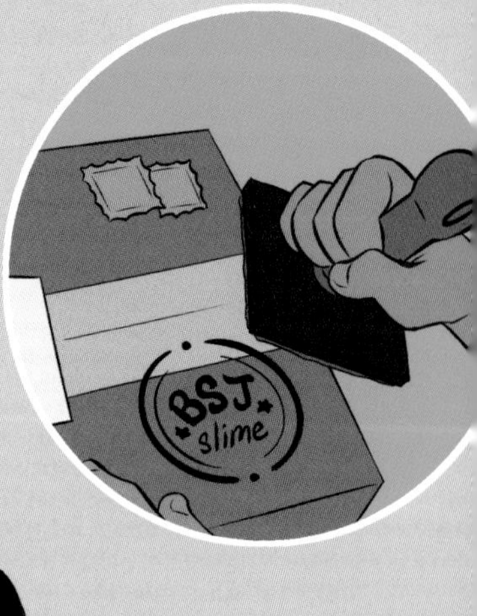
BSJ slime

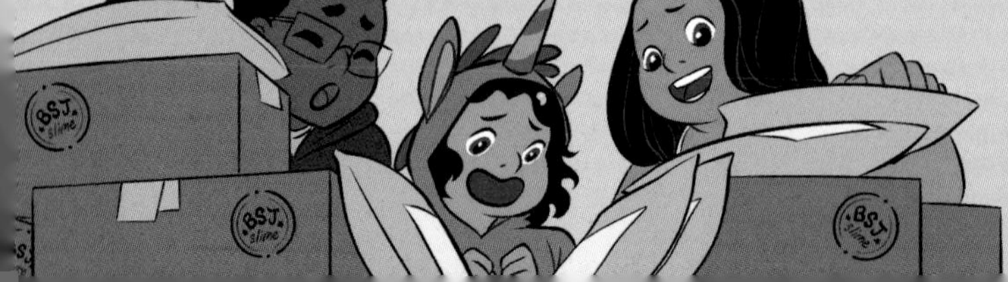
BSJ slime
BSJ slime
BSJ slime

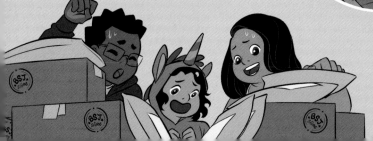

ACKNOWLEDGMENTS

Slime Shop was a joy to draw and it wouldn't be here without our wonderful team behind the scenes. Thank you to Charlie Olsen, my agent, who brought us all together! And to all the editorial hands who helped carry us to the finish line: Erika Turner, Weslie Turner, Ciera Burch, Monica Perez, Erika West, and Mary Magrisso. Our wonderful designers were Celeste Knudsen, Phil Caminiti, Catherine San Juan, and Whitney Leader-Picone, all of whom helped make sure these slimes look ready to ooze off the page! Thanks to Kori Michele for all their incredible help with color flats; there was really never any other choice when it came to a book about cute slimes. Hugs and thank-yous to Berrin and Silas, the best co-working buddies I could ask for! And most of all, thank you, Kiri, for everything. —N.S.

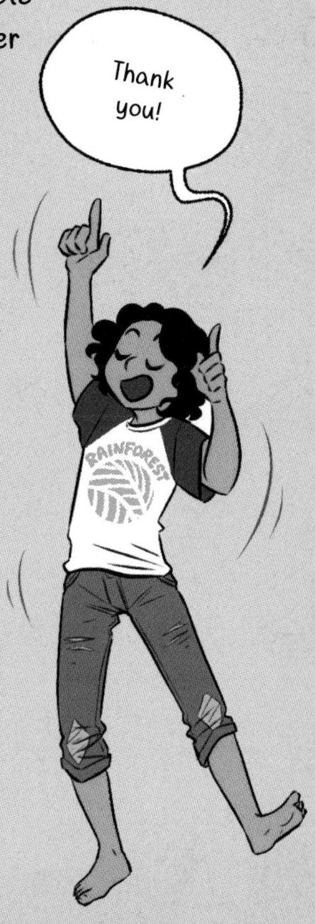
Thank you!
RAINFOREST

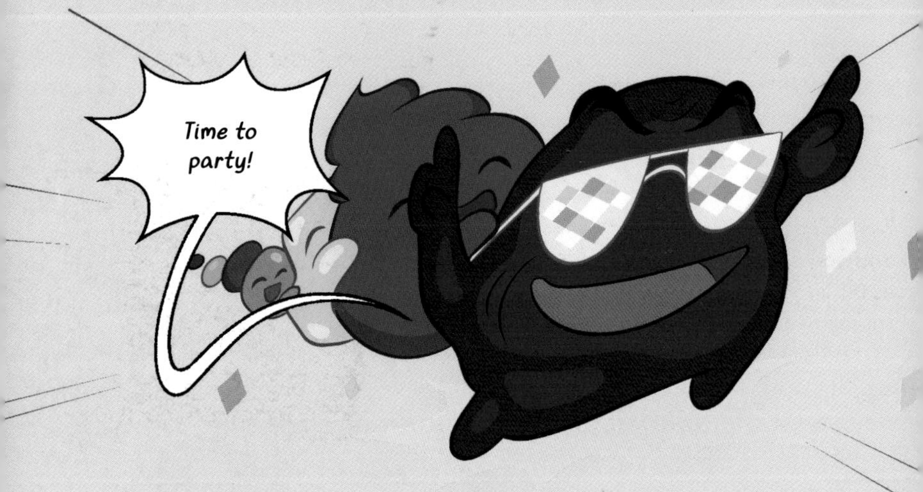
Time to party!